HAND AND GLOVE

GW00569184

Cover: Picture painted by Amelia Edwards (ABE/Pic.6). *By courtesy of the Principal and Fellows of Somerville College.*

Amelia B. Edwards
1831-1892

Author of *A Thousand Miles up the Nile*

HAND AND GLOVE

A Novel

Amelia B. Edwards

THE RUBICON PRESS

The Rubicon Press
57 Cornwall Gardens
London SW7 4BE

First published in 1858
This edition first published 2000

Preface copyright © Joan Rees, 2000
All rights reserved

British Library Cataloguing-in-Publication Data.

A catalogue record for this book is available from the British Library.

ISBN 0-948695-63-3

Printed and bound in Great Britain by Biddles Limited of Guildford
and King's Lynn

CONTENTS

PREFACE

Amelia Edwards's writing career can be said to have begun at the age of seven when a poem called 'The Knights of Old' was published in a penny magazine. At nine she won first prize in a temperance story competition and at twelve she wrote 'The Story of a Clock'. This juvenile effort was republished in 1893, some twelve months after her death, in the American *New England Magazine*. The fact that it was thought worth reprinting marks the distance travelled by this gifted child of a half-pay army officer and his lively wife, from a shabby-genteel background in south-east London to her status as a woman whose name was known and honoured in two continents. At her death, however, at the age of sixty-one, it was not as a writer that she was primarily known but as an Egyptologist, the founder, virtually single-handed, of the Egypt Exploration Society, a body still existing and dedicated now as then to the preservation and proper excavation of the monuments and sites of Ancient Egypt.

Amelia Edwards made her one and only visit to Egypt in the winter of 1873/4 and what she saw then made so great an impact on her that for the rest of her life she devoted her gifts and energies to the task of rousing public interest and gaining support for the objects of the Society. To that end she wrote thousands of letters and hundreds of articles and lectured both at home and in the United States; and she composed an account of her own Egyptian journey. *A Thousand Miles up the Nile*, as the book was called, was much read and enjoyed as it still is today. What is not commonly recognized by its modern admirers is that the divers literary skills, which are the decisive factor in making *A Thousand Miles* the entertaining and informative book that it is, had been developed and refined in a long apprenticeship as journalist, short-story writer and novelist.

Amelia Edwards was a writer before she was an Egyptologist and to her writing she brought a wide and varied experience and an astonishing range of knowledge. She wrote in all eight novels, the first of which, *My Brother's Wife*, was published in 1855 when she was twenty-four. The last, the only work of fiction she produced after her return from Egypt, was *Lord Brackenbury*, published in 1880 when she was forty-nine.

She had a high estimate of the novel as a literary form, claiming that it was the genre *par excellence* of the nineteenth century. Its function, she believed, was to draw a lively and accurate picture of contemporary society and by doing so to leave to succeeding generations an invaluable record of the past and an unparalleled insight into it. Her most trenchant remarks on the subject occur in *Hand and Glove* in the mouth of Hamel, the highly cultivated and strikingly sophisticated minister of the small Protestant community of Chalons-sur-Saône, in the region of which the novel is set. It is a fascinating feature of the book that this man, so much at odds with social and moral convention as he is, should be at many points evidently a spokesman for Amelia Edwards herself. She delights in his brilliance, she shares his satirical observation of the narrow minds who surround him and she evidently goes at least some way with him in the excoriating attack on conventional presentations of Christianity which he delivers as his first sermon. *Hand and Glove*, in fact, gives us a glimpse of a young Amelia Edwards, independent-minded and bursting with energy and talent. To express them she is not afraid to challenge accepted ideas and even, in some degree, morals.

She was a prolific inventer of stories and her novels are characteristically animated by multiple narratives which are full of action in a variety of settings, very often France, Germany or Italy, countries which she knew intimately. After the publication of *Hand and Glove* (1858) she adopted the then popular format of the three volume novel. It was a form with a notorious tendency to produce loose and untidy structures but for Amelia Edwards it had the advantage of giving room for the full deployment of her narrative energy and also for the wide range of reference which is a characteristic feature of her work. The world of art, music and literature is a constant background of her novels but her characters also range over such topics as climatic change and its probable social and political consequences, attitudes to women and the distinctions between hierarchical and republican governments. All Amelia Edwards's novels draw on a wide spectrum of interest and knowledge and *Barbara's History*, the first in the larger format, displays this characteristic to the full. Its story develops through ever-changing, vividly depicted scenes and generates an abundance of action. At the same time, through the character of Hugh Farquahar, the knowledge and experience of a widely cultivated, travelled and multi-accomplished man is mediated to the reader. The knowledge and the experience are, of course, Amelia Edwards's, a fact which highlights how much wider her coverage is than the narrow area of domestic ground commonly associated with women writers, especially in her day.

In the six years that passed between *Hand and Glove* and *Barbara's History*, Amelia Edwards had set herself to establish a secure footing in the literary market-place so that when she resumed novel-writing she would have a firm base from which to offer her work. She undertook publishers' commissions of many kinds, she worked at a career as a journalist, she built up a reputation as a short-story writer and she published her first travel book, an account of a tour through Belgium by a party of schoolboys. All this, together with her own travelling and her enthusiastic acquisition and assimilation of knowledge of all kinds, prepared her to offer *Barbara's History* to the world as her claim to be a serious contender in the field of fiction. The book did indeed make her reputation in the eyes of the critics and public alike and this and subsequent books went through numerous editions and were translated into other languages.

On all her books there is an entirely individual stamp. Story-telling skills, an acute and somewhat ironic sense of humour and descriptive gifts of an unusual calibre combine with untiring intellectual curiosity and energy to make a very distinctive mix. Her books were and remain well worth reading: they have much to offer.

Joan Rees
November 2000

CHAPTER I

A Midnight Vigil

The stealthy opening of the door awoke me.

'How does he seem now, Janet?' I asked, starting up in an instant with all my senses about me. 'Does he still sleep?'

'Yes, he still sleeps,' said the old woman mournfully.

Worn and weary as I was, I could not restrain a movement of impatience.

'Why did you disturb me, then?' I said, peevishly.

The fire and candle had both nearly burnt out, and I shivered as I spoke.

'I did not mean to wake ye,' said Janet, with unusual mildness. 'But it was awfu' to sit there and hear him havering in his sleep about them that are dead and gone long ago.'

She busied herself at the hearth as she said this, and blew the scattered embers red again. Presently she came over to the sofa, and bestowed the shawls more carefully about me.

'You're cold, Gartha,' she said, compassionately, 'and you've had no food for hours. Try to eat some supper.'

I shook my head, muttered something about trying to sleep again, and cowered down with my face to the wall, shuddering as before. But this time it was in vain. Not a thought wandered, and every sense seemed sharpened to a painful acuteness. The slow ticking of the great clock in the hall - the monotonous rocking to and fro of Janet in her chair - the lengthened blasts of melancholy March winds across the moors, all fretted and tried me to the very verge of nervous irritation. Yet I lay quite still, hand and foot, and listened to the sounds as they came and went, and repeated themselves over, and over, and over again. Listened, above all, for any stir that there might be in the silent chamber overhead. This lasted for a long time. By-and-by my father's bell rang.

We were both up in an instant. Janet, being in advance, entered the room first.

'Where's Gartha?' I heard him say. 'Where's Gartha? Why am I left alone? Where's Gartha, I say?'

The querulous tone, and the thin fingers plucking powerlessly at the curtain, struck me with a cold fear.

1

'I am here, sir,' I said, going round to the foot of the bed, and shading the light with my hand. 'Are you better now?'

He had shifted his position in his sleep, and lay in a slanting direction, with his feet towards the door. He looked up sharply when I spoke, and shook his head.

'Why do you ask?' he said, even more petulantly than before. '*You* don't care how I am! I might die up here for all the attention I get from you!'

I made no reply; but Janet charged herself with my defence.

'You ought to be ashamed o' yersel', Martin Wylde!' she exclaimed, in her rough north-country accent. 'Not care, indeed! D'ye ken that the child hasn't been to bed these five nights past, and that she's wearin' herself out for you every hour in the twenty-four?'

'Hush, Janet!' I cried; 'you forget!'

'I forget naething,' said Janet, obstinately, 'and it's because I forget naething that I speak plainly. He has nae mair thocht or heart in him now than he had when his puir young wife ...'

I put my hand suddenly over her mouth, and pointed to my father. He had contrived to raise himself on his elbow. His eyes were literally on fire. His lips quivered, and, pale with passion, he strove convulsively for utterance.

'Curse you, you venomous beldame!' he gasped at length. 'What devil possesses you? I'll turn you out! You shall starve on the moors like a dog! I'll ...'

His voice broke, a change passed over his countenance, and he fell back heavily upon the pillows.

'Nobody loves me!' he sobbed, with a bitter moaning in his voice. 'Nobody loves me!'

Accustomed as I had been for long years to his paroxysms of anger, to his neglect, to his sarcasms, I knew not how to treat so strange a mood as this. Pale and trembling, I stood aside and listened in silence to that complaining cry. Even Janet was appalled.

'Eh, Gartha!' she muttered, 'but he's awfu' bad to-night child! Don't ye think we maun speak to him again o' the doctor?'

He overheard her.

'The doctor!' he repeated, with a quick scowl. 'I hate him. He shall never cross my threshold. I'll die first!'

'May be ye will die first, Martin Wylde,' said Janet, solemnly.

He turned a shade paler than before, but made no reply. The

old servant pursued her advantage.

'You hate the cleverest gentleman and the best Christian in all this country-side,' she said. 'You're not more disliked yersel than Mr. Bryant is beloved, and that's say' muckle for him. Even now ye maun hae his help if you wish to see ere another simmer.'

There was an interval of silence, during which my father moved uneasily. At length he spoke.

'Do you think there's danger?' he said, in a tone that strove to be indifferent.

'Danger! Eh! but you suld ha' sent for him a week ago, for the matter o' that!' replied Janet, bluntly.

I went over to the bedside, and took my usual seat in the easy-chair.

'Janet is right, sir,' I said, very gently. 'Consent before it is too late!'

He looked up with a ghastly expression on his face, and then turned from me.

'Too late!' he echoed. 'Am I, then, so very ill?'

'Very ill, sir,' I replied.

'Who's to pay him? Where's the money to come from? I haven't a farthing! haven't a farthing!'

And again he moaned and sobbed, and plucked in that pitiful wavering way at the heavy curtain.

'Oh, sir,' I exclaimed, 'don't think of money now! Let Janet go for Mr. Bryant!'

'You must keep her out of the way, then,' he said hurriedly.

'Who, sir? Janet?'

'No - your mother.'

My mother! I drew back, startled and bewildered.

'Hush!' he whispered, with a wandering stare. 'Hush! She was here just now. She stood at the foot of the bed, and Eleanor with her. Poor Eleanor!'

I rose hastily, and dragged Janet towards the door.

'Go, go, Janet,' I cried, in an agony of terror. 'He raves - don't you hear him? My God! what shall I do? Oh bring him - bring the doctor!'

'Has the master agreed?' asked the old woman, doubtfully. 'I darena' gang without he's agreed.'

'Agreed or not matters little now. I will be answerable - take all

3

the blame - oh, pray go, Janet, dear!'

But Janet was unwilling to venture without permission. Outspoken as she was, nothing ever induced her to act in opposition to his entire and absolute authority.

'It's a gude three miles ow'r the muir,' said she, seeking an excuse. 'And there's nae moon worth speaking of. You'd better bide till the morn, and maybe he'll give leave his ainsel'.'

I snatched a bonnet from behind the door.

'Let me go!' I cried, impatiently. 'I care nothing for darkness or distance!'

'You'll do nowt of the sort,' said Janet, forcibly possessing herself of the bonnet, and preparing to be gone. 'I'll just gang mysel', child, while you bide here with the auld man; and I'll be sworn I shall meet naebody this side of the town.'

She wrapped herself in her cloak, and we went down together. I lit the lantern for her, and stood at the door, watching her as she hurried away. The retreating figure was soon lost in the darkness, and only the glimmer of the lantern, rising and falling, and swinging to and fro, like a will-o'-the-wisp, remained to indicate her route. Even this diminished rapidly, became a mere speck, and presently disappeared. There was a heavy oppression upon me, such as I had never felt before. I remember now how I started when the clock gave warning for midnight - how slowly I made my way back up the stairs - and how I paused outside the bedroom door, listening to my father's rapid muttering, and dreading to go in.

He still wandered. Sometimes he spoke of money. Sometimes, though rarely, of my mother. But the name of Eleanor - my aunt Eleanor, who lived with us after my mother died - came most frequently to his lips. At last he fell into a troubled sleep. I stole over to the window and looked out at the bleak and dusky undulations of the moors. They extended round our house in every direction. The waning moon was just scaling a bank of piled black cloud - the three solitary poplars beside the gate swayed with the coming and going of the wind - the owl that I had been used to hear ever since my child-hood, sent up a quavering wild cry, like the lamentation of a wandering spirit. I pressed my forehead down upon my hands, and tried to bring back something of the past - but, alas! it was a past long gone by, and the pictures were broken and confused, like reflections in the water.

I was a very little child when my mother died and my aunt Eleanor took her place in our household. She lived with us for six years or more, and I was about nine when she left us. Nobody ever spoke of her after she was gone, and my father, always harsh, grew more exacting and morose than before. She was his only sister, and, I believe, the only creature that he ever loved. I had gathered from a chance word or so of Janet's, that she married badly and died abroad, and this, with such fading and fragmentary recollections as remained upon my mind, was all that I knew of my aunt Eleanor. That she was beautiful, and serious, and cold, and stately, I felt rather than remembered; but the grave tones of her voice still vibrated upon my ears, and I could almost fancy that the frosty touch of her slender fingers yet lingered on my palm. If I still preserve a faint impression of a warmer hand and a fonder voice, if I love to imagine that hand upon the draperies of my tiny cot, and that voice murmuring a gentle 'good-night,' surely - surely, this is something more than a sweet delusion! Oh, my mother! is it not possible that I may yet retain, through all this waste of time, some fleeting memory of thee?

My father turned just now, and muttered in his sleep. An impulse of reluctant curiosity forced me back to his bedside, and I bent over him, listening. He was still speaking of his sister. Some other name (a foreign name, I thought) came in now and then; but the words were for the most part unintelligible, and I could make out nothing distinctly. I then ventured to touch his hand, and finding it very cold, heaped more coverings upon him, and returned to my station by the window.

The moon was higher now, and troops of swift ragged clouds were traversing the sky from left to right. Thin ground-mists, like strips of fallen cloud, floated here and there in the hollows, and made the dreary moors look still more ghostly. I sighed, and thought how often, in my restless girlhood, I had wearied of this familiar scene; compared it with places written about in books, and rebelled against it like an exile in a desert. I remembered how, when the evening dusk closed in, I used to sit, with half-closed eyes, and try to fancy that I saw the ridged ocean in place of the wide heath - and how often, at the same hour, I had watched the piled autumnal clouds, dreaming of sunset peaks and everlasting snows. But that was long ago. I had given up hoping now, and when a thought of change came wandering back, I banished it like an enemy, or avoided it like a temptation. It was strange, but at thirty years of age I had outlived the aspirations of youth, and learned to dread the freedom I desired. I think I almost loved the dark home, and the bare heath, and the dead life of the place. As for the great beautiful world beyond, what part could I take in it, and what had I to hope from it now? Was I not thirty years of age? Thirty years of age! The fact was not new to me. I had thought of it before, and thought of it without regret; but to-night it struck upon me with a feeling of uneasiness such as I had seldom experienced. Half of life already gone! - the latter half ... Ah! the latter half, what was there for me there? Life, sunshine, hope? No - no - not these - not these. I closed my eyes to happiness as to a thing impossible, and would not think of it. Still it came back, and back, and I could not banish it. 'A crisis must come,' whispered the voiceless thought, 'sooner or late - sooner or later.'

Sooner or later! - oh, not soon - not for years, perhaps! What should I do when ... Involuntarily I snatched up the candle and went over to the bedside. My father had turned, and was lying heavily across his left arm, with his face pressed to the pillow. It was an uneasy posture, and I wondered that he should rest in it so peacefully. No start, no broken mutterings, no deep fitful breathing now! Once again I ventured, very cautiously, to touch the outstretched hand. Something in the cold clammy contact, light as it was, startled me, and, with trembling haste, I felt cheeks, lips, and brow, and found all cold alike.

'Father!' I cried, trying to lift his head from the pillow. 'Father!'

My voice was harsh and sudden, and the jarring of it on my own ear startled me. Gently I laid it down, that heavy head in which the springs of thought were at rest for ever - gently I drew the sheet over it, and closed the curtains. Then I stood still, cold, trembling, and bewildered - stood still and listened. How silent the room was now! How silent all the house was! I could hear the clock ticking on the stairs, and the crickets chirping on the kitchen hearth, and the flapping to and fro of a loose window-shutter in a distant room. Even the wind had died away. Even the owl had ceased crying. Oh, the intolerable solitude! Oh, the silence! Oh, the bitter want of something to cling to - something to listen to - something to calm this rising terror at my heart!

Utterly stunned, and full of a blind fear against which I had no power to reason, I staggered, somehow or another, from the room, made my way down the creaking stair-case, and gained the door from whence I had watched Janet's lantern fading over the moor. I could not stay in the house now - I could not bear to be the only living thing in it. So I opened the door, closed without fastening it behind me, and sat down in the porch to wait. If I had not done so, I should have fainted; as it was, the keen air revived me, and I recovered somewhat of my self-possession. Still I dared not return within doors, even for a warmer shawl, though the atmosphere was damp and piercing, and I shivered in every limb. and, sitting there in the misty night, one only thought possessed me -

'The crisis *has* come. I am alone in the world.'

CHAPTER II

DR. BRYANT

I cannot tell how long I waited in the porch. I do not know at what time I made the discovery of my father's death. From midnight to sunrise I kept no count of hours. They are all confused together in my memory, and I retain but a vague impression of them. It seemed a weary interval, however, before Janet returned. The sky was gray with dawn, and a white billowy fog obscured all the country, breaking away, however, at times after a ghostly cosmoramic fashion, and in some places creeping so near the ground as to show the gaunt poplars piercing upwards here and there, like tree-tops above an inundated plain. Thus it was that I heard the quick wheels long before any object was visible through the mist, and was prepared to see Janet, accompanied by Dr. Bryant, for some minutes previous to their arrival at the garden-gate. As they came up the path, I rose, pale and ghastly enough, I dare say, and advanced to meet them.

Janet started back with a quick instinct of evil.

'What ails ye, Gartha?' she said, hurriedly. 'Why have ye left him?'

'I could not stay in the house - alone,' I replied, faintly.

She pushed past me without a word, and went in; but Dr. Bryant took me gently by the hand, and made me sit down again in the porch.

'I am shocked that this should have happened,' he said, kindly. 'How long have you been sitting here, exposed to the damp air?'

I shook my head, but tried in vain to answer.

'You are ill,' he said, still holding my hand, and looking at me with a kind of wistful curiosity. 'The trial has been too strong for you, and, poor child! you have had to bear it alone. You won't mind coming into the house with me?'

Again I shook my head, and he carried, rather than supported, me to the room in which I was sleeping when Janet, so many hours since, awoke me. With the tenderness of a woman, he placed me on the sofa, wrapped me in the shawls which had been my covering before, and chafed my icy hands between his own. Then the last remnant of my fortitude gave way, and I burst into tears.

'I had never seen death before!' I said, sobbing. 'I could not help it!'

'Of course not,' he replied, quickly and soothingly. 'Of course not. It is at all times awful, even to me. How much more so to you, Gartha!'

He called me Gartha, as if he had known me for years already, and smoothed my hair off gently from my brow.

'Come,' he continued, 'my duty here to-day is to make you better, and the first medicine that I prescribe shall be brandy. Where do you keep it?'

I pointed to a cupboard beside the window, and he poured out a wine-glassful and bade me drink it off.

'And, in the second place, I prescribe a fire. Why, you tremble as if you had an ague! Here, mistress Janet, we want some wood and your good help, if you please. Come, come, Gartha, no more tears. We must try to be calm now; calm and brave, my dear!'

Janet came in, looking very pale; but knelt down in silence and lit the fire, while Dr. Bryant walked up and down the room with his hands behind his back, only pausing now and then to say a word of encouragement, or to place my pillows more comfortably. Presently he turned towards the door.

'I may as well go up stairs for a moment,' he said, hesitatingly. 'Is it - is it the - the same room, mistress Janet?'

'Yes, sir,' replied Janet, without looking up, and speaking in a low constrained tone. 'It's the same room.'

He shut the door after him, and went up. In another moment I heard his footsteps overhead.

'Has Dr. Bryant been here before, Janet?' I asked. But she seemed not to hear me, and I felt too ill to repeat the question. He was a long time gone - so long that the fire was blazing, and the room well warmed before he came down again. Then he also looked pale, and I saw that his eyes were red with weeping.

'You must excuse me, Gartha,' he said, huskily, 'if I prescribe for myself this time. My - my nerves to-day are somewhat shaken, and old associations are too strong for me.'

He poured out some more brandy as he said this, drank it hastily, and began walking to and fro again between my sofa and the door. After a time he seemed to grow weary of this, and, resting his elbow on the chimney-piece, stood there with his eyes bent on the ground, thinking profoundly. As for me, I lay quite still and looked at him.

He had been handsome in his youth - was handsome yet, ruddy, gray-haired, and portly, with fine white hands, and a smile more sad than cheerful. Gentlemanly in his address, scrupulously neat in his attire, there was still a shade of indecision in his manner, a tremulousness of the voice and hands, a melancholy line or two about his kind mouth and thoughtful eyes, which impressed one at the very first with what was almost a feeling of compassion.

He stood there so long, and a solitary life had made of me so keen an observer, that I had time enough to analyze all this before he changed his position. By-and-by he looked up, and his eyes encountered mine. Then he brought a chair over and sat down beside me.

'I dare say you wonder what I have been thinking about?' he said, sighing. Then, finding that I made no reply, he added, hesitatingly, 'My last visit to this house was - was of a very painful nature, Gartha.'

'Then you have been here before?'

'Yes; I have been here twice before.'

'Not since I can remember, doctor?'

Again he laid his hand upon my hair, gently and caressingly, as if I were a mere child.

'The first time was when you were born, my dear,' he said. 'The second time was - was ...'

He played nervously with my hand, and broke off abruptly.

9

Then, almost in a whisper -

'Do you,' he faltered - 'Do you remember your mother?'

'My mother!' I exclaimed, eagerly. 'Oh, did you know her?'

His lips quivered, and his voice was so low that the words, 'Yes, I knew her,' seemed rather shaped by the motion of his mouth than uttered audibly.

'Tell me something of her!' I said, flushing and trembling. 'Tell me what she was like! She was young, was she not? Young and pretty, with a sweet soft voice, and large brown eyes, and a low merry laugh, like the warbling of a bird? And her hair, doctor - Janet says my hair is like it! Oh, pray tell me - pray tell me!'

'Your mother was very beautiful,' he said, with averted face, 'and as - as good as she was beautiful.'

'Did you know her before she married?'

He bent his head affirmatively.

'And everybody loved her, did they not?'

Dr. Bryant turned again and looked straight at me, with his eyes full of tears.

'My dear Gartha,' he said, tremulously, 'I, for one, loved your mother so well that I have lived all my life a lonely man for her dear sake.'

I understood the secret of his emotion now. There was a long interval of silence.

'She was too good for me,' he said, at length; 'but I would have cherished her truly for all that. However, God willed otherwise. When they sent for me the second time, it was to see her fading away - fading away like a little autumn flower. I only attended her for a few days, Gartha, and the last time I saw her was in the - the room over-head, my dear. I came quite early in the morning - as it might be this morning, when the mists were rising from the heath, and - and she had passed away in the night. Now you know it all, just as it happened, dear - just as it happened!'

I tried to say something consoling; but my voice died away, and my own tears were falling fast.

'Do you think,' I ventured to say at last, 'do you think she was happy after her marriage?'

The doctor coughed uneasily.

'Your father,' he replied, 'was the man of her choice.'

'But was he kind to her?'

'Was he kind to you?' said the doctor, answering a question with a question.

I remained silent.

'Did he do his duty by you?'

'Yes; he fed and clothed me.'

'But did you love him, Gartha?' asked my new friend, laying his hand upon my arm, and speaking very earnestly. 'Did you love your father?'

'My father never loved me,' I replied, bitterly. 'If I did not love him it was because I could not. I tried hard enough, heaven knows! The sin was not mine.'

'I am sure of that,' said Dr. Bryant. 'I only asked you that I might better reply to your own question. I fear your mother was not very happy in her preference. Your father was too cold and gloomy - the very house and its surroundings were too cold and gloomy for her. She drooped away, Gartha, from the very first; but you were her greatest comfort - remember that, dear - her little baby was her greatest comfort while she lived. And now all this brings me to what I was going to say at the first. You have no near relation or friend at hand, have you, upon whom to lean at the present juncture?'

'I have no friend in the world, except Janet,' I replied. 'Nobody ever came here, and I think I have no relations.'

'Don't tell me that you have no friend in the world,' said the doctor, quickly. 'I am an old friend, Gartha, though you know me to-day for the first time; and, in proof of it, I shall charge myself with all that is to be done. Leave everything to me, and as soon as I get back to Brookfield, I shall give the requisite directions. As for you, dear, you are my patient, and must obey my orders. When all is over, you shall come to Brookfield, and be my visitor awhile, if an old bachelor's establishment have any attractions for you. Hush! no thanks - I cannot bear them from your mother's child.'

'And when will you come again?' I asked, detaining him a moment longer.

'To-night - to-night, if my other patients will let me; if not, to-morrow morning early. Till then, rest and sleep, and take food, and keep up a good heart for the future. There, good-bye!'

I raised myself on the sofa, and watched him driving away in the bright sunshine.

'God bless him!' said Janet, emphatically. 'There goes the best gentleman in a' the twel' parishes, and the man your father disliked maist in the world.'

'How could he dislike him!' I exclaimed, involuntarily.

'That don't matter now,' said Janet, shaking her head. 'He'll dislike naebody ever again.'

But I remembered Dr. Bryant's story, and thought I could answer the question myself.

CHAPTER III

TREASURE-SEEKING

Through all the weary week that followed, I found myself the object of Dr. Bryant's indefatigable care. He ministered alike to my body and to my mind, fortifying the one by means of his art, and the other with his paternal affection. Not that I leaned upon him. It was sympathy that I borrowed, not strength; and sympathy in abundance he had to give. Decisive enough in any professional emergency, the doctor, I soon discovered, was of a yielding and somewhat weak nature; but his very weakness only endeared him to me the more. The sympathy of one weaker than ourselves, the sympathy even of a little child will aid the most resolute; and I believe that even then, when I felt my utter loneliness most keenly, when my future lay so dark before me, and death was in the house both by day and night, I was yet the stronger of the two.

He and I were the only mourners who followed my father's coffin to its last home, in a little bleak church-yard far amid the wilds of our moorlands.

As we came back, slowly and gravely, with words the most solemn ever spoken yet ringing in our ears, Dr. Bryant addressed me for the first time on the subject of my future destinies.

'Gartha,' he said, 'it is time now that you began to think of yourself. What do you mean to do? Not to stay in the old house, surely?'

'I don't know,' I said, listlessly.

'But I say that it shall not be so! You must see something of life, and learn to associate with your fellow-creatures. You must marry,

12

dear, and be happy.'

'Marry!' I echoed sadly: 'not now, kind friend, not now.'

'And why not now?'

'Look at me, and answer yourself. I am plain; I have no accomplishments; I possess no graces of manner or feature; and I am thirty years of age.'

'What of that?'

'This; that I have no hope to be loved; and as for marriage without love, I'll none of it.'

'Tush!' said the doctor, with a melancholy smile; 'you are more romantic than I had thought.'

'I am not romantic at all,' I replied. 'How can I be romantic when my feelings have never been brought into play, and my imagination has been starved from childhood upwards? Why I have never read a novel in my life, and scarcely a poem, save the works of Shakspeare and Dryden. No, I am not romantic, I am practical. I have lived till this hour without love; I have seen what home is where love is not; and, by the breadth, and depth, and height of my loss, I measure the magnitude of the need. There may be a wisdom of expediency which gives love no part in marriage; but there is still, thank God, a truer wisdom of the heart.'

'You are right,' said the doctor; 'but I see no reason why you should be excluded from the chances of love as well as matrimony. You are neither as old as Methuselah nor as ugly as Medusa. You look less than your age, and your expression is charming. Besides, you will have money, and with money ...'

'And with money I am less likely than ever to be sought for myself! No, doctor, no - Gartha Wylde is an old maid already, and Gartha Wylde will remain an old maid to the last! Let us change the subject. You spoke of money last! Now, excepting that we always lived in a very lonely, inexpensive way, I know nothing of my father's circumstances. Do you think there will be enough for me to live upon without remaining in the old house?'

'I should suppose so. Your father had the name of a rich man.'

'Then I think I shall let or sell the house, and go abroad; at least for a time.'

The doctor looked up quickly when I said this, then sighed, and began tracing little circles in the dust with the end of his cane.

'I hoped,' he said, 'that you would have chosen Brookfield for your home. Nay, I had even some vague notion that - that ... but, at all events you have promised to visit me first!'

'Indeed, yes. And, after all, my scheme might need more wealth than I can compass.'

The good doctor shook his head.

'I fear,' he said, 'that you will find yourself quite rich enough to go a long way from me, dear, and to remain where and how you please. Our Brookfield gossips already call you "the heiress."'

The heiress! This possibility had never occurred to me before, and I repeated the words two or three times over, without exactly realizing all their meaning. An heiress, and 'rich enough to remain where and how I pleased!' Oh the magic name of wealth! How the old dreams came rushing back again, like the waters of a river that had been turned from their channel! Art, in all her multiform glory, and Nature, under her divinest aspects, were henceforth accessible to me! The sea and the Alps, my earliest and latest desires, should become visible poems! I fancied myself like the adept in the fable, who, having discovered the word of power, found the mountains grow transparent to his sight, beheld the lost treasures at the bottom of the ocean, and saw the precious ores that lay buried in the bowels of the earth!

Something of this exultation must have expressed itself in my face, for I looked up and found Dr. Bryant watching me.

'Gartha,' he said, reproachfully, 'are you fond of money?'

'Yes; for what it will purchase,' I replied, eagerly. 'Nay,' I pursued, seeing the disappointment not yet faded from his face, 'remember what my life has been before you judge me too severely. Remember how much I have endured - how little I have enjoyed, and then ask yourself what riches and freedom must be worth to me!'

The doctor held up a warning finger, and pointed to the dark housetop and the three gaunt poplars now coming into sight.

'Hold!' he said. 'Yonder lies the solution of your future. Let us not talk of riches till we know their extent.'

We hastened on in silence, and, passing through the desolate garden, entered the still more desolate house. All was dark within. The shutters had not been unclosed for days, and the air had something oppressive and earthy upon it. To admit the sunlight and the fresh breeze, and throw doors and windows open, was the work of a few minutes. Then I gave the keys to Dr. Bryant, and we set to work to find my father's papers.

First we searched a bureau in what had been his bedchamber. It was an old-fashioned piece of furniture, high and narrow, and inlaid with brass. In the upper part we found a few books, some yellow pamphlets, and a vast number of bills, recipes, and empty phials. The lower compartment was taken up by an obsolete old dictionary in many folio volumes. Certain that nothing important had been passed over, we then went on to examine the contents of a cupboard, and next a huge oaken press down in the parlour. These were ransacked with as little success, and hours passed by in useless seeking. Then the dusk closed in, and we were fain to rest awhile over a supply of Janet's coffee. We were both very silent and tired, and somewhat out of heart.

'I am the more surprised,' said Dr. Bryant, 'since a lease or two, and the title-deeds of some unprofitable moorland property, are the only papers that your father has left in the hands of Mr. Williams of Brookfield.'

His thoughts were busy, and he spoke more as in reply to an observation, than as if he were beginning a subject.

'Do you think,' he continued, after a brief interval, 'that we have omitted any secret drawer in the bureau?'

'Impossible.'

'And you know of no other likely places?'

'None whatever.'

The doctor pushed his cup away, and walked restlessly about the room, as was his custom when anxious or impatient.

'At all events, there is one chance left,' he said, and rang the bell.

Janet came after a time, but slowly and with a discontented face, as if something had offended her.

'Mistress Janet,' said the doctor, 'we have been making a great search this afternoon among your poor master's papers.'

'I ken that,' said she, sulkily. 'Ye've made litter and dust eno', I hope, between ye!'

'But, mistress Janet, we have found no will, no deeds - nothing of any importance.'

'Just what I thocht.'

'And it has occurred to me,' continued the doctor, in his most conciliatory tones, 'that - that you might perhaps remember some trifling circumstance which would assist us. Do you think you have ever seen Mr. Wylde putting papers away in any particular drawer? or was there any place which he seemed more anxious to keep locked than another? It is of great importance that you should recall this, if possible, mistress Janet!'

'Why didn't you ask me first of a'?' said Janet, still offended, and unwilling to be softened. 'You might ha' spared yourselves some trouble.'

I knew the infirmities of her temper, and held my tongue. Dr. Bryant persevered.

'Come, come,' he said, persuasively, 'tell us all you know, like a good soul. You were not in the way when we came in, and we forgot to ask you. That's all the mistake.'

'May be the little I do ken winna be of ony great use after a',' said Janet, relenting.

'Well, we shall see.'

'I suppose you've turned out the press?'

'Yes, yes. The press, and the bureau, and the cupboard, and every place we could think of, mistress Janet,' replied the doctor, somewhat impatiently. 'Nothing in any of them - nothing but rubbish.'

'Ay, ay,' said Janet, prolonging our suspense with evident satisfaction. 'I could ha' told you there was naething but rubbish in all of 'em. But I'll be bound you never thocht of looking in the big old chest under the bed, where the gude man kept his clothes.'

The doctor brought his hand down heavily upon the table.

'Upon my conscience, Janet,' said he, 'you're right: we never thought of it! What's in the chest?'

'Naething now, perhaps,' replied the old woman. 'But there were papers there years syne - vera secret papers, too. The master used to take 'em out at night, and read 'em over with the door locked. I mind ganging into the room ane day when he'd forgotten to turn the key, and the table was covered with 'em; and when he saw me he gathered 'em all up in a heap wi' both hands, and turned upon me like a tiger. Oh! he was an awfu' man when he was fashed!'

The doctor seized a candle, and preceded me up stairs without another word. We then pulled the great chest out into the middle of the room, and, one by one, tried every key on every rusty bunch, and found not one that fitted. It was a peculiar looking lock, shaped like the letter Z, and requiring a key unusually small compared with the size of the chest. Then we endeavoured to force the bolt back with a gimlet, but in vain - and then Janet remembered to have seen a key in my father's pocket-book. To fetch the pocket-book, find the key, fit it to the chest, and throw it open in triumph, was the work of but a few moments. I turned cold and held my breath, and Dr. Bryant's hands trembled like the hands of a sick man.

My father's best suit, neatly folded, lay at the top; some razor-cases, some old linen, and a pair of antique inlaid pistols came next; then a little canvas bag, containing money, which I threw aside without pausing to examine; then a square parcel, folded in a faded silk handkerchief.

Dr. Bryant laid his hand on the parcel.

'It is full of papers,' he whispered, and opened it upon the floor.

I shall never forget the anxiety of that moment - nor the revulsion of feeling by which it was followed. A bundle of yellow newspapers tied together with a morsel of red tape, a curl of dark hair in a piece of folded paper, and about a dozen letters was all that it contained. Not a law paper - not a deed - not a will of any description!

The letters were addressed to my father, and directed, with one exception, in a delicate female hand. The newspapers were some of French, some of English, and some of Portuguese publication, and bore a date of twenty years ago. On the margin of the uppermost I read these words, in my father's writing:-

'Particulars of the trial of A.A.L., January to March 18—.' I then opened one of the letters, and saw that it was signed 'Eleanor.' Dr. Bryant looked at it long and earnestly.

'Poor Eleanor!' he said, with a sigh. 'These are her letters from abroad, after her marriage - and this,' selecting another from the heap, 'is one written by her husband. Did you ever see so crabbed a hand?'

It was certainly a strange hand - marvellously minute, firm, and clear, with odd writhing tails and fantastic capitals. It reminded me of specimens that I had seen of the old court writing, such as Chaucer wrote, and Chatterton imitated. I looked at it for a moment with curiosity, and then flung it back into the chest with the newspapers and other contents of the handkerchief. Eleanor and her husband possessed no interest for me, and my heart was full of its own anxieties.

'Is there nothing more?' I asked despondingly.

'Nothing but this,' replied the doctor, untying the canvas bag, and pouring the contents into my lap. We told them over together. There were about fifty shillings in silver; five or six old guineas; twenty-three sovereigns of the reigns of George III, George IV, and William IV; and bank-notes to the value of one hundred and sixty pounds. Just one hundred and ninety pounds altogether. Not a farthing more. As we counted it over for the second time, Dr. Bryant shook the bag, and a scrap of folded paper fell out. It contained a few words in my father's writing, and was dated about two years back. It ran thus:-

'I am not a rich man. If my daughter has fallen into the general error, and supposed herself an heiress, she is mistaken. The little that I have to leave is hers, but it is only the remnant of my property. Lawyer Williams, of Brookfield, has charge of the papers relating to the old house, and to the three cottages on the Kingsbury Road. These, with a few acres of moorland, and the contents of the canvas bag, are the whole of my possessions. If my daughter desires to know what has become of the rest, she may hear the story of my losses from Lawyer Williams above named. Having learnt this, let her take up the inheritance of hate over which I have brooded for so many years.

'MARTIN WYLDE.'

Stupified with amazement, I read this paper over twice or thrice, and then handed it to Dr. Bryant. A dark shade passed over his face.

'There have been times when I feared this,' he said. 'I am not taken altogether by surprise, Gartha.'

'What does it mean?' I asked. 'What does it mean?'

'It means that your father was a ruined man, and that the swindler was ... your aunt Eleanor's husband.'

There was a long silence. Not a word fell from my lips, and I sat there on the floor with my face buried in my hands. My dreams were all dispersed - my thoughts wandering and confused - my hopes dashed for the last time to the ground.

'Poor Gartha!' said my friend, with his hand upon my shoulder. 'Poor Gartha!'

But I had no voice to answer him.

CHAPTER IV

A PROJECT AND ITS ISSUE

It was only too true. My father died a poor man - poorer than even I, who had been brought up in utter ignorance of the popular rumour, had ever had reason to anticipate. A youth of hopeless longings, a womanhood of solitary repining, a brief dream of riches and enjoyment had ended thus. Ended in barren poverty, and brought me face to face with the realities of life. Looking back upon it now, I recognize the priceless value of that crisis. I see how all purposes of fate were wisely shaped; how the command of sudden wealth might have influenced my nature to weak and selfish ends; and how necessary to the development of my moral being was this stern and wholesome trial. I was not fitted, by education or experience, for the possession of riches. I doubt if I should then have used them worthily, or have held them, as I should now hold them, less for my own gratification than as a trust for the deserving and the needy. The disappointment was for a few hours more acute than I quite care, after this lapse of time, to confess; but I know now that it was wisely ordered, and I am thankful that events so succeeded, and so controlled each other.

In acceptance of Dr. Bryant's invitation, I consigned the old moor house to Janet's care, and went over to visit him at Brookfield. Brookfield, as I now know it, is a dreary, gossiping, formal little country town, as exclusive, as inquisitive, and as far *en arrière* as any other English country town enjoying the same advantages of remoteness, dulness, and general incapacity. But not so did it then appear to me. The few old-fashioned residents that now and then paid a brief visit to the doctor - the market-place, with its busy crowd on Tuesdays and Fridays - the passing of the London coach, of farmers' gigs, tradesmen's carts, and occasional private carriages - bewildered and amused me as much as if I had been transferred to one of the most crowded thoroughfares of London or Paris.

The sight of human life and human occupations - the faces of childhood and old age - the hum of traffic, the song of a wandering ballad-singer, and the echoes of young laughter in the quiet street at dusk, all replied to a yearning in my heart - educated me, in fact, for the society of my fellow creatures, and paved the way for that future which shaped itself before me more and more clearly every day.

I resolved to go out into the world and earn my living. How and why I came to this conclusion will require but a very few words of explanation.

My first care, on reaching Brookfield, was to call on Mr. Williams, the lawyer, to investigate the exact condition of my affairs, and to arrive at the nearest possible estimate of my real position. This, I found, was straitened indeed. The old house and the cottages were valued at something more than a couple of hundred pounds. The twenty acres of moorland were scarcely saleable. Altogether, I had not five hundred pounds in the world. This was a grim prospect; but, the first shock over, I learnt to face it steadily. An active life, under any circumstances, was welcome, and I had hardly conceived the plan before I was impatient for its execution. Dr. Bryant vehemently opposed it.

'Earn your living, indeed!' he said, impatiently. 'How can you earn your living? What experience have you had? How are you fitted for the crosses and jostlings of the world?'

'Better fitted for them,' I replied, 'than many who are thrown upon their own resources at an earlier age. Is not a woman of thirty at least as competent to work as a girl of seventeen?'

'I deny it,' said the doctor, eagerly. 'I deny it. At seventeen, hope is strong, and the disposition plastic. Seventeen shakes off care and unkindness, as a bird shakes the rain drops from its wing. Seventeen will bear transplantation; not so thirty - not so thirty.'

'But thirty can - thirty will - thirty must!' I answered firmly. 'Listen to me, dear friend. I want an aim in life - every woman does - and I cannot be happy without one. I am neither faint-hearted nor sensitive. I have never known what it was to be a home-darling. I have no ties. I am weary of England - weary of inaction - weary of myself. What I need is work; wholesome, daily, honest work, whereby to employ both mind and body. I care little what manner of work I find, so that it be true and fitting, and such as I can fairly execute. I would rather be employed in France or Germany, that I might perfect myself in one of those languages. If I meet with only moderate consideration, civility, and just payment, it is all that I have any right to expect, and I shall not feel myself injured or misunderstood if my employers hold themselves towards me in the simple relation of employers, and nothing more.'

Dr. Bryant made a grimace of disappointment.

'Let us grant all this,' he said, petulantly. 'Let us grant that you wear mail of proof, and that your determination is (for the sake of argument) reasonable - still you have not proved your competency. Again, I say, what are you fit for?'

'I can sew - I can write - I am a good accountant - I have a fair book-knowledge of French and German - I know the English history and Murray's grammar by heart - I have read much - thought a little - tutored myself for the duties of a teacher, a housekeeper, or a companion. I believe that I am "fit" for either of those three positions.'

The good doctor sighed, sat down, rose up again, took both my hands in his, and said -

'Gartha, live with me.'

I was so taken by surprise that I could find nothing to reply.

'I feel towards you,' he went on, 'as if you were my own daughter, and I have felt thus since the first moment I saw you. I am an old man, Gartha, and I know that I have many faults; but I will be the truest friend and the fondest father to you. I am not rich - I have never tried to be rich - but I am moderately well off, and I will leave you all that is mine. Come - give up your project and be my child, and my housekeeper, and my comfort till I die.'

The tears rose to my eyes, and I leaned my forehead up against the cold chimney-piece. The struggle between gratitude and independence was a hard one, and the wish to stay was almost as strong within me as the wish to go.

'Yes, or no, Gartha,' said Dr. Bryant, holding out a tremulous hand. I took the hand and touched it with both tears and kisses.

'Forgive me,' I said, after a long pause. 'Forgive me - but I - I want work. I must go.'

'It is your positive decision?'

'It is my positive decision.'

He stood for some minutes absorbed in thought, and then said, very gravely -

'If it must be so, I shall do my best to help you - under protest.

Promise me one thing, however: promise that you will take no further steps for at least another fortnight.'

'I promise.'

'And that you will allow yourself to be guided in some degree by my advice and experience.'

'Most certainly.'

Upon this he went straight to his study. Hence I saw him despatch a letter to the post about an hour afterwards; but he said nothing more, and I dared ask no questions.

I often tried at this time to lead the conversation to the subject of my father's losses, but without much success. Dr. Bryant knew nothing of them, and spoke from conjecture only.

I then had recourse to Mr. Williams; but Mr. Williams, who was quite a young man, shook his head and laughed, and said, that if I wanted information on affairs of twenty years ago, I must consult his father, who was then in Antwerp, and would not be back for four months longer. I had, therefore, to content myself with such stray scraps of information as fell every now and then from Dr. Bryant; and these, after all, amounted to very little. That my aunt Eleanor had married unfortunately, that the man was a foreign adventurer, of whose antecedents she was entirely ignorant, that he was twenty-two when she was forty, were facts that I almost knew, or guessed at already. Fascinating and unprincipled to a rare degree, it was not wonderful, said the doctor, that he should have misled my father as he misled many others - ruined him, as hundreds were ruined. He came down to our district as agent for a continental speculation, and secured a large number of subscribers. The speculation turned out to be a bubble. My aunt Eleanor lost all, and my father nearly all his property.

Other circumstances there were, said Doctor Bryant, still more humiliating, which it were useless to repeat after the lapse of so many years. Eleanor was long since dead; her unfortunate husband, he hoped, was dead also, and so it were better that the rest should lie buried with them, and like them be forgotten. More than this I could not obtain from him, and after a time my interest in the matter died away. Other events, more nearly relating to myself, thrust all else into the background, and the time arrived when projects were to become realities.

Scarcely had two-thirds of the prescribed fortnight gone by, when Dr. Bryant came in to breakfast one morning with an open letter in his hand.

'This,' said he, 'concerns you, Gartha. Read it, and tell me what you think of it.'

It was written on foreign paper, bore a foreign post-mark, was dated from Chalons-sur-Saône, and ran thus:-

'MY DEAR FRIEND AND COUSIN,-

'The sight of your handwriting is indeed a pleasant novelty. I often regret that we are both such lazy correspondents, and that we suffer our intimacy to rust as it has done of late years. Since my poor mother's death, you are the only relative of whom I have any knowledge in dear old England - the only tie left to remind me that I am not a Frenchwoman born. Thank you for your inquiries and good wishes. I am quite happy, and Monsieur Vaudon is the kindest of husbands. All goes well with me, and you must make up your mind to pay us a visit when the vintage next comes round, if only to convince yourself that your English cousin is happy in her French home. Regarding the subject of your letter, I am sorry that I cannot myself receive your friend, who is, I am sure, a most interesting person. Our daughter Adèle has just finished her education in Paris, and for our little son we have a tutor resident in the house. I can, however, introduce her to my excellent friends Monsieur and Madame Delahaye, who are seeking an English companion for their daughter. She is two years younger than Adèle, pretty, amiable, and accomplished - perhaps a little spoilt and over-indulged, like only children in general. She is engaged to her cousin, M. Gautier, but will not be married for some two or three years to come. In the meantime they are anxious to improve her in the English language, and desire me to offer that charge, with a salary of six hundred francs yearly, to your friend. The sum is small; but in France we seldom offer more, unless accomplishments of a high order are required. They live at Montrocher, one of the prettiest villages in the Côte d'Or; are genuinely hospitable, worthy people; and will, I am sure, do everything to make her comfortable. Let the lady reply to their offer as speedily as possible, and, should she accept it, prepare at once for the journey, as they are wishing to receive her immediately. Adieu. If my English is very faulty, pray forgive it. I think in French, and have the greatest difficulty to prevent myself from translating literally as I go along. Monsieur Vaudon bids me say, that our vintage festivities next autumn will be incomplete without you. You really must yield, or I shall believe that you have quite ceased to care for

'Your affectionate friend and cousin,

'MATILDA VAUDON.'

I read this letter over twice, and, looking up, found Dr. Bryant watching me.

'Well,' he said, 'what of it, Gartha?'

'There can be but one answer,' I replied. 'I accept it gratefully.'

'But consider a little. Six hundred francs is only four-and-twenty pounds a year.'

'It will be enough, with the interest of what I have already.'

'And Montrocher is but a tiny village in one of the remotest departments of France. You will be almost as lonely as in the old house on the moor.'

'I shall have employment and society, and the opportunity of acquiring a language.'

'And you will have to go immediately.'

'I am as ready now as I should be a month or two hence, and the longer I delay the less willing I shall be to go.'

'Delay then, by all means!' exclaimed the doctor, eagerly. 'Delay now and always, Gartha, and make this house your home! Ah, cruel child, what can I do to persuade you?'

'Write to your cousin, dear friend,' I said, laying my hand upon his sleeve, 'and accept this situation, with all fitting thanks, for me. Say that I will leave here as speedily as they please, and ...'

'And that you are glad enough to go,' added the doctor, reproachfully.

So he went back again to his study, again wrote and despatched a letter to Madame Vaudon, and the thing was settled.

The very next available foreign post brought me a polite little French note from Madame Delahaye, containing full directions respecting my journey, the hours of departure by steamer and railway, the list of fares, and the name of a hotel in Paris, where it was necessary that I should break the journey by one night's rest.

A brief intimation that my hotel and travelling expenses would be defrayed by M. Delahaye, and a complimentary phrase or two of good wishes and congratulation, concluded the letter.

But from our far-off north-country district to London alone constituted another day's journey, and as this necessity had not occurred to Madame Delahaye, it compelled me to hasten my departure by twenty-four hours, and made my time for preparation brief indeed. To go back for a day to the old house; to gather together all that I cared to take with me in the way of books and wardrobe; to set aside such relics of home as I desired to preserve; and to select for Janet the few household articles necessary to furnish a small cottage, occupied all my time up to the moment of my going. To Dr. Bryant, I left the care of this poor old servant, who, blunt and undemonstrative as she was, had been a faithful worker in the house for five and thirty years. She was now to occupy the smallest of the three cottages on the Kingsbury road, which was all that my poor means permitted me to do for her. It made her, however, quite happy and independent. I then left the management of my little property to Mr. Williams, and placed in Dr. Bryant's charge such few books and papers as I cared to preserve. Among these, though half tempted to destroy them, the letters and papers relative to my aunt Eleanor, and the rest of the contents of the handkerchief found in the trunk. Rapidly as all was done, I left nothing undone. I then returned to spend my last night at Brookfield. At peace with regard to my worldly affairs, hopeful for the future, and yielding ready acquiescence to a feeling that, in its novelty and pleasantness, bore no little affinity to the spirit of adventure, I rose cheerfully and promptly the next morning, and hastened down to breakfast, with my bonnet on. I found my boxes waiting, ready corded, in the hall, the doctor pacing to and fro between the table and the door, and Janet sitting gloomily on the lowest step of the stair-case. A little brown pocket-book lay on my breakfast-plate, and, beside it, a faded morocco case with a silver clasp. Seeing me about to examine these objects, the doctor came over, and prevented me from opening the pocket-book.

'Tush,' said he, 'not now - not now. Wait till you are on the road, and want amusement. It is only a memorandum-book that may be useful on your journey, and - and in it you will find a - a little trifle, just for pocket-money, as a token of my love!'

I would fain have declined it; or opened it, that I might at least render back a portion of the gift, which was, I felt assured, more liberal than I could bear to take. But he would not suffer it.

'It is so little,' he pleaded, 'and so inadequate to express my love and regard, dear, that you would quite break my heart if you refused any of it. Pray, say not another word. You don't know how you wound me!'

So I desisted, and took up the morocco case instead. It contained the portrait of a lady, much faded, not even very well painted, but representing a countenance so innocent and so lovable, that I found myself interested at the first glance.

'Who is this?' I exclaimed.

The doctor sat down on the nearest chair and covered his eyes with his hand.

'It is the likeness of one whom, ... do you remember our conversation, Gartha, on that first morning when I found you in the porch?'

A sharp sensation, more of pain than pleasure, tightened round my heart, my breath fluttered, the picture grew blurred and wavering before my eyes.

'It is my mother!' I said faintly.

The doctor bent his head, took one long look at it, closed the case reverently, and returned it into my hands.

'It has been my dearest treasure for many a long year,' he said tremulously. 'It was sketched from memory by an artist who had seen her once in church. He gave it to me - I give it to you. You have a better right to it than I.'

Wholly overcome, I laid my head down on the table, and sobbed like a child. Just at that minute Janet opened the door and looked in.

'Now, Gartha,' she said, roughly, 'here's the porter lad come round from the coach-office. Are ye ready?'

'Quite, quite ready,' I said, starting up, and sweeping the case and pocket-book into my travelling-basket.

'But ye've tasted ne'er a morsel o' breakfast!'

I shook my head, and tried to still the sobs that kept rising in my throat.

'Good-bye, Janet!' I said, holding out the disengaged hand.

The hard lines about her mouth were working, in spite of her resolution to be firm.

'Gude-bye to ye, puir child,' she said, hoarsely, pressed my hand between both her own, and turned away.

I took Dr. Bryant's arm, and followed the porter down the empty village street, lying now so still and silent in the early morning. All was ready at the coach-office. The passengers were in their places, and the coachman, whip in hand, was just about to mount.

'Mornin', sir,' said the guard, touching his hat, with a ready grin; 'I knew we shouldn't have to wait for the young lady where a gen'lman of your punctual ways was concerned.'

The good old man kissed me on the lips and brow - the inside passengers made room for me next the door - the coachman gathered up the reins - the guard touched his hat again to Dr. Bryant, and pocketed a bright half-crown - the merry horn gave the starting signal - the boys and ostlers shouted, and we were off.

Off down the sleepy streets, and past the well-known house where Janet was standing at an upper window with her apron to her eyes; off across the bridge, where the banks were just beginning to get green, and past the school-house, where the noisy little ones had not yet congregated for their daily labour. Off into the open country and the wide wide world, and far away already (as this first milestone tells me) from that corner of the Brookfield market-hill where Dr. Bryant stood, leaning on his stick, and looking after us beneath the shelter of his hand!

CHAPTER V

OVER THE SEA

Although, after some three hours in the coach, I reached a station on the Great Northern Railway and finished my journey by train, it was nevertheless quite late when I arrived at the London terminus. Worn out by the unwonted excitement, bewildered by the innumerable streets which had glinted past the carriage window during the last ten minutes or so, and, above all, confused by the living torrent pouring along the platform, I had recourse to a gigantic porter, and, under his auspices, succeeded in obtaining a cab, storing it with my luggage, and driving off straightway to Peele's coffee-house, which, by the way, was the only hotel in London that Dr. Bryant knew anything about. I suppose it was a somewhat unlikely hostelry for one of my sex, since the waiters received me with looks of surprise discreetly veiled, and the landlord smiled as he ushered me into a modest little apartment overlooking the street. Here, however, I was well content. They served me with a delicious little meal, which was dinner and tea combined, supplied me with the *Times*, and the last instalment of *Punch*, and, when the candles were lighted and the curtains drawn, wished me a civil good-night, and left me to myself.

In London! It seemed so impossible that I should be in London! Still more impossible that, by this time to-morrow evening, I should be in France, and on my way to Paris! I was in no humour to-night for the wit and wisdom of *Punch*, and, closing the pamphlet, listened awhile to the subdued murmur rising from the streets. Then I opened the window, and looked down upon the crowded thoroughfare below. It was a fine night, and the pavement was thronged with foot-passengers. To the right, Temple Bar; to the left, a rising chain of lights, Ludgate Hill, and the ghostly outline of St. Paul's. Along all the busy street a quick pulse of traffic, brisk and noisy, and full of restless life, sending up hoarse cries, and fragments of tunes ground out on hand-organs, and sounds of wheels, and whips, and humming voices, all fused together in one great murmur, like the murmur of the sea! I gazed and gazed till my eyes and head ached, and the cold night air warned me to give over. Then I went to bed, and dreamt uneasily till morning.

Next day, soon after noon, I was on the road again. I felt less nervous and bewildered now, and enjoyed the transit from London to Folkestone very much indeed. The richness of this charming district, so different in its abundance and beauty to the barren north, delighted me beyond measure. The quaint old farm-houses, the cultivated slopes and sweet, green valleys, the mossied barns and fruit-promising orchards, filled my mind with images of simple grace and comfort, which were only dispersed at last by a glimpse of the far blue ocean, a solitary martello tower, and a panting steamer in the harbour down below.

Yet a few minutes more and I am on the sea - on that sea of which I dreamt and read so often in the old time! It is very lovely; calm, and blue, and ruffled by a soft breeze, as wayward and tender as the kisses of a playful child. A melting haze indicates the direction of the coast of France; the sun shines out over the blue waste in shifting lines of brilliant green and amber; and a stately brig, with all sails set, is gliding slowly past in the mid-path of the channel.

And so the day wears on, as if all this novelty and beauty were but the passing of a panorama, and I an unpartaking spectator. I suffer myself to be borne hither and thither, landed at Boulogne, hustled through the custom-house, placed in an omnibus, and deposited in a railway waiting-room, without exactly understanding how it can all have happened, or by what means I have reached the right place at last. Being very weary now, and finding that the Paris train will not leave till nearly midnight, I make a sofa of a form in an obscure corner of the waiting-room, and sleep soundly till roused by an attentive porter, who conducts me to a comfortable corner-seat in a second-class carriage. I have but one fellow-passenger, and this passenger is a restless young gentleman with a small leather satchel slung over his right shoulder, and an inexhaustible store of vivacious incendiarism.

First of all he begs permission to smoke, and, this granted, produces a complicated piece of mechanism with a flint and steel at one end and a wormy coil of yellow worsted at the other. He then lights a dainty cigarette and smokes for about three minutes with his head out of the window. Getting tired of this, he produces a newspaper, an ingenious little railway reading-lamp, and a box of matches. To fix the lamp, fire off a platoon of lucifers, and plunge into the study of the latest *feuilleton* occupy him for nearly ten minutes more, when he suddenly extinguishes the lamp, dives into the recesses of the satchel, and brings out what appears to be a small fishing-rod in many compartments. The fishing-rod, when screwed together, turns out to be a pipe, and is ignited by quite a different process. This conduct, infinitely varied with regard to combustibles and occupations, lasts, as I should think, for three hours, waking me up perpetually, and prompting me to uneasy dreams. By-and-by, however, he also subsides into a profound slumber, and so the night passes. When I next open my eyes the day has begun to dawn, and the landscape looms indistinctly through the gray vapours of early morning. The recollection that this is France, and that I am speeding away to my unknown destination, rouses me thoroughly, and I observe every feature of the shifting picture. Trees and houses, looking thin and ghostly, but growing momentarily more distinct, seem gliding past the windows. Then fields, with a thick mist hanging over them in parts, plantations, farm-houses, villages, and towns. Now comes a broad, bright river, reflecting the slaty sky amid the dark-green rushes - next, a thick wood, with a little white chapel peeping from amidst the trees - then lime-kilns; steep cuttings; long barren fields; pasture-lands crossed by monotonous lines of stunted pollards; dreary flats; and the huts of a colony of charcoal-burners. Last of all, a continuous sprinkling of white buildings, and a view of Paris - distant, indistinct, and many steepled.

The sun is high, and it is just seven o'clock as I emerge from the station. Oh, beautiful Paris! how fair and strange it looks to me as I drive past in the early morning! The shops are not yet opened, and there are but few people on foot. The broad streets are silent and sunny - the trees along the Boulevards are all in bud, and some have just put forth a leaf or two upon their topmost branches - the gilded balconies of the hotels, and the creamy shutters of the lofty houses, remind me of the city of the caliph and the palaces of Grenada. So occupied am I with admiration, that I am quite sorry when the cab stops, and I find myself already in the court-yard of the hotel. But the glimpse that I have had is not sufficient, and I cannot rest without soon going out again, and seeing all that may be seen within the short space of a single day. A passing glimpse of the Louvre, a brief visit to the solemn aisles of Notre Dame, a turn in the gardens of the Tuileries, and a circuitous drive through the Champs Elysées bring the day quickly to an end, and send me back, dazzled and wearied, to a frugal dinner and a long night's rest. And so the third day ends, and the fourth and last arrives. It is well for me that this is the last, for I am all unused to rapid change of scene, and the effects of continuous exertion begin to tell upon me. Sitting in the solitary *salon* at my early breakfast, long before the *habitués* of the hotel have an idea of waking, I fancy that I still feel the motion of the train, and hear the rough bass of its iron progress. There is a weight upon my eyelids, a singing in my ears, and an oppression on my chest which is distressing to the last degree, and no sooner am I again installed in one of the luxurious compartments of the Lyons railway, than I once more take refuge in sleep.

CHAPTER VI

BROUGHT INTO HARBOUR

It was quite late in the afternoon, and my fatigue had almost merged into stupefaction, when, looking at my railway book for something like the hundredth time, I discovered that the next station but one would be Meursault. To get out my pocket-glass, and endeavour to smooth my ruffled hair - to gather my scattered property into the travelling-bag - to fold my railway-rug, and get everything in readiness, gave me ample occupation till the moment when the train paused at Beaune, and the guard, peeping lazily in at the carriage-window, inquired if there were any passenger for Meursault.

'I am going to Meursault!' I said, promptly.

He looked at me with a sort of indolent curiosity, yawned, turned the ticket over twice or thrice, and said -

'Ah, madame is going to Meursault! *Bien.* I will desire the engineer to stop.'

'Do you not always stop there?' said I. 'Is there not a station named in the way-bill?'

The guard shrugged his shoulders. Madame was perfectly right. There *was* a station; but, *mon Dieu!* nobody ever stopped there except on market-days. It was such an out-of-the-way, forgotten little place! But he begged madame's pardon. Perhaps madame was a native of Meursault?'

Whether this were meant as an indirect compliment to my execrable French accent, I cannot say; but I laughed and replied that I knew nothing of the place - that, in fact, I was going on to Montrocher. Had I named a settlement in the interior of Africa, the guard could hardly have expressed a more profound ignorance of the locality. Montrocher! He had never even heard of Montrocher. It must be *au bout du monde!* The train now began to move on, and he darted away to warn the engineer that an unhappy traveller desired to be cast out amid the wilds of the Meursault station.

Somewhat discouraged by this conversation, I surveyed the passing landscape with increased interest, and, having the carriage to myself, roamed from window to window, endeavouring to gather some information from the aspect of the country. Ever since we left Dijon in the rear, the scene had become by degrees more and more hilly - here the hills rose almost into mountains, and were clad with vineyards and orchards. These, however, lay all to the right. To the left, a great plain stretched away and away into the faint far distance, and was bounded by the shadowy outline of a chain of mountains.

While I was yet in this suspense, the train slackened, and a very small station came in view.

'Meursault!' cried the guard, coming straight to the window, and helping me out with my parcels. No other passenger alighted. My luggage was flung to the solitary porter, who rolled, half awake, out of a shed close by - the guard touched his cap, and said compassionately, '*Bon voyage!*' - the warning whistle rent the air, and the train flew onward towards Lyons. Flew onward, and left me standing there with my boxes and the sleepy porter, and not another soul in sight! Like Robinson Crusoe, 'I listened, and looked around me. I could see nothing, nor hear anything.' Surely there must be some one to meet me! Had Madame Delahaye mistaken the day that she had herself named? How should I get there if it were so? How far was I from Montrocher? These, and fifty other questions flitted through my mind and found no answer. Surely I might get a conveyance from Meursault - but then, where was Meursault? The station seemed to have dropped from the skies in the midst of a purely agricultural country, with not even a steeple in view! To be in search of a town *au bout du monde*, and set down at a station that led to nothing was almost too bewildering!

I turned to question the porter, and found that he was transporting my luggage to a waiting-room at the opposite side of the line, so I scrambled down as well as I could, and followed him. There was nobody in the waiting-room - not even a clerk in the little office up in the corner - no sign of life, save the ticking of the great clock over the door. I began to address my inquiries to the porter; but he took no more notice of me than if I had been one of my own boxes, and sauntered off to fetch the remainder of them from the opposite platform. Hereupon I sat down in utter despair.

'Come what will,' I said, resolutely, 'I will stay here till they send for me.'

Just at this moment the approach of a heavy footstep attracted my attention, and a glass door was thrown open at the lower end of the room. The new comer was a short, elderly man, with a whip in his hand, and a meerschaum in his mouth. He wore a shabby brown great-coat, and a broad-brimmed hat; and scowled round the room under his heavy eyebrows. Seeing my boxes in the middle of the floor, he walked deliberately up, read the labels on each, even went to the length of turning one over that had been accidentally reversed, favoured me with a stern, steady stare, and then struck the butt-end of his whip three times heavily upon the ground. Obedient to this signal, a brown, merry-looking country fellow, with little gold rings in his ears, and a clean blue blouse, lumbered in in his sabots, shouldered two of the trunks as if they had been feathers, and clattered out of sight immediately.

'Are there any more?' growled the brown-coated stranger, speaking for the first time.

Too much surprised to reply, I only pointed to the porter, then coming back with a bandbox, a portmanteau, and a carpet-bag.

The stranger shrugged his shoulders, snapped the silver lid upon his meerschaum, put the pipe very coolly in his breast-pocket, snatched up these three remaining articles, and set off down the passage at a rapid trot. I followed, perplexed and fluttered, and found myself presently in a gravelled space just outside the station. Here stood a light country cart, and a high, perilous, old-fashioned chaise, very much the worse for wear. The stranger flung down my property somewhat roughly, and the carpet-bag, falling heavily against the bandbox, inflicted a severe contusion.

'Take care, monsieur!' I exclaimed. 'The bandbox is not made of iron!'

He muttered something to himself (it sounded very like an oath) - turned the box over with his foot - looked ruefully at the fracture, and, ejaculating the single word 'Chiffonerie!' assisted to place the heavier articles in the cart. He then pointed to the gig, and without offering to help me up, jumped into his own seat, pulled out his pipe, just looked round to see if I were by his side, and drove away.

He had taken possession of my luggage and myself in so grim, authoritative, and matter-of-fact a manner, that I had never once thought of questioning his right to the same; but now, as we rattled along the pebbly road, with the light cart at our heels, and a fog of dust rising about us with every turn of the wheels, I began to entertain serious doubts, and invent all kinds of wild and unforeseen possibilities. What if this man had pounced upon me by mistake, and were driving me to some place even more inaccessible than

Montrocher?

Half smiling at my own vagrant fancies, I stole a side-glance at his imperturbable face, and found him absorbed in his pipe and his contemplations.

I have said that he was elderly; but on second observation, it seemed to me that he was nearer that time of life which goes by the name of middle age. It also struck me that the lines about his ponderous brow and determined mouth were noticeable as the signs of an abrupt temper and a dogged will, rather than as the tracings of either time or sorrow. His eyes were deep-set, restless, brilliantly black, and over-shadowed by bushy eyebrows, like the eyes of a Scotch terrier. His hair, beard, and moustache were of a thick, coarse, unsatisfactory iron-gray - which still farther increased that canine resemblance. Add to this, a square, massive jaw; a short, but not unshapely nose; a pair of immensely broad shoulders, and a thick bull-neck; and I believe that I have given as true a portrait of him as the photography of words may produce.

When I had noted these things in my mind, and surveyed him quite leisurely, and, as I thought, quite unobserved, I was not a little discomposed to see him put his pipe out, turn half round in his place, and apply himself to a deliberate, undisguised, retributive scrutiny of my own features - a proceeding which reduced me to the last extremity of shame and annoyance, and which lasted, to the best of my calculation, just about as long as I had stared at him. This over, he settled back into his old position, and chuckled aloud. Nor did his appreciation of the joke end here. The drive was a long one, lasting fully an hour and a half, and throughout the whole of this time, at intervals varying from ten to twenty minutes, he either indulged in a sardonic grin, or relapsed into that still more aggravating chuckle.

And during all this drive the light cart rattled at our heels; and the road grew more and more stony, and the dust flew thicker and higher, and the rickety gig jolted and creaked, and shambled along, till my brain reeled again, and every bone ached as if I were being broken on the wheel. My chief consolation, however, lay in the ever-increasing beauty of the district. Montrocher, it seemed, was situated in the very heart of those green mountains which I had been observing from the railway, and even through the dusk which was now gathering around us, I became aware of much that was quite new and lovely in the valleys and vineyards nestled all about. Where, and how far off, Montrocher might be - what was the name of that melancholy-looking white town through which we passed just now - whether I was really on my way to Madame Delahaye's, and no mistake had occurred, were questions that I longed to put to my impenetrable captor. But he was grim and stony as the statue in Don Giovanni; so I imitated his own surly silence, and held my tongue. Who and what could he be? Not M. Delahaye himself, surely? He was too shabby for that. Nor an upper servant; for he had too much the air of one in authority for that. I longed to look at him again; but dared not - and so the dusk grew deeper and deeper, and the landscape lost its distinctness, and the fire in my companion's pipe shimmered redly through the interstices in the lid, and a star or two came out in the sky, and we jolted, and rattled, and blundered along, as if the journey were never coming to an end.

By-and-by a sharp steeple rose into relief against the gray - some lights shone here and there from cottage windows - we passed down a narrow street with small tenements and little gardens on either side - and, emerging at the farther extremity of the village, drew up suddenly before a great wooden gate and a high white wall, which looked, by that light, more like the entrance to a convent than the gateway of a gentleman's house.

The door was opened by a smiling servant, with a lantern in her hand. Two enormous hounds rushed out, yelping and baying what might have been either a welcome or a defiance; and my companion, addressing me for the second time since our meeting, said, with more conciseness than elegance - 'Get out.' He then flung the reins to a stable-boy, and disappeared round the corner.

I got out; but not unassisted. The smiling servant brought a chair and helped me down, and said, '*Bon soir*, mademoiselle,' just as if I had been for years a well-known visitor at the house; and then, preceding me across the yard, led me up a lofty double flight of stone steps, at the top of which two ladies were waiting to receive me.

The elder and taller of these two advanced, kissed me formally on each cheek, and bade me welcome to Montrocher. The younger fell back into the gloom of the passage, and followed us to a spacious parlour opening on the left of the entrance. Here Madame led her forward, and said -

'My daughter Marguerite.'

My eyes were so weary and full of dust, and I was so dazzled by the transition from dark to light, that, although I shook hands with my pupil, I could not distinguish one feature of her face.

'Mademoiselle is very weary,' whispered a sweet voice. 'We must not ask her to sup with us to-night, mamma.'

'Certainly not!' replied Madame, warmly. 'Mademoiselle shall be served in her own chamber, and do just as she pleases. Sit still, my dear, and let Pierrette carry up your bonnet and cloak! Will you take your boots off at once? Marguerite, run into your father's study and fetch my worked slippers. See, here is a bottle of eau-de-Cologne - let me pour some on your head and hands. *Voilà!* she is better already! Now, Marguerite, conduct mademoiselle to her room, and ask her what she would like for supper, and make her quite comfortable and at home.'

And Madame Delahaye, with voluble kindness, saw me to the foot of the stair-case, wished me good-night, kissed me again on both cheeks, and consigned me to the care of her daughter.

It was a stone stair-case, circuitous, steep, and narrow, like a turret stair-case in some old castle. Guiding myself by the wall, and still feeling very faint and giddy, I followed the light figure flitting on before, passed down a dreary corridor, and arrived at a place where three doors stood facing each other - one at the end, and one at each side of the passage. Mademoiselle Delahaye put her finger to her lips.

'Hush!' said she. 'My father is asleep - he is not well to-night. That is his room. This little one at the end is mine. And this,' leading me into a large and lofty chamber, 'is yours.'

I sank into the nearest seat, and looked languidly round. I was too tired to scrutinize the room just then, but two odd little beds, standing foot to foot in a recess just opposite the door, caught my eye at the first glance.

'Do I sleep alone?' I asked uneasily, for I looked forward, above all, to privacy in my own apartment.

'*Mais, sans doute!*' Then, seeing the direction of my eyes, 'Ah!' she exclaimed, 'this is the visitor's bedroom - and we always keep two beds in the visitor's bedroom. Mademoiselle will choose which she pleases.'

She then told me to ring when I was in bed, and glided away like a little fairy, returning again, punctual to the signal, attended by Pierrette with a basin of vegetable soup, a tumbler of old Burgundy, a chicken *pâté*, and a couple of snow-white rolls.

This fare was so delicate and delicious, the reclining posture so restful, the bed and pillows so luxuriously soft, and the kind face and voice of the young lady so soothing and so grateful, that I felt as if I were transported into a new world, or as if this were all a dream and I must wake presently. 'How kind you are to me, mademoiselle!' I said, pushing my plate away at length, and repeating the words for the third or fourth time during the meal.

She looked down at me with an air of innocent wonder.

'Kind!' she repeated. 'Not kind at all! If you like, I will tell you something that would be much kinder.'

'What is that?'

She blushed, and touched my hand timidly.

'Call me Marguerite instead of mademoiselle, and let me love you dearly!'

My heart bounded with pleasure. 'Good-night, then, Marguerite,' I said, falteringly.

She bent and kissed me, as her mother had kissed me, on each cheek. 'Good-night, mademoiselle,' she said with a radiant smile, and so left me. Somehow or another, I scarcely knew why, the tears came to my eyes when she was gone; but they were tears of happiness, and brought with them a blessed sense of safety and deep peace. Slowly I sank away, lower and lower, into the under-world of darkness and dreams, and then lost all consciousness in a profound and pleasant sleep.

CHAPTER VII

MARGUERITE

The sunshine was pouring in when I started from my first sleep. Strange sounds were in my ears, and I could not remember where I was. Then my eyes fell upon certain moveables of my own, and the experience of the last four days rushed back upon my mind.

But I still heard the sounds that awoke me, and, as I sat up to listen, rubbed my eyes and wondered if I were not dreaming still!

Somebody was practising singing in the room below. There was nothing wonderful in that. But then, Somebody had the strangest voice in the world! It was not a woman's - of that I felt sure. It sounded more like a very toneless, cracked, quavering, broken-down tenor - a tenor that had once, perhaps, been clear and flexible, but which now retained no vestige of tunefulness and was ear-rending to the last degree. Shakes, runs, turns, difficult exercises, and flourishes of every imaginable intricacy did this unfortunate voice struggle and do battle with, and every time the exercise conquered, and the voice broke down, and the singer returned to the contest more vigorously than ever. There was something painful in his miserable incompetency, and something touching in the perseverance with which he clung to his task. It reminded one of the jokes of a broken down Grimaldi, or the antics of the skeleton in the Fantocinni.

Who could it be? Not Monsieur Delahaye, for they said he was unwell the night before. Not my grim driver, for if *he* had any voice at all, it must be a 'bass profound.' Altogether it was a great mystery, and an inharmonious one into the bargain. I looked at my watch, and with increased surprise found that it was only half-past five o'clock. Half-past five o'clock, and Somebody practising singing!

Weary as I was, I found this question too knotty to solve just then, so I turned my face to the wall, covered my head up in the bedclothes, and soon fell asleep again, despite all vocal obstacles.

When I next woke, the sunshine had gone off my room, and all was very silent. I lay for some minutes 'twixt wake and sleep,' speculating lazily upon the hour, and wondering when the post went out from Montrocher. Then it occurred to me that a long time must have elapsed since I last looked at my watch, and then I found that it was past eleven o'clock.

Lifting myself on my elbow to survey the room, I found a bunch of fresh violets laid upon the counterpane. In this little token I recognized the gentle hand of Marguerite, and, burying my face in the dewy blossoms, drew hence a pleasant augury. She had been in my room then already, and, finding me still asleep, had left her morning greeting where I should most readily find it. Kind little Marguerite!

I then looked round the room, and anxiously noted its shape, contents and general expression. I say 'anxiously,' because I hoped that it might be a room such as I could love; and I hold it as a point of real import that we love the room which is, in name and fact, our own. It should be in harmony with the general tenor of our dispositions - cheerful for the cheerful; retired for the retiring; grave, and book-lined, and studious-looking for the scholar. It should never war with the prevailing current of our feelings, or lead our thoughts astray into channels unformed by our experience or our taste. As it is the confidant of our most secret smiles and tears, so it should be chosen as fastidiously as a friend, changed as rarely, cherished as faithfully. We do well to hang its walls with landscapes, and to fill its recesses with books. Above all, we do well to make it holy with pure hopes and worthy aspirations, and this, because it is the birth-place of our deepest thoughts, and the sanctuary of our truest devotions. For my own part, as I am neither ignorant or scholarly, never an idler, and yet not wholly a brain-worker, I incline towards a room which may be characterized by none of these extremes, and which shall partake of the advantages of all. I like it neither gay nor gloomy - furnished with the means of study - open to glimpses of the living world without - and not so sternly studious as to reproach me when I feel inclined for some hours of simple recreation. Such a room, with few exceptions, was mine at Montrocher. Like most continental bedrooms, it was 'contrived a double debt to pay,' and answered equally well for a sitting-room by day. A small round table and two arm-chairs occupied the centre of the floor. An ample bookcase, stored with standard works, stood beside the door. A large mirror, an ornamental clock, and some vases filled with dyed grasses adorned the chimney-piece. Just over the door hung the portrait of a gentleman in an old-fashioned uniform, and at the side opposite the window was suspended an antique and very curious map of ancient Paris. A small writing-table, a gigantic wardrobe, and the ordinary bedroom furniture completed the interior of my apartment. Best of all, though, was the view from the little old-fashioned casement by my bed's head. Straight before me lay an orchard bounded by a high white wall, and behind this a lofty, but gradual mountain, covered with vines and terraces almost to the summit. To the left, retiring one behind another, and fading each into a softer blue, extended a long chain of similar hills, wooded, vine-covered, and spotted with white cottages. Leading just under the window, terminating to the right in a quaint little village street, and to the left in a sandy, winding road, bordered with young trees, lay the highway by which I had arrived the night before. When I leaned out I could see a mass of foliage and the towers of a ruined castle about half a mile down that road, and, nearer still, a lofty wooden cross surmounting a wayside spring. Even while I was looking, I saw a young girl come lightly along, threading the lines of light and shadow that chequered all the footway. She carried a copper vessel on her head, and was trilling the refrain of a merry ballad. When she reached the spring she knelt down, murmured her prayers before the cross, filled her can, and then, after a long look towards the house, went slowly and silently back. The incident was so new and picturesque that I uttered an instinctive word of admiration.

'Are you paying that tribute to our mountains, mademoiselle?' asked a voice at my elbow.

It was Marguerite, who had again stolen into the room, expecting to find me asleep. I drew her to the window, and pointed to the figure lessening along the road.

'Ah,' she said, 'it is Marie - Claude's sweetheart.'

'And who is Claude?'

'Our head vine-dresser, an excellent lad, and as merry as a lark. She expected to see him, but he is gone over to Chalons for uncle Alexander. Poor Marie! I am sorry she was disappointed.'

'You speak as if you knew how to sympathize with her,' I said, smiling, for I remembered that Marguerite was herself betrothed.

The young girl blushed and sighed.

'They are so fond of each other,' she said, sadly; 'and so well suited.'

A little pause followed. Being at a loss to continue the conversation, I asked where she had gathered those delicious violets.

She gathered them, she said, in the garden, where she had been romping with Max and Pedro all the morning!

'Max and Pedro!' I echoed. 'Who are they? Your brothers, Marguerite?'

Marguerite laughed till the tears ran down her cheeks.

'My brothers, mademoiselle? Ah, *mon Dieu!* I have no brothers. They are the dogs - uncle Alexander's dogs!'

This time I felt tempted to vary my question, and ask who was uncle Alexander; but I inquired, instead, whether the garden was pretty and extensive.

'Neither,' replied Marguerite, 'and yet it is very pleasant. Make haste to come and see it before the breakfast-bell rings, and then I will take you in the afternoon to our orchard, which lies at the farther end of the village; or, if you like climbing better, we will go to St. Christopher's altar.'

Charmed with her childish gaiety, I hastened to finish dressing, and submit myself to her guidance. The house was very still, and we met no one as we went. Our way lay down the steps, and across the court-yard which I had seen the night before. This court-yard was surrounded by small out-offices, stables, and cellarage. Marguerite, to my surprise, led me straight to the largest and gloomiest of the cellar-doors, and pointing to a huge dark vault and a flight of four or five mouldy steps, desired me to follow her. The cellar was filled with gigantic vats, tapestried with heavy cobwebs, and damp as the atmosphere of a tomb.

'This is where they stamp the grapes when the weather will not permit it to be done in the open air,' said Marguerite, explanatorily. 'We have no other way of arriving at the garden without going round by the road.'

So saying, she opened a small door at the farther end, and, passing up some more steps, led me into a narrow pathway roofed over with green boughs. Hence a rustic wicket opened into the garden. It was a very plain, unpretending place, traversed by three longitudinal walks, planted on either side with a box-bordering which had grown breast-high in the course of years, and looked like a massive green wall. There was a prim little summer-house at the farther end, and a few early flowers were blooming here and there. The high walls all round were covered with peach and nectarine trees. A little lance-like steeple peered up close behind the summer-house, and a sudden mountain, partly cultivated in vineyards, part grass, part granite boulder and heathy steep, rose so closely and precipitously as to seem to block up the very end of the garden. It was a quaint spot enough - sad and strange, silent and very lonely. The little formal garden and the great wild mountain contrasted oddly with each other. Between the two rose the steeple, slender and typical (like religion between cultivation and barbarism), uniting and reconciling both, and giving to the scene a simple pathos such as no words of mine can translate.

'Well, mademoiselle,' said Marguerite, 'do you think you will like the garden?'

'I like it already,' I replied, 'and I think I shall spend many happy hours here.'

'Oh, how glad I am!' she exclaimed, clapping her hands. 'How glad I am - for this is my favourite spot, and Pedro's too. Isn't it, Pedro? Oh, you wicked boy! you've been in the water again, have you?'

And off she darted, chased by the great dripping dog, laughing with all her might, running with all her speed, and fluttering in her light dress in and out of the walks like a summer fairy. And this reminds me that I have not yet described her - perhaps because till that moment, when I stood aside in the shelter of the summer-house, I had not once had an opportunity of quietly observing her. Knowing Marguerite as I know her now, possessing the key to every shade of expression as it comes and goes, and seeing in every feature something which is unseen to the casual eye, I find it very difficult at this time to record in any way faithfully my first impression. Perhaps we have all felt this more or less - perhaps the familiar face ever lies too near to be scanned clearly. Whatever be the reason, the thing is so, and I now experience it: therefore let allowance be made for my shortcomings.

Marguerite was very small, very fair, and just seventeen years of age. So small was she, that nothing but the perfect roundness and gracefulness of her figure saved her from being, to all outward appearance, a child. Her hands were wonderfully white and tiny, but their grasp was warm and quick, like the grasp of one swift to feel and hasty to execute. Her little busy feet glanced hither and thither like 'motes in the sunbeam,' now beating time to a merry tune, now stamping with a momentary gust of anger, now reminding one of those immortal feet of which, more than two hundred years ago, Sir John Suckling said so archly that they

'Like little mice stole in and out
As if they feared the light.'

Her hair - soft brown hair, with a warm hue running through it - rippled all over, like a tide touched by the sun and ruffled by the wind. Her eyes were neither blue nor brown - perhaps a mingling of both. They were not beautiful eyes, nor particularly large ones; but they expressed every shade of her wilful moods; were wild, and shy, and quick-glancing; loving and angry, laughing and weeping by turns; and varied with the changes of the summer sky and every caprice under heaven. Her features were irregular, owing little to form, but everything to expression; and her mouth, which was certainly far from small, or such as is usually possessed by the heroines of romance, was still very frank, and tempting, and well used to framing the sunniest smiles in the world. This is a very inadequate description; but it is the best that I am capable of inditing. I find, on reading it over, that I have by no means fulfilled my own intentions, or even the promise which I made on starting. So far from reproducing my first impressions, I have drawn largely from my after experience. Instead of sketching the outline and leaving all else to conjecture, I have filled in shadow and colour, and produced a picture which, however incomplete, is yet prematurely finished with regard to minor detail. Such as it is, it must nevertheless remain. The task is difficult, and I can fulfil it no better.

'How happy you are, Marguerite!' I said, smiling.

She was making feints of throwing a stone, and puzzling Pedro out of his canine wits by sending him off on false starts to the other end of the garden.

'I am always happy when I am with Pedro,' she replied, smoothing his great silky ears with her two little hands. 'We are the dearest friends in the world - are we not, boy?'

Pedro wagged his tail vehemently, and, throwing up his head after the impulsive fashion of his race, licked his mistress's face all over with one sweep of his tongue. Marguerite jumped up, laughing and angry together.

'Oh, naughty boy - naughty Pedro! Keep your kisses to yourself, sir! I'm ashamed of you, and so is mademsoiselle! Max wouldn't do that - he knows better, sir!'

'But where is Max?' I asked, assisting her to smooth her ruffled hair. 'Is he not as great a favourite as Pedro?'

'Max! oh, yes, he is a very good dog; but he is older than Pedro, and not half so fond of fun. Besides, he gets cross if I pull him by the tail, or make him walk on his hind legs, or in any way try to improve his manners - and we don't like anything grave, or old, or cross, do we, Pedro, dear?'

And she bent down, with a strange flitting trouble in her face, and clasped the dog about the neck. The serious look lasted but an instant. A white pebble chanced to lie beside her hand - the playful mood returned - away went the stone, off went Pedro, and in another moment the riotous game was at its height again!

Once more I took refuge in the summer-house; but even there I was not safe, for presently Marguerite, being hotly chased, ran in and sheltered behind me. Pedro followed at full speed, a tremendous romp ensued, and I found myself in the thickest of the fight.

Suddenly there came an addition to our party, in the shape of a fine white greyhound. Vaulting over the wall, he made his way at once to the summer-house, and disputed with Pedro for some of his mistress's caresses.

Marguerite rose in an instant from her knees, and, putting back her hair, stood listening eagerly. The quick tramp of a horse's hoofs echoed down the road and paused at the gate. A bell was rung; the rider clattered into the court-yard; and the greyhound darted away again over the wall.

'It is my cousin Charles,' said Marguerite. 'Let us go in. Good-bye, Pedro!'

'This is not the countenance of a girl about to meet her lover,' I said to myself, as I followed her back into the house.

CHAPTER VIII

A FAMILY BREAKFAST-TABLE

The breakfast-bell was ringing as we entered the *salon*, and three persons had already assembled. One of these was Madame Delahaye. The second was a tall, bronzed, serious-looking man, whose age might have been guessed at anything between twenty-five and thirty. Of the third, I saw only a pair of sturdy legs clad in rusty brown trowsers, a rough masculine hand, and a newspaper.

Madame Delahaye introduced me to the tall gentleman.

'Allow me, mademsoiselle, to make you acquainted with Monsieur Charles Gautier. My brother-in-law, Monsieur Alexander, is already known to you.'

Monsieur Gautier bowed a stately bow, and turned to greet his cousin Marguerite - the gentleman behind the newspaper crossed his legs and growled. The growl was enough, and in uncle Alexander I recognized my grim escort of yesterday. Madame bustled away, 'on hospitable thoughts intent;' the cousins stood talking together in the embrasure of a window; and I, not knowing exactly what to do, turned over the loose music lying on the piano.

'You did not expect to see me this morning, Marguerite,' said the gentleman, in a low deep tone, which carried with it, as I thought, a modulation of infinite tenderness.

'Not in the least,' replied Marguerite, tapping her little foot restlessly upon the floor.

'I had to ride over to Meursault upon business, and it would have been too hard not to have seen you when I was so near.'

'Oh, yes, of course,' said Marguerite, absently, her whole attention riveted upon Pedro, who was gambolling up and down the passage.

The lover sighed.

'I am afraid that my absence and presence are alike indifferent to you, Marguerite,' he said, in a still lower tone.

'Indeed, I beg your pardon, cousin Charles,' she said, hastily; 'but I have been playing with Pedro all the morning, and - look at him, poor fellow! - he can't understand why our game should have been broken off. He is so fond of fun - and - and so am I, cousin Charles!'

Cousin Charles looked down on the winning little apologetic face, and smiled, and sighed again.

'Still such a child, my little Marguerite!' he said, touching her hair somewhat sadly. 'Still such a child! When will she grow wise and womanly?'

'Never, I hope!' exclaimed Marguerite, energetically. 'I don't want to be disagreeable!'

The lover's face darkened.

'Are the two always associated in your mind?' he asked, his serious eyes looking steadfastly into hers.

'Always,' replied Marguerite, obstinately.

'And yet wisdom is truth. Surely my little Marguerite will not tell me that truth is disagreeable!'

Again the restless tapping of the foot, aided this time by a heightened colour and a pouting lip.

'Cousin Charles,' she said, impatiently, 'I will not be scolded. You have no right to scold me!'

'Scold! no right!'

'I am everybody's pet but yours,' continued she, wilfully. 'Why are you always cross? It's enough to make me hate wisdom, and -'

'And what else, or whom else, Marguerite?' asked cousin Charles, sternly. He had folded his arms upon his breast, and stood looking down upon her with an air of lofty displeasure, as a proud father might look down upon a fretful child. Marguerite was about to return an angry answer; but she encountered that glance and was silenced.

'I - I don't know,' she faltered, and turned suddenly away.

He looked after her coldly for a moment, then took up a book, seated himself in the nearest chair, and began to read.

The music on the piano was of the most heterogeneous description. Crivelli's exercises for soprano or tenor - Lablache's ditto - Panofka's ditto - systems of singing, sol-fas, shake exercises, and vocal difficulties without end, volumes of Italian music labelled 'Primo tenore *La Sonnambula*,' 'Primo tenore *Lucia di Lammermoor*,' 'Primo tenore *La Favorita*,' and many more. Other volumes of detached ballads and *scenas*, all for the same voice, and all plentifully interlarded with pencilled marks of expression, introduced roulades, and marginal notes scrawled in a tremulous and minute handwriting, generally to the effect that, 'here Alberto is overcome by emotion,' or 'with passionate dignity,' &c. &c. Having glanced over these with some curiosity, I turned to a little side-table and found a collection of quite a different character. Here were polkas, waltzes, light pieces of a drawing-room character, and little French chansonnettes copied out in an uncertain girlish hand, and signed with Marguerite's initials.

Having ended her brief conversation with M. Charles, she came over to me and began talking with a forced gaiety.

'Indeed - indeed, mademoiselle,' she exclaimed, trying to cover the page with her two little hands, 'you must not look at my copied music! I am ashamed of it - I write so badly - I was the worst copyist in Madame St. Honorée's school!'

'You need not fear my criticisms,' I said, smiling; 'for I know nothing, practically, of music.'

'How! Do you not play?'

'No.'

'Nor sing?'

'Not a note.'

'Because you are out of practise, I suppose, mademoiselle!'

'On the contrary, Marguerite; because I never learnt.'

My pupil looked as if she could hardly believe me.

'Never learnt, mademoiselle!' she repeated. 'But how was that? Do not all English ladies study music?'

'Unfortunately all, or nearly all,' I replied gravely.

'Why unfortunately? Madame St. Honorée used to say that music was the most indispensable item in a young lady's education.'

M. Alexander turned his newspaper, and muttered something uncomplimentary about Madame St. Honorée.

'I don't think it by any means indispensable, Marguerite,' said I, without heeding the interruption. 'And yet I believe it to be a delightful art. Perhaps, because I respect it so much, I wish it were put to less general uses.'

'I don't understand you, mademoiselle,' said my pupil, looking puzzled.

I was about to drop the subject; but a shadow fell between me and the light, and I found M. Charles standing beside me.

'Excuse me,' he said, 'but I should like to hear more on this head. I am interested in all matters connected with education.'

'Nay, sir,' I replied, much embarrassed; 'I speak theoretically. I am not experienced in teaching.'

'The experienced are not always thinkers,' said M. Gautier, courteously.

Scarcely knowing how to reply, I remained silent. Presently he continued.

'You do not approve of the effort to popularize music in France and England?'

'That was not what I meant to say. I think the taste for music cannot be too widely diffused. I only plead against the indiscriminate teaching of it.'

'Doubtless,' said M. Charles, 'there are many to whom the knowledge is of little avail in a worldly point of view; still pleasure has its uses.'

'True; but according to the present system this study is forced upon many to whom it is no pleasure at all; say rather loss of time, and absolute weariness. As a profession for women who labour, and as a recreation for women who are rich enough to loiter through life as elegant connoisseurs, I hold music to be invaluable; but I lament the fruitless hours spent upon it by those who neither require it as a weapon, nor delight in it as a recreation.'

'Then, I suppose, mademoiselle,' said Marguerite, poutingly, 'you would never have allowed me to learn it, for one!'

'How can I tell till I know whether you love music?'

'Oh yes,' she exclaimed, warmly. 'I adore it, mademoiselle; but, you see, I hate practising.'

Again the cloud gathered upon M. Gautier's brow.

'Marguerite hates everything that is above her comprehension,' he said, bitterly. 'Mademoiselle will discover that ere long.'

'I wonder why breakfast is so long delayed,' said Marguerite, turning away with a pretty assumption of indifference. 'It is already one o'clock, and the bell rang at half-past twelve!'

'We are waiting for papa, my love,' said Madame Delahaye, coming into the room just in time to answer the question. 'I hope,' she added, turning to me, 'that mademsoiselle was not disturbed this morning. M. Delahaye *will* rise at half-past four in summer, and at dawn in winter. He thinks the early hours so much more favourable to the voice.'

Then it was M. Delahaye, after all!

'I understood,' said I, falteringly, 'I - I had no idea that ...'

'That any old man would make such a fool of himself,' said M. Alexander, finishing my sentence for me. 'Miss, you are quite right.'

Having said which, he again retired behind the newspaper, leaving Madame Delahaye to explain to me that her brother-in-law was eccentric, but at heart an excellent creature. 'One never was angry with him, and nobody took his little oddities *au sérieux*.'

After five more uneasy minutes, M. Delahaye walked in - a little withered old gentleman in a flaxen wig, a flowered dressing-gown, an embroidered smoking-cap, and velvet slippers. His shirt-front was loaded with lace, and his fingers with rings. He carried a worked pocket-handkerchief in his hand, and he perfumed the air as he moved.

Madame presented me, and Monsieur, removing his cap with the air of Louis Quatorze, professed himself 'enchanted.'

'Mademoiselle will condescend to excuse this *déshabille*? We are here in retirement, mademoiselle. We rust. We look to mademoiselle's amiable presence to restore to us the elasticity of youth, the polish of social intercourse, and, in short, the - the renovating influences of urbane society.'

Monsieur offered this less as an observation to me than as a brief address to the company; and, having said it, sat down with a complacent sigh at the foot of the table.

Too much surprised to venture upon any reply, I took the place indicated by Madame, and found myself continuing to stare, quite unconsciously, at Marguerite's extraordinary papa.

'You are late this morning, *mon ami*,' said Madame, gently. 'The *rôti* is quite cold, and the fish overdone.'

'My dove,' replied Monsieur, wafting a kiss to Madame upon the tips of his fingers, 'I am desolated; but a concatenation of events delayed me. Business, business, my life, laid upon me its imperative hand, and ... A little more fat, if you please, brother Alexander.'

It occurred to me very forcibly that Monsieur's business had been the adornment of his own person, and uncle Alexander confirmed the suspicion.

'Business, indeed!' growled he. 'You don't know what business is, brother Jacques.'

Monsieur turned pale with indignation.

'Jacques!' he echoed. 'Brother, you shock me! Not Jacques, if you please! Never Jacques! Hippolyte - always Hippolyte! please to remember that for the future, I beg of you.'

Monsieur then turned to me.

'An explanation,' said he, uneasily, 'is due to mademoiselle. Mademoiselle must know that I bear two Christian names, the second of which Hippolyte, and the first, ahem! - the first -'

It seemed as if the first had caught his breath in some remarkable way, for he coughed and paused, and was obliged to take a glass of wine before proceeding farther. He then continued -

'What could have induced my charming mother to brand me with - with so objectionable a name as that lately mentioned by my excellent brother Alexander, I cannot by any process of reasoning discover. What still induces my excellent brother Alexander to revive that very objectionable name bestowed upon me by my charming mother - that name which, as he well knows, I loathe and abhor -

that name which I have discarded for years, to the exclusive adoption of Hippolyte - that name which, but for his, to say the least of it, very inappropriate and tenacious memory, would long since have been consigned to the - in short, to the Caverns of Oblivion, I am at a still greater loss to discover.'

Monsieur paused, shook his head reproachfully at a roast fowl which had just been placed before him, and drank another glass of wine. It then occurred to him that this explanation had been addressed to me.

'Mademoiselle,' he said, gallantly, 'accept my excuses for having wearied you with these uninteresting details of my family history. I trust that the subject which gave rise to them may have been discussed for the last time -'

Here he looked sternly at uncle Alexander, who was eating macaroni with his fingers.

'- And that some more agreeable topic may now be summoned to illuminate our domestic board with - with the scintillations of wit, the radiance of good humour, and the amenities of polite conversation.'

Having thus elegantly summed up and dismissed all that had gone before, Monsieur applied himself to the business of breakfast with the air of a man who had been conferring obligations upon society, and who now expected that society would be grateful and amuse him in return.

Madame first broke the silence that ensued.

'Well, Charles,' she said, 'any news from Chalons or Santenay?'

'Yes - I have news from both places,' said M. Gautier. 'The new clergyman is expected daily in Chalons, and there is a notice pasted on the chapel-doors, to say that service will be performed next Sunday.'

'Good news, indeed,' said Madame warmly. Then turning to me, 'We have been seven weeks without a Protestant minister at Chalons, mademoiselle, and as we have no other chapel nearer than Dijon, a distance of thirty-one miles, the loss has been severely felt. We are quite a little Protestant colony about this district, and support our chapel by voluntary contributions. We have been expecting this new clergyman for a long time. His name is - really I never can remember his name! Can you, Charles?'

'I remember it,' said Marguerite, eagerly. 'The Rev. Alexis Xavier Hamel. Alexis Xavier Hamel! - what a beautiful name!'

'Rather too romantic, I think, dear, for a clergyman,' said Madame.

'Not in the least - not in the least,' observed Monsieur with a severe glance at uncle Alexander. 'A dignified and euphonious name imparts additional respectability to the person whom it adorns. To bestow such a name is one of the most obvious of parental duties, and to address persons by their names politely and considerately is one of the first obligations entailed upon us by society.'

Madame bent her head in acceptance of her husband's opinion, and with a meek, 'Certainly, *mon ami*,' turned to M. Charles for the rest of his budget.

'Come,' she said, 'you have not told us all yet. We have heard the news from Chalons, and now, if you please, we should like the news from Santenay. How goes on the new conservatory?'

'It does not go on at all,' said cousin Charles, smiling gravely. 'It has gone off.'

'Gone off! I don't understand.'

'Why, the fact is, that I have changed my mind. It is to be erected at the other side of the house.'

'Oh, what a pity!' exclaimed Marguerite. 'The south-east aspect won't be half so favourable to the flowers!'

'It is a pity, indeed,' said Madame.

Even uncle Alexander looked up and shook his head.

M. Gautier smiled again.

'It appears,' said he, 'that everybody's vote is against me?'

There was a dead silence.

'And yet my reasons are excellent.'

Another silence, accompanied by looks of eager inquiry. Cousin Charles looked quietly round, enjoying their impatience.

'Well, then,' said he, 'the case stands thus: I fixed on the south aspect - the workmen were hired - the foundations were dug. But, in digging the foundations we made a discovery.'

'A discovery!'

'You remember what a high mound we chose for the site?'

'Yes - yes - go on!'

'And under that mound there lay -'

'Good heavens! what?'

'A Roman columbarium!'

Cousin Charles delivered these words with a brow slightly

51

flushed, and a voice heightened with triumph. It was the triumph of a scholar rich in the possession of a rare archæological treasure; richer still in his power of appreciating it. He had expected to produce a sensation, but he was mistaken. With the exception of uncle Alexander, nobody appeared to have the dimmest idea of the nature of the discovery.

'But you don't congratulate me!' expostulated cousin Charles.

'*I* congratulate you, boy!' exclaimed uncle Alexander, quite heartily and energetically.

'And I - of course. And I,' added Monsieur, looking extremely wise. 'A columbarium! Ah, yes, to be sure, a columbarium!'

'And quite perfect!' said cousin Charles, impressively.

'Urns and *ollæ* complete?' asked uncle Alexander.

'All complete.'

Monsieur ran his jewelled fingers through his wig, and hemmed twice or thrice behind his hand.

'Dear me,' he observed, 'how extremely satisfactory! Delightful, really! And, ahem! - tell me, my dear Charles - do you - do you think this - ahem! -- columbarium may prove useful, ultimately useful to yourself?'

'To myself, sir!' echoed M. Gautier, profoundly astonished.

Monsieur bowed affirmatively, and a rapid perception of the truth flashed across the countenance of his nephew.

'Really, sir,' he said, with a half-repressed smile, 'I hope it never may.'

Uncle Alexander grinned sardonically.

'Prefer Christian burial, eh, Charles?' said he, rubbing his head all over with malicious satisfaction.

'Most unquestionably.'

Here Marguerite, impatient to follow all that was going forward, put an end to the equivoque by saying -

'But I don't know what you're talking about. What *is* a columbarium? Please somebody tell me!'

'A columbarium,' replied M. Gautier, somewhat formally, 'is a sepulchral chamber, or burial vault, containing in general the remains of slaves and freedmen, and erected near the more costly monuments of their masters. More than three hundred persons have been buried in this one.'

'And all these dead bodies lie just under the windows of the *salon!*' exclaimed Marguerite, with a shudder. 'How horrible!'

'Not horrible at all,' said he. 'The columbarium, as I have discovered by an inscription over the entrance, dates from the eleventh year of the Christian era - a period when cremation was universal among the Romans. Only their ashes rest there, Marguerite. Only their ashes have ever rested there. It is but a chamber underground, with rows of cinerary urns around the walls. A chamber, dark and still - solemn only from association - suggestive of no painful images - and, so far as emblems of mortality are concerned, less revolting than our modern grave-yards. You must come and judge for yourself.'

'Not for the world!' she replied, hastily.

A shade of vexation flitted once more across his brow; but he dismissed it as quickly as it came.

'You will change your mind,' he said, gently. 'Why, this very proposition formed one of the chief objects of my visit. Can you not all arrange to spend a day at Santenay next week?'

Marguerite looked down with a half-smile. Monsieur and Madame exchanged a glance of satisfaction. A day at Santenay was evidently a thing to be enjoyed.

'I am sure, my dear Charles,' said Monsieur, graciously, 'we shall all have infinite pleasure. You make an admirable host - and - ahem! - your wines are excellent.'

'And uncle Alexander?'

Uncle Alexander shook his head.

'No, no, boy - not I! I don't care for your elaborate dinners. I'll ride round to breakfast with you to-morrow morning - that will suit me better.'

'Very well, sir - I'll tell Jacqueline to unearth a bottle of the old Romanée.'

The following Wednesday was then appointed for our visit to M. Charles; and, breakfast over, he rose to take his leave.

'We shall meet on Sunday, I suppose,' said he.

'On Sunday, of course, my dear Charles,' said Monsieur, pompously, 'we shall meet to do honour to M. Alexis Xavier Hamel - and on the Wednesday after -'

'You will, I hope, sir, do justice alike to my columbarium and my cook,' interposed cousin Charles, quite gaily. Then, turning to Marguerite - 'If I do not see you at church, *ma cousine*, I shall call again before Wednesday. I have a little pamphlet on the burial-customs of the Romans which I should like you to read before you come. It is written familiarly, and will not take you an hour altogether. Adieu.'

Without waiting for a reply, he touched her hand with his lips, saluted the rest, and was gone. His horse's hoofs were clattering across the court-yard in another minute; and, standing beside the window, I saw him galloping at full speed down the road. M. Gautier both rode and looked well; but I tried in vain to draw Marguerite's attention to the fact.

'I have seen him on horseback often enough,' she said, throwing herself pettishly into an easy-chair. 'And then, why does he tease me with his ugly books? What do I care for the burial-customs of the Romans? I won't go into his columbarium - I declare I won't!'

CHAPTER IX

ST. CHRISTOPHER'S ALTAR

It was not long before I felt at home with the Delahayes. I liked the family, I liked the shady, intricate old house, and I liked the neighbourhood. Madame was cheerful, hospitable, and good-natured. Monsieur was always polite. Marguerite - pretty, wilful, affectionate, intractable Marguerite - became my pet as well as my pupil. Her innocence, her truthfulness, her warmth of heart, won daily upon my affections. Her faults were those of a child. That she was wilful, impatient, variable, resulted from the errors of her education rather than from the promptings of her disposition. If she were at times exacting, it was because she had been humoured since the day of her birth. Her generosity, her innate lovingness, her joyous carelessness, her ready acquiescence to persuasion, were all qualities which no indulgence had been able to tarnish, which no merely childish caprices were likely to uproot. Thrown together as we were, I may perhaps be allowed to have judged her more impartially than most persons. At all events, I acquired over her a stronger influence. I neither yielded to her petty tyranny, like Monsieur and Madame; nor opposed it, like her cousin Charles. Humouring her at times, as one would humour a wayward child; restraining her at others, by the sole force of kindly remonstrance; never demanding from her more patience than she was inclined to give; and always treating her less like a pupil than a younger sister, I learned to love her dearly, and to read her impulses and errors like a book. I am, however, anticipating the position of affairs, and telling the result, not of days, but of weeks.

The scenery at Montrocher was on a small scale, but exquisitely picturesque. I have seen the Alps since then, but I have nowhere beheld valleys more romantic, precipices more boldly hewn, prospects more delicious. With Marguerite for my companion, I climbed the steeps, followed the windings of the little river, and traversed all the lanes and vineyards round about. Indeed, it seemed for the first month as if some enchantment were at work to vary these rambles. There was always some new path to be explored, or some new point of view to be enjoyed. Being on so small a scale, so rich in detail, so bold of outline - the scenery changed with every turn, and, like the patterns of the kaleidoscope, presented a continual novelty of arrangement without actual novelty of material.

Like every pretty country place, Montrocher had its stock sights, - famous within the narrow radius of a village population. Firstly, there were the cascades - a succession of tiny falls in the bed of the river, about a mile from the house. Secondly, the ruined castle of La Rochepôt, a dismantled vestige of the middle ages, perched high upon a solitary hill. Thirdly, the fall at La Tournay, of which I shall have more to say hereafter. Fourthly, the Canal du Midi, which, however, was many miles away; and, besides these, the village church, with its curious old altar-piece and monumental brasses; the melancholy *cimetière*, with its iron crosses and wreaths of *immortelles*; the mountain of St. Christopher, and its shapeless altar; and many a green nook, and lane, and valley, which might have driven a painter to despair.

The excursion to St. Christopher's altar was proposed on the Saturday afternoon - the third day after my arrival.

The weather was radiantly fine. The spring flowers clothed all the slopes; and, although we had not yet reached the middle of April, the air was soft and balmy as an English May. Accustomed only to the undulations of my native moorlands, I found these mountain walks less easy of achievement; but Marguerite stepped from block to block with the ease of a chamois; and, long before I had scaled one-half of the height, was skipping about the plateau of stony heath along the top. Once arrived there, I would fain have rested; but she would not hear of it.

'No, no, mademoiselle - not yet! See, here is St. Christopher's altar - you must come and look at St. Christopher's altar!'

It was a great upright block of granite, hewn into a rough niche at the top. The niche contained a clumsy carving, protected by a rusted iron-grate.

'If this be the shrine,' I exclaimed, discontentedly, 'the saint is not worth the pilgrimage!'

'But he is the particular patron of travellers, mademoiselle!'

'Indeed!'

'And his story is charming!'

'Then perhaps it will atone for the hideousness of his shrine. Come, let us sit on this mound while you relate it.'

So we sat down on a little bank of purple heath, and Marguerite told me the legend of St. Christopher.

'Well, then, mademoiselle, you must know that St. Christopher was a giant and a pagan ever so many hundred years ago, when giants and pagans were more plentiful than they are at present. And he was not only a giant, but stronger than any other giant, and so proud of his strength, that he vowed to dedicate it to the service of the mightiest king in the world. So he went about asking every one where this great master was to be found, and, being told of an Eastern conqueror whose very name was the terror of the nations, he sought him in his camp, took the oath of allegiance, and bore arms as a captain in his service. Now this conqueror was a Christian, and not a bad kind of man, although so warlike and ambitious. At all events, he had a very wholesome horror of the devil, and never heard his name pronounced without uttering a Latin exorcism and making the sign of the cross. This so often happened, that Christopher at last took notice of it, and asked his master the reason. "Alas!" said the king, "I do it for defence against the wiles of Satan." "Satan!" repeated the pagan. "Who is he?" The king muttered his exorcism, and made the sign of the cross. "He is the enemy of all mankind," replied he, very gravely. "But do you fear him?" asked Christopher. And the king bowed his head, and said, "Indeed, we all have reason to do so." So Christopher was very indignant, and cast off his livery and his allegiance, and swore that the king had deceived him, and that he would serve only Satan, since Satan was the mightier sovereign. He then wandered out in the great deserts seeking him, and came one day upon a vast caravan, at the head of which rode a dark and terrible warrior, and this warrior was Satan. So Christopher knelt down, and again tendered his strength and his service, and went with the caravan. And now his pride was indeed gratified, for he soon found that the empire of his new lord extended over the whole earth, and that his power was tenfold that of the Eastern conqueror; but, at the same time, he observed one suspicious circumstance that reminded him of his late master. If ever the name of Christ were spoken in his presence, Satan trembled and turned away. So, Christopher resolved to question him. "Master," said he, "what is this Christ of whom I hear?" But Satan quailed as before, and was silent. "Is he a king?" asked the giant. Satan bowed his head. "Master," said Christopher, "is he greater than you?" And Satan hid his face, and the giant left the caravan in anger, and went abroad seeking Christ. He sought him far and wide; and though he heard of him everywhere, and everywhere encountered his followers, he never came into his presence. And one day he found an old hermit in a lonely cave, who offered to instruct him in the laws of Christ, and to prepare him for the meeting. So Christopher stayed a long time with the hermit, and learnt that mercy, and gentleness, and helpfulness were the qualities that would most endear him to his new master; so he devoted his great strength to deeds of charity, built himself a hut on the banks of a deep river, and, for love of the unknown Christ, took upon himself to carry over all pilgrims who came that way. And thus, with a pine-trunk for his staff, the giant passed his days in wading through the deep water, and befriending the sick and the feeble. Well, there came a night when he was very tired indeed, having carried over more travellers than usual, and he stretched himself out upon his mat to sleep. Scarcely had he done so, however, when he heard himself called by name, and found a young child waiting by the river-side. "Christopher, Christopher," said the child, "carry me over, I beseech of you, for I have a long journey before me." Now it happened that the river was swollen, and the night dark, and the service more dangerous than usual; but Christopher would not be daunted in his task of mercy. He took the child on his shoulder, and the staff in his hand, and plunged into the stream. But, as he went along, the current rushed stronger and stronger, and the water rose higher and higher, and the child on his shoulder grew heavier than the heaviest man, so that the simple giant felt, for the first time in his life, what it was to be afraid. "Alas, child!" said he, "who and what art thou, and how can I bear thee over in safety?" But the child only smiled, and told him to take courage, and they did at last get across in spite of all obstacles. Only the giant was quite faint and exhausted, and, having landed his burden, leaned heavily upon his staff, and again said, "Child, who and what art thou?" And then the countenance of the child grew radiant as the sun, and lighted all the darkness, and the river ebbed away to a level calm, and a voice, childish still, but sweeter than any sound of earth, replied, "Oh, Christopher, I am Christ, thy king!" And the giant fell upon his face, and there was silence all around, and when he looked up the child was gone, and the day was dawning, and his staff had taken root and become a tree. And that, mademoiselle, is the legend of St. Christopher, as I heard it from my nurse when I was quite a little girl; and there, you see, is the carving which illustrates my story. That big man without a nose is St. Christopher. The child is riding on his shoulder, and the tree is in his hand. Once a year the priest comes up here, followed by all the young girls and old women of the village. He sprinkles the altar with holy water, and says a mass, and it is quite a little festival.'

'And what became of St. Christopher after all?'

'Oh, mademoiselle, I know no more. Legends, like novels, seldom arrive at a satisfactory ending.'

'At all events, your legend is quite a little poem, dear Marguerite, and very interesting. Shall we go back now?'

'No - for the best reward of your pilgrimage is to come.'

'What do you mean? Am I to be introduced to another saint?'

Marguerite laughed, and shook her head.

'Will you let me have my own way for a few minutes, mademoiselle?'

'That depends on the use to which you would put it.'

'I want to take you over there, just behind that wall of loose stones; and, if you please, I wish to blindfold you first.'

Laughingly I took off my bonnet, submitted to have Marguerite's handkerchief bound across my eyes, and to be led over a few yards of uneven ground. Then we paused, the bandage was withdrawn, and I was told to look around.

Dazzled by the transition from dark to light, I could at first distinguish nothing plainly. Then all the glory and grandeur of the scene was suddenly unfolded to me. I saw a vast plain stretched before me - a plain studded with vineyards, villages, and forests. To the left, the line of railway, to the right, the spires of Chalons. A broad, bright river coiled away into the distance like a silver ribbon, and, farthest of all, melting almost upon the boundary of the horizon, rose a line of faint-blue peaks, scarcely more substantial than the clouds.

I gazed till I could gaze no longer, and then covered my eyes with my hand.

'What river is that, Marguerite?' I asked, without looking up.

'The Saône, mademoiselle.'

'And those mountains?'

'Look at them once more, and tell me if you can distinguish one higher than the rest.'

'Yes - the faintest of them all. What is it called?'

'Mont Blanc.'

My surprise and delight were too great for words. I sat down upon a mossy stone, and dwelt on every separate feature of the landscape. Showing chiefly by its trail of white smoke, I saw a little speck-like steamer about half a mile beyond Chalons. From this distance it scarcely seemed to move; but it went very swiftly for all that, hurried along by the hurrying river whose currents set eagerly to meet the Rhône at Lyons. Then in thought I pursued all the windings of the banks, traversed the valleys of Savoy, penetrated to the glacier-lands of the Upper Alps, and fancied myself under the firs of Chamouni. When at length I rose to go, it was with a lingering reluctance, as if I feared that it must all fade away like the dreamland of the mirage, and, though I sought it for ever, be visible no more.

But Marguerite was no longer by my side. She had left me to my reverie, and I found her perched upon an angle of shingly wall, looking down over her home and the village. She held up her finger as I approached, and, listening, I heard a faint sound of fiddling and piping down in the valley.

'It is a wedding,' said Marguerite, thoughtfully. 'The newly-married pair are going about with the musicians playing before them, and the bridal-guests following in procession behind. We are very primitive here, mademoiselle, and our peasantry keep up many quaint old Burgundian customs. They are very happy, too. Happier than their masters.'

Marguerite sighed. These changes of mood were not unusual to her, and I watched them with a sorrowful, half-divining curiosity even from the first.

'You shall tell me more of these old customs, Marguerite,' I said, 'and show me all the antiquities of the place; for I suppose you are well learned in such home-chronicles?'

'Not in the least,' she replied. 'I have been educated, you know, in Paris, and for the last six years have visited Burgundy only at rare intervals.'

'At all events,' said I, laying my hand upon the wall which formed her seat, 'you know whether this be part of the Roman camp that I was to see on the summit of the mountain?'

'Oh! yes; this, I believe, is part of the boundary-wall. It extends all round here, and down part of the opposite side.'

'I should like to go over it with some one who could explain the topography of the site,' I observed, taking another long look before we moved away. 'What masses of loose stones! And see, here are several deep-hewn channels cut transversely in the solid rock!'

'My cousin, Monsieur Gautier, is a profound archæologist,' said Marguerite. 'He would tell you all that you wish to know, and show you the Roman camp at Santenay as well.'

'Ah, there is another in the neighbourhood!'

'Several, mademoiselle; but that at Santenay is the finest. Monsieur Gautier has written a book on the antiquities of Santenay, which papa will lend you with pleasure. It is full of the oddest engravings of lamps, and coins, and queer little bronzes found about there. But I never had patience to read it.'

'Ah, true,' said I, slyly. 'You don't care for books about the Romans.'

Marguerite blushed, but answered nothing.

'Your cousin is very clever, Marguerite,' I continued, after a brief silence.

'Very clever,' she replied, absently.

'And highly educated as well.'

'Yes - highly educated.'

'Handsome, too - or, if not exactly handsome, very dignified and intellectual. He reminds me of the portraits of Melancthon.'

'Indeed?'

'Altogether an interesting character,' said I, 'and one that may develop into something great. It is from such men as your cousin, Marguerite, that arise the Layards, the Aragos, and the Humboldts of this present day.'

'Very true,' replied Marguerite, listlessly.

'Therefore, it is well when their works are encouraged by success - when to the ardour of search is united the triumph of discovery. Their ambitions are unselfish; their toils are productive of no riches, save the riches of knowledge; they labour for all time and all mankind. Marguerite, I am very glad that your cousin found that Roman columbarium.'

She blushed again, this time with a little pouting of the under lip which I was not slow to interpret. We had now almost reached the foot of the mountain, where a tiny thread of rivulet filtered down through the brown mosses and trickled to its junction with the mill-stream below. I laid my hand upon her shoulder.

'Marguerite,' I said, gently, 'will you do something to please me?'

'I would do anything for *you*, mademoiselle,' she replied evasively.

'But if it be not exactly for me - only to please me, Marguerite?' I urged.

She hesitated, and pulled in pieces the wild flowers that she had been gathering on the way. All at once she flung them from her.

'Don't ask me to read that book about the burials, mademoiselle,' she exclaimed, 'or to go into the vault at Santenay. Anything else - anything else in the world!'

'I will say nothing about the columbarium,' I replied, smiling; 'since I am sure that when you are once there, you will not refuse to follow the general example. At present I am only thinking of the book. Let us read it together, Marguerite. I am sure it will not be uninteresting.'

'But it is not here yet, mademoiselle!'

'He promised to give it to you after church to-morrow. Come, promise me.' So, half laughing, half pouting, Marguerite promised with a kiss, and this was my first victory over her self-will.

Monsieur Delahaye was practising the shake when we went in

- though, as far as that went, his singing was one long involuntary quavering from beginning to end. He rose from the piano, listened graciously to my request respecting M. Gautier's volume on Santenay, and ended by volunteering the celebrated 'Fra Poco,' with Rubini's own cadenzas. Compelled to stand by and listen to it, I recalled that famous criticism of honest Samuel Johnson, and wished to heaven that the thing had been, not only difficult, but - impossible!

CHAPTER X

SUNDAY MORNING

We rose and breakfasted early on the Sunday morning, for Chalons was some miles distant. Two vehicles waited in the court-yard. One, a double-bodied chaise, very well appointed; the other, that identical high, perilous, shabby old gig in which I had been conveyed from the station a few days before.

'I always drive Monsieur Delahaye myself,' said Madame, 'therefore, Mademoiselle Gartha, you had better accompany M. Alexander. Marguerite, my love, you will ride behind us. Uncle Alexander will be quite delighted to take charge of mademoiselle.'

Uncle Alexander swore at the cat, who was licking her paws in the passage, and refused to hear Madame's polite observation.

'Great heaven!' exclaimed Monsieur, sinking back tragically in his place. 'You - you cannot be in earnest! My dear, my excellent brother Alexander, you surely do not propose to wear that - that disreputable, oleaginous, and unspeakably unbecoming old hat?'

Uncle Alexander took the hat off, looked at it from every point of view, deliberately brushed the nap the wrong way, and so, having done the only thing that could have made it shabbier than before, put it on again without a word.

Monsieur groaned aloud, Madame and Marguerite laughed outright, the four-wheeler rattled away with its occupants, and Claude brought the gig up to the steps. In another moment we also were on our way.

Silently, uneasily, and insecurely as before, we jolted and shambled along; the only difference being, that the road lay this time through a more hilly and less interesting country. We seemed to leave the sweet valleys and green trees farther and farther away at every step. The blinding sunlight poured over the stony downs unbroken by a single cloud, and was reflected from the long white road and chalky banks. The air was intolerably dry. The dust rose up in swirling columns under the horse's feet. To crown all, M. Alexander brought out his meerschaum, the smoke whereof was wafted in my face by gales, not 'of Araby.'

Now this was all very disagreeable, and I found myself in the course of a quarter of an hour or so becoming unmistakably cross. I therefore leaned back, interposed my parasol between the pipe and my own countenance, and indulged in as sulky a mood as ever I fell into in my life.

'Humph!' muttered uncle Alexander, making a cut at a pig by the roadside. 'What's that for I wonder!'

I only lowered the parasol more pointedly than before. Ten minutes of silence.

'Dislike the smell of tobacco?' growled uncle Alexander, interrogatively.

'Extremely, when the smoke is blown in my face,' I replied from behind the intrenchment.

There was a chuckle, a snapping of the silver pipe-lid, another chuckle, and a dead pause: then, reconnoitring cautiously round the protecting disc, I saw that the meerschaum was banished. Had M. Alexander been anybody in the world but M. Alexander, this concession would have elicited from me some expression of gratitude. As it was, however, I felt sure that my thanks would be ungraciously received, so I only shifted the position of the parasol, and held my tongue.

Thus, without another word on either side, we arrived at Chalons, and put up at the '*Lion d'Or*,' where the rest of the party were waiting for us.

The chapel was close by, up a dreary passage on the outskirts of the town. It was a very modest, whitewashed ugly little building, with a clock, a pulpit, some half-dozen exclusive-looking pews, and two or three monumental-tablets round about the altar. The pews were nearly all filled. The free seats were quite empty. There were no pleasant faces of school children peopling the organ loft. There was no clerk to lead the responses - no bell to call the worshippers to prayers. The very pew-opener wore sabots, and had something about her which seemed at variance with the associations of the place. Everything bespoke the expression of an isolated opinion - the resort of a cultivated minority. Here were no casual droppers-in, here no weekly gathering of the poor. The peasantry, and the greater number of the gentry, belonged to another and a rival faith, and the few congregated to-day within these homely walls professed the tenets of an exceptional religion.

Commenting thus in my own mind, and watching the congregation more than the pulpit, I observed all eyes turned suddenly in one direction, and found that the clergyman had taken his place. He was bending low over the heavy volumes on his desk, and so continued till the opening voluntary was ended, leaving visible only a luxuriant mass of curling silver hair.

Marguerite made a mouth behind her prayer-book.

'Oh, mademoiselle,' she whispered, 'he is nothing but an ugly old man, after all!'

The last lingering chord of symphony died away, and the new clergyman, looking up for the first time, deliberately surveyed his auditors.

Marguerite was wrong. Though no longer young, M. Hamel was not by any means old; and, so far from being ugly, I thought him, at first sight, the most striking, if not the handsomest man whom I had ever seen in my life. He might have been about forty-two, perhaps a little more or a little less. His beauty was of that massive, masculine order that Cagliari loved - a large head finely poised, a full, firm mouth, a square jaw, and a somewhat-heavy brow, resolute, thoughtful, and broad. A complexion pale, but dark, such as one sees among the Creole population of the West Indies; a general expression of power, both in features and build; a something which was at the same time fascinating and repellant, intellectual and sensuous, gave to this man a special individuality. His eyebrows and eyelashes were quite black. His beard was completely shaved. His nose was straight, firm, and short, with nostrils that quivered and expanded when any temporary excitement succeeded to his habitual self-possession. Above all, his eyes were beautiful; deep, dark, glowing, and unfathomable. Eyes whose tenderness would be dangerous, and whose scorn intolerable. Add to all that has gone before, that *chevelure* of silken silver - so soft, so luxuriant, contrasting so strangely with his magnificent manhood, and yet so beautiful that the blackest curls would not have seemed nearly so appropriate - and the portrait is complete. To say that his hair was gray would not, however, be to convey a correct impression; neither was it white; but shaded by a something which was no colour, and yet which distinguished it quite unmistakably from the bleached locks of age. Such was this man, who stood up there for the first time in the plain oaken pulpit of the little chapel at Chalons on that memorable Sunday morning, returning scrutiny for scrutiny, with his hand upon the sacred books, and the morning sunlight shining on his head.

He then began the morning service. He repeated it in a low, calm, level voice, apparently from memory, since, except now and then to turn a leaf, he scarcely ever glanced at the volume before him. And still, pertinaciously, leisurely, almost defiantly, he continued to examine the faces of his congregation. Beginning at the pew nearest the pulpit, and dwelling purposely on every individual head, his eyes travelled in slow progression from right to left, and from left to right again.

Now it happened that our sittings were placed as nearly as possible towards the centre of the church, so I waited with some curiosity till those eyes should encounter my own. Would they dwell upon me as they dwelt upon that pale cynical-looking man yonder, or dismiss me with that quick indifference as they dismissed that pretty woman in the adjoining pew? I half dreaded their glance, and, at the same time, felt impatient for its arrival. They drew nearer now, and nearer. They reached Madame, rested for a moment on the rugged brow of uncle Alexander, gleamed, as I fancied, with swift contemptuous verdict upon Monsieur Delahaye, and without seeming even to perceive me, passed on, and remained riveted upon Marguerite.

She coloured crimson, strove to repress the faintest trembling of a smile, and fixed her eyes upon her prayer-book.

He looked at her for a long time. I could discern neither admiration nor disapproval in his face. It was the expression with which one would contemplate a picture, being more desirous to criticise than praise. Then he went on with his survey; but I noticed that he turned back every now and then, and singled her out again, as if he had seen some face like hers before, and was trying to recall the when and where; or, as if comparing her, according to some standard in his thoughts, with others of the congregation. Then came the Litany, when we knelt down, and the pulpit was hidden from us by the lofty partition of the pew; and by-and-by the service of the prayer-book ended, the clergyman retired, and the organist gave out a sweet and simple psalm-tune.

I should be sorry to attempt any description of the vocal eccentricities in which it now pleased M. Delahaye to indulge; the more so, as I am ignorant of musical phraseology, and know not how to designate the extraordinary ornaments with which he disguised the pathetic beauty of the original melody. Suffice it that no vestige of the psalm remained, and that I believe the composer himself would have been a cunning man to recognize it. He out-heroded Herod, he more than gilt refined gold, or painted the lily. He tattooed the Apollo, and adorned him with war-paint and a nose-ring. Scarcely able to preserve my gravity, I turned half aside and looked round for M. Gautier; but he was nowhere among the congregation.

'So much the better for Marguerite,' thought I. 'She will escape the burial-customs of the Romans!'

Just then the psalm came to a conclusion, and the skilful organist lengthened out the melody into a quaint and melancholy voluntary. M. Hamel returned to the pulpit in his black gown, bent his head upon the desk till the music ended, and, after a brief and almost inaudible prayer, rose up to deliver his sermon.

In his hand were two or three slips of memoranda. From these he referred to the Bible, and left them in it here and there as markers. He then closed the book, drew himself to his full height, swept the church with one comprehensive glance, as if measuring strength against strength, intellect against intellect, and, in a voice totally unlike that in which he had read the previous half of the service - a voice full, sonorous, and deep-rolling as the under notes of an organ - gave out the text of his sermon.

THINK NOT THAT I AM COME TO SEND PEACE ON EARTH:
I COME NOT TO SEND PEACE, BUT A SWORD

I shall not endeavour to reproduce the discourse that followed. It would be useless, since I could only mar the eloquence which I but imperfectly remember - eloquence so rare, so impassioned, so spontaneous - aided by reading so extensive, and judgment so keen -

delivered by a voice so grandly cadenced and with a dignity so imposing, that to this hour I can recall something of the effect which it then produced upon me. Some of his sentences, some of his tones, some of his gestures remain branded, as it were, into my very brain; others are lost in the general impression. But the substance of his sermon I never can forget; and this, to the best of my power, I will now endeavour to outline.

It was a history of Christianity - a history of its darkest and most woful side, drawn by an iron hand, and delivered not only with the profoundest knowledge of 'effect,' but at times with something of a splendid yet terrible irony. Taking for his text the sentence from St. Matthew, just quoted, he traced from first to last the fulfilment of that awful prophecy - 'I come not to send peace, but a sword.' Beginning with the martyrdoms of the immediate followers of Christ, he told all that fearful tale of blood that follows in the history of the world - that tale whose chapters are the centuries of time, and whose records are written in tears. The victims of the arenas of Rome; the slaughters and sufferings of the Crusades; the great wars of sect against sect; the persecutions of the Albigenses, the Huguenots, the Hussites, the Lollards, and the Covenanters, were all brought before us in faithful and terrible succession. He spared neither side. He dealt by Christian and Pagan with crushing impartiality. He showed how those who suffered most in the time of their weakness inflicted most in the time of their strength - how the faith, so often overborne by bloodshed, uprose and triumphed in bloodshed - how the words of love became perverted in the mouths of the judges of the Inquisition, and how the doctrines of peace availed nothing in favour of the gentle and cultivated Mexicans of Peru.

'Suffering, or striving, or ruling,' said the preacher, concluding almost in these words, 'in darkness, or in light, loaded with chains, or crowned with victory, this religion of mercy, this religion called "of peace," has been a religion of the sword! Awful prophecy, and still more awful fulfilment! To what end has this blood been shed? To what end these exterminations, these Mammertine dungeons, these stonings, and crucifyings, and auto-da-fés? to the saving of souls - to the saving of souls, which, unless they believe, cannot be saved! And is this end achieved after eighteen centuries of sorrow and suffering? Are the nations convinced? Is the victory gained over ignorance, and indifference, and idolatry? Alas, no. It is not gained. It never will be gained. It is the old struggle of the sea and the shore, and what is conquered on the one coast is reclaimed on the other. There are at this moment in the unexplored wilds of Africa, in the gigantic colonies of the Indies, in China, in Persia, and in South America, millions upon millions of human beings who live and die, generation after generation, without ever having heard the name of Christ! Let us make a just estimate. Let us count the followers of Mahommed, of Fôh, of Brahma, of the Sun, of mere Juggernauts and fetishes, stocks and stones - let us count the unbelievers, the followers of late philosophies - let us count, finally, all those who have plunged into monstrous excesses of Mormonism and the like, all those who are negligent, who are indifferent, who profess with their lips and deny by their deeds, and then, then let us see what remains on the profit side of Christianity! Oh, despair all ye who listen! Despair all ye who follow this religion of peace, and salvation, and divine tenderness! How has it come? How has it prospered? It has come as a sword, and it has prospered as a sword. It has destroyed much, and it has reaped little. It has come as a truth; but it has prospered as a lie - as worse than a lie, for the followers of lies outnumber it as millions outnumber hundreds, and the false gods of the heathen prevail against it! Despair, again I say, despair! There is no hope in the face of these things, for where there is salvation for one, and perdition for ten thousand, there is woe for all!'

My whole being was so absorbed in the one act of listening, that, till M. Hamel had brought his sermon to a conclusion, I did not once think to observe its effect upon any one else. Now that his voice had ceased to reverberate round the church, I stole a glance at my companions. Monsieur was wiping his forehead with an air of trepidation, Madame had been weeping, uncle Alexander's head was turned away, and Marguerite - lightsome, childish Marguerite - was sitting with lips closely pressed, hands tightly clasped, and a face so pale, so wrapt, so expressive of wonder, and admiration, and dismay, that I longed to see her smile again.

Then the blessing was pronounced; but pronounced so indistinctly, that I no longer recognized the impassioned tones of the preacher. And then, to the accompaniment of a bold organ-piece, we rose and left the chapel.

Once beyond the doors, we drew aside to let the rest pass on.

'We are waiting,' said Madame, 'for M. Charles.'

For M. Charles, who, to a certainty, was not among the congregation! That puzzled me.

Madame knew everybody, and exchanged a few words with everybody as they came out. Amongst the rest, with that pretty woman whom I had observed in the adjoining pew. She was richly dressed, had an agreeable expression, and was leaning upon the arm of her stout, red-haired, good-humoured looking husband. A young girl of about sixteen, and a boy of about twelve were with them.

'Well, my dear friend,' said this lady, saluting Madame Delahaye and Marguerite, and acknowledging very graciously the profuse courtesies of M. Delahaye - (M. Alexander having long since disappeared), 'Well, my dear friend, what say you to this new meteor?'

'*Eh, mon Dieu!*' replied Madame. '*Je me trouve tout a fait eblouissée!*'

'But it is absolute genius! every word extempore, and not an instant's hesitation. The best thoughts in the best language, from beginning to end.'

'For my part,' said Madame, 'I am amazed that he should be consigned to the provinces.'

'And, for my part, I rejoice that it is so! I shall attend the afternoon services, which I have not hitherto been in the habit of doing.'

'And I,' said Madame, 'shall leave my card at M. Hamel's to-morrow.'

'Ours were left yesterday,' said the red-haired gentleman. 'I like to be on visiting terms with the clergyman - though, as for this one ...'

'*Ciel!*' interrupted his wife. 'You cannot say that you don't admire him!'

'Not exactly that,' replied he; 'but I care very little for such pieces of oratory as we have heard this morning. I am a plain man, and I like a plain sermon. If I want history, I can read Livy and Tacitus - if I want tragedy, there is Voltaire and Racine. This M. Hamel is very wonderful; but he does not suit me so well as our poor excellent M. Drouet.'

'Upon my unimpeachable honour,' observed M. Delahaye, 'I believe you are in the right. He - he positively intimidated me. My nerves are frightfully discomposed.'

'And I am charmed with him!' exclaimed Madame.

'*Moi aussi,*' echoed her friend. 'I have experienced nothing like it since the *Phédre* of Rachel!'

The red-haired gentleman smiled and shrugged his shoulders.

'A criticism,' said he, 'which expresses my own notion. I feel just as if I had spent the morning in my favourite stall at the Comédie Française.'

His wife stopped his mouth with a very pretty little hand.

'*Tais-toi*, Adolphe!' she said, laughing. 'You are incorrigible. At all events, you cannot deny that he is eloquent, gentlemanly, and handsome?'

'*Tiens*! A Don Juan in canonicals!'

'Adolphe - I forbid you to speak another word! *Entre-nous*, my dear Madame Delahaye, I have a project for a little dinner-party - organized, of course, in honour of M. Hamel. If I name Saturday next, may I rely upon you all?'

Monsieur and Madame accepted the invitation, and the lady came over to where I was standing a little way apart.

'We, at least, need no introduction,' she said, in English; but with the faintest imperfection of accent, as if the long use of another language had impaired her fluency. 'I am Matilda Vaudon, and you, I feel sure, are the lady in whom my dear friend and cousin, Dr. Bryant, is interested. Let us be good friends.'

I took the hand so frankly extended, and thanked her.

'You owe me no thanks,' she said, 'I served you for my cousin's sake, and now I hope to know you for your own. I shall expect you on Saturday with our friends.'

'I shall be very glad to come,' I replied.

'And I shall be very glad to see you. The dear old language makes such sweet music in my ears, that you will be doing me a real kindness to visit me as often as your duties allow. Only conceive, that I have been married and living here for eighteen years without once revisiting my native country! But I am very happy. Those two yonder are my children. You must know us all, and love us all, if you can, my dear; and I only wish you resided in my house instead of in my friend's. *A propos* of the Delahayes, are you happy with them?'

'I have no doubt that I shall be,' I replied, smiling. 'I have not been here a week.'

'True - you cannot judge yet. Madame is an excellent creature, and Marguerite is a giddy, affectionate child; but Monsieur is cracked, and Alexander is a bear.'

'Concise, but not complimentary.'

'Bah! I speak what I think. Well - well, we shall meet again on Saturday, and then you shall tell me more. *Au revoir!*'

And so our colloquy ended, the Vaudons took their departure with many adieux, and we moved on in the direction of the Lion d'Or. To my surprise, Monsieur Charles was of the party. He had joined them while I was talking to my new acquaintance, and was discussing the general topic with more than his ordinary animation.

'There are certain faces, certain voices, certain natures,' said he, 'against which our instincts revolt; as the instinct of the wild bird revolts against the poison-berry. We cannot reason upon this thing - we can only feel it.'

'And you feel thus towards M. Hamel, cousin Charles!' exclaimed Marguerite, colouring with vexation.

'I cannot help it. Our organizations are antagonistic.'

'But it is unreasonable! You compare it yourself to an animal faculty!' urged she.

'And because it is purely animal, let us not therefore reject it,' replied M. Charles. 'These antipathies are among the mysteries of nature, and the farther they exceed our philosophy, the more should we respect them.'

'Therefore you hate M. Hamel!'

'Heaven forbid! I only feel that I had best avoid him - that I must avoid him, if I value my own happiness! Marguerite,' continued he, very earnestly, 'I feel as if this man were destined to be my deadliest enemy.'

Marguerite looked at him with a vague terror in her face, and then, with a little scornful laugh, came and took my arm.

'See now, mademoiselle,' she said, pettishly, 'I used to fancy that my cousin was at least clever and sensible!'

'He is both,' I replied, gravely.

'But this folly about M. Hamel!'

'M. Hamel is no ordinary man, and who knows whether his power be for good or evil!'

'Oh, mademoiselle, for evil!'

'Nay, I form no judgment at present; but I confess that I do not feel improved by his sermon.'

M. Charles caught my last words, and again fell into the rear.

'You are speaking of the sermon?' he said. 'Tell me *your* opinion, mademoiselle.'

'I was just saying that I had formed none,' I replied, evasively.

'It was a magnificent piece of spontaneous oratory!'

'Magnificent, indeed!'

'And yet, mademoiselle,' said Marguerite, reproachfully, 'you said you did not feel improved by it! Now this time cousin Charles is more just than you.'

'Mademoiselle must explain herself,' said M. Charles, eagerly.

'Nay, there is nothing to explain,' I replied. 'M. Hamel's view of life and of Christianity does not please me - that is all. His sermon appeared to me more like a profound satire than a genuine lamentation.'

'Good,' said M. Charles. 'And you think that the man himself may be -'

'A sceptic at heart.'

Marguerite bit her lip, and turned to meet M. Alexander, who was loitering up and down the road in front of the inn where our vehicles were waiting.

'Come, uncle Alexander,' she cried, taking hold of him by both arms, and laying her cheek up coaxingly against his shoulder, 'let us hear your opinion now! And please take my side of the argument, for mademoiselle and cousin Charles are both against me!'

Uncle Alexander grinned a grim smile.

'Hey, monkey,' said he, patting her little hand awkwardly with his great one, 'what is it all about, eh? What is it all about?'

'About this clever, beautiful M. Hamel! What do you think of him?'

'Humph! What do I think of him, eh?'

Marguerite nodded and smiled. She felt sure of uncle Alexander's favourable verdict.

'Well then, I think him - a charlatan.'

CHAPTER XI

A DISCUSSION ON FINANCE

'Up to the commencement of the fifth century, the bodies of almost all classes were buried entire, and it was not till after that period that the process of cremation became general among the Romans. Even then, the great patrician families continued to inter their dead after the fashion of their ancestors, nor did they entirely conform to the popular custom till the epoch of the first Cæsars. From this time until the age of the Antonines, cremation continued to be universal; but was again succeeded during the third and fourth centuries of our era by the early system of burial. To this period may be referred the large sepulchral urns of our European museums - to the fifth and sixth centuries the *terra cotta* coffins still more commonly met with - and to the early Christians those niched catacombs in which the bodies have been found entire. It must not, however, be concluded that all Roman catacombs are Christian cemeteries, or that they were originally excavated for the special reception of the dead. They were in the first instance mere *Arenariæ*, or sand-pits, whence a peculiar species of volcanic ashes, called *pozzolana*, had been worked out for building purposes. Once exhausted of their *pozzolana* deposit, and abandoned by the workmen, these subterranean quarries were appropriated by the primitive Christians for ..." for the purpose of driving poor Marguerite quite out of her senses! For heaven's sake, ask me to read no more of that dry, dismal, horrible book! I can't, and I won't, and cousin Charles may be just as cross as he pleases!'

And Marguerite flung the book down upon the ground, and then kissed me, to atone for her impatience.

'You wayward child!' I said, smiling and reproving together. 'I shall read it myself, and tell you something of its contents, that you may not seem so very ignorant to-morrow. Give me the book.'

Marguerite picked it up, and sat down on a stool at my feet, like a docile student - which she was not. We were sitting together in the arbour, as was our custom during the hours of study. Perhaps it scarcely deserved the name of study after all, for I was not Marguerite's governess; but her companion. Madame Delahaye said that Marguerite's education was 'finished,' and Marguerite was only too happy to be of the same opinion. All that she was now supposed to require was additional facility in reading and speaking the English language, of which, however, she had already a very fair knowledge. Our mornings were spent in reading and conversing. We lunched at one, dined at six, and walked out generally twice a-day. The books which she read to me were always of some entertaining description. I had tried, for the first two or three days, to make this English reading a medium of actual improvement, by placing before her such works as the Natural History of Selborne, Alison's Essays, and Boswell's Life of Johnson; but in vain. She could not be persuaded to learn when the same end might be compassed by means of amusement. She pleaded for poetry and romances, and when this prayer was seconded by Madame Delahaye, I was forced to submit. Bulwer, Dickens, and Miss Edgeworth succeeded to Alison and White - Sir Walter Scott was received with modified enthusiasm, and Byron and Alfred Tennyson were elevated to the utmost pinnacle of popularity. That, under these circumstances, I should have induced her to take up the Roman pamphlet at all, was matter for wonder, and that she should have even read so many pages before flinging it down, was little short of a miracle.

'Well, Marguerite,' I said, after a brief silence, 'what shall we read next?'

'I'm tired of reading, mademoiselle.'

'Then I will read to you. Stay! while I remember to ask it, you shall explain a mystery that perplexed me the other day.'

'*Un mystère, mademoiselle!*'

'Speak English, if you please, Marguerite. Yes, a mystery. How was it that, although M. Gautier was not in church the other morning, he met us after service and knew all about the sermon?'

'Ah, don't you know?' exclaimed Marguerite. Then, with an arch smile - 'Are you quite sure he was not in church, mademoiselle?'

'Indeed, I believe so.'

'But consider; must there not have been some other person there besides the clergyman, the pew-opener, and the congregation?'

'I can think of no other.'

'Not even the organist, mademoiselle?'

'But you do not say that ...'

'Indeed, I do. Cousin Charles, it is said, has a genius for music - though I'm sure he always plays very ugly things - and he has officiated for us on Sundays during the last four or five years. Uncle Alexander made the chapel a present of the organ, on condition that one of the members of the congregation should play, and the duty was accepted by my cousin Charles. Now, mademoiselle, you have all the history.'

'Your cousin is a very accomplished gentleman,' I said, musingly.

Marguerite was silent. Involuntarily I compared the future wife and husband, and sighed to think how poor a prospect lay before them both.

'And your uncle is very generous,' I added, after awhile.

She laughed, and shook her head.

'He is a strange man,' she said. 'He is at times extremely liberal, and in general extremely close. He is a keen man of business - he likes to keep the money he makes - and he has an utter disregard for appearances. He seldom gives; but when he does give, he gives nobly. People about here call him a miser; and really, to see him in that old hat and coat, one would hardly think him worth a ten-sous piece; but he is a great deal richer than we are, mademoiselle, and no miser either.'

'You speak as if you had studied him closely, Marguerite.'

'I have not studied him at all, mademoiselle, unless for love,' said Marguerite, colouring. 'You will see as much for yourself before you have been here a month.'

There was a suppressed irritation in her voice that I could not interpret. Did she suppose that I accused her of interested motives?

'Since your uncle is so rich,' I said, 'perhaps you may be his heiress, Marguerite.'

The *ruse* succeeded. She sprang to her feet, and stamped with rage.

'You, too, mademoiselle!' she exclaimed, passionately - 'You, too! Oh, how can every one be so cruel? I love my uncle Alexander, and every one reminds me that he must die! Mamma tells me of it every day. Papa is never tired of repeating the same thing. I am told to please my uncle, to take pains to make him love me - I who love him so dearly already, and hate money, and would not have him die for all the world! Oh, uncle Alexander,' she cried, amid a storm of angry tears, 'how I wish that you were poor, and that we were all poor, and that there was no such thing as money in the world!'

'Upon my word I'm much obliged to you,' said a voice close at hand. 'Wish for yourself, monkey. I don't want to be poor.'

And there, leaning against a tree beside the arbour, stood uncle Alexander himself, meerschaum and all.

Marguerite controlled her tears by a strong effort, and I went on quietly with my embroidery.

'Humph!' said uncle Alexander, after a long pause. 'Why does the monkey wish that there was no such thing as money in the world?'

'Because I hate it!' replied Marguerite.

'The more fool you,' said uncle Alexander.

'It makes people mercenary,' continued Marguerite, still trembling and vehement. 'It makes nobody happy. I'd rather be poor than rich, a thousand times!'

Uncle Alexander chinked the gold in his trowsers pockets.

'Listen, monkey,' he said. 'Do you hear that sound? Listen to it. That's the sweetest music in the ears of the world. They like it better than the chiming of church bells, and they respect it more than the king's title. An Englishman once said that knowledge is power. He was a wise man, monkey; but when he wrote those words, he wrote like a fool. Money is power. Remember that all your life. Money is power.'

I could not restrain a movement of impatience.

'You are wrong, sir,' I said, abruptly. 'Why try to teach Marguerite these selfish theories? She is much better without them.'

Marguerite looked up in dismay. She had no idea that any one would dare to contradict her uncle Alexander; for he exercised a grim control in the household, and even Monsieur, in his loftiest moods, was careful not to exceed a certain limit of respect. But my temerity was followed by no tremendous results. Uncle Alexander only took his pipe from his mouth, opened his eyes very wide, buttoned up the pockets deliberately, and said - 'Hey?'

'I say, sir, that you are to blame if you instil those principles into her mind,' I repeated, without looking up from my work. 'They can only sully her mind, without being of any service hereafter.'

'She ought to know the value of money,' growled uncle Alexander.

'Possibly; but she must not begin by rating it at more than its worth.'

'You know nothing about it.'

'As you please, sir.'

Uncle Alexander took a turn or two up and down the garden, puffing great volumes of smoke into the air.

'You have made him angry!' whispered Marguerite, and escaped down a side path, leaving me in the arbour. Presently he came back, and stood before me.

'Miss,' said he, abruptly, 'answer me one question. Why are you robbed, you women? Why are you always imposed upon, overcharged, and made fools of? Because you are ignorant of the value of money. Because you have only been taught to spend it. Because no one ever has the good sense to tell you what I have just told Marguerite. Would you see her robbed, inexperienced child that she is?'

'And who is to rob her?' I asked, composedly. 'M. Charles Gautier?'

Uncle Alexander frowned.

'*Diable!*' said he, 'you beg the question.'

'Not at all. We were discussing this particular case. If you chose to turn the argument upon generalities, that was not my fault.'

He took another turn along the path, and stopped to tie up one of the espaliers. I waited patiently, and it was not long before he returned.

'Look here, now,' he said. 'You are poor.'

'Thank you,' said I. 'I am quite aware of it.'

'And you would like to be rich?'

'Very much indeed.'

'You work hard. You are a dependant. You give up your country, your relations, your liberty - and all for what? for a paltry five hundred francs a-year!'

'Six hundred, if you please,' said I, correctively.

'Bah! six hundred, then. You must economize frightfully upon six hundred francs a-year?'

'That is my affair, monsieur,' I replied, laughing.

'Of course it is - and a deucedly hard affair, too. Now if any woman living must know the value of a Louis d'or, it is you; and yet you would have it that my theory is selfish! Let me ask what you would do if you did not know the value of every *sou?*'

'I cannot possibly say.'

'As it is, you cannot lay up any provision for the future. What will you do when you grow old, and can earn your living no longer?'

'Follow the general example, most probably, and die.'

Uncle Alexander turned upon his heel again - came back - kicked an inoffensive flower-pot to the other end of the garden, and said, impatiently -

'*Diable!* You are all fools alike, you women!'

Whereupon I gathered up my work, dropped him a short little courtesy, said '*Cela m'est égal, monsieur,*' and walked off into the house.

At the *salon* door I met M. Hamel, just going out. He passed me with a profound bow; and I thought, in that brief glance, that he looked handsomer than ever.

The door was no sooner closed upon him than a shower of eulogiums broke forth.

'What conversation!' exclaimed Madame. 'What reading! What elegant manners.'

'A perfect gentleman, indeed!' observed Monsieur, contemplating himself in the glass with infinite satisfaction. 'He has quite the - the *grand air*; and, what is more, he comprehends the art of dress. Nothing, ahem! - nothing so distinguishes the man of refinement as propriety - ahem! - propriety and richness of costume.'

An exclamation from Marguerite drew me to the window. A fine black horse was waiting in the court-yard. It pawed and snorted, and Claude could scarcely hold it in. All at once M. Hamel made his appearance on the steps. He looked up, recognized Marguerite, lifted his hat from his head, sprang into the saddle at a single bound, compelled the fiery animal to an angry quiet, and sauntered off carelessly through the village.

'Did you ever see such a magnificent horseman?' exclaimed Marguerite, flushed and smiling.

'Yes,' I replied. 'Your cousin Charles rides quite as well.'

Marguerite laughed nervously, and turned her head away.

'You think my cousin Charles perfection, mademoiselle,' she said, impatiently. 'I shall begin to fancy you are in love with him.'

'Marguerite!'

She looked in my face, blushed, and laid her cheek against my shoulder.

'Forgive me, dearest mademoiselle,' she whispered. 'I am often very naughty; but I love you dearly - indeed, indeed I do!'

'And cousin Charles?'

'Oh, he is very well, and - and I like him also. But, mademoiselle, you should have been here just now to have listened to M. Hamel! I am sure he is a poet, for he says such beautiful things!'

At this moment Pierrette opened the door.

'Madame is served,' said she; and so we all went down to dinner.

———

CHAPTER XII

THE COLUMBARIUM

The Wednesday morning shone bright and clear as a July day. We started early, so as to arrive at M. Gautier's in time for the second *déjeuner*, and I thought we never should get to the end of our journey. The distance from Montrocher to Santenay was fifteen miles at least, and the road lay across the mountains. When we had gone about a third of the distance, we came to a melancholy village, with a great iron crucifix at the beginning of the street; and a couple of dozen whitewashed hovels, that looked as if they had turned their backs to the road; and a miserable little wine-shop, with two solitary gendarmes playing dominoes outside the door. Cocks and hens, children and pigs, were playing and feeding together in the middle of the roadway. It was like every other French village all over the country. Now and then we passed through great cloisters of over-arching trees - or under a railway-bridge - or through a little stream that sparkled across the road. By-and-by we skirted the banks of the great canal that traverses this part of France, on its way to join the waters of the Rhine - a magnificent work, ploughed through the arid plains, and fringed on either side by mighty poplars. Here we passed the boundary-stone of the Côte d'Or, and found ourselves in the department of the Saône et Loire, wherein, as was announced upon a board affixed to a tree, '*La mendicité est interdit.*' And still we toiled onward and upward, always with a long hill before us, and, the shoulder of a fresh mountain to climb - and still Santenay lay far away, and showed not even a steeple to encourage us. We did reach it at last, however. It was a somewhat larger village than Montrocher, though not so picturesque. Montrocher lay in the heart of a green hollow, amid orchards and vineyards. Santenay, built on the slope of a precipitous hill, stretched upwards in one long, straggling, weary street, exposed to the blinding sunlight, and traversed by a few lean, languid, miserable dogs. Far up, at the very end of the village, rose the tops of some fine trees. These, as we approached, proved to be the outskirts of an enclosure, luxuriantly wooded, and fenced in by a limestone wall. Skirting this wall for some distance, we came to a heavy wooden gate, more like a barn-door than the entrance to a gentleman's estate. A stout, rosy old woman, wearing a mob-cap and an enormous pair of gold earrings, admitted us, with a torrent of *patois* salutations. The road lay before us through a tunnel of green boughs - there were goats browsing between the trees - and now and then, through openings in the branches, I caught glimpses of a red brick mansion beyond. Then we crossed a little bridge spanning a deep ravine, at the bottom of which, amid thick trees and bushes, gleamed a narrow thread of water - and so stopped and alighted at the door of the house where cousin Charles, smiling and courteous, was waiting to receive us.

'Welcome a thousand times,' he said, cordially. 'I heard your wheels as soon as you had passed the gate, and poor Jacqueline is in despair, for the breakfast is not yet ready. Some accident has delayed her this morning - it is but a bachelor's den after all! - and she has begged me to keep you amused for the next half-hour. How is that to be done?'

'By a turn in the grounds,' replied Madame, 'for we are cramped after the long ride, and mademoiselle would like to walk round the house.'

So we left Monsieur upon a sofa, and made the tour of the building. It was a singular old place, illustrative of two distinct periods of French architecture. The earlier part dated from the reign of Louis XI, and the latter from that of Louis XIV. The ravine proved to be a moat, now dwindled to a shallow pool and peopled by some score or two of gold and silver fish. It was a steep romantic chasm, roofed over in places by the interlacing boughs of trees, which had taken root and grown to gnarled maturity where once the water mounted - overgrown, in others, by a tapestry of crocuses, violets, primroses, and forget-me-nots - choked here and there by fragments of fallen masonry, waterstained and lichen-grown; and still showing, close beside the buttresses of the arch, the piers and staples of the ancient drawbridge. To the front of the mansion, trees, green sward, winding shady paths, and the broad circling carriage-drive - at the back, a broad space portioned off for fruit and kitchen gardens, but left for the main part uncultivated. The more habitable quarter of the building was of the red-bricked, ornamented, corniced, balustraded school of the Grand Monarque. It had little foliated entablatures above the windows, and all sorts of eccentric flights of steps leading to doors situated on the level of the first story, like the famous steps at Fontainebleau. Most of the window-shutters were closed, and it looked altogether more like a house shut up during the absence of the owners, than one inhabited by its hereditary lord. The earlier part lay somewhat to the left of the bridge, and at once usurped all my admiration. It was a gigantic square tower, the last imposing fragment of what had once been a feudal stronghold of unusual dimensions. Clothed more than half-way up in a mantle of ivy, through which some two or three small windows near the base struggled vainly for light, this tower was pierced higher up by narrow loopholes deeply set, and surmounted by a slated roof, shaped like the roofs of the Tuileries, only steeper. Crowning the whole, creaked a fantastic dragon-weathercock. On approaching nearer, I observed that there were fractures in the great walls here and there, as if the place at some remote time had sustained a siege.

M. Gautier confirmed this conjecture.

'The chateau,' he said, 'was assaulted by a party of Huguenots during the latter part of the reign of King Charles the Ninth, and, after a resistance of twenty-seven days, capitulated on honourable terms. The whole of the right wing was greatly injured, but, being from time to time repaired, continued habitable up to the year 1664, when, with the single exception of this tower, the whole was destroyed by fire. My ancestor, the Sieur Tanneguy Arnould Gautier then built the house which you now see. It is not elegant, but it contains more than thirty rooms, is in excellent repair, and needs only the addition of modern furniture to become a very comfortable residence. Many *suites* have been kept closed ever since my father's death - others are literally bare; but I shall alter all that some day, when ...'

His voice dropped, and he looked tenderly at Marguerite, who saw something down in the moat, just at that moment, which engaged all her attention.

'Would you like to go over the tower?' asked M. Charles, turning away with a sigh. 'Jacqueline will not be ready for us this half-hour to come.'

He led us round to an iron-clamped door, opening upon a small room in which there was a fire, a roof hung with herbs, onions, and rabbit-skins, some rough deal furniture, and a clock.

'Your pardon, Madame Pichat,' said M. Charles, addressing a woman who was cooking at the fire-place, and who turned in confusion at the sound of his voice. 'Good morning to you; we are going over to the tower, and must trouble you for the key of the staircase-door.'

Madame Pichat courtesied to the ground, and herself unlocked a massive inner door which was barred and clamped more heavily than the first, and opened out of her little parlour.

'This is the wife of my groom,' said M. Charles. 'I allow them to live here, and they keep the key of the tower, which, ruin as it is, is not a wholly unimportant trust. The upper-rooms communicate with the house, and burglars entering from this part could find their way where they pleased. But we entertain no fears of that kind - do we, Madame Pichat?'

Madame Pichat courtesied again, and shook her head vehemently.

'No, no, monsieur, not we!' said she, rubbing her hands. 'It is an honest part, *mon Dieu*! and even if it were not, my Jules is brave. We would load the old carabine yonder, and -'

'And Madame Pichat would raise the siege, like another Jeanne d'Arc,' added M. Charles, with a smile. 'Well, well, we will hope that our courage is not going to be put to the proof. But where is Pierre? I have not seen the boy these two days past.'

The woman smoothed out her apron with both hands, and looked delighted.

'Ah, monsieur,' she said, 'it is a fortunate garçon, and we are very happy. Thanks to my brother Claude (Madame's Claude, if she will permit it) the boy is placed at Chalons. It is far; but his good saint watches over him.'

Madame was interested.

'Then my head vigneron is your brother, Madame Pichat?' said she.

'And the uncle of Pierre, if you please, madame,' replied the dame Pichat courtesying over and over again. 'And old Madame Georges, the pew-opener at Chalons, is both our aunts; and Claude spoke to her, and said, "*Ma tante*, you must serve the little Pierre," and so she did, and that is how the lad came to be engaged in the stable, if you please, madame!'

'In what stable?' asked Madame Delahaye, utterly confused by this intricate piece of family history.

'*Mais*, madame, in the stable of monsieur the minister?'

'She means M. Hamel!' exclaimed Marguerite.

Madame Pichat smiled and bobbed assent.

'To be sure,' said she. 'He is groom to monsieur the minister, whom the saints forgive for being a heretic!'

Cousin Charles held up his finger.

'Beware, Madame Pichat!' he said, 'we are all heretics here! But is Pierre really engaged in M. Hamel's service?'

'He is indeed, monsieur,' replied the woman, greatly abashed. 'The lad has left us these two days.' Then, after a moment of hesitation - 'I had forgotten,' she said, looking down, 'that the ladies were heretics, and as for you, my good master, I say an *Ave* every day to the Holy Virgin for your conversion!'

'Thank you, my excellent Madame Pichat,' said M. Charles, kindly. 'You mean well, I am sure. But if we delay, Jacqueline will be in greater despair than ever. Forward!'

And so, with a great bunch of rusty keys in his hand cousin Charles preceded us up the narrow staircase, and Madame Pichat was left to her cookery and her *pot-au-feu*.

The first story of the tower contained four small rooms, dusty, cobwebbed, and dark. M. Charles unclosed the shutters; but the ivy had overgrown the casements, and it made little difference. Some of the rooms were sunk below, and others raised above the level of the first by which we entered. There were doors with little steps leading upwards - others with steps leading downwards - windows sunk so deeply in the massive wall that seats of old carved oak were placed on either side of the recess, and to these, again, one mounted by a flight of two or three steps. Huge old coffers, with suits of rusty nails studding them all over like scale-armour, stood here and there. Some were lying open; all were filled with dust, and rubbish, and rolls of unintelligible parchments. Some very old pictures, all bulging from their frames, were heaped up in one of the farthest chambers; and a press in the first room was found to contain the harness of M. Charles's gig. We then proceeded to the next story, and found it dirtier, dustier, and more dreary than the first. Here M. Charles asked if we wished to investigate any farther.

'You will have to grope up that ladder,' he said, 'and the loft is full of nothing but rubbish.'

However, we would go. It was a gloomy cavernous place, raftered overhead, and filled with all manner of antique lumber. Through an opening in the beams you could see up into the recesses of the pyramidal roof, and trace the outline of a huge alarm-bell, which had probably hung there for centuries. A bat whirred by in the darkness when we first entered, and our feet sank into a carpet of dust at every step. Here were stacks of old carved chairs, *prie-dieux*, and footstools, with the velvet and brocade dropping off the seats - coils of decayed rope, and rolls of tattered carpet, that looked as if a touch would reduce them to dust - a bedstead, all charred as if by the action of fire, with a drapery of cobwebs clinging to the canopy; and, strangest of all, a disabled sedan-chair of the date of Louis XV, a quaint, narrow, comfortless vehicle, with all its windows shattered and its blazonry defaced.

We examined these things with eagerness; and even M. Charles surveyed the place with a kind of melancholy interest.

'I have not been up here,' he said, 'for years. I remember that I used to be afraid of the tower when a boy, and would not have ventured near it at midnight for the world.'

'Surely,' said I, 'there must be a ghost story connected with it!'

'I believe there is some legend current in the neighbourhood,' replied M. Charles; 'though I scarcely know what it is. You must ask Madame Pichat about it. She will tell you that carriage-wheels are heard, and footfalls pacing to a solemn measure, and other horrors, equally appropriate. But if I am to take you through the other part of the house, you must linger here no longer.'

So, with a last look, we went down to the next story. Here M. Charles opened a modern looking door, led us through a passage cut in the thickness of the tower-wall, and, ushering us into a little paneled chamber, informed us that we were now in that portion of the building which dated from the reign of Louis XIV. Hence we passed through long suites of apartments, all of which had been closed for the last twelve or fifteen years. Some were quite unfurnished. Others contained piles of chairs covered with cloths, chandeliers tied up in bags, and ghostly cabinets in winding sheets of dimity. All were wainscoted, gilded, and profusely decorated with Renaissance arabesques, and panels after the school of Watteau. Here were awkward Cupids and faded shepherdesses, concerts in trim garden-alleys, and flirtations in bowers of roses. Reception-rooms, card-rooms, music-rooms, boudoirs, bed-chambers, dressing-rooms, and ante-rooms, followed in endless succession. It was like making the tour of a little Versailles.

'What a pity that the place is empty!' exclaimed Marguerite. 'I should like to see the house lighted up, to hear music in every drawing-room, and to know that each bed-room was tenanted by a guest.'

'You shall fill the house as full as you please, Marguerite,' said cousin Charles, in a low voice, 'when you are its mistress.'

She blushed and laughed.

'Shall I, really?' she said: 'oh, how charming that will be, cousin Charles!'

Wise cousin Charles! He had touched the right chord at last!

'You shall, indeed,' he answered, in the same tone, 'if you will only love me.'

'Breakfast, if you please, Monsieur Charles,' said a voice at the door.

It was Jacqueline, fat, fair, and considerably more than forty, an excellent cook, and, excepting the groom and lodge-keeper, the bachelor's only domestic.

'In a few moments, Jacqueline,' replied M. Charles, impatiently.

'No, Monsieur Charles, directly, if you please,' said Jacqueline, resolutely; 'the turbot is served, and must be eaten at once.'

Her master smiled, and shrugged his shoulders.

'Jacqueline will be obeyed,' he said, with an air of resignation; and offered his arm to Madame Delahaye.

The breakfast was laid in a large room opening on the lawn. A pleasant odour of violets pervaded the air; a soft-green shade was cast over the table by means of the closed venetians; and a breakfast, which looked like a very profuse dinner, was prepared for our discussion. Fish, poultry, delicate made-dishes, rare preserves, early vegetables, and precious wines of famous vintages, were placed before us. For the first time in my life I perceived that cookery must be a science, and eating a branch of the fine arts. M. Delahaye was an accomplished diner. He boasted of it. He condescended to explain to me that certain dishes should precede certain wines; that the failing appetite might be occasionally revived by stimulants of oysters or melon; that to eat cream with strawberries was a barbarism not to be named in cultivated society; and that no man who valued his reputation would consent to touch champagne before the dessert was brought to table.

Madame, though not so finished a *connoisseuse*, praised and tasted every dish; Marguerite, pleased with the novelty of peas and peaches in April, feasted, and laughed, and was as happy as the birds on the trees; and Jacqueline, proud as only a successful cook can be, stood by, beaming and benevolent, and received our compliments much as a Roman general might have received the honours of an ovation.

But it was in M. Charles that I was chiefly interested. Never was man so transformed. He chatted, he unbent, he was the most courteous of hosts and companions. Silent myself, I loved to sit by and watch the development of this character, so outwardly cold, so inwardly genuine. Manly, undemonstrative, grave, honourable, and hospitable was he. Somewhat exacting at times it was true, and scarcely so indulgent as a lover might have been to the careless errors of our little Marguerite; but that he did love her tenderly, deeply, nay, passionately, could one but look into his heart of hearts, I felt convinced.

'Oh that I could but reconcile these two opposing natures!' thought I. 'That I could teach her to admire, and him to tolerate! That each could see the other with my eyes, and peace and love, hope and unity for ever subsist between them!'

The breakfast lasted for two hours, and the gentlemen prolonged it still farther over their coffee and cigars. We retired to the library, where Madame fell asleep in M. Charles's easy-chair, and Marguerite amused herself with Jacqueline's white kitten. As for me, I made the tour of the bookshelves, endeavouring to analyze the tastes of the owner, and, when attracted by any particular volume, dipping into a page or two, like a bee in a flower-garden. Not that M. Charles's library could be, by any flight of fancy, compared to a flower-garden. On the contrary, it more nearly resembled some grand primeval forest, where noble trees of medium growth, and tender saplings in their first leafage, spring up within the shade of Druid oaks, whose knotted roots have grasped the soil for centuries. Here were Homer and Plato, Æschylus, Herodotus and Aristotle; all the Latin historians and poets; the works of Lord Bacon, Spinosa, Gervinus, Herschel, Arago, Humboldt, Newton, Descartes, Kant, Richter, Goethe, Comte, Lessing, and hundreds of others, equally dissimilar. Shakespeare was there in the German translation, and Walter Scott in French. The French dramatists and poets filled one huge recess from floor to ceiling, beginning with compilations from the Trouvères, and ending with volumes of Lamartine and Victor Hugo. Dictionaries, Encyclopædias, Biographies, and valuable works of reference abounded; and here, either in translations or in their original tongues, were represented all the philosophies, all the sciences, and all the histories of the world.

While I was yet taking down book after book, the door opened, and Jacqueline announced that the gentlemen were waiting to conduct us to the vault '*là bas*.'

'To the what?' cried Madame, waking up bewildered.

'*Ma foi*, madame,' said Jacqueline, with a gesture of disgust - 'to that grave out there in the kitchen-garden - that hole full of pots and bones that monsieur is so delighted with. Though why he *should* be delighted with such pagan rubbish, the holy Joseph alone can tell!'

'Ah, I understand - the columbarium!' said Madame, yawning. 'Well, it is no doubt very interesting, and I suppose we must go. Marguerite, my pet, you must not venture in the sun without your bonnet.'

'I am not going out, mamma,' replied Marguerite, carelessly.

'Not going, my love! What will your cousin say?'

'What he chooses,' said Marguerite. 'I always declared that I would never go into that horrid place, and I mean to keep my word.'

Madame gave me a look of entreaty, and left the room.

'Marguerite,' I said, gently, 'do you remember promising me something a few days ago?'

No reply.

'You promised me that you would read the pamphlet on Roman burials. How did you keep that promise?'

'Not very strictly, mademoiselle,' replied she, hanging her head.

'You read about four pages, dear, and then you flang it away. Do you remember that?'

'Yes, mademoiselle.'

'Tell me, dear - was I vexed when you did so?'

'No, indeed! You excused me, mademoiselle, with that kind smile of yours!'

And half smiling, half-artful, she put up her rosy mouth to kiss away the coming remonstrances.

'Nay, Marguerite,' I said, drawing back, and speaking as I would have spoken to a child, 'I cannot kiss you till you have given me a promise which shall atone for the broken one. Will you come with me to the columbarium?'

'May I shut my eyes when I am there?' she asked, with provoking simplicity.

I shook my head, and moved towards the door.

'Yes, or no?' I asked, gravely.

She ran and threw her arms about my neck.

'I will go wherever you like, and be whatever you desire!' she cried, clinging to me and caressing me. 'Only never look at me so coldly, for then you remind me of my cousin Charles!'

I sighed at the comparison, and led her down stairs.

Madame rewarded me with a glance of thanks, and took the arm of M. Delahaye.

'Charles and Marguerite must lead the way together,' she said, with a smile.

M. Charles bowed and offered Marguerite his hand. An unwonted flush alone betrayed the lover's exultation. Probably his wooing had never borne so fair an aspect as it bore this day.

Close beneath the windows of the southern front lay a high mound of earth, in the face of which appeared some twelve feet of brick wall and a narrow doorway. Approaching nearer, we found what appeared to be a small, square, windowless building, half unburied, and ornamented with carved coping-stones, and sculptured slabs let into the walls. Some of these bore funeral inscriptions in the old Roman letters, and some basso-relievos of processions, sacrifices, and the like. It looked quite fresh, and the brickwork had lost none of its original colour. One would have taken it for a modern ice-house rather than a remnant of antiquity. A few displaced slabs, and some broken sherds of a light salmon-coloured clay heaped together on one side - an earth-pile on the other. The direct path to the little doorway had been cleanly swept in anticipation of our arrival.

Arrived at this spot, Marguerite shuddered and turned pale. She was about to speak, but glanced towards me and refrained. We then descended a narrow flight of wooden stairs, which might have been placed there a couple of years since, for all the signs of age which they exhibited.

It was a cool, dusk, subterranean chamber, about twelve feet square. The floor was of brick, and the walls were pierced, from basement to ceiling, in long rows of tiny niches, like the holes of a pigeon-house; and coated with a smooth cream-coloured cement. Between all these rows, and on the slightly concave roof, were painted a profusion of delicately-executed frescos. On a bench erected along the farther end of the chamber, stood three urns of a dull kind of coloured glass, a small *cippus* richly ornamented, and several earthen lamps of various sizes. The air was deliciously cool, and there was nothing of that oppressive odour from which not even the best of our modern vaults are entirely free. Marguerite heaved a sigh of relief - she had evidently expected something of the horrors of the charnel-house - and cousin Charles began his explanations.

'Everything,' said he, 'is now in the same condition as when it was discovered. I do not say that nothing has been disturbed; but whatever was removed for examination has been carefully replaced, that you might to-day see this Roman sepulchre as it was seen by those who built up its portals, as they thought, for ever, after having filled the last niche with the remains of the last occupant. From that hour to the morning when a workman came running to me with the news that a little underground house had been found on the site of the proposed conservatory, no human step had profaned the silence of the tomb. I hastened to the place. The door had just been forced - I clambered over the rubbish which had fallen in upon the stairs, waited an instant till the dust cleared away, and found myself transgressing one of the strictest laws of ancient Rome - that is to say, breaking forcibly into a columbarium. Had I lived in an earlier age I should have lost my right hand, been condemned to the mines, or punished, perhaps, with death.'

'But why is it called a columbarium?' asked Marguerite.

'Because these niches resemble the niches of a dove-cot,' replied M. Charles. 'But I want you to examine the paintings, which are very curious.'

They were indeed. Some were partially obliterated by the damp; others were still brilliant and perfect. Here was a lady at her toilette, attended by servants - yonder a group of naked boys surprised by a crocodile while bathing - a priest sacrificing at the altar - a group of birds and beasts - a man slaying a boar - a basket of flowers, &c., &c. Higher up, a band of arabesques was substituted for the figure subjects, and the ceiling was decorated with a broad bordering of some intricate pattern, with a group of hunters in the middle.

'Who would imagine,' said M. Charles, after an interval of profound silence, 'that in this chamber sleeps the quiet of eighteen hundred years? Who would recognize in this painted room the sepulchre of at least one hundred and twenty persons? Oh, wise, and poetical religion, which beheld in death only the naked Geni with inverted torch, and turned with a smile from the empty terrors of the Skeleton and the Scythe! What are our huge cemeteries and pestilential vaults to the pleasant repose of such a scene as this? Death, and its dreary adjuncts, the possibility of premature interment; the sometimes violated tomb may appal even the bravest - but here, how different! To this the warrior could look forward with content, and beauty with resignation. The fame of the one would live for ever; the charms of the other would return to innoxious ashes, and the tears of the lover might be buried with the ashes of his beloved. See, here is a lachrymatory. The tears within it have long since returned to air; but the sentiment which buried them is immortal. These glass urns contained the libations of oil and wine - this graceful bronze represents a tutelary god. All is peace, and poetry, and perpetual repose.'

'Well, but after all,' said Marguerite, 'we have seen nothing of the hundred and twenty bodies. What have you done with those, cousin Charles? Buried them?'

'Buried them!' echoed M. Charles. 'Certainly not. Here they are, exactly as I found them. Did you not see the mouths of the urns sunk in the niches all round the chamber, here - and here - and here?'

And he led her round the room, showing her the openings in the bottom of every niche, and the terra-cotta lids in the middle of each.

Marguerite put forth her hand timidly, and lifted off one of the covers.

'But these are only jars,' she said, innocently. 'What is there inside?'

M. Charles looked at her with the eye of an inquisitor.

'If you do not already know,' he said, meaningly, 'put in your hand and see.'

She hesitated, drew back, took courage, and brought up a handful of ashes and charred bone.

'What are these?' she said, falteringly.

'Did you read the pamphlet?' asked M. Charles, with the old cloud on his brow, and the stern lines hardening around his mouth.

'N-n-no, not exactly; but I read part of it - did I not, mademoiselle?'

'Enough,' said M. Charles, coldly. 'You need not prevaricate, Marguerite. I gave you the book, and requested you, for my sake, to read it. You have not chosen to do so, and I will say no more upon the subject. Had you read it, however, you would have known that you now hold in your hand the cinders of one who was once a being like yourself.'

Marguerite dropped the ashes with a palpitating cry.

'Oh, cousin Charles,' she exclaimed, 'you should have told me. You should not have let me touch them. It was cruel, very cruel of you!'

Pale and trembling, she ran up into the open air. Once fairly out of the columbarium, she became hysterical, and burst into tears. All was confusion immediately. M. Delahaye wandered round and round his daughter in a state of helpless bewilderment. Madame took her in her arms and endeavoured to soothe her. I ran to the house for water, and M. Charles, angry and compassionate at the same time, paced to and fro in the background, like an unquiet spirit.

'*Mon Dieu!*' said he, impatiently, when, having brought the water, I drew aside to let her recover - '*Mon Dieu!* what folly is this? What was there in a handful of dust to call for such a scene?'

'You were wrong, monsieur,' I said, 'to let her touch it. You should have remembered how young and impressionable she is.'

'I meant it for a lesson,' he replied.

'But your lesson was too harsh. Do you wish to make Marguerite afraid of you, and do you not think that fear may end in aversion?'

He started, coloured, bit his lip, and said -

'You speak forcibly, mademoiselle.'

'Because I feel deeply, monsieur. We women read women's natures keenly, and learn more of each other's hearts in half a week than the wisest man could read in a long life-time. We are won variously, as our natures vary - some by caresses, some by mastery, some by reverence. To woo the earnest soul with toys, or the simple soul with hard philosophy, is time misplaced. You might as reasonably hope to take Algiers with sugar-plums, or bait your line with Greek odes when you fish for trout.'

He forced a smile.

'Mademoiselle knows how to reprove,' said he. 'I would I knew my duty as well.'

'Your duty just at present is to attend on Marguerite,' I said, persuasively. 'See, she rises; she is going into the house. Offer her your arm - soothe her - forget the Roman pamphlet, and remember only that she is young, and loving, and that you have caused her to shed tears!'

'You - you assign me an awkward part, mademoiselle,' he said, irresolutely.

At that moment she looked round, as, I believe, in search of me; but I turned the action to account.

'There,' I urged, 'did you not see her look this way? How can you delay? Go at once, monsieur, and entreat her forgiveness!'

He smiled again, shook his head at me, and went. Then I saw him bending over her, drawing her arm through his, and leading her to a pleasant seat beneath a willow. Madame Delahaye left them together, and came back to meet me.

'Charles should not have been so angry with the child,' she said; 'but, for all that, he improves. There was a time, my dear mademoiselle, when he would have been cold and displeased all the day long. Now, you see, he begins to know her disposition better. You have no idea how kindly he came up just now and kissed her hand. Oh, he will develop into a devoted husband!'

'Have they been long betrothed?' I asked, with a sigh.

'Since Marguerite was thirteen years of age,' replied Madame. 'it will be a most desirable marriage on both sides. M. Delahaye, though he unfortunately dissipated much of his fortune in his youth, is still a rich man; my own property is considerable; and M. Charles is one of the largest land-owners in the department of the Saône et Loire. Of course it is highly important that we should unite these interests, the more particularly as the Gautiers and Delahayes are both branches of the same family. Besides, it is probable that Marguerite and her heirs will succeed to the estates of M. Alexander, who is wealthier than any of us.'

Scarcely knowing what reply to make to this catalogue of rent-rolls and title-deeds, I bowed, and remained silent.

'I dare say now,' she continued, believing me to be deeply interested, 'that this appears strange to you. You must wonder how it happens that my husband's younger brother should be richer than himself!'

'Not at all, madame,' I said, absently.

'It happened thus. According to our French law, the second son inherits his mother's fortune, and, in this instance, the mother's fortune was twice as large as that of the father. M. Delahaye lived in Paris, and spent lavishly. M. Alexander cultivated his lands, exported his own wines, and established, not only an office at Chalons, but efficient agents in all the capitals of Europe. Thus, the smaller fortune was reduced, and the larger doubled. Do you follow me, mademoiselle?'

'Perfectly, madame.'

'It was in Paris,' pursued Madame, with a touch of sentiment in her voice, 'that I first met M. Delahaye. I was the daughter of a banker in the Rue Lafitte, and engaged at that time to my father's partner; but what are such engagements when love comes to cancel them? So eloquent a speaker as M. Delahaye carried all before him. No one dressed with so much taste, paid such delightful compliments, or sang so exquisitely! He was called the Rubini of the drawing-rooms, and the Apollo of the Bois de Boulogne! Ah, mademoiselle, that was twenty years ago; but from what you now hear of his *fioriture*, you can still conceive what must have been the effect of Monsieur Delahaye's singing!'

I bowed again.

'His upper notes, it is true, are nearly gone,' said Madame, meditatively; 'but his style is perfect. His shake on the upper G is still as wonderful as ever. And then, on his low B, - did you notice M. Delahaye's low B, mademoiselle?'

I could not say that I had particularly remarked the note in question.

'No? Then we will ask him to sing the serenade from Fra Diavolo to-morrow, and you will hear it to perfection. Why, Signor Scampini - (you have heard of Signor Scampini, the great tenor of fifteen or eighteen years ago?) - he shot himself in the very zenith of his career entirely in consequence of M. Delahaye's low B.'

Madame Delahaye, at all times voluble, was inexhaustible on the subject of her husband's graces and perfections. Time had stolen little from his fascinations according to her estimate. She could not see that he had withered and declined - she could not hear that his voice had grown discordant. He was still, for her, the 'Apollo of the Bois de Boulogne!'

In the midst of some very long story, of which I have forgotten the beginning, and never heard the end, Jacqueline again made her appearance, and summoned us to dinner.

The dinner was somewhat longer and more elaborate, than the breakfast. The soups, the sweets, the wines, and the dessert were more profuse and *recherché*; and, to my surprise, were discussed by M. and Madame Delahaye even more heartily than before. When we rose to leave the table it was already dusk, and the glow-worms were burning in the grass like living emeralds.

Fain would M. Charles have persuaded us to wait for another breakfast, and return by day. Madame Delahaye would not hear of it. The chaise was brought round, and, by the light of a bright young moon, we bade farewell to our host. He walked beside us as far as the lodge. He and Marguerite had been upon the best terms ever since that little affair of the columbarium. He had himself chosen her *bonbons*, and peeled her peaches at dessert. He had given her a large paper of *marrons-glacés* to amuse her on the way home; and now, on parting, even dared to kiss her cheek.

Then the gates closed behind us; we made our way through the village; emerged upon the lonely country-road, with our weary fifteen miles lying all before us; and some few minutes before midnight found ourselves at home.

CHAPTER XIII

A DINNER 'EN PROVENCE'

Madame Vaudon lived about a quarter of a mile out of Chalons, and her house stood by the river-side, in a pleasant circuit of lawn and flower-garden. The steam-boat-quay, the bridge, and the town spires, with a background of blue hills, were visible from her drawing-room windows. The hall and staircase were adorned with statues, stained glass, and vases of evergreens. The drawing-rooms were plentifully strewn with books, folios of engravings, curiosities from abroad, and articles of *virtu*. There were cunning little corners furnished with tiny chess-tables, recesses just wide enough for two, a boudoir containing little Roman bronzes, terra-cotta casts from the antique, jars of rare exotics, and a divan for those who loved solitude and flirtation. Everything, in short, which good taste and a refined hospitality could suggest.

The dinner was appointed for seven o'clock. We arrived there about a quarter in advance of the time, which gave me leisure to observe the place and the company. Five persons were already assembled. One of these I recognized for the pale man whom I had seen at church a week ago. He was turning over the leaves of a large album, and conversing at intervals with an intellectual-looking German. Standing bolt upright with his back to the fire-place, stood a gray, weather-beaten soldier, profusely *décoré*. The fourth guest was a brisk little gentleman, with curly black hair, and very white teeth. He had a genial way of rubbing his hands together when he spoke, as if life were an excellent joke, and he were always seeing the point of it. The fifth, was a pale and stately old lady, who spoke little, moved languidly, was dressed in black velvet, and sat in a large arm-chair, with her thin hands crossed upon her lap, and the evening light shining down peacefully upon her white hair.

Madame Vaudon was an accomplished hostess. To the polished elegance acquired in French society, she added the frank dignity of an English gentlewoman. She carried with her an atmosphere of ease and *bienséance*. She had the art of showing attention to all, of effecting happy introductions, and of placing together persons of congenial tastes. Her daughter Adèle took no part in the duties of reception; but stood with Marguerite in a distant window. Presently Madame Vaudon came over and sat beside me.

'The last five or ten minutes before dinner,' said she, 'are the most trying moments in the life of a hostess. The sight of all these hungry people makes one feel like a social Van Amburg. If anything chances to delay the dinner-bell the situation becomes perilous.'

'At all events,' said I, 'you seem to keep your guests under control.'

'Because I make them amuse each other. But, stay, I must tell you who is here, for you are a stranger in the land.'

'I should like to know the history of that old lady in the arm-chair,' I said, eagerly.

'It is sad and strange. She is one of the few who escaped the guillotine during the reign of terror. Her father, her two brothers, and her husband all died upon the scaffold; while she, forgotten in her prison, was liberated with the rest of the *'suspects'* after the fall of Robespierre.'

'And that pallid man, with the broad forehead, and disdainful mouth?'

'Is Monsieur Deligny, an author, a critic, a collector of paintings, and the owner of a delicious retreat called '*Les Peupliers*,' about half a league from Chalons. He is now talking to the Baron von Steinberg, a youth of good birth and polyglot acquirements. He is musical, philosophical, and artistic. He has dabbled in some few of the higher branches of science; written a play that was damned; travelled through England, Italy, and Spain; and acquired most of the languages of Europe. He has just completed the tour of France.'

'Truly an encyclopedic character. And the old soldier now speaking to him?'

'General Max de Chamfort - we call him General Max. He is an excellent old man, and a brave officer; but prosy on the subject of his campaigns. Now, I think, you are *au courant* with all my visitors.'

'No, you have forgotten that little gentleman with the white neckcloth. He looks like a physician.'

'And he is a physician. His name is Grandet, he professes to believe in nothing, not even in his own art, and is the merriest little Æsculapius that ever signed a prescription. But see, it wants only five minutes to the hour, and our principal guest is not yet arrived!'

Hereupon Madame Vaudon glided away to revive the failing conversations, and disguise the flight of time; but her efforts were less successful than usual. The *tête-à-têtes* flagged. People began to cluster at the windows, and to watch for the opening of the door. More than one whisper bore the name of M. Hamel, and a silence of expectation, resembling that which follows the last note of the orchestra and precedes the rising of the curtain, fell upon all the company.

Slowly the five minutes waned - the last slowest of all. Then the little ormolu knight upon the timepiece raised his lance and bowed his head - the first silver stroke rang out like a tiny trumpet-call, the door of the *salon* was flung open, and a servant announced -

'The Rev. Alexis Xavier Hamel.'

He paused a moment at the threshold, and surveyed the room in one comprehensive glance. Handsome and imposing in the unbecoming robes of the preacher, he was far more handsome and imposing in the dress of a private gentleman. His coat, with its broad lappels of silk *moiré*, his black velvet waistcoat, fastened only by three small buttons encrusted with brilliants, his slender watch-guard, with its pendant cluster of *recherché* trifles, all indicated a taste unusually costly and fastidious. Taken separately, the items of his toilette were, perhaps, too carefully studied. They wanted that austere simplicity which best becomes the person of a gentleman. Still there was something royal in the look and bearing of the man that bore out the elegance of his costume, and stripped it of every vestige of foppishness. His voice, sonorous and subdued; his very manner of carrying his head, and of crossing a room, were such as might have characterized an ambassador or a minister of state. He came forward with that perfect ease which stamps the man of society, and Madame Vaudon went half-way to meet him.

'I perceive, monsieur,' she said, at the close of some brief compliment, 'that to your other accomplishments you add the genius of punctuality.'

M. Hamel bowed.

'There are, madame,' he said, 'according to my creed, two occasions upon which no man of education deserves to be pardoned for an error of time.'

'And they are -'

'A dinner and a rendezvous.'

'He might have brought forward an instance more befitting his cloth,' muttered the critic.

M. Hamel turned quickly.

'Courtesy forbid, monsieur!' he retorted, with a glance half menacing and half sarcastic. 'What gentleman would carry his profession into society? It is only to the brave and tried soldier' (here he turned to General Max) 'that we accord as a privilege and receive as a favour the story of the battle and the bivouac.'

M. Deligny bit his lip, and was silent; but the old officer, taken by surprise, blushed under all his bronzing, and bowed profoundly.

At this moment the door was thrown open, the powdered butler made his appearance in ceremonious silence. Madame Vaudon accepted the arm of M. Hamel, and we went down to the dining-room.

There is something very imposing in the aspect of a really well-arranged dinner-table, with its pyramids of glass and silver, its creamy napery, its clustering wax lights, and its vases of brilliant and perfumed exotics. The great tureens send up a fragrant incense - the silent footmen come and go, powdered and inaudible, like the ministers of some mysterious religion - the guests sit round in solemn conclave, like the assistants at the sacrifice. The table is a pagan altar; the claret ceases to be claret, and becomes a libation; and the dining-room is a temple dedicated to the gods. Even the most intellectual people are subjugated by the influences of the place, and for the first fifteen minutes everybody is profoundly silent. The soup and fish come and go, phantom-like, and it is not till the arrival of the third course that, literally and metaphorically, we find our tongue.

I am not going to describe the dishes, or, armed with my feeble vocabulary, attempt to criticise the mysteries of that sublime art in which the Frenchman excels all the nations of the world, and which the Frenchman alone is competent to appreciate. Enough if I record that Madame Vaudon's dinner was a triumph of art and hospitality; that it lasted for four mortal hours; and that ere a sixth of that time had elapsed, the conversation flowed as freely and sparkled as brightly as the fountains of Helicon, or the rare and delicious wines of which M. Vaudon was pardonably proud.

'This,' said he, as the glasses were changed and filled afresh, 'is a vintage which I can recommend. M. Delahaye, you will recognize your brother's famous iced *Romanée*.'

M. Delahaye tasted, looked wise, and said -

'Ah, yes - very true - my excellent brother Alexander's iced *Romanée* - extract of *Romanée*, correctly and scientifically speaking.'

I ventured to ask M. Grandet for an explanation.

'My dear young lady,' said the physician, savouring the precious liquid by degrees, 'this is no vulgar vintage. It is, as has been just observed, an extract. The wine, being chosen of the first quality, is subjected to a refrigerating process, which congeals the weaker ingredients round the inside of the cask. That modicum of spirit which refuses to freeze is then bottled off, and - here you have it!'

'Drinking such nectar as this,' said M. Hamel, 'I do not envy the Cæsars their "smoky Falernian."'

'Nor I, if the Latin wines were half as bad as the fermented vinegars of modern Italy, none of which have anything good about them but their names,' said M. Deligny. 'As for the *Montepulciano*, so far from being "the king of all wines," it is a mere lacquey to Burgundy and Bordeaux.'

'Talking of Italy,' began the general, laying down his knife and fork, and preparing for a story, 'I remember when we crossed the

Alps, and found ourselves in sight of the enemy at Arcole ...'

The doctor came to the rescue.

'Upon my word, general,' said he, 'you are right. The wines about Arcole are excellent. My dear Deligny, you must make an exception in favour of Arcole, which produces a vintage little inferior to the famous wines of Oporto.'

'Alas!' said M. Vaudon, 'the wines of Oporto will soon become extinct.'

'Bad news for the Englishman who neither drinks nor understands anything better!' exclaimed the doctor.

'Because,' said M. Deligny, with his cold sneer, 'like himself, it is heavy and spiritless. The tastes of the Englishman are essentially gross, and he monopolizes the Oporto market in pursuance of the same vulgar instincts by which he is impelled towards beef and beer, fox-hunting and pugilism.'

I felt myself colour with indignation, and, looking up, found M. Hamel's eyes upon me.

'It seems to me,' he said, with the slightest possible vibration of irony in his voice, 'that Monsieur Deligny describes the stage-Englishmen of the Palais Royal vaudevilles - the Sir Smith who wears an apple-green coat, has cock-fights in his bedroom, and marries his cook. M. Deligny's imagination is vivid; but he cannot seriously entertain so unjust and ignorant an estimate of the English character. Above all, he cannot forget that he speaks in the presence of two English ladies, one of whom is his hostess, and the other her guest.'

M. Deligny darted a quick, glittering glance at M. Hamel, who, smiling, courteous, and disdainful, went on quietly with his dinner.

'Really, sir,' said he, 'you are at infinite pains to charge yourself with my defence!' Then, turning to Madame Vaudon, 'I must entreat your pardon, my kind hostess,' he added; 'but it is not my fault that your accent is so just and your French so perfect as to deceive the nicest judge of nationalities.'

Madame Vaudon smiled uneasily, and turned the conversation.

'You will spoil me,' she said. 'The more competent the critic, the more subtle the praise. But, *à propos* of criticism, what an elaborate paper we have on H—'s poems in the present number of the *Revue de Deux Mondes*.'

A peculiar smile flitted over the face of M. Deligny.

'I know the article,' he said, carelessly, 'and I subscribe to it with all my heart. This young man has achieved, within the space of one volume, a reputation greater than that of even Lamartine or Victor Hugo.'

M. Hamel shook his head.

'Take care,' he said. 'You are calling great names in question.'

'Not without justice,' retorted M. Deligny, sharply. 'To deny poetic merit is the atheism of the age, and it is time that we learnt to appreciate excellence at first sight. H— is a great poet. I judge dispassionately; while you, monsieur, just arrived from abroad, can scarcely be supposed to have had any opportunity of judging at all.'

'I beg your pardon,' said M. Hamel, calmly. 'I have read both the poems and the review, and I find the former mediocre, and the latter insincere.'

'Insincere!' echoed Deligny, angrily. 'Pray do me the favour to explain.'

'With pleasure. Beginning, then, with the poet. H— has some merit of ear and eye, makes no false rhymes, and is gifted with more than the ordinary share of fancy. But he wants style, and he wants that healthy appreciation of life which is indispensable to the poet. He seems to have been nourished on the faded sentiment of the Pastor Fido, and to have studied mankind from the sickly canvases of Watteau and Lancret. Surely there must be some great fault of education here! Why should he despise the men and things of his time?'

Mr. Deligny shrugged his shoulders.

'Ah, bah!' he said, contemptuously. 'The present age is not poetical.'

'Nay, there I must dissent. Poetry is the Pæan of humanity, and must exist so long as men live, love, suffer, and die. But the poet must go to nature for his work. He must study, like Parrhasius, from the living agony, and not simulate the ghastly quiverings of a galvanised corpse. Let him seek out the romance of common things - read off the poetry of railways, and feel the pulse of Paris streets. Living among bricks and mortar, he must make these things plastic; for there can be no true art where the artist disdains the surroundings of his daily life.'

M. Hamel spoke with enthusiasm, and every eye was turned upon him. It was no longer a private conversation across the table;

but a trial of wits, in which M. Deligny was getting the worst of the argument. He had seen this, and lost his temper long ago.

'Enough, monsieur,' he said, impatiently. 'Enough; you have criticised the poet, and we need not pause to dispute his merits. I am anxious now to hear what you have to say to the article in the *Revue de Deux Mondes!*'

M. Hamel filled and drank another glass of the iced *Romaneée*, regarded his questioner with a steady smile, and answered him with even more composure than before.

'Taken upon the surface,' he said, 'this article is simply ridiculous. Seen more nearly, we find a substratum of something worse. We find that the critic has only set up a temporary idol, that he may more safely undermine the temple of a true religion. H— is but the weapon wielded in ignoble hands - the catspaw to a premeditated fraud. It is not he who is exalted by these eulogiums; but Lamartine who is defamed. With all his fervour, I doubt whether the critic be even the honest partisan of the man he praises; but I know that he is the slanderer of Lamartine.'

Quivering with rage, Deligny rose in his place.

'Monsieur,' he said, hoarsely, 'you insult me!'

'I, my dear sir!' exclaimed M. Hamel, with well-acted astonishment. 'You are dreaming! What is it to us if H— be commonplace, and his critic venial?'

Deligny forced a laugh, resumed his seat, and said, hurriedly -

'You are right - I am wrong. The truth is that - that I am acquainted with the gentleman whose criticism you condemn so severely. I believe him to be an honest man - headstrong, but honest. I was wrong to take up the matter so warmly. M. Hamel, I - I - beg to apologize.'

His hard, nervous laugh found no response. A dead silence ensued; and presently the general again laid down his knife and fork, and prepared for a story.

'Heaven help us!' muttered the doctor.

'*A propos* of poetry,' said the general, leaning back, and closing his eyes, for the better arrangement of his ideas; 'I remember a very curious incident which took place in my own regiment, just before I exchanged into the 72nd. It was on the fourth of March, 1811, the night before our melancholy defeat at Barossa, when - '

'I beg your pardon, general,' interrupted the doctor, 'did you say Barbarossa?'

The general opened his eyes, and frowned.

'No, sir,' said he, tetchily. 'I said no such thing. Barbarossa, indeed! Preposterous!'

'Not preposterous at all,' retorted the doctor. 'The word is just now in everybody's mouth! Have you not heard that Rossini is composing a new opera; and that Scribe has taken Barbarossa for the hero of his libretto?'

The German looked interested.

'This is the first I have heard of it,' said he.

'I expect so, baron,' replied the doctor, with a roguish twinkle at the corner of his eye. Then turning to me, he dropped his voice, and whispered - 'Pure fiction, mademoiselle; every word of it!'

The conversation now became broken up. The general, mystified and interrupted, resumed his dinner; the dessert was brought to table; and, after another half-hour of desultory chat, the ladies withdrew.

Madame Vaudon then sat down to a game of piquet with the old lady in black velvet; Mademoiselle Adèle sang some little French songs to her own accompaniment; and Madame Delahaye went to sleep on the divan in the boudoir. I tried to draw Marguerite into conversation; but she was silent and pre-occupied, answered at random, and glanced frequently towards the door.

'Do you expect any one, Marguerite?' I asked, at last. 'Is Monsieur Charles coming?'

She blushed and hesitated.

'He was invited,' she said; 'but I think he declined.'

'If he should come, I will tell him how you watched for his arrival!'

'No - no! pray say nothing of the kind. I - I don't wish him to think - Ah! here he is!'

'What, M. Charles?'

'No - M. Hamel!'

She flushed crimson when she had said it, and turned away to hide her confusion. Just then, the gentlemen all came pouring in, and fresh guests began arriving; so that she was speedily surrounded, and our conversation ended abruptly.

Alas! little Marguerite, art thou fascinated too? Sorrowful and perplexed, I withdrew into the shadow of a deserted window, and looked out into the night.

All without was very calm. The crescent moon floated like a silver boat in a sea of dark-blue sky, with here and there an island of clouds, or a planet that burned, beacon-like, across the wastes of heaven. The river rippled by, and stretched away into darkness. The hills behind the town were profiled sharply against the tranquil sky. The steeple looked as if I might have touched it with my hand. There were lights on the bridges, and faint gleams from river-side windows in the town. I shut my ears to the hum and bustle of the crowded room, and, curtained away from observation, fell into a train of idle musings. I asked myself, what lay before me in this foreign land? What influence these strangers were destined to exercise upon me? Wherefore I had come, and whither I was going? 'Why was I born,' I murmured, 'if only for a life-long solitude? Am I but a waif upon the great ocean - a weed by the wayside - an outcast, drifting betwixt earth and heaven?'

At this instant a little skiff darted through the path of the moonlight, and disappeared again in the shadow. Gloomy alike were the ways of its arrival and departure, and bright only the moment of its brief passage by the windows.

'I will question Fate no more,' I said, sighing. 'The past and the future are alike mysterious. The present alone is ours to enjoy and to suffer, and the safety of the boat is in the hand of the Helmsman. I will wait - I will have faith - I will be content.'

Presently every murmur was hushed in the *salon*; I looked, and saw M. Hamel place himself carelessly at the piano. Without taking even the trouble to remove his gloves, he struck a few wild wandering chords - paused, as if to question his memory - and then, to an impetuous air, alternately wailing, tender, and triumphant, chanted in a rich and manly voice the following -

BALLAD

Oh, Faithless! all this winter long
  My pain has been thy pastime!
I loved with heart, and soul, and song -

Thine all the sport, mine all the wrong -
　　Beware! it is the last time!
　　　　For now I know thee. Thou would'st fain
　　　　Thyself undo the darling chain,
　　　　And cast me on the world again,
　　　　　A lonely man, to-morrow!
　　　　But, no! I swear that must not be!
　　　　Thou can'st not, if thou would'st, be free!
　　　　Ah, faithless! heartless! thou shalt see
　　　　　What strength despair can borrow!
　　　　And be it well, or be it ill,
　　　　I feel that I must love thee still
　　　　　In sin, and shame, and sorrow!

Ah, Cruel! though my love were shown
　　In strangely silent fashion,
Thou could'st have read it - thou alone!
In ev'ry glance and ev'ry tone
　　That told the tale of passion!
　　　　Alas! had I more boldly woo'd
　　　　Had I with fiery vows pursued,
　　　　Oh, then, perchance, I had subdued
　　　　　And made thee mine for ever!
　　　　But, by the bitter fate that drove me,
　　　　By ev'ry star that shines above me,
　　　　I swear that I will make thee love me
　　　　　Despite thine own endeavour!
　　　　Nor life, nor death shall set thee free;
　　　　And neither heaven, nor earth, nor sea,
　　　　　My lot and thine shall sever!

Carried away by the passionate earnestness of song and singer,
I listened till the last word and the echo of the last note died away.
He rose from the piano, smiling at the enthusiasm of his audience,
and received their compliments carelessly enough.

'Upon my sacred honour, sir, as a connoisseur and - ahem! - a
gentleman,' said M. Delahaye, emphasizing his criticism with a series
of little taps upon the lid of his enamelled snuff-box, 'I felicitate you! I
have devoted my life, sir, my fortune, and all the evanescent blossoms of

youth and impetuosity, to the cultivation of - ahem! - my vocal organs. I have had some experience, monsieur - I may say, some fame. I have been the Spoilt Child of Fashionable Society, and, sir, I beg to repeat once more that I felicitate you!'

M. Hamel opened his large dark eyes, bowed profoundly, and accepted a pinch from the proffered snuff-box. I noticed, however, that he held the fragrant dust untasted in his fingers, and that listening, or appearing to listen, to a long discourse on the part of M. Delahaye, his eyes wandered slowly round, seeking something or somebody. The rooms were by this time tolerably crowded, and the small *coterie* of the dinner-party had long since been merged in the tide and bustle of a *soirée musicale*. Calmly and methodically, M. Hamel scrutinized every face, then dismissed the conversation with some courteous answer, bowed once more, and made his way towards the very window in which I was standing. My first impulse was to step out, fancying that he must have seen me; but I drew back upon reflection, and waited quietly. The event proved that M. Hamel's eyes, however fine, were not more marvellously endowed than those of his fellow men. Instead of discovering me, he bent down, and murmured some words of salutation to a person of whose neighbourhood I was not hitherto aware, and who, it appeared, was sitting in the recess between my window and the next.

Anxious to avoid observation, unwilling now to step out till M. Hamel was gone, and distressed to find myself playing, however involuntarily, the part of an eavesdropper, I lingered during a moment of painful incertitude, and heard him say -

'It has not been my fault, mademoiselle. I have been waiting for this fortunate moment ever since I came up!'

The reply was inaudible; but the voice startled me. Surely it was not Marguerite's!

'Nay,' said he, in reply; 'the knowledge that you were here to-night has alone made the evening tolerable. I have lived in society till I am weary of it. I know all that it has to give, and have long since learned to seek my own compensation for its frivolity and its heartlessness. If I can but contemplate one face unsullied by its vanities - exchange a thought with one mind uncontaminated by its vices, I am more than repaid for a whole evening of *ennui*.'

'And yet,' said the voice, which I now knew to be Marguerite's, 'you can so well adapt yourself to the amusement of others. Your singing ...'

'Alas, mademoiselle,' he interrupted, 'what care I for the applause of a drawing-room full of idle people? Is it for these, or such as these, think you, that I compose the wandering rhymes and melodies which are the solace of my solitary hours?'

'Then you are a composer! - a poet!'

'Neither. I have an instinct for melody and rhyme; but poet and composer I am not. Perhaps, had my lot in life shaped itself otherwise, I might have been both. As it is ...'

He sighed, and was silent. Marguerite timidly repeated his last words, and I, curious to see something of the *tête-à-tête*, peeped between the curtains. M. Hamel was looking down thoughtfully - almost gloomily - but raised his head when she spoke, and looked straight into her eyes.

'As it is,' he said, earnestly, 'I write to satisfy the instinct that nature has planted in my heart - to charm away regret - to exorcise the phantoms of solitude. And when I sing, as I have sung to-night, for the amusement of an unthinking crowd, I sometimes console myself in the hope that there may be present some one gentle and sympathizing soul, to whom my melodies may carry a deeper feeling, and my rhymes a tenderer truth. Say, mademoiselle, do I expect too much?'

Startled and blushing, Marguerite stammered, looked down, and knew not what to say. M. Hamel paused a moment, and then resumed the conversation.

'Of music,' he said, 'under its loftiest aspect, of painting, and of poetry, I know no such eloquent interpreter, as George Sand. She alone, in this age, has done justice to the life, the needs, and the rewards of the artist. She alone has penetrated to the secrets of his inner-world, urged him to nobler ends, and placed him in his true light before the eyes of others. You have read "*Adriani*"?'

Marguerite shook her head.

'Then, I will bring it to you. It is a book to be loved by all who love sweet music.'

'Oh, thank you,' said Marguerite, eagerly. 'Is "*Adriani*" an English novel?'

M. Hamel looked surprised, and yet her very childishness seemed to please him.

'No,' he answered, simply. 'George Sand is your own countrywoman. Why do you ask? Would you have refused to read it if it had been English?'

'No, but I should have had to read it with mademoiselle,' replied Marguerite, laughing.

'Mademoiselle who?'

'She is my English companion. She has a name that cannot be pronounced, and we call her mademoiselle.'

'And you read novels with her?'

'Yes, monsieur. English novels and English poets. Our present book is "Peveril of the Peak;" but it is very long, and sometimes very tiresome. Besides, we break off so often!'

'True - you lose the thread of the narrative, and with it the interest of the book. A novel should be read quickly, and without interruption - or left unread. Nay, I could almost go so far as to say that it is not worth reading if you can bear to lay it down at any moment, like a piece of needlework. The author should hold you captive, and the people of his book should become your own familiar friends. A novel is then an ideal world, which, while it lasts, seems no less real than our own. Surely this is worth our while! "Art is long and life is short," and we do wisely to live in as many worlds as we can!'

M. Hamel spoke well and warmly, and Marguerite listened. He paused a moment, smiled to see her child-like admiration, and continued:-

'I dare say,' said he, 'that you have never before heard so serious a discourse upon so light a matter. It is the fashion to treat fiction as a thing of no mark or likelihood; and, at the very time when we are producing more fine artistic novels than were ever produced in such quality and quantity by any preceding age, we are daily reminded that romance is ephemeral, and all fiction the bubble of an hour. Do not believe so, mademoiselle. Novels frequently embody the highest truths of life, and novelists do, indeed, labour for something more than the amusement of their readers. For those who, young and candid like yourself, have seen little of that toiling world which lies beyond the charmed circle of a happy home, good novels are better than experience. For those others who, like myself, have laboured and suffered, and trodden the dust of the highways, they are still good, since they re-awaken our belief in the ideal. More than this, a good novel is a work of art, and as deathless as a canto of Tasso, or a statue of Michael Angelo. Inasmuch as it delights us to-day, because it is familiar, just so much will it be valuable hereafter as a record and an authority. Perhaps, granting everything that can be said for the early poets and historians, there are no two works of the middle ages so interesting as "Chaucer's Canterbury Tales" and "The Chronicles of Froissart." In these we read the life of the romantic ages, lamenting only that the sources of our information are so few, and that the great men of the past were so careless of the commonplaces of their time. Consider - had Petrarch and Spenser written novels depicting the life and manners of their respective centuries, how gladly we would have excused the sonnets of the one, and the epic of the other! Well, mademoiselle, what those books would have been to us, the works of George Sand and her European contemporaries will be to our descendants! They are the true Froissarts and Chaucers of this nineteenth century. In their pages the manners of our day will be embalmed long after we ourselves have passed away. It will be to them that some future Macauley will turn for those picturesque details which have revolutionized history, and some future Scott for the colouring of the historical novel. To put my meaning in a single sentence - as History assumes in time the features of Romance, so will that which we now style Romance assume in time the features of History. But I have wandered far from "*Adriani*," and wearied you with speculations in which you can feel but little interest!'

'Oh, no,' exclaimed Marguerite. 'I am never weary when you talk.'

'And do you always follow me?'

'Not always,' she replied, falteringly. Then added, 'But that makes no difference. All that you say is beautiful.'

I could not see M. Hamel's face; but he bent lower still at these words, and his voice dropped almost to a whisper.

'If this be really the case,' he murmured - 'if, mademoiselle, you indeed care to listen to the idle meditations of a dreamer such as I, you will have it in your power to add infinitely to the happiness of a very joyless existence. I am an exile here - have been in some sense an exile all my life. My attachments have been few, and I have been little understood from my very boyhood. Could I but hope, even now, to find one sympathetic friend - were there any to whom my dreams would be something more than dreams, and my ambitions not altogether indifferent, I should indeed feel that the past had not been utterly fruitless - that the future was no longer a desert!'

Marguerite remained silent, but tears were glittering upon her eyelashes.

'Will you, can you be that friend - that sympathizer - that consolation, - *Marguerite*?'

She coloured more deeply than before; trembled, hesitated, and looked down.

'Will you not give me one word?' pleaded M. Hamel.

But before that word could be spoken Dr. Grandet came bustling up to them, and the *tête-à-tête* was over.

'Aha, M. Hamel!' said he, 'you have electrified us to-night, I can tell you! Snuffed out all the men, and enchanted all the ladies.'

'How so, sir?' asked M. Hamel, somewhat stiffly.

'*Pardieu!* with your singing, to be sure. Why, my dear sir, begging your pardon for the supposition, one would say that you had just stepped off the boards of the Opera!'

'You flatter me,' said the other, haughtily. 'But, monsieur, I beg to inform you that I do not come from the boards of the Opera.'

The little doctor laughed, and rubbed his hands, and shook his curly head.

'No offence, no offence,' said he. 'Only a joke - of course, only a joke. Come, M. Hamel, I find but one fault with your singing, and that is, that we get too little of it.'

M. Hamel bowed.

'Having once begun,' continued the doctor, 'you are bound to go on; for nobody will utter a note after you. Snuffed out, I tell you, sir. Snuffed out. Baron, for instance, won't be prevailed upon at any price. Young Lenoir, very nice tenor, swears to a cold; but, between you and me, has no more cold than a salamander. As for Deligny, *he's* as dumb as a bird of Paradise!'

'Upon my word, doctor,' said M. Hamel, smiling, 'I should be sorry to believe that I had silenced all these gentlemen.'

'No doubt, no doubt, M. Hamel. But,' and Grandet looked up with the old twinkle in his eye - 'but don't you think that you had silenced one of them pretty effectually before there was any question of singing at all? No offence, my dear sir. No offence. Of course *you* couldn't tell who wrote the article in question. Anonymous *critique* - open to every one's censure - stranger to this part of the country - all fair, all perfectly fair, of course.'

'Which, sir, the *critique*, or the censure?'

'Not the *critique* - not the *critique*, of course. Very malignant - can't deny that. Very malignant indeed. But, excuse me, M. Hamel, I could have whispered a word in your ear (had I been near you) which would have silenced *you* also. No offence, you know. No offence!'

M. Hamel smiled disdainfully.

'Did you suppose,' said he, 'that I had not guessed the authorship of that article?'

'You don't mean to say that - that you knew it was written -'

'By Monsieur Deligny himself.'

'And yet you did not scruple to anatomize every motive - to expose every error! Called it a slander, and a fraud! My dear sir, why make an enemy of such a bitter hater as Théophile Deligny?'

M. Hamel shrugged his shoulders.

'Indeed,' said he, 'it would puzzle me to tell, unless I did it for the pleasure of punishing him. I entertain a natural antipathy towards all his tribe, and would crush a venial critic as readily as a scorpion!'

Madame Vaudon now joined the little circle. The conversation became noisier, and, taking advantage of a moment when they were all laughing together, I softly turned the handle of the sash and stepped out upon the balcony. To close it as carefully, to make my way all along the front of the drawing-room windows and peep cautiously into the boudoir, was but the work of a minute. Fortunately the little room was deserted, and the window already partly opened. So I walked quietly through into the *salon*, where the first person I encountered was Madame Delahaye.

'*Mon Dieu*! mademoiselle,' said she, rather impatiently, 'where do you come from? We are going home, and I have been looking for you everywhere! Monsieur is just gone to fetch Marguerite. She is over there, talking to Madame Vaudon and the new clergyman. Dear me! how late it is, to be sure, and we have more than six miles before us!'

M. Delahaye brought not only Marguerite, but M. Hamel and Madame Vaudon, who tried in vain to delay us for one half-hour longer. Madame was inflexible, and would not wait another moment. So we made our adieux, were packed into the little four-wheeled chaise, and driven off triumphantly. Marguerite and I occupied the back seat, but we scarcely exchanged a word on the way home. She was busy with her thoughts and I with mine. How nearly they coincided, and to what extent they differed, it would be difficult to say.

CHAPTER XIV

'ONE OF THE FAMILY'

From this time M. Hamel became a frequent visitor at the house, and, ere long, came and went as he pleased. He was always welcome, for he was always entertaining. Even I, who never fell into the train of his worshippers, cannot deny that his visits were the pleasantest events of every week.

He was gifted with the rarest conversational powers I ever knew. He was both imaginative and sarcastic, and had the art of concentrating his resources upon whatever subject came to hand. With a look, a gesture, a trick of intonation, he produced the happiest 'effects' imaginable; and if perhaps, not always logical, was at least always brilliant.

He had travelled; but he never made his travels the subject of conversation. If betrayed into accidental mention of places or customs abroad, he was sure to lead off the discourse upon some other topic; or, being pressed to follow up the hint with a more minute description, yielded reluctantly.

On the subject of his past life he maintained a marked reserve. Of his profession he spoke rarely, or never. Unsparing in his sarcasms, courtly in his address, democratic on the side of politics, and perfect master of the tactics of society, one came to regard M. Hamel solely as a man of the world, and (excepting when reminded by his presence in the pulpit) forgot that he was a clergyman at all.

He rode over twice or thrice a week; he supplied Madame with gossip; he talked music with Monsieur; he brought books to Marguerite. *Indiana, Lelia, Mauprat,* and others of the early productions of George Sand were by him recommended, and by her eagerly read. So fascinated was she by these extraordinary romances that, but for her English studies, she would have given up her whole time to them. It grieved me to sit by and witness this; but opposition only served to estrange her from me, and answered no end. I was unwilling that M. Hamel should direct her tastes - above all, I was unwilling that he should mould her character through the medium of a class of literature which, however admirable in its way, deals too largely with feeling to be quite healthy reading for the inexperienced and the young. But his influence soon grew too strong for me, and my efforts to counteract it were in vain.

I often wished at this time that 'Cousin Charles' had been a more frequent visitor; for I fancied that his fine uncompromising intellect would have proved an excellent counterpoise to the eloquent worldliness of our brilliant acquaintance. But cousin Charles lived fifteen miles away, and seldom made his appearance, except on Sundays - whereas, M. Hamel was quite a week-day guest, and never could come over on Sunday at all, on account of the two services that he must perform at Chalons.

And so affairs went on at Montrocher, and M. Hamel became like one of the family.

CHAPTER XV

MORE ABOUT M. HAMEL

'It is something new to see you reading, Marguerite, and at dusk, too!' exclaimed cousin Charles, good humouredly. 'What happy author has worked the present miracle?'

She had laid the book aside when he came in, and met him, I fancied, with more coldness than ever.

'Oh, it is nothing that would interest you, cousin Charles,' she replied, evasively.

'How can you tell that?'

'Because - because it is a novel.'

'Do you suppose, then, that I have lived upon archæology all my life? Quite the contrary, *petite*! I have many a fine standard fiction in my library, and should be well content to see you read every one.'

'M. Hamel has a high opinion of novels,' observed Madame, from the sofa.

She quoted M. Hamel, now, upon all occasions.

'*Who?*' said cousin Charles, with a quick movement of his head.

'M. Hamel - the Rev. M. Hamel,' replied Madame, complacently. 'A man of refined taste, I assure you.'

'And aristocratic deportment,' added Monsieur, who had been asleep ever since dinner.

'Is eloquence itself!' said Madame, with a little sigh of admiration.

'And ties a cravat to perfection,' murmured her husband.

Cousin Charles glanced from one to the other in silent surprise - then at Marguerite, who looked down and said nothing - then at me, and shrugged his shoulders significantly.

'I have no doubt,' said he, 'that M. Hamel deserves all you say of him. I have myself observed both his eloquence and - his cravats.'

At this moment Pierrette brought in the lamp, and the conversation turned upon general subjects.

It was one of the very few occasions upon which M. Gautier dropped in by chance. He had been down to a neighbouring parish on business, and had snatched this opportunity to visit his betrothed. He told her so presently, but a troubled smile was her only answer.

'If I had known that I should ride over here to-night,' said he, 'I would have put something in my pocket - a - a sort of legendary tale that I wish to read to you, Marguerite.'

'Ah, indeed!'

'Written,' continued M. Charles, 'somewhat after the style of Walter Scott.'

'Then I'm glad you did not bring it,' said Marguerite. 'I hate Walter Scott - he's so tedious!'

M. Charles looked vexed, hesitated a moment, and then went on.

'I think the subject would have piqued your curiosity, for all that,' said he. 'It is about my old tower at Santenay.'

Marguerite looked up.

'How odd! I did not know there was a legend connected with

113

the place.'

'Nor I, till a few weeks ago, when I found the anecdote related in a very old commonplace book of my father's. Mind, only the anecdote - not the tale.'

Marguerite suppressed a yawn.

'The story, as it now stands,' pursued M. Gautier, 'was composed by a true knight for the amusement of his lady-love. The knight lived at Santenay, and the lady in a castle at Montrocher. Can you guess the name of the knight?'

'Oh, dear, no!' said she, carelessly. 'I have not the least idea!'

M. Charles sighed.

'I wish you were sufficiently interested to ask,' said he.

'I beg your pardon, cousin Charles. I - I am interested. Indeed,' faltered Marguerite; 'but I'm sure I could never guess who the knight was, without first reading the poem. Could you, mademoiselle?'

'I think I could,' I replied, smiling. 'The knight is Monsieur Charles himself, and you are ...'

'And I -' repeated Marguerite, confused and half angry. 'Who am I, pray?'

'The lady in the castle among the mountains,' said her lover, quite gallantly, raising her hand to his lips.

Marguerite snatched the hand away, and Madame burst out laughing.

'What do I hear?' said she, gaily. 'Has Charles turned author and courtier?'

M. Gautier coloured up.

'Neither, madame,' he replied coldly. 'I have never flattered Marguerite in my life - nor would, though it were the only means on earth to win her affection. As for the tale, it is such a trifle that I am ashamed to have named it at all.'

'My dear nephew,' said Madame, 'you are hasty. We wish to hear it very much. Don't we, Marguerite?'

'Oh - very much indeed,' replied Marguerite, coldly.

M. Charles was pacified in a moment.

'In that case,' said he, 'I will bring it with me on Sunday, and you shall give me your opinion on it.'

'Our opinion!' exclaimed Madame, deprecatingly. 'Nay, our opinion is worth very little. You should go to M. Hamel in that matter - he is a critic indeed!'

M. Charles opened his eyes.

'Upon my word,' said he, 'this M. Hamel is an oracle!'

'He is a gentleman of extraordinary attainments,' returned Madame, with a slight toss of the head.

'Very extraordinary - for a clergyman. He is already a member of the boating-club at Chalons. He plays billiards at a hundred francs the game; and his name is down for the steeple-chase to be ridden next week by the officers of the Thirty-third.'

'And what of that?' asked Madame, impatiently. 'Is it a crime to ride in the steeple-chase?'

'No crime; but very unbecoming.'

Monsieur Delahaye took snuff, looked majestic, and shook his head.

'My dear Charles,' said he, 'the recreations of a gentleman, when pursued in a gentlemanly manner, are never - ahem! - reprehensible. The steeple-chase is an aristocratic diversion, and too dangerous to be vulgar. As for billiards - to play billiards at a hundred francs the game can disgrace no one. I have played at five hundred before now, and I am proud to confess it.'

'Besides, M. Hamel has been used to the best society,' said Madame.

'My love,' observed Monsieur, 'he is a man of the world, and a gentleman. He is also - ahem! - the occasional recipient of such poor entertainments as my roof - ahem! But Charles will appreciate my sentiments on this delicate subject.'

M. Gautier bowed, and bit his lip.

'I had no idea, sir,' he said, haughtily, 'that I was speaking of a friend of the family.'

Monsieur waved his hand with the air of a man who receives an apology.

'Indeed,' continued cousin Charles, 'I find it difficult to understand how so strict an intimacy can have been formed in so short a time.'

'It is not time,' said Monsieur, philosophically. 'It is not time. It is - ahem! - congeniality.'

Cousin Charles looked incredulous.

'Besides,' added Monsieur, warming into metaphor and concluding with a flourish, 'when the Goblet of Friendship - I say the Goblet of Friendship - has been passed about the festive board, the

115

libation is presided over by the - ahem! - the household Gods, and the name of the guest is enrolled among the archives sacred to hospitality!'

M. Charles bowed again, and Madame, to whom this latter argument appeared quite clear and conclusive, nodded, and said -

'To be sure - to be sure! That is the way to put it. That settles everything.'

It seemed, however, not only to settle, but to damp everything; and a dreary evening followed. At ten o'clock, uncle Alexander came home, and coffee was served. As fate ordained it, he also was in a worse temper than usual, and flung himself into an arm-chair without a word to any one. Monsieur, who always retired early, then wished us good-night; and cousin Charles soon after rose to go.

'Ride gently, and take care of yourself, boy,' growled uncle Alexander. 'The roads are bad, and overhead it's as black as the devil!'

'I should think the moon is up, sir, by this time,' said cousin Charles, going over to the window. 'At all events, I'm used to night riding.'

He drew the curtain aside, and looked up into the sky. As he did so, a book that had been lying in the recess became entangled in the heavy folds, and fell open at his feet.

'A dark night, indeed,' said he, 'and ...' He paused with the book in his hand. His whole countenance changed.

'Is this what you were reading, Marguerite?' he asked, sternly.

She coloured up, but made no reply. He struck the open page with his hand, and repeated the question.

'Is *this* what you were reading?'

She murmured a reluctant affirmative.

'And how much of it have you read?'

'I - I have only just begun it.'

'Thanks be to fortune!'

And cousin Charles commenced deliberately tearing it leaf from leaf.

Marguerite uttered a cry of dismay.

'Oh, what have you done?' she exclaimed. ''Tis M. Hamel's!'

He drew back as if he had received a blow, and the torn pages fluttered to the ground.

'M. Hamel's!' he repeated in a low voice. 'M. Hamel's!'

Marguerite trembled. The tears rose to her eyes; but her pride restrained them.

'Come, come, what's the matter now?' interposed uncle Alexander. 'What's in the book, hey? What's in the book?'

'Everything most unfit for a young girl to read,' replied cousin Charles. 'Lies, intrigue, false sentiment, vicious views of society.'

Marguerite sprang to her feet, flushed and passionate.

'I'll not believe it!' she cried, vehemently. 'I'll not believe it! M. Hamel would not lend me a wicked book! None of the others were wicked!'

Cousin Charles turned a pale face and a searching eye upon her.

'Then there were others?' said he, calmly.

'Yes, there were others - beautiful books. He lent them to me, and I read them. I have a right to read what I choose.'

'Say, rather, what this new adviser chooses for you. Pray, were "the others" by the same author?'

'No - yes - some of them. But am I a child that I should be questioned in this fashion?'

'Yes, in every sense,' replied M. Gautier, with the same resolute face and voice. 'A child needing restraint and guidance. Listen to me, Marguerite. The books that you *have* read may, or may not be suitable for you; but the book you have here to-night is a bad book. It's author is a dissolute man of rank, whose name has alone preserved him a footing in society. Heaven forbid that you should ever see life as he depicts it, or seek to see it! I cannot allow you even to read books of this class, or to borrow in future from M. Hamel.'

Marguerite laughed scornfully.

'You are not my master, cousin Charles,' said she. 'Pray remember that before you speak of "allowing." As to restraint and guidance, I will accept both from my parents, but neither from you.'

Madame rose from the sofa where she had been sitting throughout this altercation.

'Marguerite is right,' said she, warmly. 'You presume too far upon your position, Charles. Advice you have a right to offer: authority is ours. Besides ...'

'Besides there has been enough said already,' interrupted uncle Alexander. 'Let the thing drop, can't you?'

'Not till Marguerite promises neither to read this nor any other book of M. Hamel's,' said M. Gautier, firmly.

'I will not promise. M. Hamel is a clergyman, and he knows what is fit for me to read better than you do, cousin Charles,' retorted Marguerite.

Uncle Alexander rubbed his head all over in desperation.

'Tush, tush, monkey!' said he, soothingly. 'Not so fast - not so fast. You don't see that your cousin means kindly, and you are a hot-headed rogue for your pains. Sister-in-law, keep that child quiet, and don't talk. Charles, boy, you are as provoking as a mule. What's the good of irritating your aunt and little Marguerite? Perhaps you are unjust to the parson after all. He may never have read the book himself!'

'Then he had no right to place it in the hands of a lady,' returned M. Charles.

'True; but you had no right to tear it up before you knew to whom it belonged.'

'Excuse me, sir; I love Marguerite, and I am justified in protecting her from even the shadow of evil. I object to M. Hamel. I object to his books; and I am both surprised and displeased by the discovery of an intimacy which is not only injudicious, but dangerous.'

'Upon my word, Charles, this is going too far!' exclaimed Madame, now really angry. 'It must be allowed that we are at liberty to make such intimacies as we please, without being told that our friends are injudiciously chosen. I am glad your uncle Hippolyte is not here. He would have been seriously offended.'

M. Alexander groaned aloud.

'Sister-in-law, I told you not to talk. Boy, you are a fool. Don't you see that you are injuring your own cause, and fighting your enemy's battle? Have patience, all of you, and shake hands, and say good-night, and part friends.'

'I shall be very willing,' said Madame; 'but Charles must confess that he is in the wrong.'

'Wrong!' echoed uncle Alexander; 'of course he is. You're all wrong!'

'If I have been hasty, I am ready to apologize,' said M. Gautier, formally.

And so Madame and her nephew were reconciled; but Marguerite turned sullenly away.

M. Charles drew himself to his full height, and looked coldly after her.

'Good-night, Marguerite,' said he, and moved towards the door.

'Good-night,' she replied, with averted face.

And so they parted. At the threshold he lingered, but it was only for a moment. Then uncle Alexander took him by the arm, and hurried him away, dreading a renewal of the dispute.

In a few minutes we heard him ride out of the court-yard.

M. Hamel came the very next day, and, as usual, carried all before him. Easy, brilliant, and ready-witted, he silenced objection almost by a word. A jest at the expense of too-virtuous critics, a frank admission of certain minor inconsistencies, an elegant eulogium on one or two fine passages taken at hazard from the mutilated leaves, sufficed to quiet Madame's latent apprehensions, and to convince Marguerite that her cousin was not only disagreeable, but unjust.

What wonder, then, that the estrangement grew wider and deeper - that the lover's visits became fewer and less welcome - that the one influence increased with the waning of the other?

CHAPTER XVI

THE CHAPEL OF BOISGUILBERTE

I had heard from time to time of La Tournay and Boisguilberte, but vaguely, and without having formed any clear notion of what was to be seen there. I was not sorry, therefore, to find myself *en route* to both these places one bright, laughing June morning, in company with M. and Madame Vaudon and three carriages full of merry pilgrims, all bent upon a picnic and a summer holiday.

Marguerite was there, under my care. M. Hamel was there, on his beautiful black horse. Jovial little Dr. Grandet, and General Max, and Adèle attended by the German traveller, and three or four more young people made up the party. M. Charles had been invited, but declined; and the Delahayes had all been so often that none, except Marguerite, were disposed to undertake the journey.

It was a glorious morning, full of sunshine, and green leaves, and bird-singing, with a soft haze over the mountains, and scarce a cloud anywhere to be seen. We met early, to avoid the heat. Every one was in high spirits, and M. Hamel, riding on before, broke off some branches of pink May, and flung them into the carriages. A light cart followed at some little distance, with the hampers of wine and cold fowl; and one of the young ladies had brought a guitar. Altogether, it was one of the pleasantest picnics imaginable.

Our way lay for some time along the Santenay road, and then branched off into the very heart of the mountains, over stony by-roads, where we could only drive at a foot-pace; past dark woods and solitary farms; through gorges rendered all but impassable by huge fragments of fallen rock; and beside vineyards where the brown labourers started up to shade their eyes with their rough hands, and gaze after us as if we had been creatures of another world.

Now the road narrows to a path little wider than a foot-way, and the trees meet overhead in gothic vistas. Now a troop of ragged children plunge out of a way-side hovel, and rush after us with shouts that are only to be quieted by a shower of halfpence. Now we come to a group of large walnut-trees beside a steep grassy slope crowned with rocks and waving grasses. Under the shade of these walnut-boughs we alight. The servant in charge of the light cart supplies the horses with water, and we ascend the green slope all together. Coming down by a slippery path at the other side, we find ourselves upon the threshold of a rocky cavern, which pierces through the hill as if it had been tunnelled for the purpose, and is traversed by a clear deep stream about six feet in width, silent as a well, and cold as snow.

'This stream,' says M. Vaudon, 'waters a little valley to which Alexander Dumas has given the false topographical name of the *Vaux Chignon*, and the imaginative, but just title of the Burgundian El Dorado. It has another source about a third of a mile farther on, and a cascade not inferior to that of the famous Pelerins at Chamouni. Will you come?'

We follow with acclamations, and, bearing our May-blossoms in our hands, scramble through brakes and brambles and patches of meadow ancle-deep in flowers, and arrive at last at the foot of a steep gray rock three hundred feet in height, whence falls a gauzy, radiant, transparent veil of silver spray, fenced in on either side by close green trees, and gliding away towards the bottom amid mosses and flowers, till it is once more lost among the rocks.

Here we gather sheaves of the wild foxglove, primrose, forget-me-not, and daisy; and Dr. Grandet, having explored farther up the rock than the rest of the party, comes back in triumph with an armful of the purple fraxinella - stray native of the Pyrenees and the Rhône.

And now, when we have admired and lingered as long as the increasing heat will allow, we hurry away again to the carriages, bound for Boisguilberte.

This time our progress is even more laborious than before, for our way lies always among the mountains, and there are no public roads worth that name. Sometimes we take the cart-ways through fields and plantations; oftenest through lanes where no second vehicle could have passed; and once we even drive across a broad tract of pasture where no wheels have pressed the fresh young grass for many a month before. At last we come to a mountain higher than any which I have yet seen in Burgundy - a mountain clad for the most part in a dense forest of the larch and fir, and only to be traversed on this side by a narrow foot-path carpeted with mosses of rich golden brown.

At the foot of this mountain we once more alight. There is another way farther on by which the carriages can ascend; but it is steep and wearisome. We are to walk up in the shade of the forest.

How pleasant it is under this green roof, with its groinings of arched boughs and frettings of blue sky and golden sunshine! The young people wander on, two and two, along the leafy corridor, and M. Hamel gives his arm to Marguerite. I cannot tell the subject of their talk, for I am far behind, walking with Madame Vaudon; but I see him lean towards her, I see the daylight glittering on his silver curls, and I see, by the thoughtful bending of her head and the occasional upturning of her face, that she is listening (as to him she always listens) in a dream.

'Charles Gautier must beware,' says Madame Vaudon, significantly. 'Our hero with the silver locks hath a charmed tongue, and might prove a dangerous rival!'

I look after them and sigh.

'I should not be sorry to think so,' I reply, sadly, 'if M. Hamel were likely to make her happier than the other; but I fear that both are very unfit for my little Marguerite.'

'Unfit! How so?'

'Nay, perhaps I have no right to judge either; but it seems to me that M. Gautier is the last man in the world whom Marguerite should marry. He is serious, proud, exacting; and he treats her as though she were a little child. Hers is the buoyant vivacity of youth - his the gravity of premature age.'

'But he loves her?'

'Without knowing how to woo, or how to win! Then, as to M. Hamel ...'

'Ah, what have you to say to M. Hamel? He surely is courteous, and cheerful, and ardent enough! A young man still, despite his silver locks!'

I hesitate. I scarcely know how to answer.

'M. Hamel is very fascinating,' I reply, at length; 'but - but I don't feel as if he were to be trusted.'

Madame Vaudon darts a penetrating glance at me, and shrugs her shoulders *à la Française*.

'It is true,' says she, 'that we know nothing about him. His antecedents are a profound mystery.'

'But where did he come from? How did he obtain this appointment?'

'Through one of our large land-owners here in the Côte d'Or, who met him somewhere abroad - where he was travelling, I believe, with a rich Anglo-Indian pupil. Our friend was delighted with him, kept up a correspondence with him for more than eighteen months after, and when this little ministry was vacant, procured it for him. That is all that anybody knows; but there are endless reports about him - all ridiculous enough.'

Here she beckons to Dr. Grandet.

'Dear friend,' she says, laughingly, 'do repeat to Miss Wylde the foolish things that are said in Chalons of M. Hamel!'

The little doctor shakes his head, rubs his hands, and looks immensely sly.

'Scandal, my dear Madame Vaudon,' chuckles he. 'Scandal, pure scandal, upon my honour!'

'Of course! Go on.'

'Well, if you will be so wicked! - but, let me see - in the first place, there is Madame Nodier, (that old lady's inventive powers are really wonderful!) she says that he's a Jesuit in disguise.'

'Admirable! what next?'

'Mademoiselle Boulanger next. She will have it that he was an actor. Lecroix vows that he is no Frenchman - inclines to the opinion that he is of Spanish or Creole blood. Deligny declares that out of a salary of four thousand francs, he spends at the rate of forty thousand. Then there are plenty of young ladies who can see in him only a hero of romance. He is a nobleman in distress - he is disappointed in love - he is an exile - he is, perhaps, one of the heroes of the last Italian revolution!'

Madame laughs aloud - the whole affair is so absurdly untrue. Dr. Grandet coughs mysteriously.

'There is one strange circumstance which I have observed,' says he, taking off his hat, as if for coolness, but holding it before his face to shut in the sound.

'You little angel!' cries Madame, enthusiastically; 'what is it?'

'You'll not repeat it?'

'*Foi d'honneur!*'

'Do you swear it by the bones of your ancestors?'

'Solemnly,' replies Madame, with mock gravity.

'Well then, have you not noticed that M. Hamel ...'

'Don't hesitate! That M. Hamel ...'

'*Never ungloves his right hand?*'

We stop, involuntarily, and look in each other's faces. Neither of us have yet observed this peculiarity. What does it mean? Can Dr. Grandet guess? No. Dr. Grandet is as profoundly puzzled as we; and, in the midst of our conjectures, the forest-gloom clears suddenly away, and we find ourselves at the end of our journey.

It is a broad, open glade, high up on the shoulder of the mountain. All around us lie the close woods. At our feet sleeps a reedy tarn, dotted over with floating lilies, and peopled by gigantic pike, which go plunging down to the bottom when they hear the echo of our voices. To the left, lying a little way back, and protected by a dismantled gateway, stands a large dilapidated building, with stone-crop growing on the broken roof, and rotten planks nailed over most of the windows, and a group of wild-looking children crowded together on the threshold. A waggon, half loaded with hay, blocks up the gateway. There are pigs and poultry all about; and a savage watch-dog, who barks furiously at us, and would do more than bark if he could break his chain. Farther back still, with rough barn-doors fitted to the pillared portal, and a broken roof, and the stored hay jutting through the traceries of what has once been a goodly oriel-window, stands in melancholy degradation and decay, an exquisite gothic chapel!

'Pilgrims all!' says M. Vaudon, oratorically, (for he is the leader of this expedition,) 'behold your goal! Behold the monastery and chapel of Boisguilberte!'

And so we go over all of it that may be seen; for it is a farm-house now, and inhabited by a family of simple folks, who can hardly be brought to understand that we have travelled all this way for the mere purpose of visiting their ruinous outhouses.

Only a small angle of the house is occupied - the rest is abandoned to the bats and owls; roofless, cobwebbed, and in many places quite choked up with fallen beams and heaps of rubbish. The cellar, where the monks kept their good wine, is now a barn. Cheeses, and flour-sacks, and a cider-press lie stored at one end of what was once the refectory. So much of the cloisters as can yet be traced are divided into pig-sties. The chapel is a stable; and where the altar stood, now stands the manger.

By the time that we have seen all these things, the carriages arrive by the other road, the horses are led round to the farmer's stables, the hampers are unpacked, the fresh-caught pike are cooked and ready; and a pleasant green knoll, just out of sight of the farm-house, is chosen for our picnic. Here, with the tarn glittering near us in the sun, and the trees overhead, and a little sculptured crocket or two peering up among the foliage on the other side of the water, we enjoy as charming a picture as any artist need wish to see. So the snowy cloths are spread upon the grass; and the champagne is cooled among the rushes on the brink of the pond; and the clatter of knives and forks, cork-drawing, conversation, and laughter is soon at its height.

By-and-by, when our interest in the cold fowls and pigeon-pies has somewhat abated, the young lady with the guitar is called upon for a song - which she is kind enough to administer in eight or ten broken-hearted verses, very dismal and dispiriting. Then somebody wonders if there be any legends connected with the monastery; and somebody else proposes that the farmer be sent for and questioned - a motion promptly negatived by M. Hamel.

'In the first place,' says he, 'the poor man would be too nervous to remember anything; in the second place, his *patois* is unintelligible;

and, in the third place, if you want an old legend, I will make one for you with pleasure.'

This speech is received with acclamations; the glasses are filled once more with foaming nectar; and M. Hamel, reclining on his elbow beside Marguerite, prepares to relate a story.

'Let it be a very old legend, if you please, M. Hamel!' laughs Madame Vaudon.

'It shall be as old as you like. What say you to the reign of Francis the First?'

'I should prefer the time of the Crusades.'

'Be it so. In the time of the second Crusade, ladies and gentlemen, when Louis, the seventh of that name, was surprised and betrayed in the gorges of Lycaonia ... but stay; perhaps you would prefer it in rhyme?'

'Oh, in rhyme! By all means in rhyme!' is the general chorus - so M. Hamel lays the guitar across his knee; ungloves his left hand, and sweeps a few wild chords with his still gloved right; pauses an instant; looks at Marguerite, as if for inspiration; tosses back his curls with a careless smile, and chants, rather than sings, the following -

LEGEND OF BOISGUILBERTE

Beside this tarn, in ages gone,
   As antique legends darkly tell,
A false, false Abbot and forty monks
   Did once in sinful plenty dwell.

Accurs'd of Christ and all the saints,
   They robb'd the rich; they robb'd the poor;
They quaff'd the best of Malvoisie;
   They turn'd the hungry from their door.

And though the nations wept aloud
   And famine stalked across the land -
And though the best of Christian blood
   Redden'd the thirsty Arab sand -

These monks kept up their ancient state,
   Nor cared how long the troubles lasted;

But fed their deer, and stocked their pond,
    And feasted when they should have fasted.

And so it fell one Christmas-eve,
    When it was dark, and cold, and late,
A pious knight from Palestine
    Came knocking at the convent-gate.

He rode a steed of Eastern blood;
    His helm was up; his eye was bold;
And round about his neck he wore
    A chain of Saracenic gold.

'What ho! good monks of Boisguilberte,
    Your guest am I to-night!' quoth he.
'Have you a stable for my steed?
    A supper, and a cell for me?'

The Abbot laughed; the friars scoff'd;
    They fell upon that knight renown'd,
And bore him down, and tied his arms,
    And laid him captive on the ground.

'Sir guest!' cried they, 'your steed shall be
    Into our convent-stable led;
And, as we have no cell to spare,
    Yourself must sleep among the dead!'

He marked them with a steadfast eye;
    He heard them with a dauntless face;
He was too brave to fear to die;
    He was too proud to sue for grace.

They tore the chain from round his neck,
    And then (oh, brave unhappy knight!)
O'er the black waters of the pond
    Their torches flash'd a sullen light.

And the great pike that dwell beneath,
　　All startled by the sudden glare,
Div'd down among the water-weeds,
　　And darted blindly here and there:

And one white owl that made her nest
　　Up in the belfry tow'r hard by,
Flew round and round on swirling wings,
　　And vanish'd with a ghostly cry.

The Abbot stood upon the brink;
　　He laughed aloud in cruel glee,
He wav'd his torch; - 'quick! fling him in -
　　Our fish will feast to-night!' said he.

They flung him in. 'Farewell!' they cried,
　　And crowded round the reedy shore.
He gasping rose - 'Till Christmas next!'
　　He said - then sank to rise no more.

'Till Christmas next!' They stood and star'd
　　Into each other's guilty eyes -
They fled within the convent-gates
　　Lest they should see their victim rise.

The fragile bubbles rose and broke;
　　The wid'ning circles died away;
The white owl shriek'd again; the pike
　　Were left to silence and their prey.

```
***    ***    ***    ***    ***
***    ***    ***    ***    ***
```

A year went by. The stealthy fogs
　　Crept up the hill with footsteps slow;
And all the woods of Boisguilberte
　　Lay hush'd and heavy in the snow.

The sullen sun was red by day;
 The nights were black; the winds were keen;
And all across the frozen pond
 The footprints of the wolves were seen:

And vague foreshadowings of woe
 Beset the monks with mortal fear -
Strange shadows through the cloister pac'd -
 Strange whispers threaten'd ev'ry ear -

Strange writings started forth at dusk
 In fiery lines along the walls;
Strange spectres round the chapel sat,
 At midnight, in the sculptur'd stalls!

'Oh, father Abbot!' cried the monks,
 Let us repent! Our sins are great!
To-morrow will be Christmas-eve -
 To-morrow night will be too late;

'And should the drowned dead arise ...
 The Abbot laugh'd with might and main.
'The ice,' said he, 'is three feet deep -
 He'd find it hard to rise again!

'But when to-morrow night is come,
 We'll say a mass to rest his soul!'
To-morrow came, and all day long
 The chapel-bell was heard to toll.

At eve they met to read the mass.
 Bent low was ev'ry shaven crown;
One trembling monk the tapers lit;
 One held his missal upside down:

And when their quav'ring voices in
 The *Dies Iræ* all united,
Even the Abbot told his beads
 And fragments of the Creed recited.

And when . . . but hark! what sounds are these?
  Is it the splitting of the ice?
Is it a steel-clad hand that smites
  Against the outer portal thrice?

Is it the tread of an armèd heel?
  The frightened monks forget to pray;
The Abbot drops the holy book;
  The *Dies Iræ* dies away;

And in the shadow of the door
  They see their year-gone victim stand!
His rusty mail drips on the floor;
  He beckons with uplifted hand!

The Abbot rose. He could not wait;
  He could not strive, nor even pray;
For when the mighty dead command,
  The living must perforce obey.

The spectre-knight then gaz'd around
  With stony eye, and hand uprear'd.
  'Farewell,' said he, 'till Christmas next!'
Then knight and Abbot disappear'd.

***   ***   ***   ***   ***
***   ***   ***   ***   ***

And thus it is the place is curs'd,
  And long since fallen to decay;
For every Christmas-eve the knight
  Came back and took a monk away!

Came back while yet a blood-stain'd wretch
  The holy convent garb profan'd;
Came back while yet a guilty soul
  Of all those forty monks remained;

And still comes back to earth - if we
   The peasant's story may believe -
   And rises from the murky tarn
    At midnight ev'ry Christmas-eve!

The legend is over. The improvisatore lays aside the guitar, laughs at the sight of our attentive faces, holds up his glass to be refilled, and says:-

'Is my legend old enough, and horrible enough, to please you?'

'So old,' replies Madame Vaudon, 'that I believe every word of it, and begin to be half afraid that you yourself are the ghost of the Crusader!'

'And so horrible,' adds Dr. Grandet, 'that I am sorry I ate any of the pike!'

By this time we have all sufficiently recovered from our surprise to thank M. Hamel for his improvisation. Marguerite alone is silent; but her looks are praise and thanks enough.

Then, we break up the little dinner-party, and stroll about in two and threes while the servants take our places, and demolish the rest of the viands. Some sketch the ruins of the chapel. Some set off on a climbing excursion to the top of the mountain, whence an extensive prospect may be seen. Some wander in the shade of the trees on the border of the forest. Among the last are Adèle and the young German traveller, Marguerite and M. Hamel.

And now the sun sinks lower and lower in the sky; the air cools upon the mountain; and the waning of the sultry afternoon warns the stragglers back. By-and-by we have all assembled in front of the farm-house; the horses are put to; the grateful peasants are rewarded with a liberal gratuity; and the last three bottles of Chambertin are handed round as a stirrup-cup before we begin our journey.

'To the Naiad of the waters!' cries M. Hamel, flinging a libation of red wine into the tarn, glass and all.

Whereupon we drive laughingly away down a steep roadway on the other side of the forest, where the birds are wheeling, and twittering, and fluttering home to their nests in the branches.

We are four in each carriage. Madame Vaudon, General Max, Marguerite, and I occupy the last in the procession, and M. Hamel rides beside us, jesting all the way.

Then the dusk begins to steal over the landscape, and the talk grows more exclusive, and General Max entertains me with a tedious story, beginning -

'I remember, mademoiselle, when we bivouacked, on the heights of Fontenoy, on the 29th of March, 1814, just the evening before we defeated your armies with such terrible carnage ...'

Then Madame Vaudon falls sound asleep in the corner, beside Marguerite; and I have the greatest difficulty in the world to keep awake. Then the shadows gather round us thicker and thicker; and the general's story grows longer and prosier; and M. Hamel bends lower, and speaks softlier, and rides with his hand resting on the carriage-door, and his head inclined nearer and nearer to the drooping face of my little Marguerite.

> 'My mind misgives,
> Some consequence, yet hanging in the stars,
> Shall bitterly begin his fearful date
> With this day's revels.'

CHAPTER XVII

MONSIEUR'S LITTLE STUDY

M. Delahaye had a little room down stairs which he called his study. It contained no books; but was furnished instead with a great many pairs of lacquered boots, some highly-coloured engravings of singers and ballet-dancers, and a bookcase full of pomade-pots, curling-irons, and *cosmétiques*. Here monsieur was in the habit of retiring after breakfast with the newspaper; here he 'meditated' after dinner; and here he was supposed to transact all the business of the estate. A large writing-table, containing a ledger, a file of bills, and an empty ink-bottle, contributed to favour that illusion. The windows of this chaste retreat opened upon the little shady path between the house and the garden.

'My dear mademoiselle,' said Monsieur, meeting me one morning in this path, 'you are a woman of genius. Your powers of mind are - ahem! - gigantic. Intellectually speaking, mademoiselle,

131

you soar above us like ...'

Monsieur paused for a simile, and then added majestically - 'like a balloon!'

Scarcely knowing how to answer this dubious compliment, I dropped a demure courtesy, and waited to hear more. After a few flowery speeches, Monsieur came to the point.

He had discovered, somehow or another, that I could keep accounts.

'To be candid with you, my dear young lady,' he said, 'I am no arithmetician. At the time when I should have been studying the multiplication-table, I was already cultivating my voice and the fine arts, pursuing the enchanted mazes of the Beautiful, and losing myself in - ahem! - the - Realms of Fancy. Do you follow me?'

'Perfectly, sir,' I replied. 'You want me to cast up some accounts for you.'

Monsieur kissed his hand in token of assent.

'But confidentially,' whispered he. 'Confidentially; oh, my charming guest! Not a word to Alexander!'

'You may depend on my silence, sir,' said I, smiling - whereupon Monsieur squeezed my hand in an ecstasy of gratitude, and preceded me to the study.

Here he explained to me that his land produced annually a small quantity of wine, and that his brother aided him in the sale thereof, requiring only, for the sake of clearness, that their accounts should be balanced once a-year. This awful period, it seemed, was now at hand, and Monsieur, more than ever bewildered, declared that he had reached the very verge of despair.

'In which emergency,' said he, contemplating his cravat in the looking-glass, 'knowing the delicious amiability of your disposition, and encouraged by the uninterrupted urbanity of our diurnal inter-course, I ventured ...'

'Pray don't apologize, sir,' I interrupted, getting more impa-tient than was quite consistent with the delicious amiability of my disposition. 'I shall do it for you with pleasure, and if I may take the books up to my own room, I dare say I shall be able to return them in the afternoon.'

Monsieur looked alarmed.

'But - but my brother is at home to-day,' said he. 'You might be seen carrying them backwards and forwards!'

'Then I must work here?'

Monsieur kissed his hand again.

> *'C'est bien l'endroit bénit,*
> *Consacré par l'amour!'*

- hummed he, with an air of faded gallantry.

'And if I work here, sir, I must be alone,' I added, rather crossly.

'Alone!' murmured Monsieur. 'Oh, ye sylphides that inhabit little dew-drops! did she say alone?'

I affected not to hear this invocation, and remained standing with so determined an air that he had no longer any excuse for remaining.

'I will retire,' said he, sentimentally. 'Polyhymnia, perchance, will prove less cruel to her votary! My talented guest, adieu!'

He sighed, bowed, made an effort to see his back in the looking-glass, and took snuff with the grand air of Louis XIV. Finding that I was already sorting the bills, and quite heedless of these fascinations, he sauntered slowly to the door - paused - repeated in a mysterious whisper:-

'Remember - not a word to Alexander!' and withdrew.

He then went to the *salon* and practised for hours, and Madame took her work, and sat and listened to him.

I was as busy as a bee for the rest of the morning, and Marguerite had a holiday. I ran and fetched my own ink-bottle; sorted the bills; made out the entries in my very best writing; verified the sum total three times over; that I might be sure of its accuracy, and finished just ten minutes before the dinner-bell was rung. Monsieur, it is needless to add, was enchanted.

After this I had many a task of the same kind to perform, and scarcely a week passed that I was not installed for an hour or so in Monsieur's queer little study. I like what is called dry work, especially account-keeping, and I was quite pleased with the occasional change. As soon as my employers were convinced of this, they no longer scrupled to trouble me, and I found myself before long intrusted with all matters relating to their private affairs - acting, in fact, as a kind of private secretary to M. and Madame Delahaye.

Thus it happened that Marguerite had many a holiday, and that my guardianship became in a measure withdrawn from her.

Thus it happened, also, that I one morning beheld an incident which furnished me with some misgivings, and caused me to watch the progress of events more closely than before.

I have risen somewhat earlier than usual on this particular morning, and stolen down stairs before the heads of the household are awake, intending to finish some accounts begun late the evening before. Early as I am, however, Marguerite is in advance of me, for I find her bedroom-door open as I go by, and see one of her gloves upon a table in the hall.

The morning sun is shining full into Monsieur's little study, illuminating the faded smiles of the ballet-dancers on the walls, and covering my scattered papers with patches of bright light and shifting shadows from green leaves without.

Pausing with the pen in my hand, I look up at the roofing boughs of the trees beside the window, and at the background of deep-blue sky that peeps between them. I listen to the lark high up in the heavens, and to the shrill hot cry of the *cigales* on the pavement of the little path-way, and I feel more than half inclined to let the writing wait while I also bask awhile in the sunshine and drink in the fresh air of the new day.

As I am yet lingering beside the open casement, uncertain whether to go or stay, I hear the gate creak on its hinges, and see Marguerite coming in from the garden. There is something so abstracted in her attitude, and she looks so unlike my little playful companion of a few weeks since, that I draw back involuntarily and observe her.

Her step is slow, her eyes are fixed upon the ground, and in her hand she carries a bunch of the large ox-eyed daisy. Pedro gambols round her, but she takes no notice of him. She goes lingeringly past the window without even a glance to see if I am there. Alas, her thoughts are far away, and I am quite forgotten! Now, at the distance of a few yards, she pauses. She leans against the low wall that divides the path from the garden, looks round to see if any one be near, and then, smiling faintly to herself, begins plucking her flowers leaf from leaf.

Ah, I recognize it! It is an old German game, of which I remember to have read long ago in some quaint romance about the river Rhine - a floral charm by which young Frauleins test the truth of lovers' vows! See, her lips move with the falling of every leaflet! What are those words so softly murmured that I can scarcely hear them?

In the eagerness of my curiosity, I even lean forward to listen. In the earnestness of her invocation she neither sees nor hears me.

'He loves me - very much - passionately - not at all!'

This is the formula, and with every variation of the sentiment a leaf falls, like a tear.

Now there are but four or five left. Her colour comes and goes - her lips tremble - she has half a mind to fling the oracle away and know no more!

She plucks another, and another - and now, having calculated to the end, flings the last triumphantly into the air.

'PASSIONATELY!'

How charming she looks with that flush on her cheek, and that smile on her lips! How she repeats the word to herself, as if it were a precious secret; and then, with a peal of ringing laughter, hugs the old dog round the neck and bounds away down the path like a young fawn!

I remain there for some seconds, mute and sorrowful. She is gone, and she did not see me. So much the better!

My eyes fill with tears. There lie the scattered leaves - Alas, poor cousin Charles!

CHAPTER XVIII

ON A SUMMER'S EVENING

Now that the summer evenings were come, and M. Hamel was so frequent a guest, I often walked alone in the neighbourhood of Montrocher. It was pleasant to wander out thus at sunset, when the heat of the day was past and the *cigales* were still. Sometimes I met the village priest, with his breviary in his hand and the little children clinging to his skirts, returning home after the Angelus - sometimes a party of sun-browned *vignerons*, plodding wearily back after their long day's work on the mountains - sometimes in the quiet lanes, where I liked best to stroll, couples of young lovers, blushing and shy, who shrank back at my approach, and gave me a timid 'good-evening,' as I passed.

They were my happiest hours, and my most solitary. Hours full of musings on the present and the past, and fed by conjectures of the future.

Sauntering along thus one evening, when the red sun burns through the belt of amber vapour that skirts the landscape all around, and my shadow lengthens before me along the dusty road, I am overtaken by a gentleman on horseback, who calls me by my name, and uncovers courteously when I look up. It is M. Charles, and he is riding in the direction of La Rochepôt.

'Good-evening, mademoiselle. Yours is a lonely walk.'

'But a very pleasant one, thank you. Do you come from Montrocher?'

'I - I come from Meursault,' he replies, with some embarrassment. 'I have ridden through the village; but I have not called at our friend's this evening.'

There is a momentary silence, and M. Charles controls his horse to a slow walk.

'I was not sure that I should find them alone,' he next adds, playing nervously with his whip-handle. 'And - and I was not sure that I should be welcome.'

Finding me still silent, he springs to the ground, passes the bridle over his arm, and walks beside me.

'Mademoiselle,' he says, in an agitated voice, 'tell me. Am I right? Is - is Monsieur Hamel there?'

'I really do not know. He was not there when I left.'

'Then - forgive me for questioning you - why are you walking alone? Why is not Marguerite with you?'

I was unwilling to tell him that they were expecting M. Hamel; but he interpreted my hesitation in an instant.

'Enough,' he said, impatiently. 'You need not take the trouble to shape the unwelcome truth. I am glad I did not go near the house. I could not have met that man with common civility. How often is he there? Once a week? Twice? Three times? Tell me, I entreat you!'

I knew not how to answer. I endeavoured to palliate matters; but my mediation took the form of a reproach.

'You should come oftener yourself,' I said, 'and then no other could occupy your place. M. Hamel *is* a frequent visitor; but why are you not the same? This intimacy could never have progressed so far if ...'

'If what?'

'Will you forgive me, if I speak plainly?'

'Ay, and thank you also.'

'If you had taken as much pains to win Marguerite's affection as you took to estrange her from you.'

'I! I estrange her! You are dreaming!'

His astonishment was so real that, but for the sorrow of the thing, I could scarcely have forborne a smile.

'I can well believe,' I replied, 'that you are quite unaware of all that you have done; still it is indeed too true that you have yourself to blame for much that offends you.'

'Tell me, at least, mademoiselle, of what I have been guilty.'

I saw that the old proud spirit had again come over him; but I resolved not to notice it.

'You have chilled the warmest heart, and wounded the most sensitive nature in the world,' I said, calmly. 'You have been exacting when you should have been yielding. You have shown none of the devotion, none of the indulgence, none of the submission of a lover. You have treated Marguerite as if she were a child to be schooled and governed, not as a woman to be wooed and won. Spoiled and petted as she has been all her life, living in a home where her every wish is law to those around her, you alone, monsieur, have attempted to oppose and control her ...'

'And was I not right?' he interrupted, hastily. 'Was it not my duty to correct her faults?'

'Yes, had you been her husband; but was it judicious while you were only her lover?'

He paused, and bit his lip.

'She would have loved me all the more for it, if she were sensible and grateful,' he said, after a while.

'But if she were only childish, sensitive, impulsive, self-willed?'

He looked down, and made no answer. I pursued my advantage.

'It was not because Marguerite was promised to you while quite a child, and unable to choose for herself, that you should have treated her as if she were already your property. It was not because

137

you were sure of her that you should have deemed it unnecessary to please her. The effort ...'

'Pardon me, mademoiselle, but I am not so ungenerous as you imply,' interposed M. Charles. 'It is not in my nature to fawn and flatter. I love Marguerite, and she knows it. That knowledge should suffice. I am neither a Romeo nor a St. Preux, and I hold it beneath a man's dignity to sigh and serenade like a lover in a romance. I have omitted that folly, not because I was negligent of pleasing her, but because it would have been unworthy of myself to stoop so low.'

There was no reply to be made to a speech like this, so I only listened, and looked doubtful. A long silence followed, during which he glanced at me uneasily from time to time, and sighed heavily.

'You think me too uncompromising?' he said, at length.

'I think you too proud,' I replied, bluntly.

He smiled.

'It is my great fault,' said he.

'And your pet fault,' I rejoined, with impatience. 'You are proud of being proud - like every one else that I ever met before. Correct yourself of it, monsieur, since you have so great a talent for reproval.'

He smiled again with entire good humour.

'You are a severe Mentor,' he said; 'but a very straightforward and kindly one, I am sure. It would have been well for me had I sooner enjoyed the honour of your acquaintance and the benefit of your advice.'

'It would, indeed,' I said, sadly. 'That is, if you would have listened to me. Even now, perhaps, it is not too late.'

He started, and changed colour.

'Too late!' he echoed. 'Too late! What do you mean by "too late?"'

'I mean that - that if you will strive to make her love you - if you will let her see how much you love her - if, in short, you will put aside your pride, your false dignity, your reserve, you may win her even now.'

He stood still, and I saw that his lips trembled.

'Good God!' he said, eagerly, 'do you doubt it? Do you - do you think she dislikes me?'

'I don't think that she dislikes you,' I replied, unwillingly; 'but it is natural that she should compare your coldness with the indulgence of others, and prefer those who ...'

'One word, mademoiselle - one frank word, I beseech you! Have I quite lost her? Does she - does she love ...'

He could not speak the hated name, but laid his hand imploringly upon my arm. I hesitated, I dreaded lest I should say too much; but my face betrayed what my tongue would fain have denied.

He gave utterance to a kind of smothered sob, and turned his head away.

'You need not tell me,' he said, bitterly. 'I see how it is - I feel how it must end. Oh, Marguerite, Marguerite!'

I could not see his emotion without attempting some consolation; and I pitied him from the bottom of my heart.

'You do wrong,' I said, soothingly, 'to anticipate the worst. Remember, that perhaps it is not yet too late! Remember what an advantage is yours even now! She is your betrothed, and if you are but prompt ...'

He turned, and held out his hand to me. I saw that his face was very pale.

'You have told me many truths to-day, mademoiselle,' said he, in a low voice, 'and I thank you. I - I must consider what is best to be done, and heaven grant that I may choose the right. At present I scarcely know how to act - or how to think!'

With these words he sprang into the saddle, put spurs to his horse, and rode wildly away; leaving me standing by the roadside, speechless and sorrowful.

CHAPTER XIX

CONFIDENCES

'Sister-in-law,' said uncle Alexander, speaking for the first time since breakfast had begun; 'it is just three weeks to-day since Charles Gautier last set foot in this house. What is the meaning of it?'

Marguerite looked down. Madame shrugged her shoulders, and was silent.

'What is the meaning of it, I say?' repeated uncle Alexander -

this time somewhat louder.

'*Ah Ciel!* how should I explain the caprices of M. Charles Gautier?' retorted Madame. 'It is his pleasure, I suppose, to remain away.'

A shade passed over uncle Alexander's brow, and he plucked angrily at his iron-gray moustache.

'He is not a man to entertain "caprices," sister-in-law,' said he. 'You know that as well as I. Perhaps, however, you do *not* know that he rode past the door of this very house the day before yesterday, and that, too, without even looking up at the windows. This was not caprice. He had some reason for avoiding us, and I wish to know what that reason is.'

M. Delahaye set down his glass untasted.

'Rode past the house!' said he, with astonishment. 'My nephew Charles - my son-in-law *in futuro!* Brother Alexander, the thing is incredible - incredible! I can't believe it.'

'Believe or not as you like best,' growled uncle Alexander. 'I saw him myself, and my eyes are better than most people's.'

Monsieur drew a long breath, and looked much disturbed; but Madame maintained her attitude of indifference.

'If,' said she, 'he chooses still to be offended about that foolish matter of the book (in which, by the way, he was altogether to blame) we cannot help it, brother Alexander - and if he supposes that Marguerite is responsible to him alone, or that her parents are to be guided by his caprices in the choice of their acquaintance, he has vastly mistaken his position in this family.'

'Caprices - caprices again!' exclaimed uncle Alexander, impatiently. 'Sister-in-law, you talk like a woman! Charles Gautier never had a caprice in his life. He is an honourable, straightforward man; and it would be well if you had the sense to appreciate him!'

'Appreciate him, indeed!' echoed Madame. 'Why his prejudices against M. Hamel -'

'Confound M. Hamel!' interrupted uncle Alexander. 'I wish with all my heart that he had been at the devil before he came here!'

Marguerite flushed with indignation; and M. Delahaye leaned back and waved his hand.

'Brother Alexander,' said he, with an air of dignified reproach. 'Your phraseology is indecorous - reprehensibly indecorous; both as regards the object of your remarks, and the presence of the - ahem!

the fair sex. No gentleman (much less a member of the clerical profession) could be supposed, under any circumstances, to go to the - ahem! I am shocked, brother Alexander. I am shocked.'

Brother Alexander gave utterance to a sarcastic grunt, and ate peas with his knife, doggedly.

'If, indeed,' continued Monsieur, regarding him all the time with supreme disgust, 'my nephew Charles do really entertain such prejudices, and participate in such sentiments as - as you appear to nourish, brother Alexander, I have only to add, that he is a young man of ill-directed tastes and obtuse perceptions, and that he had better remain away till - Good heavens, brother Alexander! what are you about?'

Uncle Alexander was at that moment wiping his plate with a piece of bread, that he might lose none of the gravy. He looked up with a diabolical grin.

'Hey?' said he. 'What's the matter now? Anything wrong?'

'Wrong!' exclaimed his elder brother, fanning himself pathetically with his pocket-handkerchief. 'Sir - your vulgar idiosyncrasies will be the death of me!'

Whereat uncle Alexander laughed outright, pushed in his plate, smacked his lips, and rose from table.

'I'm going out,' said he, 'for the day; and if I see Charles I shall invite him to dine here on Sunday - so I give you all fair warning.'

With these words he took his hat, and turned to leave the room. At the door he paused, and drew a newspaper from his pocket.

'There is a column of statistics here that I want copied,' he said. 'Who will do it for me? No - not you, monkey, I am afraid to trust you.'

His eyes were fixed on me as he spoke, so I rose and held out my hand for it.

'If you will trust me, sir,' I said, 'I will endeavour to do it correctly.'

He nodded, muttered something which sounded like 'much obliged,' and hurried from the room.

The breakfast-party then broke up, and I carried the newspaper to my own chamber, and copied the column of statistics fairly out on two large sheets of ruled paper.

Just as I had finished, Marguerite tapped at my door with her English books in her hand.

'Shall I read here, mademoiselle, or in the *salon*?' she asked.

'Here, dear; because we shall be cooler, and less interrupted. But wait for a few moments while I verify these figures.'

She put her books on the table, drew a stool beside me, and sat down at my feet.

'I will be very quiet, mademoiselle,' she said, gently, and laid her head, with a sigh, upon my knees.

By-and-by she possessed herself of my left hand, and more than once, while I continued perfecting my work, pressed her lips fondly against the palm. They were hot and dry, and when I at length looked down and laid my pen aside, I saw that her face was very pale.

'*Petite*,' said I, passing my hand caressingly over her hair, 'you are silent and sad to-day.'

'I am tired, mademoiselle.'

'Tired! Of what, *chérie*?'

'Of thinking,' said she, with a sigh of deep weariness.

There was a pause.

'And shall I tell you what you have been thinking of, Marguerite?' I asked, taking her head between my two hands, and bending over till my lips rested on her forehead.

'Yes - if you are a sorcerer, or a *clairvoyante*!'

'I am neither - and yet I am almost sure that you have been thinking of what your uncle told us at breakfast about poor cousin Charles.'

She stirred uneasily, and I saw the blood mount faintly to her cheeks.

'I cannot believe it,' she said. 'I think uncle Alexander was mistaken.'

'No, Marguerite,' I replied, gravely. 'He was not mistaken. Your cousin did really pass the house - for I saw him.'

Her breath came quickly. She opened her lips as if to speak; but closed them again without a word.

'He would not call here,' I continued; 'because he feared to be unwelcome - because he feared to find another in his place.'

'Nay, mademoiselle,' exclaimed Marguerite, impatiently, 'you cannot know that!'

'Dear, he told me so.'

She started at this - looked up suddenly in my face - and repeated the words after me.

'He told you so, mademoiselle!'

'Yes. I was walking; he was riding, and had just passed through the village. Oh, Marguerite, he is very jealous and unhappy!'

She looked down and bit her lip.

'And, dear, you give him reason to be so,' I added. 'Your coldness towards himself - your encouragement of M. Hamel ...'

'Charles is unjust to M. Hamel!' interrupted Marguerite.

'Perhaps so; but it is because he loves you.'

'No - no - no,' she exclaimed hastily. 'He never loved me! He never loved me in his life!'

'He did, Marguerite; and he does. Your cousin is undemonstrative; but his feelings are warm and deep – the warmer, perhaps, because they are so silent. He does indeed love you most dearly! Would you believe it if he told you so himself? - if he overcame his natural reserve, and showed all the tenderness that lies hidden in his heart?'

Her agitation was great, and she began nervously rending the feathers from a pen.

'I - perhaps, I might believe it,' she replied in a low voice; 'but ... but ...'

'But what?'

'But I could never give him any affection in return!'

'And why so, *chérie*? Is he not your betrothed husband?'

She shuddered, and was silent.

'Marguerite!' I said, earnestly, 'Marguerite, have confidence in me! Is it - is it because you have no heart left to give him? Do you love M. Hamel?'

Her colour came and went. Her lips trembled.

'I am afraid I do!' she cried, bursting into a passion of tears, and hiding her face in my lap.

'My poor darling!'

It was all that I could say; for my own tears interrupted the words I was about to utter.

Then I took her in my arms, and laid her head upon my bosom as if she had been a little child, and kissed her wet eyelashes, and did my best to soothe her; but she wept for a long time, and was not easily comforted.

'Oh, mademoiselle,' she said, brokenly, 'I am so wretched! I feel as if it were so false - so dishonourable! ... and yet I cannot help it!

Why did they promise me to Charles when I was a child, and neither knew nor loved him? He has never been gentle and kind to me, mademoiselle - never! - never! and now, when ...'

She hesitated, and a burning blush crimsoned all her face and neck.

'Go on, my darling, and tell me all!'

She made a violent effort over her own reluctance.

'And now, mademoiselle,' she said, 'when I am old enough to - to see and judge for myself, am I so very much to blame if - if I ...'

She threw her arms about my neck, and half-smiling, half-sobbing, hid her face on my shoulder.

I was sadly perplexed and troubled.

'Alas! my foolish birdie,' I said, sighing, 'this is a sorry business, look on it from which side we may! But there is one important item which you have not yet told me.'

'And that is? ...'

'Has M. Hamel ever said anything definite to you?'

'Never, mademoiselle; and yet ...'

'And yet you know that he loves you - is that it? Oh, *petite! petite!* the worst is all to come!'

We sat together and talked it over for a long time, and Marguerite poured out all her heart to me. Alas! how simple and loving a heart it was, and what an unreal dream was life to her! When at length we rose from our places, the sun was already bending westward, and the shadows lay long upon the grass.

'Heigho! little one,' said I, 'the day is almost past, and we have had no English lesson!'

'I am glad of it,' she whispered, nestling closer to my side, and laying her cheek up against mine. 'I am very glad of it, mademoiselle. I feel much happier now!'

'And I am glad of it also, my darling; for it seems to me that you and I have been somewhat estranged since ...'

She interrupted my sentence with a kiss.

'I will have no more secrets from you, my dear, kind mademoiselle!' said she, fondly.

And so we went down stairs together, and there was confidence once more between us.

M. Alexander neither brought M. Charles, nor came back himself in time for dinner. When he did return, he went straight to his own room, and there remained with his books and papers till quite late in the evening. About ten o'clock, when M. Delahaye had retired for the night, and we were all reading round the table, he made his appearance in the *salon*, took possession of a sofa, and smoked himself to sleep.

Presently Madame got up and left the room; but on tiptoe, and so softly that she could not have roused the lightest sleeper. Nevertheless, M. Alexander opened his eyes, and was miraculously wide awake in an instant.

'*Eh bien*,' said he, quickly. 'Where are my statistics?'

They were laid, folded and ready, on the table, beside my book. He took them from me without a word - glanced at the first page - thrust them into his capacious pocket - refilled his pipe, and smoked for some minutes in silence.

Then he rose abruptly, and lit his bedroom-candle.

'Humph!' said he, as he passed my chair. 'Now, I understand the improvement in my brother's arithmetic! Good-night, monkey.'

CHAPTER XX

THE FATE OF A BOUQUET

The three weeks lengthened to a month, and still no cousin Charles made his appearance. We did not even see him on Sundays, as in the spring-time; for it was now our custom to attend the second instead of the first service at Chalons, and M. Charles never played but in the morning. The pleasant coolness of our homeward journey during the sultry July weather was the reason assigned; but, as the change was not made till after the estrangement had begun, I was more than half inclined to think there was avoidance on both sides. But, if cousin Charles staid away, M. Hamel's visits, on the contrary, were as frequent and entertaining as ever. He had always something to bring, or to relate. Now it was a new volume of Sand or Lamartine; or a foreign plant which he had reared on purpose for Madame; or the latest *critique* of a new opera for Monsieur; or a song which he had himself composed, and wished to submit to our general criticism. On the particular evening of which I am about to speak, he brought with him a small, but precious volume of engravings and etchings; and as Marguerite, delighted, turned the pages, he hung over the back of her chair and commented upon each.

'This charming head,' said he, 'is engraved by Bartolozzi, after a painting by Angelica Kauffmann. Would you have believed that mere dots and lines could produce such effect? How the shadows deepen, and then melt again into half-light! The bloom seems to rest upon that cheek; and you can almost see the breath that parts her lips!'

'It is, indeed, very beautiful,' murmured Marguerite. 'And this - this is surely a scene in Venice?'

'Yes, a view of the Mocenigo palace, sketched by Prout. Here Lord Byron performed some of his most eccentric exploits. More than once, when returning from the palace of some friend or neighbour, he has been known to plunge into the canal and swim to his own door - sometimes even by night, with a lantern held up in one hand to light him on his watery way!'

'How daring!'

'Say rather, how absurd, when it was in his power to choose between a gondola and a catarrh! Ah, now you come to one of the gems of my collection! This is a proof copy of the famous "Three Trees," designed and etched by Rembrandt himself.'

'Dear me,' said Marguerite, innocently. 'It is very ugly!'

'Oh, treason! 'Tis one of the most wonderful light-and-shadow pictures in the world! Only observe those piled clouds, that sweep of infinite distance, this entanglement of weedy foreground, the liquid blackness of this glassy pool, and the marvellous opposition it affords to that space of pure and dazzling light above! Why, mademoiselle, impressions inferior to this have sold before now for no less a sum than four or five hundred francs!'

She opened her bright eyes, and laughed with unfeigned surprise. M. Hamel smiled, and continued:-

'This, perhaps, may interest you more. It is a portrait of the Princess Elizabeth of England, daughter of James the First, and afterwards wife to the king of Bohemia. It is copied from the painting by Vandyck, and engraved by Robert Vander Voorst, engraver-royal to King Charles the First. The lines are coarse; but full of power and freedom. Do you admire the face?'

'Not much; but it looks as though it might be more pleasing in the picture.'

'A just criticism, mademoiselle, which I am happy to confirm from my own experience. This group of horses, by Bewick, will hardly please a lady - or this rough-looking caricature of a politician, by Hogarth. But here we have a landscape by Barrabe, and here a view on the Roman campagna, which I beg you to observe particularly.'

'That is perfection!' exclaimed Marguerite.

'In every sense; for it is the perfection of nature expressed by the perfection of art. This is a modern engraving from a modern painting, and both are masterpieces in their way.'

'How I should like to see the painting!' said she, with a sigh.

'Wish, instead, to see the actual spot,' continued M. Hamel. 'Wish to stand upon that enchanted desert, bounded by blue mountains and a bluer sky; sown with ruins of temples, aqueducts and tombs; flower-grown like the primeval paradise; and solitary as the prairies of America, or the pastoral plains of Asia.'

Marguerite shook her head sadly.

'I should wish in vain,' said she; 'for I am never likely to reach Italy. However, I am glad to see the engraving, and should like better still to see the painting.'

'The engraving is to the painting, what the painting is to nature,' said M. Hamel. 'But, after all, how little that is! At best an imperfect hint to the imagination or the memory!'

'*L'art n'est pas une étude de la réalité positive - c'est une recherche de la vérité idéale*,'* said I, reading aloud from a book that was lying open upon the table.

M. Hamel looked up quickly, for it was not often that I took part in these conversations.

'Right, mademoiselle,' said he. 'Mine was a sceptical lament, and I deserve correction.'

'Nay,' I returned smiling, 'it is George Sand who corrects you, sir - not I.'

'But your own views?'

---

* Art is not a study of positive realism – it is a search after ideal truth.

'I have had few opportunities of forming them,' I replied; 'but, in so far as I may be said to have any, they are somewhat realistic.'

'And so are mine,' chuckled uncle Alexander, who had not spoken a word since M. Hamel's arrival. 'I like the bread-and-cheese pictures best of all.'

'The bread-and-cheese pictures!' repeated M. Hamel, in astonishment.

'Yes - with a foreground of vegetables, a middle distance of bottles and glasses, and a horizon of dead game! I never bought a picture in my life; but, when I do, it will be one of that sort.'

A half-contemptuous smile was M. Hamel's only reply.

'This scene,' said he, turning another page of the album, and addressing himself once more to Marguerite, 'represents a famous classical landscape by Joseph Vernet.'

Uncle Alexander grinned maliciously.

'I hate classical landscapes,' said he. 'I hate brown trees, and nymphs, and temples that stand just where they ought to stand.'

'But, my good sir,' expostulated M. Hamel, 'high art must be, to a certain extent, conventional; and the ideal ...'

'Is all humbug,' said uncle Alexander.

At this moment the dogs barked in the hall, the outer bell was rung, and some one rode into the court-yard.

Marguerite changed colour, and our eyes met. It was cousin Charles.

He came into the room without embarrassment; but stopped suddenly at the sight of M. Hamel. It was but for an instant, however, and greeting his rival with a stately bow, he met the rest almost as usual - perhaps a shade more coldly.

'Boy,' said uncle Alexander, 'you have not been here for a month.'

Cousin Charles had a bouquet of exotic flowers in his hand; but he took a seat near Madame Delahaye, and laid it on a table just behind him.

'I have been rebuilding my conservatory,' he replied, 'and taking measures for the preservation of the columbarium - which, by the way, has been visited by a deputation from the Archæological Institute of Lyons.'

'Humph! And on Sundays?'

Madame Delahaye interrupted him with an uneasy smile.

'Brother Alexander,' said she, 'we have no right to interrogate Charles in this manner. He visits when he pleases, and he is always welcome. Marguerite, my love, your cousin would like to see that beautiful book!'

Marguerite rose reluctantly, and gave the volume to her mother; but Madame made room for her on the sofa, and bade her explain the prints to cousin Charles. Both were uncomfortable. Marguerite scarcely spoke; M. Gautier hardly looked; and the pages were turned in silence.

A sense of oppression seemed now to fall upon the whole room. Uncle Alexander relapsed into his usual taciturnity - I withdrew into the embrasure of a window, and watched the gathering twilight - Madame went on with her knitting - and M. Hamel trifled with his watch-guard, and glanced keenly every now and then towards the group on the sofa.

Presently he rose, sauntered after me to the window, and looked out.

'What a delicious evening!' he said, aloud, 'and how the nightingales are singing in the lindens at Heidelberg!'

'Ah,' said I, quickly, 'have you been to Heidelberg?'

'I lived there once for a whole year. That is,' said he, checking himself as he always did when betrayed into any allusions of the kind; 'I - I have visited it many times.'

'And is it so very beautiful?'

'It is, indeed. But,' and here he dropped his voice almost to a whisper - 'but I had no idea that M. Gautier was related to the Delahayes!'

'He is monsieur's nephew,' I replied, 'and Marguerite's first cousin.'

He bit his lip at this, gave a hurried glance into the room, and resumed.

'Is he - is he very intimate?'

'Very intimate, indeed,' I answered, quietly. 'Is it possible that you have not met him here before?'

He darted a searching eye upon me; but I maintained an air of perfect unconsciousness.

'Never,' he said, earnestly. 'Never before.'

'How singular! But I think you were speaking of Heidelberg?'

He glanced back again, gave an impatient sigh, and came a

step nearer. For my part, I watched his discomfiture with great secret satisfaction.

'Is Mar - Mademoiselle Delahaye much attached to her cousin?' he asked, with assumed indifference.

Now that it was in my power, I resolved to probe his passion to the quick, and test if it were genuine.

'They have been betrothed for years,' I replied, evasively.

The blow told. He stepped back as if he had been stung - the blood rushed into his face - the veins on his forehead rose and throbbed.

'So - betrothed!' said he, hoarsely, and looked round at cousin Charles.

That gaze was long and steady, and, as he looked, the colour ebbed slowly from his face till his very lips were white.

'You are surprised, Monsieur Hamel!'

He drew a long breath, and forced a haggard smile.

'I *am* surprised,' he replied. 'Very agreeably surprised, I assure you; but,' (regaining his composure by an effort,) 'but, *à propos* of Heidelberg, which is the most beautiful ruin on this side of the Alps, have you seen La Rochepôt, which is the ugliest?'

I answered in the negative. He made some other passing remark, and then turned away. I stayed in the recess, and observed all that followed.

He went straight to Marguerite, and, with his usual easy self-possession, asked her for a song. She, only too happy to escape from the sofa, complied without hesitation. He led her to the piano; he sought out the music for her; he turned the pages; he applauded; he hung over her, like a lover. She, trembling, confused, happy and fearful at the same time, dared not look round; scarcely dared to answer; and sang in a voice so tremulous that one could with difficulty distinguish a single word.

As for cousin Charles, he leaned back in his place, and was too proud to betray his annoyance even by a glance. Once only, when M. Hamel sang, and every one's attention was for the moment diverted, I saw him extend a quick hand to the table behind Madame, crush the bouquet in an iron grasp, and fling it through the open window.

Soon after this he rose, took his leave with perfect politeness, and departed as frigidly as he had arrived - leaving the field to his rival.

Something seemed to tell me that from this moment all was over between Charles and Marguerite. I even fancied that he would never come again; but on that point I was mistaken.

He did, indeed, come again - but it is not yet time to speak of that.

M. Gautier was no sooner gone, and uncle Alexander with him, than M. Hamel's spirit rose to the highest. He jested, he sang, he was buoyant with love and victory. He paid Marguerite the most devoted homage, and when he left that night, it was with the consciousness of his power, and with the determination to overcome every obstacle.

That he loved her passionately and disinterestedly, and that, too, upon one of those mysterious impulses called 'love at first sight,' I have never for an instant doubted. There have been some who taxed him with a more worldly motive; but I was not one of them.

He loved her well, be his faults what they might; and he wooed her royally. Impassioned and accomplished, his powers of fascination were almost magnetic; and it is no wonder that she should have forgotten all else in favour of his rare gifts and splendid person. To her he displayed all the treasures of his imagination. He flattered her with his devotion, and subdued her by the magic of his eloquence. If she could not always comprehend, she admired none the less, and was content to know that it was beautiful. She listened as a savage might listen to a symphony of Beethoven or Mozart; or as a lonely traveller might lie, musing and solitary, on some mountain ledge,

> 'lulled by the sound
> Of far-off torrents charming the still night.'

And so things came to pass, and the threads of this life-drama became twisted and twined, and I, the sole observer, sat apart and noted all.

CHAPTER XXI

THE RUSTLING AMONG THE LAURELS

'Do you really think that he will stay away for ever, mademoiselle?'

'*For ever* is a strong phrase, *chérie*,' I replied, gravely; 'but, indeed, I fear that it will be a long time before we see your cousin Charles again.'

And then I related to her the fate of the bouquet.

We were walking in the middle path between the garden-gate and the summer-house, waiting for the breakfast-bell. The morning was, as usual, gloriously fine - indeed, we had now had seven or eight weeks of unclouded skies, and the grapes were ripening fast. Sauntering backwards and forwards in the stillness of the sultry noon, we talked over the meeting of the night before, with no other interruption than the shrill droning of the *cigales* or the darting of a little green lizard now and then across our path.

Marguerite listened to me in silence, and a half-smile hovered upon her lips.

'I wonder if M. Hamel saw the bouquet,' she said, musingly, 'and if - if he guessed anything about cousin Charles?'

I could have replied very readily to the latter part of this conjecture; but I had long since resolved never to promote M. Hamel's cause by any word of mine - so I held my tongue.

We took another turn from the summer-house to the gate, and back again.

'I hope he was not offended with uncle Alexander!' she then said, after a silence of some minutes.

'*He!* do you mean your cousin?'

'No, mademoiselle,' she replied, blushing. 'I - I meant M. Hamel.'

There was a rustling among the laurels beside the summer-house. I turned at once, for I fancied that I had heard it when we were standing on the same spot a few minutes before; but there was nothing visible.

'It would be a strange thing, would it not, mademoiselle, if cousin Charles were to be the first to - to annul the engagement?' murmured Marguerite, following the current of her thoughts, and playing with the tendrils of a vine that overgrew the lattice-work of the little arbour.

'Strange, indeed!' said I, absently, with my whole attention riveted on the laurels.

'I don't think,' continued she, 'that any two in the world could afford a greater contrast. Cousin Charles is cold and gloomy - I never saw him more cold and gloomy than last night! And M. Hamel -'

She hesitated, and again, as the name passed her lips, the leaves rustled.

'What about M. Hamel?' I asked, speaking with indifference, but listening keenly.

She laughed, and looked down.

'Ah,' said she, with an idle tapping of her little foot upon the gravel, 'you know how kind and delightful M. Hamel always is, and what *I* think of him!'

I heard the stealthy parting of the boughs, I turned - I caught sight of an eager face peering through the leaves, and hidden instantly!

'Marguerite,' said I, quick as thought, 'run into the house, darling, and bring me the handkerchief that lies upon my dressing-table.'

She nodded, and darted off like a bird on the wing. As her white skirt fluttered out of the gate, I went round, with a swift step and a beating heart, to the path behind the summer-house.

The laurels grew thickly, and at first I could see nothing. Then I came to a little zig-zag opening between the bushes - ventured in after an instant of hesitation - and saw, at the farther end, just where the apparition of the face had started through the leaves, a crouching figure!

One moment's consideration satisfied me that the intruder was harmless enough; so I put on a stern face, and desired him to come out directly.

He obeyed me at once; for he was a very small boy, and terribly frightened. I took him by the arm, and led him into the light, and looked at him from head to foot. He had a sun-burnt little face, with twinkling dark eyes, and curling black hair, and the oldest and most acute expression that I ever saw in my life. He was not a peasant boy; for he wore leather shoes, and cloth trowsers, and a drab waistcoat with sleeves which were a great deal too long for him. Altogether he looked more like a stable-boy than anything else.

'Who are you?' said I, in a very fierce tone of voice; 'and what are you doing here?'

He darted a despairing glance at the high wall under which we were standing, and made no answer.

'If you won't speak, I will take you into the house.'

Hereupon he shuffled his feet uneasily, cast down his eyes, and looked the picture of cunning trepidation.

'I - I wanted to - to -'

'To what?'

' - To see the garden, ma'mselle!'

'That is not true; and if you don't tell the truth, I will call Monsieur Delahaye. What is your name?'

'Pierre.'

'And what besides Pierre?'

'Pichat, ma'mselle.'

'Pichat!' I repeated. 'I am sure I have heard that name before. Where do you live?'

'Chalons, ma'mselle.'

Pichat - Chalons! I could not make it out anyhow, so I went back to my first inquiry, and said -

'Now, Pierre Pichat, if you don't at once confess everything, I will hand you over to Monsieur Delahaye, and Monsieur Delahaye will hand you over to Claude, and you will be soundly flogged! Answer me at once, sir, and acknowledge why you hid yourself in the bushes!'

He became so seriously alarmed by these menaces (especially by the mention of Claude) that he burst out crying, and promised to tell all.

'I - I didn't come for myself, ma'mselle,' he faltered through his tears. 'I - was sent, ma'mselle - indeed I was! Please, let me go, and don't call uncle Claude!'

'*Uncle Claude!*' I echoed. 'So, then! Now we shall have no trouble to find out who you are, or who sent you! Come with me, sir, directly.'

'Oh, no - no, please, ma'mselle!' he cried, frantic with terror. 'Pray let me go! It was M. Hamel that sent me!'

'M. Hamel - uncle Claude - Pichat,' I repeated, running over everything that I could think of in aid of this mystery. 'Why, you are the son of M. Gautier's groom - your mother lives in the tower at Santenay - and you are stable-boy to M. Hamel!'

'I can't help it, ma'mselle!' said he, piteously. 'I can't help it!'

At this moment I heard Marguerite calling to me in the garden.

'Mademoiselle!' she cried. 'Where are you, mademoiselle? Have you gone in?'

I turned to Master Pierre Pichat, and laid my finger on my lip.

'If you move or breathe,' I said, softly, 'you will get that flogging!'

He thrust his knuckles into his eyes, and held his breath till he got black in the face, to stop himself from sobbing. Then the gate swang again, and Marguerite was gone.

The first breakfast-bell rang.

'Do you hear that bell?' I asked, sternly.

'*Oui*, ma'mselle.'

'Well - it will ring again in five minutes, and if by that time you have not confessed what you were sent for, I will hand you over to your uncle Claude.'

'And if I do confess, ma'mselle?' he asked, with a cunning twinkle in his little brown eyes.

'Then I will let you go.'

He looked up at me again, as if to see whether my word could be trusted; then dived into the lining of his cap, and brought forth - a letter!

'I - I was to watch about the house and give that to Ma'mselle Marguerite whenever I saw her alone,' he said, rapidly, 'and if I could wait, without being found out, I was to carry the answer back to my master.'

'And is that all?' I asked, securing the letter.

'*Dâme!* but it is all, indeed, ma'mselle!'

'Then you had better tell M. Hamel exactly what has become of the letter,' said I, 'and make your escape as fast as you can!'

I was just about to loosen my grasp when another thought struck me, and I held him back at the moment he thought himself free.

'When you were in there,' said I, pointing to the laurels, 'you were listening as well as watching. Did you overhear anything that was said?'

An indescribable expression flitted over his face; but he looked down, and shook his head.

'Not a word, ma'mselle,' he replied demurely.

'Did you catch the sound of anybody's name?'

'No one's, ma'mselle.'

At this instant the second breakfast-bell rang out its noisy summons. I looked down very doubtfully upon the roguish face; gave him a parting shake; said, 'Now, sir, make the best of your time!' - and let him go.

He darted away without another glance at me - swang himself up from branch to branch of a walnut-tree close by - dropped from the tree to the top of the wall, and disappeared in an instant.

I turned the letter over and over. It was written on pink paper, scented with verbena, and sealed with M. Hamel's crest - a serpent twining round a coroneted helmet. He had taken the precaution of not even directing it, and there was no writing visible.

I was in a difficult position, and knew not what was best to be done. Should I destroy it, and then tell Marguerite that I had done so? - or should I lock it up and say nothing about it to any one? or should I simply deliver it to her for whom it was destined, and trust to my own influence for the rest?

While I was yet deliberating, I heard Pierrette calling me to breakfast - so I thrust the letter into my pocket and put off my decision for the present.

Still I could not forget it. I was absent and anxious throughout the meal, and the possession of that perfumed note troubled me as much as if I had been the owner of the bottle-imp.

The breakfast passed off; the afternoon, with its duties of tuition went by; the evening came, and we parted for the night - and still I hesitated.

The next morning I took a solitary walk, that I might think the matter fairly out; for I felt a great responsibility upon me. I went up the mountain at the back of the house, and, sitting on a fragment of the Roman wall, decided not to give Marguerite the letter.

It was late when I returned. Madame was in the store-room, absorbed in the concoction of peach-jam and came out to me in a white apron and linen sleeves.

'*Dieu merci!*' she exclaimed, somewhat out of temper. 'I am glad to see you back, mademoiselle; for here is M. Hamel in the house, and no one to receive him but Marguerite!'

'M. Hamel!' I repeated in dismay.

'Yes - and Monsieur is out; and Alexander gone of course to

the office; and I am so busy and *déshabillée* that I cannot be seen! You will make my excuses?'

I turned away without another word, and went straight to the *salon*.

They were standing in one of the windows, hand in hand. Had I entered by the front way, they must have seen me; but, as it was, I surprised them. Both started guiltily. Marguerite turned her face away - M. Hamel let her hand fall - and for some seconds no one spoke.

I was the first to break silence.

'Madame Delahaye desires her compliments to you, monsieur,' I said, coldly (improvising the message as I went along), 'and request me to tell you that she is unavoidably busy this morning, and cannot have the pleasure of seeing you in person.'

M. Hamel bowed with all the nonchalance in the world.

'The loss is mine alone,' he replied, turning over the music on the piano, and humming the airs softly to himself.

But I was determined not to let him defeat me so easily.

'Madame hopes that you will shortly do her the favour to renew your visit,' I added. 'At present, I regret that I must claim the society of Mademoiselle Marguerite.'

He bit his lip, and darted an impatient glance at me; but the hint was unmistakable, and he had no longer any excuse for remaining. 'So I *must* go!' he said, and bending low in his farewell to Marguerite, murmured some parting word which brought the colour to her cheeks. He then made a sign to Claude in the court-yard, passed me with a haughty bow, vaulted into the saddle, and rode leisurely away.

There was a long silence after this, during which neither of us stirred. Then Marguerite ran into my arms, and began to sob.

'Don't - don't look so vexed with me, darling mademoiselle!' she cried. 'Not this morning - pray, not this morning!'

'And why not this morning?' I asked, trying to speak coldly.

She turned up a face wet with tears, but radiant with the sunshine of the heart.

'Because' - she faltered, 'because I am so happy!'

'Foolish child!' I said, sighing. 'I would have prevented this if I could; but now - heigho! what is to be the end? Stay, I have a letter in my pocket ...'

'Which I need scarcely read now,' interrupted Marguerite. 'He has told me the story of its capture, and all about its contents. Poor little Pierre Pichat!'

'Oh, if you already know the contents, I need not give it to you at all!' I said, holding it at arm's length.

But she snatched it from me all the same, and laughing, ran away to her own room, and locked the door.

CHAPTER XXII

MONSIEUR DELAHAYE MAINTAINS THE DIGNITY OF THE FAMILY

There was something mysterious on foot. No one could exactly define it, but all felt it, and a general uneasiness pervaded our establishment at Montrocher.

In the first place, M. Hamel did renew his visit, but he paid it to Monsieur alone; and after being closeted with him for more than two hours in the 'study,' went away without making his appearance in the *salon* at all. In the second place, a great alteration fell upon M. Delahaye himself. He grew silent, and moody, and irritable; started at the lightest sound; lost his appetite and his sleep; and took to bolting himself into his study of an evening. He had evidently something upon his mind; but what that something was no one could discover. Any allusion to it made him worse than ever; and once, when Madame ventured upon a public remonstrance, he became more energetically wrathful than I could have believed possible. As to his interview with M. Hamel, it was a point upon which he was utterly inaccessible.

'Church business!' said he, shaking his head as comprehensively as Lord Burleigh himself, and declined farther particulars.

Marguerite, too, was dreamy and abstracted, 'steeped in golden languors,' as a modern poet hath it, and all unlike her old joyous self. I seldom saw her play with Pedro now, or heard those peals of 'silver-treble laughter' which used to echo so merrily along the corridors. But they were happy reveries all - true 'luxuries of contemplation.' If she also started at every swinging of the courtyard-gates, or flushed and trembled when any horseman clattered down the road, it was certainly not with the same emotion as that which whitened the cheek of M. Delahaye, and caused him to retreat so often to the fast-nesses of his private room.

I do not pretend to say that these things puzzled me greatly, or that I was so much in the dark as poor anxious Madame Delahaye; but though I saw and conjectured much, I sought no confidences even from Marguerite. Shrewdly suspicious of the truth, I waited till events should explain themselves.

But I did not wait long. Scarcely a week went by before the storm broke.

It was a deliciously calm, cool evening, with a gray sky that hung hazily about the hill-sides, and melted every now and then into a noiseless shower. Madame, Marguerite, and I sat together in the *salon.* I had been reading to them, and had only just laid aside my book, for it was getting almost too dusk to see. We were very silent, and in the midst of our silence heard a sound of distant galloping.

Faster and louder it came, as if the rider were flying for his life, and the horse tearing the road up with his feet. Then it ceased before the gates, and the bell was rung furiously.

I looked at Marguerite. She had half risen from her seat, and the hand that rested on the window trembled.

'*Ah, mon Dieu!*' she said, shudderingly. 'It is Charles!'

'He ought to know better than to ride in that mad way,' observed Madame, with the utmost composure.

Before the last word had fairly escaped her lips, he was in the room.

He walked straight up to Marguerite, and stood before her. He seemed to see no one else, and brushed past Madame without so much as a glance of recognition. His face and lips were livid in the twilight, and his right hand crushed a written paper.

'I have come,' he said, hoarsely, 'to ask if this be true.'

And he flung the paper at her feet.

She drew back, startled and shocked, and clinging to me, as if for protection, said -

'What do you mean? What do you want? I do not understand you.'

M. Gautier spurned the paper with his foot, and smiled bitterly.

'Read your lover's letter, Mademoiselle Delahaye,' he said, in the same harsh, level voice. 'You will understand me then.'

'My lover's letter!' repeated Marguerite, faintly; but without attempting to take it from the spot where it lay.

I picked it up, crumpled as it was, and offered it to her; but she shrank back, and would not touch it.

'Give it to me,' said Madame, who had been looking from one to the other in speechless surprise. 'This is a most extraordinary scene, and quite beyond my comprehension.'

I gave it to her, and lit the lamp. So some three or four seconds of oppressive silence went by, during which M. Gautier folded his arms, and waited. But the forced calmness of his attitude was more terrible than any extreme of passion.

Then, holding the letter close under the lamp, Madame began to read.

At the first sentence her countenance changed, and towards the end became flushed with anger.

'This is not only false,' she exclaimed, 'but a forgery! I know Monsieur Hamel better than to believe that he would have written it. And to make use of Marguerite's name, too - it is abominable!'

M. Charles bent his head stiffly.

'I am glad to find you of that opinion,' said he; 'and I wish I could think with you.'

'"*Appeal to your feelings as a gentleman to resign one who has never loved you - reciprocity of affection - authorized by her family - sanction of the young lady herself,*"' continued Madame Delahaye, running over passages half-aloud, and paying no attention to his words. 'Oh, it is a cruel slander, Charles! No such proposition has been breathed to either your uncle or myself, and you know that this marriage has been the cherished project of our lives. As for Marguerite ...'

Madame turned to her daughter, and held out a loving hand.

'My poor child,' she said, tenderly, '*you* have never deceived me. *You* have never sanctioned any such "appeal" as this!'

But Marguerite neither spoke, nor accepted the outstretched hand. Her eyes were cast down, and she trembled from head to foot.

'Well!' cried Madame, eagerly, 'why don't you answer?'

'Because she dares not,' said M. Charles, between his closed teeth; and I believe that at the moment he almost hated her.

Marguerite met his eyes with unwonted courage.

'You mistake,' she said, mastering her agitation by a strong effort. 'I am no longer a child, or afraid to speak in your presence. If I hesitate, it is for - for mamma's sake - not my own.'

M. Charles pointed to the letter.

'Is it true?' he asked.

Marguerite drew a deep breath, and nerved herself for the reply.

'It is true,' she said, steadily.

'And you desire to be free?'

'I do.'

A sort of convulsion passed over every fibre of M. Charles's body. Madame uttered a moan of bewilderment and distress, and Marguerite's self-possession broke down in an instant.

'Oh, forgive me, forgive me, dearest mother!' she cried, clinging to her neck with both arms. 'Indeed, I cannot help it. I never could have been happy! Never - never!'

M. Charles turned upon her instantly.

'Why not, Marguerite?' he asked, in a strange, distinct whisper.

'Because you never loved me!' was the quick rejoinder.

He dropped his face upon his hands with a low, passionate cry that seemed to turn the very currents of my blood.

'I never loved anything else in my life!' he groaned, rather than said.

He spoke the truth, and even Marguerite bent forward with such a world of pity in her eyes that, had his own been then uncovered, all might yet have ended differently. But it was not to be; and presently, when M. Charles (ashamed of his own weakness) drew himself once more to his full height, Marguerite had shrunk down, with her head against her mother's shoulder.

Then Madame rang, and desired Pierrette to summon Monsieur Delahaye.

The *femme de chambre* returned with a refusal.

Monsieur was in despair at being obliged to forego the pleasure; but he was immersed in calculations, and could not come this evening.

Madame glanced at me imploringly.

'*Chère* mademoiselle,' she said, 'will you go? My husband does not guess how much, or why, he is wanted!'

I complied willingly, threaded the long passages in the dark,

161

and tapped at the study-door.

'Monsieur,' I said. 'Monsieur Delahaye!'

He muttered something which sounded like 'Come in,' so I turned the handle; but found the door locked.

'I cannot open it,' I said; 'but Madame entreats you to come to the *salon*, if only for half an hour. M. Charles is there, and ...'

'Who is it?' interrupted he, sharply. 'Is it Pierrette again?'

'No, monsieur - it is I. Gartha.'

'Are you quite alone?'

'Quite.'

The door opened suddenly, and Monsieur beckoned me in. I hesitated and drew back; but he stamped impatiently, and looked so agitated that I obeyed. As soon as I had fairly entered, he turned the key again.

'Now,' said he, hurriedly, 'what do you want? What is the matter? Why am I sent for? Who is here, and what is it all about?'

'M. Charles is here,' I replied. 'He has received a letter ...'

'A letter!' interposed Monsieur, biting his nails in a frenzy of excitement. 'A letter - eh? Well, I didn't write it, did I? What's his letter to me? Let them settle it between themselves. I'll have nothing to do with it!'

'But you have something to do with it, sir,' I urged, 'and M. Charles -'

'I'll not come. I hate quarrels, and I hate scenes, and I'm determined not to have my nerves torn to pieces for anybody! I know what Charles is when he's thwarted. I'd as soon face a Bengal tiger!'

And he paced backwards and forwards, sat down, rose up, and rubbed his hands over and over again, fifty times in a minute.

'Indeed,' I said, unable to forbear smiling, 'you have nothing to fear from M. Charles. He was perfectly tranquil when I left the room, and Marguerite ...'

'Poor Marguerite! poor Marguerite!' exclaimed Monsieur, whimpering feebly. 'I only wish to see her happy! If she prefers M. Hamel, she must marry M. Hamel. Of course it's a trial for her, poor dear; but she can bear those things better than I. My nerves won't allow me to interfere - they won't, indeed!'

It enraged me to see him sitting there on the edge of the sofa, flourishing his pocket-handkerchief, and shedding selfish tears; so I turned to leave the room.

'Then I am to say that you will not come, sir?' I asked, with my hand on the key.

'Come! not for the world! Say that I have a headache - that I'm gone to bed - that you couldn't find me - that - why he'd lay all the blame on me, mademoiselle!'

'Well, I suppose he would, sir, if you have had any share in the letter.'

Monsieur groaned piteously.

'I wish I never had had any share in it!' he exclaimed. 'Why did I allow myself to be persuaded? Why did I listen to M. Hamel at all? What am I to do, and how is Charles to be pacified?'

'Only by a frank explanation,' I suggested.

'An explanation! Alas, you little know the sufferings of a sensitive temperament! Look at me, mademoiselle:' (here he threw himself into an attitude, and glanced at the cheval-glass to observe the effect) 'look at me, and behold one whose life has been a martyrdom to susceptibility and - and indigestion. A being, in short, who is All Nerve!'

I walked out indignantly, and shut the door. Before I was halfway down the passage I heard him turn the key - he dreaded lest his nephew should come to question him in person!

Returning to the *salon*, I hear a voice that startles me.

'Yes, sir. Honoured by the permission of M. Delahaye, I wrote that letter.'

'By his permission! My uncle's! I'll not believe it!'

'Before you accuse me of falsehood, remember, monsieur, that mine is a profession of peace.'

It is M. Hamel. His attitude is haughty, and his eye glitters dangerously. One can see that his impulses are less pacific than his words.

At this moment Madame catches sight of me in the doorway, and interposes eagerly.

'There is but one person who can decide this difference,' she says, entreatingly. 'There is but one whose judgment you must both respect. That one is M. Delahaye. M. Hamel, let me entreat you to wait till he comes. Nephew Charles, I beseech you to be patient.'

And she glanced eagerly towards the door, and from the door back again to me.

I made the best apology that I could invent for him; but still it was a refusal.

M. Hamel smiled sarcastically. He was too keen a judge of character not to guess the truth.

'I flatter myself,' said he, 'that M. Delahaye will not prove inexorable to *my* persuasions,' and left the room.

Then cousin Charles, with all his reserve uprooted, and his pride quite broken down, turned despairingly, and for the last time, to his betrothed.

'Marguerite,' he faltered, 'Marguerite! Is there *no* hope for me? Is your heart lost to me beyond retrieval? Give me one word, only one word, and I will do anything, be anything, that you desire!'

'Oh, cousin Charles,' sobbed Marguerite. 'It is too late!'

'Too late - and I love you so dearly!'

She wept, and though he took her hand did not resist it.

'You never told me so,' she said, brokenly. 'If you had been less cold and harsh with me, I should never have disliked you!'

He covered his face with his hands, and one large tear came trickling through his fingers.

'I am punished indeed!' he murmured. 'I thought to mould you to the likeness of a vague ideal - I strove to teach, and, in the vanity of my heart, forgot that I also needed teaching! If I have not seemed to love you, it is only because I have loved you so well, and sought to make you perfect!'

But Marguerite sobbed as if her heart would break, and hid her face upon the sofa-cushions and repeated -

'Alas! cousin Charles, it is too late! - too late!'

The closing of a distant door, and the sound of his rival's voice in the corridor sufficed to efface every sign of weakness from M. Gautier's brow. There was something Spartan-like in his power of self-mastery after all.

M. Hamel came in, with M. Delahaye upon his arm. A glance at their two faces was confirmation enough - the one triumphant, but sedate; the other cowed and conscious, like a beaten hound.

M. Hamel placed a chair for him with all the ceremony in the world, and then said, bowing profoundly -

'Will you now, sir, do me the favour to convince this gentleman?'

Sitting there like a prisoner before a judge, and quailing before the steady gaze of the nephew whose cause he had deserted,

164

M. Delahaye looked at that moment, in spite of his curls and his jewellery, the most pitiable old man in existence. The tears which he had shed in his excess of self-condolence had left little tracks along his rouged cheeks, his false teeth chattered in a miserable smile, and every feature looked pinched and faded.

At the first word he was called upon to utter, he began whimpering again.

'My dear M. Hamel,' he stammered, 'my very dear nephew Charles, this - this is really a - a crisis - a position - a moment for which I - that is to say, the feelings of - of a father, and the - the delicacy of my nerves - (my dearest Charles, *you* know what my nervous system is!) - in - in short, I am happy - that is, I am sorry, that private feelings must - must yield - stern sense of duty - happiness of an - an only child. I - I - oh, M. Hamel, my inestimable friend! what do you wish me to say?'

'Simply this, sir,' interposed M. Charles, gravely and sorrowfully. 'Have you, in my absence, dishonourably given away that which was mine; or have you, in good faith and courtesy, waited to consult me on the matter?'

M. Delahaye cowered down behind his embroidered pocket-handkerchief - the very skeleton and caricature of an Apollo!

'My - my dear and valued nephew,' he said deprecatingly, 'I - I esteem you - I love you like - like my own son! I - I wish you were my own son - I do, upon my unimpeachable honour; but -'

'But you no longer love me well enough to make me your son-in-law! It is a nice distinction, sir,' said M. Gautier, bitterly.

'My dearest Charles,' began M. Delahaye, more affectionately than ever, 'you - you see this matter in a false light! My - my friendship for yourself is -'

M. Gautier waved him down with an imperious gesture.

'No more, sir,' he said, calmly and coldly. 'It is time that this unhappy subject were ended. I withdraw my claims, and should withdraw them more willingly did I believe that by so doing I secured the future peace of her whom I resign.'

He then turned to Marguerite.

'You are free,' he said, gently. 'You are free, and that you may be happy is all I now desire.'

'Do you forgive me?' cried Marguerite, passionately.

'Fully and freely. Farewell.'

With these words he passed out of the room.

A dead silence ensued; and we heard him ride out slowly, and the gates swing after him.

Then M. Delahaye drew a long breath, and looked round, simpering feebly.

'A most unpleasant affair!' he said. 'A most trying and harrowing affair, upon my sacred honour! I have suffered inconceivably; but, notwithstanding the delicacy of my feelings, and the - the palpitating susceptibility of my nervous organization, I do flatter myself that I have brought matters to a satisfactory conclusion, and maintained - ahem! the dignity of my name and family.'

M. Hamel bowed to hide a smile.

'The most heroic are not exempt from natural emotion,' he said, evasively.

'And even Virginius,' added M. Delahaye, with delighted self-complacency, 'was no more than man. Marguerite, come to my arms. If you are happy, I am repaid for all. Bless you both!'

Whereupon he draped his flowered dressing-gown around him, and assumed the attitude of a Roman father.

CHAPTER XXIII

FAMILY VERDICTS

They were affianced.

It was done very quietly, and without any of those rejoicings which usually attend these events in the provincial parts of France. Excepting that a few visits of ceremony were paid, that Marguerite wore a superb brilliant on her wedding-finger, and that M. Hamel went with us everywhere, there was little actual change of any kind. And it was better so, considering all that had gone before.

M. Delahaye was delighted with his son-in-law elect, and lived in an atmosphere of self-congratulation. He firmly believed himself to have been the contriver and promoter of the whole affair, and took great pains to impress this fiction upon the parties concerned. Madame, on the contrary, was for a long time anxious and unsettled;

remorseful on the score of the old love, and not yet reconciled to the new. She was too kind and too honourable not to feel that a wrong had been committed. However, her confidence in her husband, and her admiration for M. Hamel prevailed at last, and her doubts subsided into contented acquiescence.

Not so uncle Alexander. Furious at first, he settled down after awhile into a silent, sulky, tobacco-smoking mood, and remained in it. Discontent became his normal state. Nothing, he said, could ever bring him to countenance this engagement - and nothing ever did. He had disliked M. Hamel from the beginning; he disliked him to the end; and he would have disliked him for a thousand years had he been allowed the time to do it. He dealt in antipathies, as in wines, wholesale; and was as sound and consistent a hater as I ever knew in my life. To do him justice, however, he could be as firm in his friend-ships as in his enmities, and, in proof thereof, never ceased to be the steadfast advocate and ally of M. Charles.

'Ah, monkey! monkey!' he used to say, shaking his head, and pinching her little pink ear between his great brown fingers. 'Charles was an honest gentleman, and would have been a good husband! You are not the first who has changed away substance for shadow, and given up a true heart for an oily tongue! Love, indeed! Tut - Tut! I remember when little damsels like you never dreamt of such a thing as falling in love for themselves; but took the husbands chosen for them, and were thankful!'

All of which Marguerite parried by coaxing or crying, and generally contrived to have the last word. Still she could neither coax nor cry uncle Alexander into any degree of civility towards M. Hamel.

As for M. Gautier, he became to us as if he had never been; and, save for such stray scraps of news as chanced now and then to fall from the lips of uncle Alexander, we heard less of him than of the veriest stranger. He lived for awhile in great retirement, and then went abroad. Once we heard that he was at Frankfort, and once that he had been seen in Vienna, and after that we learned no more for very many months. The dust gathered upon the keys of the little organ in our chapel at Chalons; for he was gone, and there was none to succeed him. Great griefs are solitary ever, and he of Athens was, after all, but the type of a mood from which few among us need hope entirely to escape.

In the meantime, M. Hamel was the most devoted of suitors, and Marguerite the blithest of living creatures. She was petted and spoiled now to her heart's content, and seeing him so fond, and her so happy, I learnt to master many of my early prejudices, and to regard, almost with favour, the fortunate successor of poor cousin Charles. If at times it did occur to me that his tenderness was more indulgent than elevating, and that his very love had something sultan-like and condescending in it, I kept that obnoxious opinion to myself and observed in silence.

After all, be his faults what they might, he lived for her only.

> 'And in his eye, where love and pride contended -
> His dark, deep-seated eye, there was a spell,
> Which those who love and have been lov'd can tell!'

CHAPTER XXIV

A BURGUNDIAN VINTAGE

The rich autumn ripens and wanes, and the velvet dahlias are all in flower, when I am one morning awakened soon after sunrise by a confused echoing of merry voices, a strange sound of rumbling and rolling in the court-yard, and a continuous volley of steady hammering, which rings like metal upon metal. After lying and listening for some time in sleepy bewilderment, I am just about to doze again, when Marguerite bursts into the room, clapping her hands and tossing her hair like a wild little Bacchante.

'Oh, mademoiselle! dear mademoiselle! The coopers are come, and the vats are all out, and they are cleaning the *pressoir*, and scrubbing the grape-baskets, and the vintage will begin to-morrow!'

I am up in a moment, and almost as excited as herself. The vintage! There is an intoxication in the very name of it! I had almost begun to think that it would never come; for it is now the second week in October, and the grapes are so ripe that they fall from their stalks upon the merest touch.

To dress is the work of but a few minutes; and we are presently standing together on the uppermost step of the stone flight that leads down into the court-yard.

It is a pleasant sight, seen by the slanting beams of the early sun. There is the sturdy village cooper, attended by his apprentices; and there are the great vats and mash-tubs strewn about, in various stages of mending and cleansing. Yonder lie piled some scores of baskets of all shapes and sizes. These are likewise undergoing a strict inspection, and while the perfect ones are being scrubbed and pumped upon by a group of merry, bare-footed maidens in one corner, a grave, white-haired peasant, sits industriously repairing the ragged rims and broken handles in another. All the workers are brown-skinned, joyous, and noisy. The men wear slouching straw-hats, casquettes, and night-caps; the women, all manner of snowy caps, and head-dresses of bright twisted handkerchiefs. Some clatter in sabots; some are shoeless altogether, and some are natty in blue-worsted stockings and strong leather *chaussures*. Moving to and fro amongst them all, keeping an attentive eye upon the coopers, help-ing to roll the vats, laughing with the girls, and preserving order and industry as effectually as a master, I see Claude, handsome Claude, with his bright eyes, and gold ear-rings, and jaunty cap - Claude who is uncle to Master Pierre Pichat, and head vine-dresser to M. Delahaye and M. Alexander.

'Take care, mademoiselle!' says Marguerite, laughingly. 'Claude is already betrothed, and Marie would be jealous if she saw you admiring her lover!'

'Marie! who is she?'

'The prettiest *paysanne* in all the department, and the grand-daughter of ... but surely you have heard us speak of the *mère* Blanchet?'

'Never. Is she your relation?'

Marguerite puts on a little comic pout of offended dignity.

'Our relation, mademoiselle! No, indeed; but she is the most venerable woman you ever saw. She is nearly a hundred years old, and can read, and spin, and write as well as the youngest. Besides, she is very clever, and knows all about the properties of herbs, and can tell you the pedigree of every noble Burgundian family, and every legend and local ballad, as readily as she repeats her pater-noster.'

'An interesting old lady, truly! Where does she live?'

'She lives with her son and his wife in a curious old cottage close by the ruins of La Rochepôt. They are our tenants, and have been for many generations. Pierre Blanchet is a stone-cutter, and Marie is his eldest child. But you have seen her, mademoiselle - though I dare say you forget all about it.'

'Indeed, yes. When and where was it?'

'It was the morning after your arrival here, and you were looking out of your bedroom-window ...'

'At a pretty girl who came to fetch water from the spring, and knelt down in the road before the cross! I remember her perfectly. Does she come all the way from La Rochepôt?'

'Yes. The water is chalybeate, and the grandmother uses it for medicines. She is quite a physician among the poor, and cured Claude last winter of the fever.'

'Whereupon Claude thought fit to catch a still more prevalent malady, and fell in love with his physician's grand-daughter - eh, *petite*?'

'Not at all, mademoiselle. It is an old attachment. Claude and Marie have been in love with each other since they were quite little children and played together among the castle ruins. They are to be married when the vintage is over; and I am to be bridesmaid! It will be a *fête* for us all, and you will see a rustic wedding, than which there is not a prettier sight in France!'

'Excepting one other wedding, petite, in which I shall see you play a still more interesting part!'

Which last remark Mademoiselle Marguerite does not choose to hear at all.

I have risen so early, that the day seems interminable. Still it is a cheerful day, full of noise, novelty, and excitement. There is talking, hammering, and singing going on from morning till dusk; and towards the afternoon the house is literally besieged by bands of wandering *vignerons* in search of work. They are a very motley race, speaking the *patois*, and wearing the costumes peculiar to their several districts. Being tempted to the wine-districts at the gathering season, they follow the echo of the cooper's hammer from house to house, like bees attracted by the rattling of the housewife's frying-pan. When hired, they labour cheerfully ten hours a-day; and either sleep in the out-houses, or encamp, gipsy-like, around a wood fire in the open air. It must be confessed, however, that these strangers entertain easy notions on the score of property, and that the orchards and hen-roosts are sometimes known to suffer by their proximity.

What, therefore, with the workmen in the court-yard, and the applications for labour, Claude has enough upon his hands, and uncle Alexander holds a ragged levee all day long in Monsieur's little study. Here he reviews and interrogates the candidates, examines their papers, hires, dismisses, and enters names and agreements in a great dusty ledger up till a late hour of the evening. By nine o'clock, when he at length comes up to his supper and his pipe, no less than a hundred are engaged for the harvest, exclusive of those labourers who belong to the surrounding villages, and those who are permanently retained throughout the year as servants of the estate.

The next day begins the vintage in earnest, and henceforth I spend half my life in the air, wandering with Marguerite from vineyard to vineyard, and enjoying to the uttermost all phases of this picturesque and joyous festival.

All day long the dwarf alleys of the vine are alive with gatherers, and the air with the hum of voices. All day long the patient oxen come toiling homeward with the great rough wains laden high with grapes. All day long the weary treaders labour in the *pressoir*, which stands on the shady side of the hot courtyard, and, with crimson feet and trowsers turned up to the knee, stamp out the streams of juice. All day long, like an overseer in a Massachusetts cotton-field, Claude paces backwards and forwards between the courtyard and the vineyards, observant of everything, and careful of his master's property as if it were his own.

How merry it is out among the vintagers! How they sing and laugh, and what quantities of grapes they contrive to eat! Their mouths are never empty, and their tongues are never still. Some of the little children who help to carry the baskets are so stained and smeared with the purple juice as to be scarcely recognizable, and fall asleep towards the afternoon through sheer exhaustion of feasting. We ourselves eat grapes at every meal, and it is only in those precious districts which produce M. Alexander's old Romanée and famous Chambertin, that depredations are prohibited. Here he himself stalks grimly, and where he makes his appearance an unusual amount of silence and industry prevails.

Towards mid-day the clicking of the shears, and the creaking of the heavy wheels, and the plashing of the treaders ceases suddenly, and all the men and girls, old people and children, come thronging to the meadow at the back of the house, and throw themselves in careless groups under the shade of the willows. There Claude and Pierrette, aided by the cook and certain chosen auxiliaries, bring out and distribute great basketfuls of brown bread and a multitude of clean wooden bowls. Then comes a huge cauldron of soup, steaming hot from the kitchen, and a mountain of *bouilli*. Then a cask of last year's *piquette*, which is a thin, sour, miserable wine kept for the labourers' drinking, and produced from the third pressing of the exhausted skins and seeds of the grape. The bread is then broken up and tossed from hand to hand, the soup is ladled out, and the *bouilli* shared amongst the hungry crowd. This all consumed, they wash their bowls in the running water, and turn the tap for themselves, filling and emptying as often as they please.

Thus an hour of rest and refreshment glides away; the bell rings, they rise reluctantly, they spread themselves once more over the hill-sides, they make a plentiful dessert off the clustering grapes, the singing and chattering breaks out afresh, and the afternoon is consumed in a renewal of the morning's labour.

At dusk they assemble again, and their supper is precisely like their dinner. When this is over, they sometimes dance upon the green sward to the drone of a rustic *musette*, upon which the young men perform in turn; but they are oftener too weary to do aught but lie and rest, and watch the rising of the stars. Then the strangers drop off by twos and threes to their straw-litter in the great barn beyond the church; and the regular labourers plod home to their cottages, and mutter an Ave as they pass the crucifix by the roadside, or the image of the Virgin over the gate of the village *cimetière*. But the young lovers ramble on in the light of the broad moon, and take the longest way round, and say 'good-night' a hundred times over. Yet they will meet again in the morning, and be as happy as the birds in the spring time!

Oh, a pleasant idyll is the Burgundian vintage!

CHAPTER XXV

THE MURDER-STONE

The vintage had been about a week on foot, when Marguerite proposed a visit to the *mère* Blanchet. M. Hamel had an engagement that day and was certain not to come, so we agreed to make it an evening walk, and started away directly after dinner.

Oh, the misty hills and winding valleys of Montrocher! How fair they showed by the broad light of that golden afternoon; how fair, and how fertile! A painter might spend his life among them and not exhaust their pictorial resources. A poet might there study every aspect of rural life, and every phase of natural beauty, and never need the stimulus of 'fresh woods and pastures new.' Between Beaune and Chalons, within a circuit of twenty-five or thirty miles, lies all that is loneliest and loveliest this side of the Jura - a land untrodden by tourists, unrecorded by artists. Here may be traced the footsteps of the Roman and the Gaul side by side with the romantic monuments of mediæval Burgundy. Here legend and ruin enrich the lavish beauty of wood and mountain, and the very birds sing as of old they might have sung

'In Tempe or the vales of Arcade.'

Thinking thus, and pausing every now and then to listen to the songs of the grape-gatherers, I sauntered leisurely along, and sighed as I passed the spot where I was overtaken some few weeks ago by M. Charles. It troubled me to remember his solitude and his sorrow; but Marguerite had no such gloomy reflections. She danced on before, she sang, she gathered the wild hedge-flowers, and ran back every few minutes to show me some new treasure, or to prattle of the pastoral loves of Claude and Marie.

After walking about a mile along the road, we came to a steep pathway leading to the castle. Following this for some distance, we struck into a by-lane and reached a little lonely village on the side of the hill. It was a very miserable place, and, save by one poor old woman who sat spinning on the threshold of her cottage, seemed quite deserted.

'They are all gone to the vintage,' she croaked, feebly, in reply to my questioning. 'I should be out too but for the fever that I had in the spring. But I will go with them next year, please the holy saints! I will go with them next year!'

We left her nodding, and repeating this promise to herself - 'I will go with them next year!'

Further on came a broad space peopled by a few lean geese, and surmounted by the shell of what had once been a feudal stronghold. Wild flowers, ivy, and fallen masonry gave something of picturesqueness to the spot, and a tiny column of blue smoke rose from the midst of a cluster of trees behind the castle.

There was nothing very interesting in the appearance or history of Chateau La Rochepôt. Habitable up to a comparatively recent period, it had been demolished some forty years before, and the materials sold for business purposes. Under these circumstances a ruin loses more than half its pathos. Its mosses are of recent growth - its ivies are not venerable - the weather stains are faint upon its walls, and the night-winds as yet seem scarcely to have hushed away the human echoes. Devastation has been there; but not decay. The ruin has ceased to chronicle the ravages of time, and perpetuates only the record of its own disaster. It is no longer a type of human life; but rather a satire upon human fortune!

The column of blue smoke arose from Madame Blanchet's chimney. The cottage was built in a snug hollow under the lee of the castle walls, and sheltered by a group of pear-trees. It was wide and low roofed, built of rough stone, and approached by a flight of seven steps. The windows were very small and very high, and there were weeds and yellow mosses growing in the interstices of the masonry and along the ridges of the roof. Marguerite led the way, and we went in.

It was a quaint interior - a subject for the pencil of Edouard Frere. The floors were paved with the same rough stone, and the ceiling was hung with bunches of flax, dried grapes, and herbs. Two great armoires of old dark wood filled all one side of the room, and a clock, a table, and a settle with high carved back and arms furnished the others. On either side of the chimney stood a large stone seat. A log fire crackled cheerily on the hearth. Just under the window, in her own arm-chair, sat the white-haired grandmother. Her thin hands were crossed upon her lap, and she was smiling placidly upon a conclave of noisy children seated round a table on

174

the farther side of the fire-place. They were clamouring for supper, and their mother, a fine handsome woman, with a steaming saucepan in her hand, was endeavouring to appease their hunger with great ladlefuls of hot mushrooms and cubes of hard rye-bread. Lastly, in a dark corner behind the grandmother's chair, sat a couple whom I had not observed at the first glance; but whom I recognized for Claude and Marie. Young and loving, seated side by side and hand in hand, they completed the poetry of the picture, and seemed placed there to represent that delightful season which follows the wayward years of childhood, precedes the cares of maturity, and beholds from afar off the serenity of age.

Beautiful as it was, I saw the scene but for an instant. At the first sound of Marguerite's voice all was changed. The children held their peace and stared - the mother came forward, saucepan and all, to welcome us - the girl blushed and snatched away her hand, and Claude, abashed before his master's daughter, escaped by a side door. Only the grandmother was unmoved. Age is a great leveller, and Madame Blanchet, at ninety-eight, smiled upon us as she smiled upon her grandchildren, and kept her seat, although it was 'Ma'mselle Marguerite' who came to the cottage.

The first greetings over, I found myself ensconced in a corner of the settle, and Marguerite seated beside the *mère* Blanchet; while the children, shy and wondering, forgot that they were hungry, and left the mushrooms smoking on the platters.

'Why Pierre, why Paul, why little Clémence!' said Marguerite, reproachfully, 'you do not eat!'

'Eat, my little ones - eat,' urged the mother; 'or Ma'mselle Marguerite will think she has frightened the appetites away!'

'And then Ma'mselle Marguerite will herself be frightened away, and say she was not welcome, which would be terrible!' added the grandmother.

They needed very little persuasion; but presently, when no one was looking, fell to quite silently and industriously, like a brood of hungry chickens, using their spoons and forks very prettily, burying their shiny faces in the great mugs of wine-and-water which stood in the midst, and only squabbling, *sotto voce*, every now and then, when one happened to get a larger mushroom or a deeper draught than the rest.

'The children grow like the spring flowers, and the old wither away as the leaves in autumn,' said the grandmother, with a melancholy smile. 'Here is Ma'mselle Marguerite grown up and affianced - here is Marie already provided with a lover; and yet it seems but a day since they were both smaller than the smallest of these little ones! Alas, ma'mselle, old as I am, life has many ties for me; and I would gladly live on to witness the unfolding of yonder little buds!'

'You will stay with us for many years longer, *mère* Blanchet,' said Marguerite, caressingly. 'We cannot spare you yet - you who cure the sick, and advise the young, and are beloved by high and low through all this countryside! Is it not a common saying that the good *mère* Blanchet bears a charmed life, and was it not true that although you took the fever eleven months since, you are as strong and healthy to this day as when I first remember you, ever so many years ago?'

The *mère* Blanchet still smiled and shook her head.

'The young are ever hopeful,' she said. 'But I have too often watched the decay of others not to recognize the coming of my own.'

'At least, then, you can prescribe for yourself also,' urged Marguerite.

'Blessed are the wholesome herbs that the good God has planted for our easement,' replied the grandmother, reverentially. 'They give sleep to the sleepless, and strength to the strengthless, and cool the burning blood in the veins of the fevered; but neither in field, or fallow, or running water, grow the simples that shall renew the sinews of extreme age. Life is good, Ma'mselle Marguerite; but death is good also, if M. le Curé could only persuade us to think so.'

There was something very impressive in the language of the *mère* Blanchet - something which is marred by even the most faithful translation, but which is by no means infrequent in the mouths of the French peasantry. Living, generation after generation, amid all that is most soothing and beautiful in nature, they learn to draw their metaphors from the surroundings of their daily life, and talk unconscious bucolics. Trees, crops, flowers, are to them familiar things, and tincture all their thoughts with a simple poetry of colour which would be eloquence in the lips of a Sand or a Lamartine. To this the very structure and intonation of their native tongue contributes much, and their pastoral poverty and semi-serfdom even more.

The *mère* Blanchet ceased speaking, and in the midst of the pause that followed, two little urchins had a scuffle for the mug, and ended by upsetting it, whereupon a general confusion ensued, and the offenders were expelled. The rest were somewhat noisily disposed after this event, but the grandmother raised her hand, and there was silence.

'It is well,' said she, 'for the children to be taught submission in their youth, that they may grow to be orderly and respectful men, obeying their masters, labouring soberly in their vocations, and learning to subdue their passions like humble Christian souls. Pierre and Jacques are good boys; but little Paul is wilful and hot-tempered, and my daughter-in-law spoils him sadly.'

'Nay, mother,' expostulated Madame Blanchet the younger. 'Paul is still almost a baby, and will know better by-and-by.'

The grandmother looked incredulous.

'And then he is so quick and clever!'

'Say, rather, so mischievous,' said *la mère* Blanchet. 'Why, it was only yesterday that he frightened the little daughter of Simon the wheelwright almost into a fit, by hiding himself and howling at the back of the Murder-Stone?'

'The Murder-Stone!' I exclaimed. 'What is that?'

'It is a rock about half way down the other side of the hill,' replied the *mère* Blanchet. 'Has not Ma'mselle Marguerite yet -'

'No, not yet,' interrupted my pupil. 'This is the first time Mademoiselle Gartha has been up to La Rochepôt; and I mean to take her home by the other path on purpose.'

'But why do you call it the Murder-Stone?' I urged. 'Surely there is some story connected with the name!'

'Ah, ma'mselle! there you must ask the grandmother!' exclaimed the younger woman, significantly. '*Ma foi!* she knows all those things, and tells them like reading from a book!'

Thus appealed to, the *mère* Blanchet smiled, leaned back with closed eyes and folded hands, and seemed to be recalling some long-forgotten story. The daughter-in-law placed her finger on her lip in token of silence - the children gathered round with open eyes and mouths - Marie slipped noiselessly from the room, and a hush of expectation followed. Presently the grandmother looked up and nodded, and, as nearly as I can remember, told us in the following words this story of

'About a mile to the north of La Rochepôt, on that strip of meadow-land, still called the *pâturage Regnier*, stood, some seventy years ago, the comfortable farm-buildings of the père Regnier Barras. He was not badly off, that Regnier Barras, if one might judge from the education he gave his twin sons, André and Maurice, both of whom could read and write, and keep accounts as well as M. le Curé himself. Besides, you could nowhere see a nobler pair of oxen, or two prettier milch-cows than those upon his farm, and it was well known that not only had he at the least twenty-five acres of land all his own, but that he sometimes kept twenty combs of wheat in his barn all the winter through, of which he was not slow to boast, as you may imagine. He was by no means an old man, that Regnier Barras, and I remember him as well as if it were but yesterday. I was a handsome woman then, between twenty-five and thirty years of age, and just married to my dear husband, Bénoit Blanchet - heaven rest his soul!

'Well, Ma'mselle Marguerite, you see, the père Regnier died suddenly one fine Sunday morning, as the bell was ringing for mass up here in La Rochepôt. "My sons," said he, with his last breath, "the farm is not enough for two families. If you never marry, it will support you both; but if either of you take a wife, one must seek his fortune elsewhere. Never divide the little patrimony which has come down to you untouched through five generations."

'Well, the boys vowed they would not, and for some years no two brothers in the world lived more happily. To be sure, they loved each other very dearly, and had never been parted in their lives.

'As babies in the cradle, they used to lie clasped in one another's little arms - as children, they could not bear to be separated for an hour - and as young men, each thought the other the best and noblest fellow in the world. Thus they found no difficulty in obeying the last injunctions of the père Barras, but spent all their time in industry and brotherly love, caring nothing for the society of other youths; shunning the pretty girls, as if they had been wolves in disguise; and promising to keep single, and cultivate their hereditary acres without partition or disagreement all their lives long. But there were folks who laughed and said that things could not long remain thus: and they were right, for, somehow or another, André fell in love.

Now it is well known that those who are born twins love each other more tenderly than do those children of the same mother who are born with an interval of years between them; but it is also certain that when either twin comes to love one of the other sex, he loves as other men cannot love, and, successful or unsuccessful, carries his love with him to the grave. And this was the case with poor André, who dared hardly confess even to himself how it was with him, and who would not have had his trouble discovered by Maurice for all the world. How it was to end he knew not, and the worst part of it all was, that the little Geneviève was only a poor orphan who kept sheep and geese on the brothers' farm, and was more destitute than St. Mary in the desert. So he pined away, and grew so pale and wan that the neighbours whispered among themselves that either André Barras was in love, or had some sin upon his conscience, which came at last to the ears of his brother Maurice. Now Maurice was a brave, strong, generous fellow; not more generous, to be sure, than André; but more frank and gallant in his manner, and if not quite so handsome, hardier and merrier. In disposition, he was just the opposite of André. His temper was hasty; André's was placid. He was communicative; André was reserved. His was the courage of daring; André's was the courage of endurance. Thus it happened that, since their first childhood, Maurice's impetuosity had taken the lead of André's judgment, and, when anything was to be done, Maurice always was the one to act, and André the one to acquiesce. Now, had the twins loved each other one whit less dearly, this could not have lasted long; but, as Maurice valued nothing in the world so much as André's pleasure, it followed that their only quarrels were quarrels of generosity, in which Maurice generally came off the victor.

'Well, when old Jules the miller took upon himself to talk to Maurice about André, and to repeat all the foolish things that had been said, the young man staggered as if some one had struck him a heavy blow; but as soon as he had recovered his presence of mind, resolved, for the first time in his life, to be silent and observant, and find out the truth for himself.

'"If it be a sin," said he, "which our Lady forbid, I can perhaps help him to bear and expiate it. If it be love, why he must marry the woman he loves, and I will seek my fortune. I am strong, I love adventure, and I have no taste for matrimony. The land is clearly for him, and it shall go hard but I will find the means of doing well - ay, and perhaps come back some day with my pockets full of gold for André and his children!"

'But the generous fellow was after all not quite so strong as he fancied; and when he really did find out at last how it was with André, he was for a time quite broken-hearted, and could nowhere find courage to say or do the brave things he had intended. So he, in his turn, grew pale and spiritless, and there were the two brothers pining away with the same secret, and neither daring to confide it to the other.

'This state of affairs was, however, too miserable to last very long, and Maurice resolved one day to put an end to it. So he made a parcel of the things he needed, and sent it on by the carrier to Chalons; took a hundred francs, as his share of the last year's profits; and, going down to where André was ploughing in the fallow by the river, cut a good strong bough from the ash that grew beside the foot-bridge, and began shaping it with his knife.

'André was so listless that at first he scarcely seemed to see what Maurice was doing, and guided his oxen full three times up to the farther end of the fallow and back again before his curiosity was aroused. At last he stopped just a yard or two off, and said -

"'Brother, you are cutting that bough very carefully this morning."

"'Brother," replied Maurice, "I have reason to do so. This stick will be my help and companion for many a mile and many an hour. I am going a journey."

'André let fall the goad out of his hands.

"'Going a journey!" he repeated.

'Maurice stood up, brave and cheerful.

"'Yes, brother," he said, "and I have come to bid you farewell. There has been a secret between us for nearly a year past. Don't look troubled or turn away, brother. You couldn't help loving her, and I couldn't help finding it out, and it has been nobody's fault, and only the will of the good God. Now I am going upon the world, for you remember the promise we gave to our father. If one married, one must turn out. I am ready to turn out, and not only ready, but willing, if you will only give me your word to marry little Geneviève before the month is over."

"'Brother," said André, scarce able to speak for tears - "brother, you shall not go. I will think no more of *la Geneviève*, and we will return to our old life and be happy together."

'But Maurice shook his head, and would not hear of it.

'"Impossible," he replied. "My clothes are at Chalons by this time; I have a hundred francs in my pocket, and I have my stick in my hand. Above all, I have resolved, and you understand what that word means in my mouth, eh, brother? Come, let us embrace and part at once. God bless you. Think of me sometimes, and name your first boy after poor brother Maurice."

'So he embraced André, kissed the two old oxen between their great placid eyes, leaped through a gap in the hedge, and never turned to look back till he reached the top of this rock of La Rochepôt, where the fine old castle then stood as firmly as if it never was to decay or be pulled down.

'And there, when he looked round towards the *pâturage* Regnier, he saw the plough standing still in the furrow, his brother André lying stretched upon the ground in an agony of sorrow, and the hot sun shining down over the country, as if there were no such thing as grief in all the world. I have heard those say who saw him at that minute, that Maurice leaned against a tree and cried like a child; and that, when at last he turned away, he went into the chapel and knelt for a long time before the altar of the blessed Mary - so long, indeed, that the idlers who had watched him enter, grew tired and dispersed, and nobody knew when he came out, or by which road he went away.'

Here the grandmother rested for a few minutes, for she was not used to talk for long together, and the children took advantage of the interruption to express their opinion of the story.

'Well,' said Pierre, 'if I had been André, my brother should never have gone away like that on my account, and I think he was very cruel to let him!'

'And I,' said little Paul, who had stolen in again from his banishment, 'I would have done just as Maurice did, only I would have had my half of the money, and not left everything to that ungrateful André.'

'But, my child,' said his mother, reprovingly, 'you forget they had promised never to divide the farm.'

'Well, then, I would have made master André turn out, since he was the one to break the contract first! What business had he to fall in love with that ugly Geneviève?' said Paul, whose rebellious nature saw nothing but injustice in the whole transaction.

'Ugly! nobody said she was ugly!' exclaimed Clémence. 'I am sure she was a dear little thing!'

So they were just about to quarrel again about the merits and demerits of Geneviève, André, and Maurice, when the *mère* Blanchet raised her hand in token of silence, asked for a draught of the children's wine and water, and saying -

'Patience, my little ones! wait till you have heard the end,' - resumed her narrative.

'André married Geneviève before the month was out, as Maurice had desired, and though some folks thought proper to call him heartless, others considered that he did well to obey his brother's wishes. Amongst these was our good Curé, and my husband Bénoit Blanchet. How he heard the news, or where he was when he heard it, nobody ever knew, but about a week after the wedding there came a letter from Maurice, thanking André for having complied with his wishes, and calling down every blessing on the new-married pair. This letter had been given to one of the villagers by a travelling pedlar who was passing along the high-road. It contained no address, and did not even hint at his plans for the future. Of course, everybody had his own notion about it. Some said he was gone to Lyons, some to Marseilles, and some would have it that he crossed the Jura, and hired himself among the farmers of Switzerland; but André shook his head at all of them, and consoled himself by saying -

'"Maurice is a wise lad, and as kind as he is wise. He will not write till he is settled, and so soon as he has good news to tell me, I shall know where he is."

'But he was mistaken! months went by. Years went by. Children were born in the little farm-house. Geneviève grew matronly, and André came to middle life; but never, never, never again came letter, or message, or news from Maurice!'

At this point in the story we all drew nearer - Marguerite turned pale and held her breath, and the children burst into exclamations of curiosity.

'Ah, my little ones,' said the grandmother, 'you may well wonder what had become of the brave Maurice! Never was he forgotten in La Rochepôt, and never met half-a-dozen neighbours round a winter hearth, but his name came up, and the story of his exile was talked over, and over, and over again. As for André, nothing seemed to go well with him. He was always pining about Maurice, always reproaching himself, and every day getting poorer and poorer. His health failed, his crops failed, and, above all, his courage failed. He said he felt as if there were a curse upon him, and, indeed, it seemed like it, for year after year his family increased, and his substance dwindled away. First of all he borrowed money at seed-time, and, when his harvest was blighted, sold so many roods of land to pay the debt. Then he borrowed again, and then he parted with the pasture-land. When he had parted with the pasture-land, he had no food for his cows, and sold them also. In short, from one step to another, from straitened means to poverty, from poverty to want, from want to real destitution, descended the unlucky André and his family. At last, land and stock were both gone, and, except the half-ruined house in which they lived, nothing remained that they could call their own. It was now just fifteen years after Maurice had gone away. André was completely ruined, and my husband and I often feared that the little ones down at the meadow-farm had nothing to eat. To be sure, we did call them in and give them a slice of bread and a bunch of raisins whenever we saw any of them up at the village; but that was seldom enough, and André was now grown so morose that none of his old neighbours dared go near the house to see how matters went with them.

'Well, the autumn came, and the vine-gathering was over, and André's wife fell sick of the fever.

'"Come, husband," said I, "if you are too delicate to go down to the meadow-farm, I am not; and that poor good Geneviève shall never lie there sick without a soul to nurse her. You may do as you like; but it would need another than André Barras to frighten me."

'So I put a couple of new white loaves, a basin of soup, and a plateful of *bouilli* in my basket, and away I went. Happily there was no one in the house but the two youngest children, and poor wasted Geneviève on her mattress in the upper room. I talked to her, however, as hopefully as I could - got her to swallow a cupful of soup and a few morsels of bread - attended to the children, and put the room a little in order before André came back. I own I did feel a little uncomfortable when I heard his heavy tread in the room below; but to make the best of it, and to avoid any dispute before the sick woman, I went down to meet him.

'"Good-day, neighbour," said I. "I am sorry to find your wife so ill."

'He turned round, fierce as a wolf, and said -

"Who are you? What do you want?"

'He had his gun in his hand; his face was haggard; and his eye wandering. He looked twenty years older than when I last saw him, and his very voice was changed and hoarse.

"I am Elise Blanchet," I replied, calmly, "and I have come to see if I can be of use to Geneviève."

"No one can be of use here," he said, gloomily. "Go away, and never come back."

"I shall do neither," said I. "Your wife is very ill, and unless somebody sees after her, she has little chance of getting better."

"She had better die, then," he muttered. "I wish we were all dead, every one of us!"

"Hush!" I exclaimed, hardly thinking of what I was saying. "Hush, André Barras! Are you not afraid that the spirit of your brother will hear you?"

'He staggered back, and put his hand wildly to his head.

"Maurice!" he said, "Maurice!"

"Yes, Maurice," I replied, hoping to turn the minute to advantage, "Maurice, who went away and died abroad for your sake! How dare you be so hopeless? how dare you be such a coward after that? Be a man, and behave like a man, and try to support your family in some honest way."

'But André's eyes were fixed upon the door, and he never heard one word of my reproaches.

"I shall see him again before I die!" he said, shaking his head mournfully. "He lives - I know that he lives. How shall I face him? What shall I say to him of the inheritance he gave up? Alas! what is to be done? What is to be done?"

'He spoke as if he were in a dream, and not to me, but to himself.

"How do you know that he lives?" I asked, eagerly.

'He drew himself to his full height, and looked up into the sky.

"Because," said he, solemnly, "if my brother had died abroad, I should have seen his spirit."

'And with that he passed by as if he did not even see me, and went straight out of the door.

'Well now, to make a long story short, I did all I could for poor Geneviève, and she slowly recovered. Then two of the children took the fever; and then I fell sick also, which was worst of all, for not another soul in La Rochepôt would have anything to do with André Barras. And the truth is, that his reputation grew worse and worse every day, and among all the bad things laid at his door, it must be acknowledged that a good many were true. Having neither land nor stock, he depended on his gun for the support of Geneviève and the children, and was not, I fear, very particular as to the game he shot. Sometimes it was a tame duck, sometimes a turkey, sometimes a young lamb that had strayed from the fold; but there was never any exact proof, you see, and knowing that the mother was still weakly, and the children sick of the fever, none of us cared to search too closely after the offender.

'Then came the report that two of his children had died, and that Geneviève, though the fever had left her, was growing feebler every day. And all this time I also was in my bed, and it was hard to say if I should die or live. You will understand, then, that all I am now going to tell you happened when I myself was sick, and that I am repeating what was afterwards told to me.

'It was soon after the grape-gathering that the sickness broke out in our part of the country. Geneviève had been one of the first to take it, and I one of the last; but from first to last it lingered about the meadow-farm, and as quickly as one of them got better, another fell ill. Two of the children were dead; Geneviève was sinking fast; the other three little ones were ailing; and, to make matters as bad as they could be, the first snow fell, and the bitter cold set in earlier than usual. Then, what with seeing his wife and children starving, and what with his own sorrows and needs, André grew desperate, and no longer cared what he did, or what became of him. Indeed, it seemed as if misfortune had made quite a ferocious brigand of the proud and serious farmer. Proud he was still; but wickedly proud, since he would have killed himself and all his family sooner than ask a neighbour for a loaf. Yet he was not too proud to steal our poultry, or take our turnips out of the fields by night. His seriousness had become savageness, and it was said, by those who happened to catch glimpses of him now and then, that he looked more like a wild man than a Christian soul.

'At last there came a day of what we call "black frost" - which is the bitterest cold of all, and worse than even the cold that comes with snow and ice. The ground was hard frozen, the sky low and leaden, and the bitter wind blowing from the east. On that day, when André went into the woods, he felt that he also was going to take the fever. His head swam, the ground seemed to rock beneath his feet, and his gun felt so heavy in his hand that he was forced to trail it after him. He went a long way without any success. If a bird did cross his path, he missed it; for his hand shook and everything swam before his eyes. So, after many hours of wandering, he turned his face homewards, and found himself close under the castle of La Rochepôt, on that sheltered path which winds round the hill midway between the foot and the summit. It was by this time two o'clock in the afternoon, and a heavy sleet began to fall. Worn out, sick at heart, and racked by fever-pains, the unfortunate André longed to crawl home and die. But he had no strength to go farther; so he lay down shiveringly among the bushes. And here he would have lain all night, but that he presently remembered the hollow rock a little way down, and so contrived to drag himself on till he reached it. It was a great gray rock, of the same kind as that on which the castle is built, and was hollowed into a shallow cave. It remains so to this day, and nobody knows how it came to be of that shape. Some say it was cut away to make a niche for the image of Christ and the Holy Mary; and some, that it was used as a sentry-box in the old warlike times, hundreds of years ago. But that is all guessing, and for my part, ma'mselle, I think it came so by nature, like all other caves, and never was anything else than a shelter for the wild birds and the drifting leaves. Well, it was into this place, at all events, that the wretched André crept, thinking to stay there for the night, and get home, somehow, on the morrow; so he lay with his gun beside him and his head propped on his hand, listening to the howling wind, and watching the clouds that pursued each other across the dreary sky.

"'Who knows?" said he to himself. "Perhaps when to-morrow comes, I shall be too ill to stir. Nobody comes this way in winter, and if I were to cry, nobody would hear me! Perhaps I shall die here, like a dog, of starvation and fever."

'His heart was full of bitterness - so full that he even doubted the justice and mercy of the good God, and cursed himself for ever having been born, which is the wickedest thing a human being can do, my dear little grandchildren, and brings down upon us the most terrible punishment.'

'Was André punished?' interrupted little Paul, very eagerly.

'Indeed he was, *mon enfant*,' replied the grandmother, solemnly. 'Have patience, and you will soon hear in what manner.

'It was beginning to get dusk before the sleet-storm abated, and still André crouched in the hollow rock, hating himself and all mankind, and even the good God who made him. And, every now and then, he got up and went to the verge of the pathway, where it overhung the by-road underneath, hoping that he might see some one go past, and yet hardly daring to ask himself what he should do or say if his wishes were fulfilled. Not that it was very likely they should be, for the by-road was but a bridle-path between Chalons and Montrocher, known only to the people of the country, and very little frequented, except by those who wanted to take a short cut from one town to the other, or who were on their way down to the mead-ow-farm - and, for that matter, I believe there was not a soul in La Rochepôt, just then, who would not have gone round by the road, even if it were ten miles out of the way, sooner than venture past the house of André Barras, over which, they said, a curse was surely hanging!

'However, it was the will of the good God that a traveller should pass down that road that afternoon. A traveller mounted on a good horse, wrapped in a handsome overcoat, and whistling merri-ly as he came along - never dreaming that he had lost his way, as no doubt he had, or he would not have been there. Well, when André saw him coming along so gaily, he felt as if that man were his bitter-est enemy, so envious, and selfish, and wicked had his heart become! That any man should be happy when he was miserable, warm when he was cold, healthy when he and all his family were dying, seemed like a wrong done to himself; so, seizing his gun with a sudden strength, he leaned over the bank, and waited eagerly. The rider came up fast and fearlessly - a brave, hearty-looking man, with a couple of saddle-bags before him, well filled, no doubt, with money and valuables. The sight of these decided André. He waited till the other had ridden past, took aim (like a cowardly assassin) at his back, and fired.

'Yes, *mes enfants* - fired; and this time, alas! his hand was steady and his aim true. The murdered man fell like a stone, and lay in the road, with one foot entangled in the stirrup; but his trembling horse stood quite still beside him and never stirred an inch, even though

André came clambering down the bank with his gun still in his hand.

To fling the gun aside, secure the saddle-bags, and free the traveller's foot from the stirrup was the work of an instant; for André had the sudden strength of a madman, and was mad, I have no doubt, with sickness and misery. He then pulled open his victim's coat, rifled him of his watch and pocket-book, and, laying his hand on his breast, found his heart still beating. A diabolical idea occurred to him. He snatched up his gun again, resolved to batter out the last lingering breath of life; and had raised his arm to do it, when the traveller opened his eyes, and looked straight at him.

'The murderer cannot face the eye of his victim; and before this glance André staggered and trembled. The traveller made an effort to lift himself on his elbow; but he fell back as often as he attempted it, and all the time kept his eyes on the assassin.

'"Villain," he gasped, "you have murdered me! God forgive you - at your last moment - as - as Maurice Barras forgives - you!"

'André uttered a great cry of despair.

'"Maurice Barras!" he said, stretching out his hands before him like a blind man. "What do you know of Maurice Barras?"

'The traveller could not speak; but, lying there in a pool of his own blood, pointed feebly to himself.

'"God help me," said André, falling on his knees. "God help me! My brother!"

'A convulsion passed over the dying man, and he sat upright in his place. His lips moved as if he would have spoken - his hand seemed to invoke a last blessing on his murderer - and then he fell back, stiff, and quite dead, with André still kneeling beside him.

'And so it really was. After fifteen years of exile, after fifteen years of hard toil and faithful friendship, Maurice returned at last, as he had himself foretold, with his pockets full of gold for André's children - only to be murdered within a couple of miles of his home by André's hand!

'And now tell me, little ones, was not André punished for his wickedness against the good God?'

The other children were awed and silent; but little Paul looked up with large startled eyes, and whispered an eager question.

'Grandmother - was André guillotined?'

The *mère* Blanchet shook her head.

'He died of the fever within two or three days,' she said;

'having first of all crawled up to the house of the Curé and confessed his crime. Had he recovered, he would certainly have died for the murder of his brother; but no doubt the good God thought him sufficiently punished.'

'And Geneviève and the children?' asked Marguerite.

'Geneviève died also; but the three remaining little ones recovered, and were sent to an asylum in Paris, where they were brought up to useful trades, and kept in ignorance of the dreadful story of their youth. And now, Ma'mselle Marguerite, I think I have told you all about André and Maurice, and explained to you how it is that the hollow rock, which sheltered the assassin, has ever since been called the Murder-Stone.'

We were all very silent after the story was ended, and presently Marguerite rose to take leave.

'For,' said she, with an effort to be gay, 'it will be soon dusk, and I am sure, if we delay much longer, I shall be afraid of meeting the ghost of Maurice!'

The grandmother looked grave.

'It is not well to speak lightly of the spirits, Ma'mselle Marguerite,' she said, with uplifted finger. 'They sometimes appear to those who heedlessly name them!'

'Have *you* ever seen a ghost, *mère* Blanchet?'

'Never, ma'mselle - and yet ...'

'And yet what?'

'And yet,' said the grandmother hesitatingly, 'I have heard that - that towards dusk, on the bridle-path beneath the Murder-Stone, a - a man has been seen riding past ...'

'On a good horse, and wrapped in a handsome overcoat!' exclaimed Marguerite maliciously, quoting the very words of the story. 'Oh, Madame Blanchet, this is excellent! A ghost on horseback, too!'

The old lady shook her head, and made the sign of the cross; but Marguerite only laughed again as we were crossing the threshold, and said -

'Adieu, *mère* Blanchet. 'If I meet the ghost, I will let you know!'

The grandmother waved her hand, and the children crowded round the door to shout another farewell. Just where the pathway took a turn among the apple-trees, we found Claude and Marie standing, side by side, against the well. We came upon them so

suddenly that they had no time to escape; but stood aside, blushing-
ly, to let us pass.

'Ah, Marie,' said Marguerite, 'you have lost such a pretty story!'

Marie courtesied again without speaking; but as we moved
away, glanced up at her lover, half confidingly, half shyly, with eyes
that seemed to tell how far rather she would listen to him than to the
best tale that ever was told.

Our path lay down the hill-side. It was getting dusk. We were
both in a thoughtful mood, and found ourselves in sight of the
Murder-Stone almost before we were aware of it. The *mère* Blanchet
had described it exactly - a beetling, sullen crag of dark-gray stone,
hollowed away into a shallow cavern, overgrown with gray and silver
lichens, creeping plants, and ferns. A savage spot, shut in by bushy
trees, and overlooking a narrow road that wound along the side of
the hill, and was lost in the curve of the valley beyond!

Marguerite shuddered.

'This, then, was the very spot,' she said, almost in a whisper.
'Oh, mademoiselle, what a fearful story!'

'And yet, Marguerite, you jested about it a few minutes ago!'

She hung her head, and looked confused.

'I am very giddy at times,' she said penitently. 'I do not believe
in ghosts, it is true; but I fear I was wrong, for all that. It was too deep
a tragedy for smiles.'

One could never be long angry with Marguerite!

'Never mind, *petite*,' I said; 'to be giddy is not to be unfeeling.'

'Indeed it is not, mademoiselle - for - for I am sure no one
could have felt that story more than I felt it! Besides, it was so well
related by the *mère* Blanchet! Why, as I stand here, the whole scene
comes before me. I see André, haggard and malignant, with his gun
beside him. I see him start up at the sound of the horse's hoofs on
the frosty road, and part the bushes with his eager hands. I hear ...
Heavens, mademoiselle! what noise is that?'

She jumped back, startled and pale, and flung herself into my
arms.

I listened. There was no mistaking what the sound really was,
and I confess that, for the moment, my own heart beat faster than
usual. Something in the dusk, the silence, and the spot, seemed to
turn all the currents of my blood.

'It is some one riding down the road,' I said, trying to speak cheerfully. 'What a strange coincidence!'

Marguerite trembled from head to foot, and clung to me like a frightened child.

'It is not a coincidence!' she murmured.

The sounds approached. The rider, whoever he might be, was coming at a slow trot, and every clang of his horse's hoofs echoed sharply along the defile.

The regularity and resonance of these steps cured me of my terrors.

'Nonsense, little one,' I said, gaily. 'Ghosts don't make so much noise; take my word for it. Let us peep through that opening in the bushes, and see who it is.'

He came - a fine broad-shouldered man, sitting his horse with a certain careless grace that bespoke the accomplished rider, and followed at some distance by a large dog of the St. Bernard breed. Deep in thought, his head drooping, his eyes bent on the ground, his hand resting lightly on his thigh, he rode on, and would have passed out of sight without farther incident, save for his four-footed follower, who, scenting the proximity of lookers-on, paused and barked close under our retreat. The gentleman checked his horse, and turned in the saddle.

'What, Cæsar, is that you?' he said, sternly. 'Did I not forbid you to come out to-day, sir?'

The dog whined and lay down in the road, the very type of submission; but his master would not be conciliated.

'Go back, sir,' he said, resolutely; pointing up the road. 'Go back directly.'

Cæsar whined again, and rubbed his nose in the dust, but never stirred an inch. His master showed him the whip.

'Will you go?' he asked, slightly raising his voice, which, strange to say, sounded familiar to me.

'Will you go, I say?'

Dogs have a language as intelligible as speech and on this occasion Cæsar lay and looked at his master, with a countenance that said, as plainly as words could have uttered - 'I won't go back. You may beat me, if you like; but I won't go back to-day.' And the gentleman understood him too, for he rode his horse up to a tree by the way-side, deliberately dismounted, tied him up by the bridle, and, testing the flexibility of his whip by bringing it down sharply through the air, said, coldly - 'Very well, sir, we shall see,' and walked up to the rebellious Cæsar, still lying in the road.

That last tone - that momentary glimpse of his upturned face, as he glanced towards the darkening sky, was enough. I knew him now. It was M. Hamel.

He stood over the dog with uplifted arm.

'Cæsar,' he said, in the same pitiless tone, 'you are a good dog; but you have disobeyed me, and you must suffer for it.'

Cæsar whined anticipatively, and the first blow fell, and the second, and the third, and half-a-dozen, each sharp and steady, and cruel, as if they came from the hand of an executioner. At the sixth his master paused.

'Will you go now?' he said. But Cæsar uttered a low pitiful cry, and laid his nose upon M. Hamel's foot, imploring clemency. The latter looked at his watch, and bared his wrist.

'As you please,' he said. 'I will stay here all night, but I will conquer you.'

And he struck again and again, the whip curling round the dog's palpitating body at every blow, and those piteous yells of almost human agony following after each. I could look no longer. I felt sick and cold by turns, and drawing back with a shudder, saw Marguerite standing behind me pale and motionless, with fixed eyes and parted lips, and a countenance so rigid that it startled me to look upon it.

'Marguerite! Marguerite!' I whispered, taking her in my arms, and trying to soothe her. 'Look up, my darling. Look at me.'

Her features relaxed, and her eyes filled with tears.

'Oh! mademoiselle,' she said, in a low, quivering voice, 'how cruel he is! Listen to him. How cruel!'

At this moment the sound of the lashes ceased. I peeped out again. Cæsar was gone, and M. Hamel was untying his horse. When he had done so, he looked up the road; rubbed his right arm twice or thrice; laughed a low, short, mocking laugh; mounted lightly, and cantered away as if nothing had occurred to interrupt his progress. We watched him down the hill, and along the valley, till the curve of the road hid him from our sight. Then I turned to Marguerite.

'Well,' said I, with a deep breath, 'it is getting dark, and we had better be going.'

So she took my arm, and we went home without exchanging another word.

CHAPTER XXVI

THE STORM

The vintage had progressed favourably, and was approaching its completion, when the wind veered round to the west, and the weather changed. It became oppressively warm and cloudy. A stagnant moisture weighed down the atmosphere, and the barometer threatened us with storms.

All day long the gatherers toiled with redoubled activity; but, toil as they might, unless the rain kept off for forty-eight hours longer, M. Alexander must lose the produce of two of his most valuable vineyards. Towards dusk the clouds grew denser, and the heat more stifling. Low ominous moanings were drifted by every now and then upon the languid air, and night came on before the last waggon was unloaded in the court-yard.

We met at dinner, and the meal was two hours later than usual. M. Alexander came in with the second course. He was gloomy and absent; referred several times to the note-book which lay open beside his plate; had scarcely any appetite; and paid no attention when spoken to.

Monsieur Delahaye was, on the contrary, rather more conversational than usual, and entertained us with no end of flowery speeches. His own grapes had been gathered in at the first, and it is easy to philosophize on the misfortunes of others.

'Pre-eminently picturesque affair, the vintage, mademoiselle,' said he to me, leaning back, and picking his teeth by the aid of an elegant little machine incrusted with turquoises. 'The women are not unprepossessing, and I yesterday observed a Normandy family which was positively handsome. - Ahem! Handsome, upon my unimpeachable honour.'

'I saw them, papa!' cried Marguerite eagerly. 'There are two grown up brothers, a sister, and a little boy, who is as beautiful as an angel!'

'I must aver that the - ahem!- the latter individual escaped my observation,' said Monsieur, with great suavity; 'but the sister reminded me of the celebrated Baroness de Renneville - a glorious creature, and one who carried the art of dress into the - ahem! - the Regions of Imagination! She was the most renowned beauty of her day, and I had the honour to be her most devoted servant. We led the fashions, mademoiselle. We tyrannized over the toilettes of the *beau monde*. We abolished buckles, and we gave the last blow to powder.'

I bowed, and tried to look interested. Monsieur sipped his wine and continued.

'I remember,' said he, 'that upon one occasion the *Gazette des Modes* was polite and discriminating enough to designate us the Reigning Sovereigns of the Empire of Fashion; for which I present-ed the editor with an enamelled snuff-box, and a complimentary poem. Charming, was it not? The Reigning ...'

'Raining!' interrupted uncle Alexander, starting abruptly from his reverie. 'Is it raining already?'

Monsieur smiled compassionately.

'You are terribly absent, my dear Alexander,' he observed, languidly. 'The weather was, of all topics, the remotest from my thoughts.'

'Then it wouldn't be if forty thousand francs of your money were depending on it!' retorted uncle Alexander, surlily.

Monsieur sighed, and peeled a peach.

'Commercial - horribly commercial!' he murmured, half-aloud.

Uncle Alexander shrugged his shoulders, pushed back his chair, and stalked to the window.

'We shall have it before many hours are over,' he said, casting a rapid glance at the sky.

'And you will lose forty thousand francs!' exclaimed Marguerite, with childish dismay. 'Won't you be very sorry, uncle Alexander?'

'I shall not be very pleased, monkey. But there may be worse consequences than that to follow!'

'Worse!'

'Yes - much worse;' and uncle Alexander paced gloomily before the open window. 'If - if the rain lasts to-morrow,' he continued, reluctantly, 'the men must tread in the cellars.'

Marguerite uttered a low shuddering cry, and buried her face in her hands. Madame looked distressed.

'I thought,' said she, falteringly, 'that - that you would never allow it again, Alexander. Could not the barn ...'

'The barn is too distant,' returned he, 'and the work too far advanced. Claude is positive that fermentation has begun.'

'Alas!' said Madame, rising from table and leaving her dessert untasted. 'Last year a life was lost; and three years ago ...'

Uncle Alexander recoiled as if from a blow, and turned lividly pale.

'Thunder of God!' said he, hoarsely, 'do I need to be reminded of it?'

Madame looked alarmed.

'Forgive me,' she said. 'I - I meant it as no reproach to you. You did all that was generous, and the survivors ...'

Uncle Alexander stopped her with an impatient gesture.

'Silence, sister-in-law,' he interrupted. 'Silence. The new outhouses shall be built by this time next year. Would to heaven that they were built now! Let us drop the subject.'

He turned away and leaned out of the window. Marguerite came up, and whispered in my ear:-

'The grape-juice gives out some bad gas, mademoiselle, which does no harm in the open air; but is terribly hurtful in the cellars. We have had four men die from it. Uncle Alexander cannot bear to hear it named.'

She then stole lovingly to his side, and a dead silence followed. Monsieur finished his dessert and despatched a couple of glasses of Maraschino with infinite gusto. He then went over to the piano, and began practising the shake.

'Hush!' cried uncle Alexander, and held up a warning hand.

He had scarcely spoken, when, in the midst of the sullen calm without, there came a fierce, shrill, solitary gust of wind, followed by a low muttering of very distant thunder.

'Do you hear that?' said he. 'Do you hear that?'

Monsieur Deláhaye struck a fresh chord, and yawned with aristocratic indifference.

'My good brother,' said he, composedly. 'I am not deaf.'

Uncle Alexander surveyed the piano, the performer, and the

exercises with a scowl of undisguised contempt.

'I wish with all my heart that I were!' he retorted sharply, and marched out of the room.

It was very dull in the *salon*, and I had found a volume of Crebillon on an upper shelf of the bookcase in my bedroom; so I slipped away after dinner, lit my night-lamp, and settled down to an hour of quiet reading.

The storm had not yet come up, and I began to hope that it might not travel in our direction at all. It was so hot, that I sat with door and window wide open; and so still, that the tender tongue of flame within the globe of my lamp never wavered for an instant. Thus the time flew, and it was ten o'clock before I was aware of it.

Suddenly, and without any kind of warning, like the tornado of the tropics, a rush of wind poured through the casement, blowing the curtains in, and fiercely fluttering the pages of my book. Another moment, and a blaze of livid light burst over the landscape - seemed to fill all the room - lit up for one brief moment every tree and shrub, and stripped the darkness from the mountains round - was overtaken by a deafening explosion of thunder just above the house, and succeeded by a strange and awful calm, without a sound or an echo.

I flung the book down and ran to the window. The sky - low, dense, and starless - seemed almost to rest upon the tree-tops. The wind was gone. The air was hot, and a silence, as it were of death, had fallen upon everything. Not a leaf stirred - not a bat flitted - not a sign of life was abroad. I took up my lamp and went down stairs. I peeped into the *salon*, and saw them all three sitting silently together. The outer door was open. I could not resist the temptation of venturing out. I removed the globe from the lamp - passed noiselessly down the passage, and stepped out on the little terrace above the court-yard. As I had anticipated! Steadily and brightly burned the flame, casting a wide circle on the flags round about my feet, and not betraying by the lightest tremor the presence of the gale which had just now shaken the house to its foundations!

It was an awful pause. I seemed to be standing under a huge black dome. I breathed with difficulty. I expected the storm to burst every moment, and yet a strange fascination bound me to the spot.

The lull continued unbroken. I could hear the very ticking of my watch. I took it out, and found it was already twenty-five minutes past ten. All at once, measured, distinct, and solemn, the chapel-bell began to toll.

I could scarcely believe my ears. A service at this hour! I listened with suspended breath, and recognized the very *timbre* of those keen vibrations. The sounds throbbed past me on the air. I could almost hear the bell swing from side to side in the little Romanesque belfry!

'Mademoiselle is courageous,' said a mocking voice close beside me.

I started and turned. It was M. Hamel.

'The tempest will be up in less than five minutes,' he continued. 'I had no intention of coming to-night; but I had also no inclination for a drenching, and, as I was passing home through La Rochepôt, I thought I might as well push on here for shelter. I have just ridden my horse into M. Delahaye's stables.'

'You did well,' I replied, with a slight shiver. 'It will be fearful presently.'

'Yes,' said he, carelessly. 'A grand performance, no doubt. But hark! that respectable old St. Christopher is just about to be supplicated in behalf of the vines. He is the lightning-conductor of the parish!'

He laughed, and his laugh jarred with the solemnity of the moment.

'It is a simple and pious superstition,' I replied, 'and though it be worth nothing ...'

'Oh, I beg your pardon,' interrupted M. Hamel. 'It is worth ten francs to the curé!'

'I cannot help thinking,' said I, pointedly, 'that a member of your profession should be among the last to place such matters in a ridiculous point of view.'

'Not at all. It is precisely because I am behind the scenes that I am so far *désillusionné*.'

'Oh, Monsieur Hamel!' I exclaimed, almost involuntarily.

He laughed again, and tossed his curls back, defiantly.

'Ah, bah!' said he, lightly. 'What would you have? *C'est mon métier!*'

'I am sorry for it. Perhaps, had you chosen some other path ...'

'I should not have walked in this! - *n'est-ce pas?*'

'How can you make a jest of it?'

'Because I find it too much trouble to be serious. But, stay! here comes the storm, and that will be no jesting matter, I assure you!'

As he spoke, a tremendous sheet of lightning changed the whole sky into one broad field of fire. Then a volley of quick thunder shook the very ground beneath our feet, a deluge poured from the heavy clouds, and the tempest began in earnest.

I retreated precipitately into the passage, and M. Hamel after me.

'Mademoiselle is no Ajax, I perceive,' said he, with one of his inscrutable smiles.

'Why, what did Ajax do?'

'He defied the storm, and was consumed by lightning for his impiety.'

'And a very proper ending too!' I replied, half-laughing, and half-terrified; for the flashes were becoming incessant. 'I leave you to imitate him if you like. For my own part, I shall take refuge in the *salon*!'

With this I ran in, and he presently followed me.

The supper was laid; but they were all too much alarmed to eat it. In the farthest corner shrank the little trembling group of servants. Monsieur leaned back in his easy-chair, very pale and silent. Madame had just enough self-possession to welcome the new arrival, and to fill out glasses of Burgundy for the sustainment of everybody's spirits; but Marguerite hid her face in the sofa-cushions, and would not look up, even to please M. Hamel.

Without, the scene was fearful. The flashes succeeded each other at intervals of about twenty or thirty seconds; sometimes running in long quivering lines round and round the horizon; sometimes bursting forth in all directions, as if from a fiery ball high in the heavens; sometimes springing upward from the earth, and bounding along the valley and up the mountain-side with a terrible living energy, such as I had never seen before. Simultaneously with every flash, crackling in sharp and sudden explosions like the opening of a battery, came the discharges of thunder. Now and then, during the brief lulls, we heard the snorting of the horses in the stables, the whining of the hounds, the fall of trees torn up by the hurricane, and the rushing of the water-courses along the steep and stony road.

> 'Such sheets of fire, such bursts of horrid thunder,
> Such groans of roaring wind and rain, I never
> Remember to have heard.'

Finding no one else inclined to listen to him, M. Hamel persisted in talking to me. It was an honour that I could have dispensed with very readily, and one to which I was by no means accustomed; but he followed me to the window, beside which I had crouched in trembling admiration, and I found it impossible to avoid him.

'This is elementary art on a grand scale,' said he, with the same levity as before.

'I never beheld anything so magnificent,' I replied, seriously. 'Heavens! what a flash was that!'

He shrugged his shoulder.

'Bah!' said he. 'They do it almost as well at the theatres.'

I was silent from very indignation. He saw it, and laughed aloud.

'I really believe,' said he, 'that I have succeeded!'

'Succeeded! In what way?'

'In inspiring you with the worst possible opinion of me. That is the precise expression of countenance that I meant to produce.'

'Upon my word, sir,' I replied, with some impatience, 'you choose your occasion badly. This is not a moment for trifling.'

'All moments are alike to the philosopher,' said he; 'and I am a disciple of Lavater.'

'Then I beg that you will not practise upon me,' I answered shortly, and turned away.

He let me alone for a few minutes after this; but pursued me, by-and-by, to the other window. He then began talking again; but in a different strain, and with the endeavour to please.

He spoke of art, of books, of scenes abroad; and related an anecdote of wild adventure in a tempest among the Apennines. How brilliant he could be, and how fascinating! Absorbed in the interest of his story, and carried away by the picturesque vigour of his language, I soon forgot, not only my temporary vexation, but the storm itself; and not till he came to a pause, and I found the whole room listening, did I even observe that the fury of the wind and rain had abated, and the lightning altogether subsided.

Amid the silence that followed this narrative the door opened, and uncle Alexander walked in. He looked pale, and stern, and weary, and his hair and clothes were as wet as if he had been in the river.

'Sister-in-law,' said he, with a shiver. 'Give me some brandy.'

Marguerite flew to bring it, and a chorus of questions burst from every lip.

'*Ciel!* How wet you are!' cried Madame. 'Where have you been?'

'What damage to the vines?' asked M. Hamel, with a quick appreciation of the truth.

'*Grand Dieu!* what a state to be in!' shrieked Monsieur Delahaye, recoiling into a distant corner. 'Don't come near me - you'll give me cold, and I shall have another attack of rheumatism!'

But M. Alexander never opened his lips till Marguerite came back. He then half filled a tumbler with cognac, drank it at a draught, lit his chamber-candle, smiled grimly, and said -

'There will be no treading in the cellars to-morrow, and no gathering. The Romanée grapes are all destroyed; two of the horses are dead; and the new wine is working in the vats.'

'Alas! my inestimable Alexander, what will you do?' cried Monsieur, keeping at a respectful distance, but bringing out his pocket-handkerchief very pathetically.

'Go to bed,' growled that unromantic individual, and walked off at once, without saying 'good-night' to any one.

It was now past midnight, and a steady rain was all that remained of the tempest. Late as it was, we sat down and supped, and after supper M. Hamel went away. A bed had been prepared for him, but he could not stay.

'Tempt me not!' said he, gaily. 'Tempt me not, I beseech you! To-morrow morning I must marry a pair of lovers from St. Nys; and, wishing to do as I would be done by, I dare not disappoint them. Adieu!'

With this he summoned Claude from the kitchen, himself assisted to bring his horse from the stable, shouted a last cheery good-night, and rode away in the rain.

———

CHAPTER XXVII

THE VINE-FEAST

It was but too true. The Romanée grapes were literally thrashed out, and as there was nothing left to gather, the vintage came to an abrupt conclusion.

It was a dull, uncertain morning; bitterly cold and raw, and visited by frequent showers. We went out towards noon, and met traces of last night's calamity at every turn. Here lay a huge tree, uprooted by the hurricane - here a charred and blackened shed that had been struck by lightning. Yonder stood a group of labourers round a broken tumbril; and in the court-yard of the dwelling-house a double relay of treaders crushed out the last waggon-loads of yesterday's gathering. We passed on to the vineyards. They were scarcely recognizable! The vines were beaten down, torn up by the roots, buried under great blocks of rock and fragments of timber, and choked by driftings of rubbish and rich mould. All those sloping lands which lay so temptingly to the sun round about the skirts of St. Christopher's mountain were seamed by water-courses and stripped of their produce. The peaceful stream that bounded the village was swollen to a torrent. The lanes and field-paths were ancle-deep in mire. The miller was repairing his broken wheel - the cottagers were lamenting their lost poultry - the farmers and vine-growers paced disconsolately amid their desolated crops, and cast up the sum of their disasters.

Altogether it was a dreary scene, and we were glad when another shower came to send us home.

What with the groups of lookers-on, the row of empty and loaded waggons, and the *pressoir* with its temporary awning, beneath which a crowd of flushed and weary treaders were steadily tramping, the court-yard presented, in spite of the shower, a gay and animated picture. There was uncle Alexander with his great red cotton umbrella, and there was Claude helping to unlade, and there was the great cellar-door standing wide open, showing glimpses of the gigantic vats down below, and of the garden-path beyond.

Marguerite ran lightly up the steps; but stopped suddenly when she reached the top.

'Oh, mademoiselle!' she cried, 'here he is! here he is!'

'Here who is?'

'Why, my little Normandy boy, to be sure!'

I went up, and found her bending over a tiny object crouched down upon the threshold. It was a small, sad-looking child, with long light hair, and large lustrous black eyes. His clothing was wet and scanty, his head was bare, and his little naked feet were thrust into a pair of *sabots* two sizes too large for him. He seemed neither confident nor shy; but very languid.

'You might have found a drier shelter, *mon petit*,' said Marguerite, kindly.

The boy just looked up, but never stirred a limb.

'I am not sheltering,' said he, 'I am resting.'

'Are you tired, then?'

'Yes; I am very tired.'

'And what has tired you?'

'The storm. It kept me awake all night.'

Marguerite took up the little listless hand, and when she let it go, it fell heavily down, as if there were no life in it.

'Your clothes are very wet,' said she.

'The rain came into the barn.'

Marguerite turned to me with the tears in her eyes.

'Alas!' she exclaimed, 'he lay all night in the barn, wet, and sleepless, and frightened - for you were frightened, were you not?'

'Yes, we were all frightened,' replied the child, leaning his head against the door, and closing his eyes.

'And what is your name?'

'François.'

'Well, then, little François, come with me into the kitchen, and dry your clothes by the fire.'

He shook his head.

'I am well here,' said he, wearily.

'No, no; you must not stay in the rain. If you will come with me, I know where to find some nice soup, and a slice of cake.'

An expression of languid annoyance passed over his face.

'I am not hungry,' he said, with an impatient gesture.

I put Marguerite aside, and passed my hand over the boy's forehead. I then pressed my fingers on his wrist.

'He has taken cold,' I said, 'and should be put to bed immediately.'

'He shall have the little bed in the attic,' cried Marguerite; 'and

I will nurse him myself!'

But François turned his head sullenly aside.

'I won't go to bed,' said he. 'I won't leave sister Babette! I am not ill, if you please, and I only want to be quiet!'

I gave Marguerite a glance.

'I will speak to mamma!' cried she, and darted into the house.

An angry flash shot from the boy's dark eyes; and though I tried to soothe him, he refused to utter another word.

'Would he be more tractable,' thought I, 'if we called in the aid of "sister Babette"?'

Full of this idea, I cast an eager glance into the court-yard. Uncle Alexander was gone; but Claude was still there, so I ran down and sought him out from amid a busy knot of *vignerons* and a labyrinth of baskets.

A touch of the gold-laced cap, a ready smile, and an attentive silence greeted my hurried explanation.

'*La fille Babette* and the rest are all up at the St. Gervais fields,' replied Claude; 'but I can send to them if ma'mselle pleases.'

'The child is certainly far from well,' I said, hesitating.

Claude shrugged his shoulders.

'Ma'mselle should have seen the barn this morning. *Parbleu!* the water lay half a foot deep in places.'

A light touch on my arm, and a breathless - 'What have you done with him, mademoiselle?' diverted my attention in another direction.

It was Marguerite, flushed with running.

'What have you done with him? Where is he? Mamma consents, and he is to have the bed in the attic, and I am to pet him as much as ever I please!'

'What have I done with him?' I repeated. 'Why, I left him in the doorway but a moment ago!'

Marguerite stamped her little foot impatiently.

'Then he has slipped away for fear of being put to bed and parted from his dear Babette! Oh, how tiresome!'

It was tiresome, and, what was worse still, he had hidden himself so effectually that, though we searched for nearly an hour, we could not find him. Marguerite actually wept for disappointment, and was only consoled by the promise that the child should be hers when the morning's work was done, and Claude had time to hunt him out.

Thus the busy day went by; and at four o'clock Pierrette came to tell us that 'M'sieur Alexan're was just going to make the prison - *faire le prison.*'

'*Faire le prison!*' I echoed. 'What can that be?'

But Marguerite only took me by the hand, and ran out to the court-yard, whither the rest of the household followed.

Here we found uncle Alexander, surrounded by the workpeople. Beside him stood a small tub containing about a couple of pints of grape juice, and in his hand he held a bunch of rusty keys.

He nodded to Marguerite, and, turning to me, said -

'This is a local ceremony. When the juice is all got, and the vats are full, we lock the cellar-doors and leave the liquor to ferment. It is fermenting now. Come and hear it.'

We went in. The farther entry was already closed, and an oppressive vinous perfume loaded the air. It was very dark, so that the great vats looked strange and shadowy, and the strip of spectral daylight scarcely reached down to the lowest step.

I laid my ear against the nearest vat, and there, far beneath the surface, I heard the seething and gurgling of the living liquid.

'The monkey may baptize the wine if she likes,' said uncle Alexander, good humouredly.

Marguerite clapped her hands.

'Oh, thank you, thank you!' she exclaimed. 'I shall like it above everything!'

Whereupon uncle Alexander gave the word to Claude, and Claude brought down the little tub of juice, and the *vignerons* crowded round the door and half-way down the steps, and it was a very exciting moment indeed.

Then uncle Alexander took up a wooden mug that had been left there for the purpose, and filled it with juice; and then he took Marguerite in his arms, as if she had been an infant, and so ascended a ladder which led to the top of the great vat next the door.

Claude handed up the mug.

'Ma'mselle must first say "*vive le vin*,"' said he, cap in hand.

She looked down, half shy and half laughing; took the mug with one hand, and clung tightly about uncle Alexander's neck with the other.

'*Vive le vin!*' she said, gaily; took a sip of the juice, and flung the rest into the vat.

'*Vive le vin!*' cried uncle Alexander and all his vignerons, and that was the baptismal ceremony.

They then came down, and every one left the cellar. Uncle Alexander was the last to come out.

'Anybody left behind?' he shouted from the top step.

His voice resounded hollowly along the vaulted roof, and was followed by a profound silence.

The great doors were then pulled to, the outer bolts drawn, the padlock passed through the rusty staple, and the key turned.

'Now for fermentation and carbonic-acid gas!' said M. Alexander, rubbing his beard against Marguerite's soft cheek, like a playful bear. 'In six hours more those cellars will be unapproachable; by midnight it would be death to enter.'

On the evening of the day when the wine is left to work, the vine-growers of the Côte d'Or give their vintagers a supper. This chiefly by way of farewell, for the strangers are then dismissed, and wander away once more, either in search of fresh labour or of their own far-distant homes.

Not that the vintage is yet quite over, for wine-making is like beer-making, and goes through some subsequent processes, by which certain inferior liquors are produced for household uses. But this branch of the work is intrusted to the habitual *vignerons* of the estate, and does not take place till the first rich wines are drawn off and bottled. The refuse grapes lying at the bottom of the vats are then taken out and subjected to the action of a powerful press. Hence a thin table-wine is extracted. When this is, in its turn, drawn off, a third, meagre, miserable drink is forced from the twice-squeezed skins and seeds. This is called *piquette*, and is kept, as small-beer is kept in our English farm-houses, for the consumption of the servants and vine-dressers throughout the year.

Now the harvest-supper at Montrocher fell full ten days before the time that M. Alexander had expected, and before any kind of preparation could be made, so that the public room of the *Cheval Blanc* had to be hired; and mine host of the *Cheval Blanc* was intrusted with the victualling department; and poor M. Alexander, who in more prosperous seasons had always entertained his labourers upon home-made fare in his own great barn, was this time condemned not only to lose his forty thousand francs, but to pay the expenses of a great supper into the bargain. He bore it, however, with singular *sang froid*; for although he could grumble more than enough upon minor occasions, he was too thorough a Frenchman not to submit to the inevitable.

At dinner M. Delahaye indulged in a variety of lamentations and condolences, all of which aggravated his brother to the last pitch.

'*Mille tonnerres!*' said he. 'Was it my fault if the rain smashed the grapes and swamped the barn?'

'But, my dearest Alexander, the sympathy that ...'

'To the devil with your sympathy!' snarled the ungrateful loser. 'I hate sympathy! Let me never hear the word again!'

Which effectually silenced the master of the house.

By-and-by M. Alexander marched into the study with a great cash-box under his arm, and paid off the work-people; and later in the evening took Marguerite and me down into the village to see the progress of the *fête*.

The *Cheval Blanc* is a rambling old *auberge*, with white-washed walls, and polished floors, and great yawning fire-places where you might roast entire oxen every day. Being met at the door by M. Roget, the eager, bustling, obsequious little landlord, we are ushered with great ceremony into the *salon*. The *salon* is a huge raftered vault of a place, very little smaller than M. Alexander's barn, and lighted by a blazing log-fire. A couple of long, narrow tables traverse it from end to end, and round these tables the *vignerons* are sitting, thirty along each side, about a hundred and twenty in all, counting men, women, and children. Soup, hams, *bouilli*, great wooden bowls of vegetables, stacks of bread, and cans of *piquette* stand at intervals all down the tables; and when we come in the glasses are filled simultaneously, and the guests all rise to drink our health.

Then we take our seats in the chimney-corner, and watch the progress of the feast. We are no restraint upon them, and they go on eating, talking, and chinking their glasses as merrily as if no one were present but themselves. In this respect the difference between the French and English peasant is considerable. Boisterous in his mirth, quarrelsome with his fellows, and shy in the presence of his masters, our simple field-labourer seems incapable of real enjoyment: whereas Jacques Bonhomme is always gay, self-possessed, and open to amusement. Nothing abashes him, and yet he is always polite. Besides, he is a republican at heart, and believes himself as good a man as his employer.

Sitting thus by the fireside, and listening to the clatter of knives and plates, and the quick confusion of merry voices, I look round in search of little François. Neither he nor any of his family are to be seen at either table, and though there are wanderers here from many distant departments, none wear the quaint and picturesque costume of Normandy. Concluding that the child is unwell, and has probably been removed by his brothers and sisters, I dismiss the subject, and return to the picture before me.

And now, the hearty appetites being set at rest, the tables are carried away, and the young men clamour for a dance; so a couple of *musettes* and a violin are brought, and a space is cleared in the centre of the room for the dancers. Hereupon Claude, who wears his holiday clothes, and represents the best class of *vignerons*, comes respectfully forward, and solicits the honour of 'Ma'mselle Marguerite's hand for the first *bourrée*.' So Marguerite is led out, and they open the ball in the midst of a circle of spectators. No sooner has she returned to her seat than the jollity of the evening begins in earnest. Twenty couples instantly take their places, the musicians strike up a rapid measure, the *sabots* patter to time, and the barefooted children clap their hands with unchecked delight. When they are tired, there are plenty of others ready to take their places, and, altogether, the players have a hard time of it.

All, however, are not dancers. Some are too young, and some too old for that amusement; so the children gather round a great basket of nuts and apples, and crunch and pelt to their heart's content in one corner; while their elders assemble in another, to discuss their pipes and *piquette*, and talk over the storm of the night before. By-and-by one very old white-haired peasant gets an audience about his chair, and tells a curious legend of some ruined castle by the sea, down in his own native province of La Vendée. Then some one volunteers a song, which is very long and very dreary, and every verse winds up with a dismal chorus of

'Oh, les beaux jours de ma jeunesse!'

It is listened to, however, with the utmost admiration, and then

207

the dancing begins again more merrily than before.

What a motley gathering it is! Yonder have clustered some half-dozen rough, black-eyed mountaineers from the high Pyrenean districts. They are talking eagerly together in a guttural patois, of which I cannot understand a single word; but M. Alexander explains to me that wolf-hunts and adventures form the topics of their discourse. That handsome family now sitting aside to watch the dancers, are Gascons all; and those odd-looking youths who stand sheepishly together in a corner, as if doubtful whether the girls will dance with them or not, are Bretons, *pur sang*. What with their short jackets, leather gaiters, and baggy breeches, they look more like a troop of ragged Zouaves than anything else. As for that miserable, wild-looking savage, who squats in a corner and stares sullenly at the gaiety in which he will not join, he is a native of the Landes. He wears a loose Robinson-Crusoe-like costume of undressed fleece. His legs are bare, and his shaggy hair falls about him like a mane. He drinks wine like a Caliban, for the Landes produce no grapes, and, excepting at the vintage time, he must drink water all the year. He speaks a language which is more Spanish than French, and though he has perhaps never fared so well in his life as at the supper this evening, he hates his entertainers, despises the fair and fertile province in which he is a sojourner, and yearns to get back to the sandy plains and dismal pines of his own Biscayan deserts.

It is now close upon ten o'clock. The fun is at its best, and by-and-by they will get uproarious; so we prepare to take our departure. While we are yet waiting for the end of the present dance, M. Roget enters, looks anxiously about the room, fixes upon Claude, who is at that moment executing a vigorous *pas seul*, and whispers in his ear.

What that whisper may be I know not, but I see the handsome *vigneron* pause in the figure, and raise his hand hurriedly to his brow. In another moment he has left his partner, and is making his way towards us.

'Oh, M'sieur Alexander! Oh, Ma'mselle Marguerite!'

His face is pale; his lips tremble; it is all that he can utter.

'Hey! What now?' says uncle Alexander. 'More bad news, Claude?'

'Alas! yes, m'sieur. The - the child - the little François ...'

'What of him?'

'He is missing, m'sieur; and his brothers have been searching for him these last three or four hours. And - and now ...'

'Well - go on!'

'And now Jacques Fayot remembers to have seen him run down the cellar-stairs, while he was treading this morning!'

Marguerite utters a cry of horror; but M. Alexander only turns a shade sallower than usual, plucks silently at his moustache, and glances at his watch.

'The doors have been closed these six hours,' he mutters between his teeth. 'It is too late - too late!'

'Not too late for one effort, M'sieur Alexander,' says Claude, entreatingly. 'If M'sieur will but let me have the keys ...'

'Run for them to M. Delahaye's study,' interrupts his master, abruptly. 'You will find them on the nail behind the door. Marguerite, stay here with mademoiselle.'

With this M. Alexander hurries from the room.

In another instant all is confusion. The news flies from lip to lip - the women burst into cries of lamentation - torches are snatched from the fire - lanterns are lit - we are carried out, as it were, by the eager revellers, and presently find ourselves, despite M. Alexander's injunction, hurrying down the village-street in the midst of the crowd!

The court-yard is filled in a few seconds, and the torches cast a weird flickering light upon the faces round. Claude cannot find the keys, and there is a delay, during which they batter at the cellar-doors with the ends of their torches, and shout with all their might - 'François! little François! cheer up! we are here, little François!'

'Stand back, and hold your tongues!' vociferates the stentorian voice of uncle Alexander. He has the keys in his hand, and with one sweep of his powerful arm clears a space about the door.

Claude then snatches a torch from the hand of the nearest bystander, and holds it for his master - the key grates in the lock - the heavy bolts are dragged back - the great doors swing lazily on their hinges, and the abyss shows murkily beyond.

M. Alexander then tests the state of the air by flinging a brand down into the vault. It flashes on the roof and steps, sends up a shower of sparks as it strikes the ground, flickers for some thirty seconds, and expires slowly.

'Let some one give me a closed lantern,' says uncle Alexander, standing on the top steps, and preparing to descend.

Four or five are brought forward instantly, but Claude is determined to dispute the dangerous honour.

'*Pardon*, m'sieur,' he pleads, with tremulous eagerness. '*Pardon*; but it is for me to go down! I am more used than m'sieur to the air of the cellar - and the little François knows my voice, and ...'

But uncle Alexander only puts him quietly back, and goes a step lower.

'Tush,' says he, 'this is my affair. Give me the lantern.'

'But, m'sieur ...'

'And if I am not back in four or five minutes, break open the farther door from the garden side, and let no one enter till the air is purified.'

'But, m'sieur ...'

Uncle Alexander snatches the lantern from his hand, and his eyes flash dangerously.

'*Mille tonnerres!*' he exclaims, 'did you not hear me? I tell you it is my affair. Stay where you are!'

Claude draws back, abashed and reluctant - Marguerite clings to my arm in silent terror - uncle Alexander, calm and determined, trims the candle, secures the little hasp of the lantern, casts one last rapid glance round the court-yard, and goes down!

There is an interval of eager suspense, during which we hear his steady footfall echo down the stairs and across the floor. We are not near enough to see down; but the crowd closes instantly about the doorway, and in the silence of that painful moment a sound of suppressed sobbing, and the words, 'Oh, François! my little brother François!' are distinctly heard. They proceed from a woman who is dimly seen, crouched down beside the gate.

One - two - three minutes go slowly by. I count them by the ticking of my watch; but the seconds lag, and the silence grows terrible. We look in each other's faces - a whisper runs round - I can hear the very beating of my heart!

'One minute more,' says Claude, hoarsely, 'and then ...'

The sentence dies away upon his lips. He holds up an eager hand.

Hush!

There is a sound as of something striking against one of the vats - a stumbling footstep - a sudden surging back of the spectators; and uncle Alexander, pale and ghastly, staggers up the steps, and falls insensible just as he reaches the top.

Something he holds, clasped tightly in his arms.

Something ... alas! poor sister Babette!

CHAPTER XXVIII

THE SHADOW OF DEATH

Ours was a sad and silent house the day after the vine-feast. We spoke in whispers; we stole about with muffled footsteps; we stopped even the striking of the clocks, and gathered together in little knots upon the stairs and landings, uncertain what to say or do, or how to pass the weary hours away. For there was death, and the shadow of death, among us, and our hearts were 'exceeding heavy.'

Up stairs, in the very attic which Marguerite had so desired he should occupy, lay the little François; but it was with arms folded across his breast, and flowers scattered over his pillow, and tapers burning at his feet. He looked as if he were only in a pleasant sleep; but he was dead, and sister Babette crouched beside him with her face buried in her hands, and refused to be comforted.

One story lower, in a darkened chamber just above my own, lay uncle Alexander, silent and senseless, breathing hard, like a man struck with apoplexy, and motionless as if every limb were chained. Sometimes an eyelid was seen to quiver, and sometimes a few drops of moisture gathered slowly round about the corners of the mouth; but these were the only tokens either of suffering or amendment, and for eighteen hours the balance trembled 'between two worlds.'

Towards evening the pressure on his brain and lungs was lightened. He stirred languidly twice or thrice, muttered some incoherent words, and fell into a placid sleep. Then Dr. Grandet pronounced him out of danger, and, as he had watched since a little before daybreak, resigned his charge to Madame Delahaye, and returned to Chalons.

We took it by turns to sit at his bedside throughout the night, and still he slept profoundly. In the morning he woke, weak, but comparatively well, and at first remembered nothing of what had happened. We could hardly convince him that he had been ill, or that he had passed thirty hours in his bed since the night of the vine-feast.

He rose, however, and came down to breakfast at midday; refusing to be treated as an invalid, and sullenly resenting any allusion to the events of two days before. After breakfast he brought out a sheaf of business letters, and sat down to answer them; but found that his eyes would not serve him, and was reluctantly compelled to let me write them for him.

Thus the second day went by, and on the third little François was buried. The poor Normands were Romanists by faith, and their little brother was interred with the ceremonies of their religion. He was borne out of the house and round to the church at the foot of our garden, with crosses and tapers going before the coffin, and childish voices chanting a melancholy psalm. Suffering as he still was from his own share of the danger, uncle Alexander walked among the mourners. He had already been generous to this poor family, and had given them, not many hours before, a gratuity that secured them, at all events, against the privations of the coming winter; but, somehow, it seemed to me that this simple act of reverence was more generous still, and that uncle Alexander's heart was in the right place after all.

They laid the poor child under the shade of a laburnum, in a corner of the church-yard, next the river. It was a pretty spot, and the violets clustered there in the springtime, as they cluster about the graves of Keats and Shelley in the Protestant burial-grounds near Rome. The ceremony was beautiful and sad; but it was when all was over, and the priest shut up his book, and the earth was closed in, that the grief of the mourners broke out in lamentations. They sobbed, and called upon the name of the dead; they laid flowers and wreaths of *immortelles* upon the fresh-heaped hillock; they came back and back again a hundred times for a last prayer or a farewell look, and cried, 'Pray for us, pray for us, little brother François, that we may be reconciled to our sorrow!'

When, at length, they tore themselves away, they refused all farther rest or refreshment, and went forth straightway upon their weary pilgrimage.

'A safe journey home, *mes amis*,' said uncle Alexander, compassionately.

But the elder brother shook his head, and pointed northwards.

'Home!' he repeated. 'Alas! what shall we say when our father asks us for the child of his old age?'

With this he pulled his hat over his eyes and turned away, and the rest followed him, weeping loudly. When they reached the turn of the road, they paused with one accord and waved a last farewell; but poor sister Babette looked back and lingered longest.

CHAPTER XXIX

THE FIRST SNOW-FALL

Next to being branded as a scoundrel, nothing offended M. Alexander so much as being reputed a hero. He could take abuse tolerably well. It chimed in with his own humour, and, indeed, I think he rather liked it than otherwise; but praise was intolerable to him, and he never forgave it. Thus, when the neighbours complimented him upon his descent into the deadly atmosphere of the cellar, he either turned his back upon them, or gave utterance to some bitter impertinence which scarcely his well-known eccentricity could excuse. And thus, when the 'Lyons Courier' appeared on the following Sunday, with a flaming article headed, 'Fatal accident and heroic act of daring in the department of the Côte d'Or,' he thrust the paper between the bars of the grate, kicked the cat, swore at the dogs, and threatened to horsewhip the editor. The presentation of the Monthyon prize, was alone wanting to crown his indignation, and I believe that would almost have driven him mad.

While he was in this delightful temper (and it lasted for some weeks), the fag-end of October went out in east winds and rain, and November came on with all the promise of a severe and premature winter. We had bitter frosts at night and morning, leaden skies, fog-hidden mountains, and winds that whistled round the house and shook the windows, and moaned along the passages like a legion of impatient ghosts. The leaves were all gone now, and the vineyards looked like plantations of walking-sticks. Distant cottages, unseen before, showed whitely through the skeleton branching of the trees.

213

The mountains looked bare and stony. A dreary stillness brooded in the air. Even the swallows that built over the study-window, and fluttered backwards and forwards all the summer through, were fled to a warmer clime; and all nature seemed bound up in an iron sleep.

At Montrocher the change of season was severely felt, and by no one more than Marguerite. She had been ailing ever since the fatal end of little François, and now grew more and more languid. The dull skies, the silence, the gloom, affected her both mentally and bodily, and preyed upon her young cheeks day by day. Nothing amused her, and, in the absence of M. Hamel, nothing gave her pleasure. Yet even he could not always charm away her melancholy, or succeed in bringing back the light to her eyes, or the smiles to her lips. When he strove most to interest her, she was oftenest silent and inert; and, when alone, would sit for hours in her bedroom, looking over to that corner of the grave-yard where the child lay buried. She had never seen death before, and none of us could either banish it from her memory, or disabuse her of the fatal impression that she had been the cause of the disaster.

'But for me,' said she, 'he would not have concealed himself - but for me, he had been living now. Perhaps he was already dead when I baptized the wine; or (worse still) lay fainting in some gloomy corner, without the power to speak and be saved. Oh, this thought is terrible, and never leaves me either by night or day!'

And then she would shudder, or burst into a passion of tears; but we were glad when she wept, for it seemed to relieve her for awhile, and during the rest of that day she was always better. Uncle Alexander, who loved his 'little monkey' better than anything else in the world, grew fretful and impatient; scolded me, which did no good; and scolded her, which did worse. He then brought Dr. Grandet home with him one day to dinner; but the little man only shook his head, and pursed up his mouth, and said -

'Get her out. Amuse her. Don't let her think, or sit still, or be silent, if you can help it. A hearty laugh would be worth more to her just now than twenty bottles of medicine.'

'But if she won't laugh? If she won't speak? If she won't be amused?' urged uncle Alexander.

'Humph! - in that case you must try change of scene.'

'And if change of scene does no good, doctor - what then?'

'Bah, if you come to suppositions, I have done with you, friend

Alexander,' retorted Dr. Grandet. 'Change of *scene* must do good. Time enough to grumble when you have tried it. I tell you that nothing can actually be said to ail her. She is little more than a child; giddy, impetuous, and impressionable. She has received a shock; she cannot easily get over it; and her spirits are depressed in proportion to their former elevation. Your business now is to raise them; to find her constant occupation, both of mind and body; and to efface those gloomy fancies, which are doing all the mischief. I have no other advice to give you.'

The consequence of this interview was to create a perfect revolution in our plans and mode of life. Madame talked of hiring a house at Chalons or Lyons for the winter; M. Hamel pleaded for the hastening of his marriage; I was released from my voluntary secretaryship, and gave up all my time to the task of amusing Marguerite; and Madame and I took it by turns to drive her out in the chaise every day.

Thus it happened that we one morning drove to Chalons to pay a visit to the Vaudons. It was a bitterly-cold day, with a white glare upon the sky that prophesied snow. We left the chaise, as usual, at the '*Lion d'Or,*' and went forward on foot. Marguerite was not yet any better, and had come out reluctantly. Like most nervous invalids, she dreaded to meet any but home-faces; and even when we came in sight of M. Vaudon's house, would fain have persuaded me to turn back, and visit uncle Alexander at his office instead.

But I would not hear of this; so we went on, and found that our friends were all gone to spend the day at Grétigny, some six or eight miles down the river.

Marguerite was so glad to have escaped, that her spirits rose at once, and she smiled as she had seldom smiled of late.

'Now,' said she, as we turned away from the door, 'now, mademoiselle, we can go to uncle Alexander's! You have never been to uncle Alexander's office, have you?'

'Never,' I replied, with a glance at the sky. 'Is it far?'

'Oh no - quite near; that is to say, about three-quarters of a mile along the quay; just a few houses beyond the church.'

'I think we had better go home,' said I. 'It will snow before long.'

And almost as I spoke, the first few flakes came fluttering slowly down. Still Marguerite entreated, and we hastened forward. Before we were half across the bridge, the cloud blew thick and fast, and, as we had left our umbrellas in the chaise, we were soon well whitened, and obliged to run for it. Unluckily the quay was lined with warehouses, and there was no shop anywhere near in which we could take refuge.

Blinded, breathless, covered with snow, and hesitating which way to turn, we found ourselves suddenly sheltered beneath an umbrella, and a green-gloved hand, holding the same, introduced between us.

'Wretched outcasts! whither away?' exclaimed the familiar voice of M. Hamel.

Marguerite uttered a cry of delight.

'Oh, Alexis,' said she, 'I am so glad it is you! We were going to uncle Alexander's, but -'

'But now you will go home with me instead,' interposed her lover, coolly leading us off in an opposite direction. 'Monsieur Alexander's is too far, and, when one gets there, too comfortless for a day like this. Whereas, my lodgings are close by, and I left an excellent fire blazing away, not five minutes since.'

'If - if mademoiselle has no objection,' hesitated Marguerite.

'Mademoiselle has no objection in the world,' laughed M. Hamel, without giving me time to answer. 'On the contrary, she is but too happy to exchange wind and snow for shelter and a fireside. Besides, I have some admirable Johannisberger, upon which she must give me her opinion.'

'I am no judge of wines,' said I, drily; 'and I never tasted Johannisberger in my life - so pray don't make that your reason for carrying us away in this summary fashion!'

'Reason or no reason, you are my prisoners,' retorted he, 'and here is your place of durance!'

Saying which, he drew us into the shelter of a large portico, and rang the bell. The door was opened by a small boy in livery, whom I recognized for Pierre Pichat. M. Hamel preceded us up stairs.

'My rooms are on the first floor,' said he, 'so you have not far to mount; but I fear the place is in sad disorder. Pierre, we must lunch directly.'

With this he ushered us into his sitting-room, and wheeled a sofa to the fire.

We had never been in M. Hamel's lodgings before, though we knew the house well, and used to look up at the windows, going by, and wonder which were his. Therefore we were not prepared for the splendour of his accommodation; for a room lined with mirrors, curtained with silk damasks, furnished with oak and velvet, and carpeted with a luxurious fabric into which our feet sank deeply at every step. Fauteuils of oriental comfort, elegant little works of art in bronze and marble, a superb piano, a stand of beautiful and curious arms, both modern and antique; a Louis XIV cabinet, with panels painted *à la* Watteau; a side-table of exquisite *marqueterie*; books, foils, boxing-gloves, drawing materials, folios filled with engravings and sketches, curiosities, nicknacks, and luxuries of every conceivable description covered the walls, the sofas, the tables, and even the floor in every direction.

Marguerite was petrified, and had not a word to say.

'Well,' said M. Hamel, with a smile, 'do you like my rooms?'

'Like them! they are fit for a prince! How could you find anything so splendid in Chalons?'

M. Hamel shrugged his shoulders disdainfully.

'Chalons, indeed!' said he. 'You may well ask that question, *chérie*! all that you see here was sent to me from Lyons, the first week of my arrival.'

'And they are all your own, these statues, these - *Ciel!* how rich you must be!'

M. Hamel darted a keen glance, first at his betrothed and next at me, and laughed somewhat nervously.

'I *am* rich,' said he. 'Richer than an emperor in the possession of my little Marguerite!'

But his little Marguerite shook back her curls with a pretty gesture, half wilful, half childish; and would not be put off with a compliment.

'Of course,' she replied; 'but that's quite another sort of wealth, Monsieur Alexis! You can't exchange me for carpets, and pictures, and looking-glasses, and such fine things as these.'

'Nor should I wish to do so, my darling,' said M. Hamel, lifting her hand to his lips. 'You are more precious than all the "fine things" in the world, and I am happier than if Aladdin's lamp were mine.'

Whereat Marguerite snatched her hand away, and crimsoned with happiness.

'I shall look at everything now that I am here!' she exclaimed, turning to a table on which stood a tortoise-shell and silver casket. 'What can be in this beautiful little box?'

'You may open it if you please,' said M. Hamel; 'but I'd wager a thousand francs you'll never guess its contents.'

Marguerite paused with her hand on the hasp.

'It looks like a jewel-case,' said she.

'No.'

'Or a card-box?'

'Wrong again.'

'Then it's for scent-bottles?'

M. Hamel smiled, and affected to hesitate.

'Well,' said he, 'I cannot deny that the objects contained in it are of a perfumed nature; but ...'

Marguerite lost patience, and raised the lid.

'Cigars!' she exclaimed in a tone of disappointment. 'Nothing but cigars, after all! What a shame to keep them in such a lovely casket as that!'

'Nay, then, I will devote it to a better purpose,' said M. Hamel, tossing his Havannahs into an empty vase. 'Convert it into a jewel-case or scent-box, as you please, for it is yours.'

'Mine!' echoed Marguerite; 'do you mean that?'

'As surely as that I and all my possessions are your property.'

Marguerite laughed for joy - one of her old, ringing, laughs that had been so rare of late.

'Hear him, mademoiselle!' she cried. 'Hear him! There's a fatal admission! All here is my property! I can take anything I like - do anything I like - break, sell, give away, and appropriate as I please! Oh, what a delicious power!'

'Use it, then,' said M. Hamel, with a profound salaam, 'and dispose, oh queen! of the humblest of thy slaves.'

But she skipped away to the Louis Quatorze cabinet instead, and began ransacking every drawer that it contained.

Models of junks, strange little gods in china and silver, carved narghillies, medals, and oriental toys of all kinds were here accumulated.

'I brought them from the East,' said M. Hamel, carelessly. 'You may have whatever you fancy from among the lot. They are of no use to me.'

'From the East!' repeated his betrothed, pausing, and looking up amazedly in his face. 'You never told me that you had been in the East before!'

'I have been in most places that you could mention, *petite*,' replied he, gaily, 'from Paris to Palmyra.'

'Oh, tell me about your travels,' cried Marguerite, eagerly, forgetting everything else in the desire to know more of his history. 'Tell me where you went, and what you went for, and how you happen to be so rich; for I so wish to hear it, and I know so little!'

M. Hamel laughed; but looked annoyed nevertheless.

'Pshaw!' said he. ''Twould fill a dozen volumes, and take a year to tell. Wait till you are my little wife, and then we shall have time enough.'

'*Will* you then tell me all? Really all?' said she, wistfully.

'Yes - yes, of course. Why do you ask? Why do you doubt?'

'Because - because,' faltered she, 'I have heard that husbands never trust their wives to keep the secrets of their hearts.'

'But if they have no secrets to intrust? What then, little questioner?'

Marguerite shook her head and sighed. The impatient gaiety of M. Hamel's evasion dissatisfied her.

'I'm sure that you have secrets,' she said, 'and the proof is that I do not even know ...'

She checked herself, and, whatever she might have been about to say, felt that she had ventured upon dangerous ground. As for M. Hamel, the veins rose upon his forehead, and he started as if he had trodden on a viper.

'What is it that you do not even know, Marguerite?' he asked, sternly.

She changed colour, hesitated, and knew not what to answer.

'I - I think,' said she, confusedly, 'that is, I wonder - when you have travelled so far, and - and seen so much, how you can be contented in a little provincial town like Chalons - and - and why you came here at all.'

M. Hamel drew a deep breath, and fixed his eyes on hers, as if he would pierce into her very thoughts. He knew quite well that these last words were a substitution, and he deliberated for a moment whether he should compel her to a direct explanation, or accept that which she had already given. He decided on the latter.

219

'A natural question enough, *chérie*,' he said, calmly. 'I am a Frenchman, and I love France better than any other country on earth. I have seen the world, and I am weary of it. I had a fancy for retirement, and here I have found it. Fortunately I have found you also, and now what can I wish for more?'

'And you are contented?'

'Quite.'

'But is it not wonderful,' said Marguerite, clasping her hands over her knees, and sitting on the floor in the midst of the junks and idols, 'is it not wonderful that a clever, eloquent, accomplished man like you ...'

M. Hamel laid his hand quickly over her lips.

'I cannot let you flatter me in that outrageous way,' he interrupted, laughingly. 'Have you a mind to spoil me?'

'No, no - I mean every word of it, and you know that you are clever, Alexis - cleverer than even M. Deligny - so pray let me finish what I was going to say.'

'Finish in peace, little one.'

'Well, is it not surprising that you - *you* who ...'

'We'll take the acquirements for granted, if you please,' put in M. Hamel.

'Who might have settled in Paris, and have been famous and have married some beautiful, rich, fashionable lady,' continued Marguerite, gravely and earnestly, and with her whole honest little heart; 'is it not wonderful that you should be able to content yourself with an obscure country appointment, and with an ignorant child like me?'

M. Hamel took her head between his two hands, and looked as if he could have devoured her for love.

'My darling,' said he, tenderly, 'I bless the day when I first heard of the obscure country appointment! I never cared for Paris, and I have been so long a wanderer that, had I gone there, I should have found myself as solitary as here. Then I was longing for retirement, and I had heard of this place long before I ever thought to visit it; and ...'

'Yes, I know. You met a brother of M. de Senneville's somewhere abroad, and when M. Drouet died, his influence gave you the situation,' interposed Marguerite.

'Exactly; and, having learned to love Montrocher before I had even seen it, I accepted without hesitation. The salary, I need hardly say, was no object to me. It keeps me in cigars, *mais voilà tout?*'

Marguerite laughed delightedly.

'I really believe,' said she, 'that you are a prince in disguise!'

'Not I, *petite*. I am simply one who follows his profession, not from necessity, but choice. If I am not the Crœsus that you seem to fancy, I can at least afford to indulge my taste for the arts, and surround my home with all the minor luxuries of life.'

'Yes, you may say that, Hamel,' replied a strange voice. 'May I never smell powder again if you haven't a genius for extravagance! But I fear I am intruding. Beg a thousand pardons, *mesdames*. Had no idea that you were so agreeably engaged, *mon ami*, and at this early hour of the day, too! *Fi donc*, parson! I thought better of you.'

The intruder was a small, bronzed, dapper, military man, of about five feet and a-half in height, and some thirty or thirty-four years of age. The coolness with which he sauntered into the room and leaned upon the back of a chair, the familiarity of his address, the *nonchalant* politeness with which he removed his cap, and the unmistakable insolence of his stare and laugh, made my blood boil. He came, too, at an awkward moment. The tiny difference between the lovers had just blown over. The little lady was still sitting in the midst of the toys, and M. Hamel, kneeling on one knee beside her, was holding up a curious ivory fan, and looking into her eyes with a smile which it required no very keen powers of observation to interpret.

It was like a stage situation, and changed as suddenly. M. Hamel sprang to his feet, and Marguerite half rose in her place; I alone kept my seat and my countenance, and met the bold black eyes of the little officer with a composure almost equal to his own.

There was a moment of awkward silence.

'I - I certainly did not expect to see you so early,' at length, said M. Hamel; 'were you not to have been here at four?'

The stranger showed his teeth and twirled his moustache.

'Yes, to be sure; but the snow came down like a thousand devils, and I happened to be passing by on my way to Favart's, so I ran in here instead, and find you, *parbleu!* on your knees and, I presume, at your devotions.'

M. Hamel's eyes flashed ominously.

'You mistake, Sylvestre,' said he, with forced calmness; 'these ladies ...'

'To whom you have not yet introduced me,' put in the stranger, with another stare at Marguerite.

M. Hamel drew himself to his full height.

'I am now about to do so,' returned he, coldly. 'Marguerite, allow me to present to you M. Emile Lorraine Sylvestre, lieutenant-colonel of the foot regiment now quartered in Chalons - a gentleman of whom I dare say you have never heard, and whose acquaintance you would scarcely have been likely to make but for the accident of this morning. Monsieur le Colonel, this lady is Mademoiselle Delahaye, of Montrocher. Her name and family are numbered among the most honourable and ancient of the department.'

Having said which, he offered his hand to Marguerite, and led her, with stately deference, to the sofa.

The colonel saw his mistake, bowed profoundly, and had sufficient good breeding to offer no apologies; but he felt the sting of M. Hamel's reproof, and chafed under it.

'Your luck last night was wonderful,' said he, crossing over to the window, and trying to speak carelessly. 'De Sauley used to pride himself on his lansquenet till we came here; but neither he nor any of us can hold a hand against you.'

'M. de Sauley is a better player than I,' replied M. Hamel, contracting his dark brows. 'Lansquenet is not a game that I have studied, and, when I am successful, it is my good star that I have to thank, and not my skill.'

'Then you thanked your good star to some purpose last evening! Your winnings can't have fallen far short of six thousand francs.'

'Really, colonel,' replied M. Hamel, stiffly, 'you appear to be better informed upon the subject than myself. I protest that I have not yet made the calculation.'

The colonel reddened, bit his lips, and, after a moment's hesitation, brought out his pocket-book.

'I know,' said he, 'that you are the most careless fellow in the world with regard to money matters, and that if we losers kept no account of our debts you would never be wise enough to remind us of them. Here, however, is my share of the spoil.'

And he laid a folded paper on the table.

'In the meantime,' he continued, 'we wait our revenge. Will you come round to my rooms to-night to supper?'

'I fear not to-night,' replied M. Hamel, taking no notice of the payment. 'When these ladies have rested, and the snow ceases, I shall do myself the honour of seeing them home, and perhaps of remaining at Montrocher for the evening.'

'To-morrow night, then?'

'To-morrow night I was about to invite you here, together with De Sauley, Regnier, and three or four others. I expect my new billiard-table by then, and shall be glad of your opinion on it.'

'*Ainsi soit il!*' returned the colonel, somewhat profanely, and took up his cap to go. 'By the way, Hamel, have you come to any decision yet about Regnier's bay hunter?'

'Yes; I bought her yesterday, and she came round to my stable this morning. Did you think of having her?'

'I had some notion of it; but could not afford the price. He asked me three thousand five hundred.'

'And took three thousand,' said M. Hamel.

The little officer twirled his cap, and drew a deep breath.

'Even that is a heavy price,' said he.

M. Hamel shrugged his shoulders.

'I have known a worse horse sell for more,' he replied, carelessly, 'and this one suits my purpose.'

'Ah, you are thinking of next week's meet! Well, good morning. *Mesdames, j'ai l'honneur.*'

With this he saluted us again, and M. Hamel accompanied him down stairs. Marguerite was the first to speak.

'Oh, mademoiselle,' she exclaimed, 'what a horrible man!'

'Not a pleasant specimen of M. Hamel's associates, certainly,' I replied.

She changed colour, started up, and began pacing nervously to and fro between the table and the fire.

'Six thousand francs,' said she, to herself. 'Six thousand francs!'

'Yes, it is a large sum to be won at cards in a single evening.'

'But he is not a gambler, mademoiselle,' she said, earnestly. 'I am sure he is not a gambler!'

I remembered what M. Charles had told us upon this very subject, many a month ago, and so kept silent.

'Besides,' pleaded Marguerite, 'he is so rich!'

'True, he is rich; but he has "a genius for extravagance," and, if he play high, may lose all to-morrow.'

She sighed and pressed her hands together, as she was wont to do when in distress.

'*Ah, mon Dieu!*' said she, 'I begin to wish we had not come here to-day!'

At this moment M. Hamel came back, and announced that lunch was ready in the study.

The study was a smaller and scarcely less elegant room on the same floor. Lined throughout with books, and commanding what would be, in finer weather, a delightful view of the valley of the Saône, it was just the retreat that Montaigne or Shenstone would have loved. Over the fire-place hung a fine copy of the *Madonna della Seggiola*, and a collection of curious pipes, hookahs, narghillies, and other appliances of the Indian weed. The table displayed a delicious array of raised pies, cold game, confectionery, smoke-coloured Rhine and Moselle bottles, and delicate Venice glasses flowered with gold.

We took our seats, and M. Hamel placed himself between us. By this time he was in admirable spirits, played the host to perfection, and did his best to efface every unfavourable impression that might have been left upon our minds by the advent of his late visitor. He dismissed the attendant, and himself waited upon us. He helped us to the choicest morsels, kept us amused by a torrent of witticisms, and with his own hands uncorked the famed Johannisberger. Marguerite's anxiety was not long proof against these pleasant influences. She soon forgot everything but the present; and listened, laughed, and admired with all the childish *laissez aller* of her impulsive nature.

Thus the time slipped away, and three o'clock struck before we were aware of it. The snow had ceased falling, and towards the east the sky was barred with gold. We had now no time to spare, so M. Hamel despatched Pierre to the *Lion d'Or*, for the chaise, and ordered his own horse round that he might see us safely home. This done, we hurried away as fast as we could. Marguerite's new treasures, including a great many more than she had herself selected, were packed away in a basket and placed in the gig-box; a huge fur wrapper of M. Hamel's was rolled round us; master Pierre, who had rather avoided my eye all the morning, touched his cap and handed me the whip; our cavalier sprang into the saddle; and in another moment we were on our way to Montrocher.

———————

CHAPTER XXX

THE MINIATURE

It was past eleven o'clock. M. Hamel had stayed late, and was just gone, and I went up, shiveringly, to bed. The night was damp and rafty, and the morning's snow had long since yielded to a thick, fine mist. The stone stair-case chilled me as I hurried up, and I shuddered at the recollection that my bedchamber was paved with brick.

'It will be a horrible room in the depth of winter,' I muttered to myself - opened the door, found the place all alight, with a rich, ruddy glow, and saw a blazing wood-fire piled up and crackling on the hearth.

An exclamation of surprise escaped my lips, and was answered by a merry echo in the direction of my bed. I turned, and saw Marguerite peeping from between the curtains.

'This is indeed kind, *petite*!' I said, crouching before the fire, and warming my cold hands. 'To whom am I indebted for such an indulgence?'

'To papa and mamma in general,' replied Marguerite, 'for they have always said that mademoiselle should have a fire in her room throughout the winter; and to uncle Alexander in particular, for when the snow fell this morning, he told mamma that he was sure you felt the cold severely, and that it was quite time to begin to take care of you.'

'Very considerate of uncle Alexander, I am sure! But shall I really have this delightful companion every evening?'

'Till the warm weather returns, mademoiselle. And now are you in a great hurry to go to bed?'

'Not at all, since I have a fire to sit by. Why do you ask?'

'Because I have not yet looked over that basketful of curiosities that we brought from Chalons this morning; and - and my room is so cold ...'

'And mine so warm and comfortable that you would like to examine them here, *n'est-ce pas*?'

'If you please, mademoiselle. May I fetch the basket?'

'By all means. I think it will be very amusing.'

She darted away, and was back again almost directly, with the basket in her arms. Then we shut the door, drew the table to the hearth, trimmed the lamp, and set ourselves to a cosy investigation of the treasures.

First of all came a carved-ivory puzzle of Chinese workmanship, ball within ball, a very marvel of useless ingenuity. Next a sandal-wood fan and paper-knife, and a pair of embroidered Chinese slippers. Then the beautiful tortoise-shell casket, emptied of its contents, but still odorous of tobacco; a fat little porcelain mandarin; a silver idol about the size of a walnut, sitting cross-legged on a pedestal; a fan and head-dress of Mexican feather-work; an elephant-tusk elaborately engraved; a piece of polished green marble, labelled 'from Hadrian's villa at Tivoli;' some curious shells; a string of silver coins from the Greek isles, and a flat volume in a wrapper of silk brocade, which proved to be an Oriental poem, written on vellum, and gorgeously illuminated.

This last delighted me. I had seen nothing like it before - nothing like this exquisite Eastern writing, with its marvellously accurate curves and slender hair-strokes - nothing like these elaborate borderings encircling every page; these capitals radiant in purple and gold; these highly-finished vignettes of birds, and mosques, black-bearded kaliphs, dancing-girls, and rose-gardens. There were about fifty pages in all, and no two alike. A subtle perfume, that I had never smelt before, pervaded all the volume, and was exhaled by the turning of every leaf. I felt as if I were transported to the land of Arabian nights, and became so absorbed as to take no heed of whatever else the basket might contain.

In the midst of this reverie, I was startled by an exclamation from Marguerite. I looked up hastily. In one hand she held a little carved-ivory box, which she had but just opened, and in the other a miniature, upon which her eyes were intently riveted.

'A portrait!' she faltered. 'A woman's portrait, and so lovely!'

I snatched it from her, and held it close under the lamp. It was indeed a female head, painted upon ivory, and set in a large oval locket, with a device of hair at the back. The hair was dark and fine, and arranged to represent a single feather, tied by a true lover's knot. The face was serious and beautiful, with small aristocratic features, and large contemplative brown eyes, and a mouth so delicately curved, so sweet, and yet so stately, that only the subtlest portraiture could have reproduced its peculiar character. The hair was dark and wavy, like that at the back, and was dressed in an obsolete fashion of at least twenty years back. The distinguishing peculiarity of this likeness was, however, the singular smile which informed every feature, and yet appeared to move no muscle and change the lines of no portion of the countenance. It was, perhaps, scarcely so much a smile as the expression of a great and radiant serenity not wholly unalloyed with coldness, such as we see shining from the eyes and lips of Joanna of Arragon, in that wonderful portrait that hangs in the great gallery of the Doria Palace in Rome.

Altogether it was a rare and beautiful transcript of a still more rare and beautiful woman. It was a masterpiece both of art and nature. It was like a face seen in a dream, and, strange to say, affected me at the first glance with a tumultuous sensation, as if I *had* actually seen it in some vague, forgotten dream of long ago.

So strong, and, I may say, so painful was this impression, that for some three or four seconds I could not utter a word, or take my eyes from the locket. When I did at last look up and see the agonized expression of my little Marguerite's pale countenance, I was both shocked and surprised.

'*Comment, petite!*' I said, passing my arm about her neck. '*Qu'est-ce que tu as?* Why fix your eyes on this picture as if it were the head of the Medusa?'

'*Hélas!*' she murmured, with a sort of sob and catching of her breath, 'who is she? Why is she so lovely? How came he to -'

She broke off with a shudder, and buried her face in her hands. I drew the hands forcibly away, and made her look again at the miniature.

'You foolish child,' I said, 'are you jealous of a woman who must have been in her prime before you were born? Look at the fashion of her hair, and compare it with that engraving of the Princess Charlotte of England that hangs in your father's study down stairs. Don't you see that it is precisely the same thing, and that, even at the time when this likeness was taken, the original was no longer in her first youth? If still living, she must be sixty years of age. Most probably it is the portrait of M. Hamel's mother!'

Marguerite drew a deep breath.

'Oh, mademoiselle, if I could only think that. But -'

'But what, *petite*?'

'But Alexis is - is so much older than I, mademoiselle! May he not at some time or other have - have loved -'

'Somebody else, eh? Well, to tell you the truth, Marguerite, I should not believe M. Hamel if he declared the contrary ever so firmly! It is impossible that he can have gone through life up to this time without some previous attachments. At the same time, I do think it unlikely that this lady could ever have been one of them.'

'Really, mademoiselle?'

'Really and sincerely. Come, let us take the facts as they stand, and I believe I can convince you. M. Hamel's age is, let us see, about -'

'Forty,' replied Marguerite somewhat reluctantly. 'He told me he was forty; but he does not look that, for all his silver hair, does he, mademoiselle?'

'Humph - I don't know. Perhaps not, *chérie*; but that is not the question at present. M. Hamel, we will say, is forty years of age; and this portrait was painted, at a guess, twenty years ago. M. Hamel was then only twenty, and the lady (to judge by her likeness) could scarcely have been less than thirty-five - perhaps even a few years older. She could hardly have been his mother; but -'

'But she might have been his near relation, his godmother, or his aunt!' interposed Marguerite, eagerly. 'Oh, mademoiselle, dear, kind, darling mademoiselle, how happy you have made me!'

'And how unhappy you made yourself, little one! When will you learn to think before you jump to conclusions?'

She laughed, answered with a kiss, and declared herself quite satisfied and ready to go to bed. My fire was now burning down, it was past midnight, and I felt too tired to invite her to remain. So we replaced the treasures in the basket, portrait, casket, mandarin and all, and deposited it safely on the spare bed that stood at the foot of my own. Then Marguerite bade me good-night.

'Sleep well, mademoiselle,' said she, archly, 'and don't be tempted near the Eastern poem, or I am sure you would lie awake all night admiring those hideous kaliphs, which are enough to give one the night-mare!'

I shook my head, promised not to touch the book again that night, and laughingly shut her out. I then prepared to go to bed; but a painful restlessness had taken possession of me, and, fatigued as I was, I felt I could not sleep. I drew the blind and looked out. The rain had ceased, the snow had quite vanished from the face of the landscape, and the moon shone fitfully between rents of driving cloud. How often I had watched her pale disc on just such nights as this, when the autumn rain-clouds hurried overhead, and the ghostly mists crept along the dank hollows of my native moors! A crowd of old remembrances rushed across my mind - scenes of my wasted youth, of my broken longings, of my father's death-night, and of my fearful waiting in the solitary porch! I could not bear these thoughts, and could not banish them. I dropped the blind, threw another log on the fire, took up a book, and tried in vain to read.

Then, by a strange transition, I remembered the portrait. I longed to look at it once more. It fascinated me; and though I knew that it concerned me not, I could no longer resist the impulse that prompted me to take it out again. It lay at the very top of the basket, and, as I brought it to the light, seemed to look through me with those earnest eyes. Great heaven! why was it that I could not divest myself of the impression that I had seen that living face at some time or other long gone by? Was it in a dream, or in some remote and forgotten stage of being?

My own doubts and questions agitated and unnerved me. I put the miniature out of sight, recovered my calmness by a strong effort, and determined to think of the subject no more. But we cannot always control the operations of the mind, and this night mine was in open rebellion. Long after I had laid my head upon the pillow, I was distracted by the vision of that haunting face and its peculiar smile, nor did I fall asleep till after I had heard the clock strike three.

———————

CHAPTER XXXI

THE CZARINA MANTLE

Marguerite's cheerful moments were only transitory, and the day at Chalons proved but a bright exception after all. The next morning found her more dispirited than ever. She complained of headache and languor; absented herself from table; and refused to leave her room, though M. Hamel himself came round in the afternoon to see her. She would neither read, nor work, nor go out, and could scarcely be induced to take any kind of nourishment. She lost all interest in her beautiful Eastern toys, and, as she seemed to have forgotten the mysterious miniature, I abstracted it quietly from the basket, and locked it up in my own desk, fearing lest the sight of it might in any way add to her present despondency. It was a strange illness, an access of mental and physical debility, which seemed at times to be shaken off readily enough, but which at other times descended upon her like a pall. For my own part, I felt sure that it was neither more nor less than one of the manifold developments of hysteria, and I even doubted whether the fatal occurrence to which her sufferings were ascribed, was, after all, the primary cause thereof. She had ever been a wayward creature, made up of smiles and tears, and it seemed possible that the insidious malady should have been latent in her system for longer than any of us had hitherto had cause to suspect. But this was mere conjecture, and I kept it to myself. In the meantime, she became weaker every day, and more melancholy. When another fortnight had gone by thus, and Dr. Grandet confessed himself baffled, change of air and scene was determined upon, and it was arranged that we should all, with the exception of M. Alexander, migrate to Lyons for the winter. M. Hamel, who was half-beside himself with anxiety, then started away in advance to secure suitable apartments, and it was arranged that on the fourth day after his departure we should follow him.

An indescribable bustle and confusion ensued, and for three days our quiet home at Montrocher was in a state of siege. Packing went on perpetually, nothing was to be found in its usual place, nothing was done at its usual hour, everybody kept getting in everybody's way; and stacks of carpet-bags and portmanteaus blockaded all the passages. Poor Madame went from room to room like one distracted, and would fain have carried the whole contents of the house with her to Lyons. To add to her distress, the winter had set in early, and both she and Marguerite were unprepared with travelling wraps. In this emergency I was despatched to Chalons with *carte blanche* to purchase everything suitable, and uncle Alexander, who was going in that direction, agreed to drive me.

The morning was bitterly cold, and it had been freezing hard for the last six-and-thirty hours. The ground rang beneath the horse's feet as we went along, and the few whom we passed now and then by the way, looked blue and frost-bitten. My own breath came like a white steam from my lips, my fingers lost all sensation, and my teeth chattered dismally. Not so my companion. He was protected like a Laplander; wore huge fur gloves that made his hands look like paws; smoked vigorously; and was enveloped from head to foot in a ponderous overcoat with a high-peaked hood, that stood up over his hat like a gigantic extinguisher. Thus fortified against the weather, he puffed on in the most placid and provoking silence, and never opened his lips till we were more than half way on our road to Chalons. He then looked back at the sky, refilled his pipe, and said -

'We want more snow.'

'Indeed, we don't!' I exclaimed, with a shiver. 'At all events, not before we are all safely settled in Lyons.'

'Nonsense, we do want it. *I* want it. Why, the funds went down yesterday to sixty-four, solely on account of the frost.'

'I'm glad of it,' said I, spitefully.

'Glad of it!' echoed uncle Alexander. 'Are you mad? What do you mean by saying you are glad of it?'

'I mean that I am delighted to find the cold take some effect upon you, for you seem to feel it no more than a salamander!'

Uncle Alexander burst into a gruff laugh, and dealt the horse a sharp cut with his whip. A speech like this was just the thing to put him in good humour; and the more really peevish it was, the better he liked it.

'I suppose *you're* cold, then,' chuckled he, when his enjoyment of the joke had somewhat subsided.

'Cold, monsieur! I am nearly frozen.'

'Your own fault. Why not wear a thicker shawl?'

'I have none thicker; but I shall buy a cloak to-day.'

'Humph! a cloak indeed! Why don't you learn to smoke? Look

at this little bowl of fire - it contains more heat than half a hundred cloaks, and yet I dare say you would not smoke it out to save your life!'

'I beg your pardon, sir. To save my life, I would undertake to smoke a hogshead of tobacco.'

Uncle Alexander darted a keen side-glance at me, and whipped the horse on afresh.

'Are you so fond of life?' he asked, doubtfully.

'Indeed, I am.'

'Why?'

'I scarcely know. Perhaps because it is the only precious thing that I possess.'

'A most illogical conclusion.'

'Not at all. The world is a pleasant place, and I should wish to enjoy it as long as I can.'

Uncle Alexander made a furious grimace, and plucked, as usual, at the ends of his moustache.

'It's a devilish dull place,' growled he; 'a sneaking, cringing, lying, selfish place, and I hate it! *Mort de ma vie!* I hate it!'

'That's because you are rich,' said I, very composedly. 'It never cringes or lies to me, and I have, therefore, a much better opinion of it. But then, you know, I am poor.'

'What an advantage!'

This was so satirically said that I did not choose to reply to it. After a momentary silence, M. Alexander continued -

'Of course,' said he, 'you despise riches - would not be rich if you could - admire poverty, and contentment, and every other humbug of that description - hey?'

I shook my head, and smiled bitterly.

'Alas! no,' said I. 'I am not philosophical enough for that. I once, for a few hours, believed myself wealthy; and they were the happiest hours of my life.'

'Hah! When was that?'

'Not a year ago.'

'And what followed?'

'The disagreeable discovery that my father had been cheated of his property, and that I was left almost penniless.'

Uncle Alexander gave utterance to a prolonged whistle, relapsed into silence, and spoke no more till we reached Chalons and pulled up at the *Lion d'Or*. He then, with unaccustomed civility, helped me to dismount, and handed me my umbrella.

'At what hour shall I be here again, sir?' I asked, concluding that we should part at once upon our separate errands.

'Where do you want to go?' said uncle Alexander, answering a question with a question.

'To the draper's and the furrier's.'

'Well, I'll walk with you as far as the furrier's. It lies in my way. Ostler, you may give the cob a feed of corn.'

Hereupon he went forward with mighty strides into the town, still keeping up the extinguisher-hood, and I kept pace with him as well as I was able. Presently he dived into a newspaper-office, and came out with the *Moniteur* in his hand; and in a few moments more we reached a shop which bore the name of Gilbert Lejeune, and the sounding title of *Magazin des Pelletiers de la Sibérie*.

Here M. Alexander, instead of leaving me and going on his way, unfolded his newspaper, lounged against the shop-door and began to read. I then took out Madame's list of orders, and selected two handsome sable muffs, two boas, and two pairs of cuffs to match, for her and Marguerite. This done, I would have turned to leave the shop; but the furrier, who was a very magnificent gentleman, with a bald head and a ruby-velvet waistcoat, insisted that I should be shown his 'latest novelties.'

'One moment's patience, mademoiselle,' he said, persuasively. 'Only do me the favour to observe these elegant winter-cloaks. We call them the Czarina mantles. They are lined throughout with excellent squirrel, and are made of the finest Saxony cloth. Only three hundred francs each, mademoiselle - only three hundred francs!'

I hesitated, wondered whether Madame would not think them too expensive, saw that she had only specified 'warm travelling-cloaks' in her written list, and finally decided that I was not authorized to give so large a sum.

'But they are absurdly cheap,' urged M. Lejeune. 'I protest to you, mademoiselle, that I am giving them away - positively giving them away at that price! Besides, I have served Madame Delahaye for more years than I can remember, and I know that this is precisely the article she would purchase.'

'Indeed, it is of no use,' I said, firmly. 'I cannot take upon

233

myself the responsibility of ordering anything so expensive.'

'Then mademoiselle will at least permit me to put this one down for herself?'

I smiled, and shook my head.

'Oh, dear, no,' I replied. 'It is very handsome; but I could not possibly afford it.'

Uncle Alexander looked over the top of his newspaper.

'What's all this about?' growled he. 'Who are the cloaks for? Why don't you buy them, and have done with it?'

'I dare not buy them,' I answered, 'for fear that Madame should be displeased at the price.'

'What is the price, then?'

'Three hundred francs a-piece, monsieur,' interposed the furrier. 'Only three hundred francs a-piece!'

'Is that dear, or cheap?' asked uncle Alexander, looking to me for explanation.

'Cheap, considering their value,' I replied; 'but, according to Madame Delahaye's written directions, I -'

'There, there, that will do! They're cheap, and that's enough! M. Lejeune, you'll send the cloaks up with the rest of the rubbish to the *Lion d'Or,*, and desire the ostler to put the parcel in the gig-box.'

'But, monsieur -' I began in great alarm, 'six hundred francs for only two cloaks -'

'*Sacrebleu!* do you suppose, mademoiselle, that I cannot afford to give away six hundred francs if I please?' shouted uncle Alexander, in a towering passion. 'Of course I mean to pay for them!'

Whereupon M. Lejeune bowed with great alacrity, and uncle Alexander wrote a cheque upon the spot.

'Be so good as to see that the amount is right,' said he, as he gave the paper into M. Lejeune's hand.

The tradesman took the cheque, stared, and seemed about to speak; but uncle Alexander seized him by the arm, and drew him suddenly away. Their conference did not last a moment. A word from the purchaser, a bow from the seller, another glance at the cheque, and it was over. Then M. Alexander crumpled his newspaper into his pocket, and strode out of the shop.

'What more do you want this morning?' said he, stopping short at the corner, where several streets diverged.

'Nothing but a shawl or cloak for myself, which it will take but a few minutes to choose,' I replied, curtly. 'If you will tell me when to meet you at the *Lion d'Or*, I need detain you no longer.'

A most peculiar and inexplicable grin overspread M. Alexander's countenance; and, to my utter amazement, he offered me his arm.

'This way,' said he. 'This way,' and dived down a dirty turning leading to the river.

'But I want to go to the draper's!' cried I, yielding very reluctantly.

To which he only replied -

'All right - short cut - this way, this way,' and hurried on like a man worked by steam.

The dirty lane opened on a wharf; the wharf led to a quay, and the third office on the quay bore the name of A. DELAHAYE painted on the door-post.

'Come in, come in,' said uncle Alexander, hustling me through an anti-chamber full of clerks, and depositing me in the corner of a dismal little private room, as cold as a well, and as dark as a dungeon. 'Won't delay you ten minutes. Business-letters to read through. Sit down, and make yourself comfortable.'

Comfortable, indeed! I should as soon have thought of comfort in the Black Hole at Calcutta! A bare floor, a single office-chair, a high desk and stool, a few dusty maps, a shelf full of ledgers, an empty grate, and a window overlooking a dead wall - these were the materials with which uncle Alexander expected his visitors to make themselves 'comfortable!'

I sat down in indignant silence, and gave myself up to a prolonged contemplation of this attractive retreat. Meanwhile, my singular companion, perched on his high stool beside the window, broke seal after seal, and filed letter after letter of his voluminous correspondence. This done, he summoned a clerk from the counting-house, scribbled a list of orders, and prepared to be gone.

'I've kept you three-quarters of an hour instead of ten minutes,' said he, with a glance at his watch. 'Are you cold?'

'Intensely. How can one be otherwise in a place like this?'

He chuckled, unlocked a cupboard, and brought out a large square bottle and a couple of glasses.

'Did you ever see anything like this before?' he asked, filling out a glassful, and holding it to the light.

It was a clear, colourless liquid, and had little fragments of gold-leaf floating about in it.

'This is the famous *goldenen wasser*, or golden water - a Dutch cordial,' said he. 'Drink it. It's very good, and will warm you.'

I drank it, unsuspecting victim that I was, and choked immediately; which delighted uncle Alexander to such a degree, that he held his sides and stamped about the room.

'Don't you like it?' said he, when he could laugh no longer. 'Don't you like it?'

'Like it, indeed! I feel as if I had swallowed a furnace.'

Whereupon uncle Alexander underwent a relapse, and then drank three glasses in succession without winking. He next locked up the bottle and glasses, and we went out. To my surprise, the chaise was waiting at the door.

'Get in, get in,' said M. Alexander, impatiently.

But I drew back, and reminded him that I had still another purchase to make in the town - 'which,' I added, 'is really of importance.'

'All right,' replied he. 'Set you down at the door, and wait for you. Get in.'

So I got in; and the cob, having had his feed of corn, rattled away gallantly. But rattled away in the wrong direction! Rattled away to the right instead of to the left; carrying me every moment farther and farther from the very quarter of the town that I required to go to!

'Surely, sir, we must have taken a wrong turning!' I said, after a few moments of uneasy silence. 'The draper ...'

'To the devil with the draper!' interrupted M. Alexander, with a vicious flourish of his whip. 'I've heard enough of the draper for to-day. Talk of something else.'

'But my cloak, sir! I must have my cloak!'

'To the devil with your cloak! I've heard enough of that also!'

I now lost all patience, and felt myself getting very red and angry.

'Upon my word,' said I, half rising in my place, 'this is unbearable! You carry a jest too far, monsieur, and I insist upon going back directly.'

Uncle Alexander grinned from ear to ear, and forced me back into my seat with one of the furry paws. By this time we had threaded the extreme suburb of the town, and emerged once more upon the open country.

236

'My good little woman,' said he, 'keep your temper. Your cloak is in the gig-box; and as soon as you get home, you shall have it.'

I looked at him in blank amazement.

'My - my cloak!' I stammered. 'In the gig-box!'

'Of course. You didn't suppose that I should get cloaks for the two others and let you go without, did you?'

The tears rushed to my eyes.

'Oh, monsieur!' I exclaimed, 'you - you surely have not given three hundred francs for a cloak for me?'

'My money is my own,' growled uncle Alexander, 'and I suppose I can do as I like with it - hey?'

I felt such a tightness in my throat that I could scarcely speak; but I strove to say something grateful.

'This - this gift,' I faltered. 'I have not deserved - I ...'

Uncle Alexander plucked furiously at his moustache, and glared upon me like a tiger.

'*Mille tonner-r-r-res!*' said he, with his fiercest roll of the R. 'If you attempt to thank me, I'll set you down in the middle of the road, and leave you to walk home by yourself!'

So I held my tongue; for he looked terribly in earnest, and we were a good many miles from Montrocher.

After this we were both silent; and it was not till we came almost in sight of our journey's end that my companion spoke again.

'See,' said he, pointing with his whip to a flock of heavy white clouds that were rising with the wind. 'We shall have snow after all!'

CHAPTER XXXII

A WINTRY MIGRATION

The transit to Lyons was long and fatiguing, and, as the railway was not at that time completed farther than Villefranche, we had to change into a public diligence and travel the last eighteen miles by the road. This was the dreariest part of our journey, for it was quite dark, and the snow which had been falling all day clogged up the wheels at every turn, and rendered our progress not only difficult, but dangerous.

Our little party just filled the interior, and Pierrette had a seat in the *rotonde*. We were all very tired. Marguerite, after having kept up throughout the day, was now thoroughly exhausted, and had fallen asleep with her head resting on her mother's shoulder. Madame dozed and nodded from time to time; and I, wrapped from head to foot in my fur-lined mantle, would gladly have done the same, but for the lurching and jolting of the diligence, and the querulous restlessness of M. Delahaye, who was sitting beside me. First, he was too hot, and must have the glasses down - then he feared the draught, and closed them - next, he must bathe his hands and forehead in *Eau de Cologne*; or light a match to see the time; or hunt for his voice-lozenges; or, seeing the conductor walking patiently through the snow beside the door of the vehicle, thrust his head out of the window over and over again, asking 'how much farther we had to go yet?' or 'what the deuce they meant by keeping us so long upon the road - positively!'

Thus, between alternate sleeping and waking, amid stoppages at post-houses, and delays where the *cantonniers* have not yet cleared the road, many hours wear by, and it is past midnight when we enter the outskirts of Lyons. A narrow interminable suburb - a line of fortification, and a gloomy gate that echoes as we pass - a glimpse of lighted buildings on the heights - a broad glittering river crossed by many bridges - a line of quays, wet and solitary - a sudden turn under an archway, and into a great court-yard, and a crowding up of ostlers and stable-boys with lanterns in their hands - these are the sights and sounds that tell us of the termination of our weary pilgrimage.

Then the door opens, the conductor is pushed aside, a gentleman springs upon the step, and an eager voice exclaims -

'Welcome - welcome to Lyons! I have been expecting you these three hours and more. You must have had a terrible journey from Villefranche!'

At the sound of her lover's voice, Marguerite looks up and smiles languidly, and M. Delahaye bursts into a torrent of lamentations.

'*Ah, mon Dieu!*' he cries, with uplifted hands. 'Such roads! such horses! such a vehicle! My nerves are torn to pieces, and I am sore and stiff all over! What a torture this day has been, M. Hamel! - what a torture!'

To all of which M. Hamel replies by smiling cheerfully, and pointing to a fly that has drawn up close beside the door of the diligence.

'Forget your troubles, *amici*,' says he, 'and prepare for comfort and supper! Here is a carriage waiting to convey you to your lodgings, where you will find all that such weary travellers can desire!'

And with this he lifts Marguerite out tenderly in his arms, and carries her to the other vehicle - helps to transfer the rugs and wraps in which we have been smothering ourselves all day - gives an arm to Madame, a shake of the hand to me, a nod to Pierrette, and a five-franc piece to the conductor - sees to our luggage, shuts the door upon us, jumps up beside the driver, and gives the word to start. So we rattle on again, up one street and down another, and across a broad stone bridge, to a quay bordered with trees. Then the fly stops; M. Hamel once more opens the door; and with the welcome words - 'You are now at home,' ushers us into a lighted hall, and up a broad staircase with a gilded balustrade.

Our lodgings are on the first floor, and consists of ten rooms *en suite*. The *salon* is cheerful and spacious, with crimson damask hangings, and painted panels, and large mirrors reaching from floor to ceiling. At the farther end blazes a huge fire, and yonder stands a goodly supper-table, gleaming with glass and silver, and displaying manifold creature-comforts desirable to the hungry. Then come waiters from a neighbouring *restaurateurs*, bearing pyramids of hot plates and covered dishes that send up 'a steam of rich distilled perfume' the moment they are brought into the room. And then we draw the table to the fire; and M. Delahaye temporarily forgets his sufferings; and Marguerite - lying upon the sofa - gets waited on by everybody; and we all praise and enjoy the supper to the full extent of its merits, and compliment M. Hamel upon his excellent management.

'Then you are content with your *courier*?' he says, laughingly.

'So well content, my esteemed friend, that I will with pleasure add my name to your certificate,' replies Monsieur. Whereat, seeing that he intends a witticism, we endeavour to look amused, and applaude politely; for he, be it known, especially prides himself on the maintenance of an elegant gravity, and looks upon a joke as the most flattering condescension which he can offer to society.

And now, having supped well, and talked about our journeys and adventures, we find that it is past two o'clock, and time to separate. So M. Hamel takes his leave till next morning, and the 'good-nights' travel round, and ere half an hour more is gone by, the tired heads are all laid to rest upon their pillows for the first time in Lyons.

Pleasant sleep and peaceful dreams, my pretty Marguerite, and may this night prove to thee the harbinger of that divine gift of health which is, of all God's blessings, 'most rare, precious, and celestial!'

CHAPTER XXXIII

OUR LIFE AT LYONS

Our life at Lyons went by very pleasantly; the winter was severe, but fine; and Marguerite's health improved slowly and surely. For a nervous invalid no residence could, perhaps, have been better chosen; and, for my part, I cannot conceive why travellers should concur in the dispraise of a city so finely situated, and, in many respects, so nobly constructed as this, which is islanded between the waters of the Saône and the Rhone. Encircled by heights fort-crowned and tree-clad, adorned with quays and bridges more elegant than those of Paris, and enjoying by water one of the finest approaches of any capital of Western Europe, this admirable picture, which already seems as if it could leave nothing more for the imagination to supply, is filled in by a background of the hills of Chambery and the Chartreuse, and the snowy pinnacles of the Alps of Savoy!

Everything was now done to amuse our dear invalid. M. Hamel, who had himself engaged apartments in the Place des Terreaux, studied her every wish, almost divined her every thought, and was the most devoted of lovers. For the sake of remaining near her, he gave up all his acquaintance at Chalons, and all his accustomed pursuits; only absenting himself for the weekly performance of his clerical duties seventy-nine miles away. He even brought a couple of horses over to Lyons, and when there came a particularly fine morning, induced her to ride out with him amid the delicious environs that reach for many a mile in every direction round about the city. These excursions, together with such amusement as was afforded every evening by the entertainments then going forward, soon brought back to Marguerite much of her old brightness and elasticity, and all her physical health.

'She must be cheerful,' said Dr. Grandet, 'if you never give her time to be sad.' His advice was now followed to the letter; but, for all that, her mind seemed never quite to recover its former tone. She smiled; but the smile no longer danced in the eyes as well as on the lips. She laughed; but her laugh lacked the sweet silvery ring of other times. Something was wanting, something was gone - and yet she was not unhappy. It was as if the glittering illusions of youth were already over - as if the first thought of death had prematurely sobered down the sparkling hues of life, and turned the world to earnest.

Perhaps, too, she began to question the future; to ask herself if she had done well and wisely; and, passionately as she loved him, to doubt whether her lot with M. Hamel would be so sunny and so thornless after all. Once she said to me - 'I do not like his associates, and I fear they lead him into expenses. I shall never forget that horrid Colonel Sylvestre!' And on another occasion, when we were alone together and expecting his arrival, she leaned her head dreamily upon her hand and said -

'The more intimate we become, the less I seem to know him. There are depths in his nature to which I can never penetrate - there are moments when I almost fear him. With all his calm, he can be fierce and terrible. Do you remember that evening by the ruins of La Rochepôt? How pitiless he was, and yet there was something fine about it, after all! I often wish that he would tell me more of himself, and have more confidence in me; but if I ask him of his past life, he either answers with a jest or silences me with a frown. I sometimes think that he cannot always have been what he is now, and that political troubles have worked some wrong upon him. Why, mademoiselle, he may once have held a title - who knows?'

'Who knows, indeed!' I replied, with a sigh, and there the subject ended.

Of all days in the week, Saturday was ever the saddest to Marguerite, Sunday the dullest, and Monday the happiest - for on Saturday M. Hamel left us to go to Chalons, on Sunday he was absent beyond recall, and on Monday the early train brought him back by two o'clock at the latest. Thus it happened that when the drawing-room door flew open one Saturday evening, and uncle Alexander stalked suddenly in, extinguisher-hood and all, nothing could have been more opportune, and none, save one, more welcome.

'Any room for me?' said he, carpet-bag in hand.

Marguerite flew to meet him, and, clasping both her arms about his neck, drew his rough face down to her own level and kissed him heartily.

'Oh, how glad I am!' she cried. 'Dear, dear uncle Alexander, how glad I am! Room for you, indeed! How dare you ask such a question?'

'Hey, then! you're pleased to see me, monkey? You're pleased to see me?' said uncle Alexander, submitting, with grim complacency to his niece's caresses, and dismissing the rest of us with a nod a-piece. 'Business slack - time to spare till Monday or Tuesday - thought I'd run down and see how you were getting on.'

'I am sure, my dear Alexander,' began M. Delahaye pompously, 'that the maximum of gratification which ...'

'Ay, ay - exactly,' interrupted his brother. 'That's why I'm here, you know. How d'ye like Lyons?'

'We like it,' said M. Delahaye, 'unequivocally. I may say unequivocally. It harmonizes with my own constitution, and has had the effect of restoring to Marguerite the - ahem! - the Roseate Gifts of Hebe!'

'It suits you plainly enough,' growled uncle Alexander. 'You're getting fat.'

M. Delahaye recoiled, changed colour, and cast a hurried glance at the nearest looking-glass.

'Fat! Good God! did you say *fat*?' he exclaimed, in agonized accents.

But his brother went on, with cruel indifference, to other subjects.

'This is a lively situation,' said he; 'but in the wrong place. You should have got up on one of the heights - better air, and cheaper rent. Good large rooms also; but too fine. Two - four - six ... no less than six looking-glasses, *parbleu!* What's the good of so much trumpery? You're none of you so handsome that you need care to see your own faces multiplied by six all round the room!'

'The apartments were chosen for us by M. Hamel,' said Madame, apologetically, 'and though they are somewhat dear, we are very comfortable in them.'

'M. Hamel is an extravagant spendthrift, with more money than taste,' blurted out uncle Alexander. 'At least,' added he, with a conciliatory pinch of Marguerite's pretty little ear, 'in every instance but one, monkey! In every instance but one!'

Marguerite looked vexed, but tried to laugh it off; and M. Alexander, who had by this time thrown aside his great coat, and extricated himself from a huge woollen comforter about five yards long, called for something to eat.

'For,' said he, 'I came down by the steamer, and I'm as hungry as an elephant.'

'By the steamer!' cried two or three of us at once. 'What could induce you to do that?'

'The difference between thirteen francs and four,' replied he, shortly.

'But, dear uncle,' expostulated Marguerite, 'why should you, in this bitter wintry weather, expose yourself for the sake of a few francs to ...'

'Tush, tush, monkey! nine francs saved are nine francs gained,' interrupted uncle Alexander. 'I can't afford to throw money away, like some folks.'

And with this he drew his chair to the table, made a mighty plunge at a raised pie, and for the next half-hour was too busy to speak another word. Then, having thoroughly excavated the pie, demolished some three or four side-dishes, and disposed of three parts of a bottle of Bordeaux, he ensconced himself beside the fire and smoked contentedly.

There was a long silence, during which Marguerite sat down on a stool at her uncle's feet, and I knitted quietly in a corner. Madame was the first to speak.

'Have you no news from Chalons!' asked she - 'nothing whatever to tell us?'

'Humph! not much. Charles Gautier is at Genoa; but I suppose none of you care to hear about him.'

Everybody looked uncomfortable, and nobody answered.

'And he has been elected an honorary member of the Royal Academy of Sciences at Turin. He will make a great name yet, take my word for it.'

'Does he talk of returning?' said Madame, with some embarrassment in her voice.

Uncle Alexander shook his head gloomily.

'Not a word of it,' said he. 'He's banished for many a year to come, depend on it - thanks to you and your precious parson!'

There was another dead silence, during which I looked up, and saw that M. Delahaye had thought it prudent to go to sleep. By-and-by M. Alexander laid down his pipe, stared fixedly at me, and said -

'Who is Dr. Bryant?'

I started at the unexpected sound of that dear name, and the work fell from my hands.

'The best and kindest friend that I have in the world!' I replied, eagerly. 'What of him?'

Uncle Alexander uttered a sort of grunt, and twisted his moustache.

'Oh, nothing particular. Only I saw the Vaudons yesterday, and they spoke of him.'

'Indeed! What did they say?'

'H'm! I don't know. Bid me tell you he was coming to see them, I think.'

'Coming to see them! When?'

'Really, I can't tell. Directly, I believe.'

Directly, and I seventy-five miles away! I was confounded, knew not what to say or think and, in my impatience, began unraveling my knitting without knowing what I was about. Meanwhile, uncle Alexander refilled his pipe, lit it deliberately, and watched me from under his eyelashes.

'Did they - did they tell you nothing more, sir?' I faltered, presently.

'Not that I can remember.'

I hung my head, and felt the tears of disappointment rising to my eyes. Then there was no invitation for me - no special word of any kind; and, unless my friend came himself all the way to Lyons, which, at his age and in this season was not to be supposed, there was no chance of our meeting after all.

Uncle Alexander grunted again, and fidgeted in his chair. Then, as if he had left his former sentence incomplete, added - 'But I've a deuced bad memory for messages,' and closed his eyes as if to end the subject.

Not long after this M. Delahaye woke up and challenged me to a game at chess, which lasted till it was time to go to bed.

CHAPTER XXXIV

ADRIENNE LECOUVREUR

A great actress, *en route* to Marseilles, was announced for one night at the grand theatre of Lyons. The sum by which she had been induced to interrupt her journey was something fabulous in the annals of a provincial management, and the tickets of admission were put up to auction in the saloon of the theatre. M. Delahaye took a box; but whether he took it for Marguerite's sake, or for the maintenance of his own dignity among those of his acquaintance who might be present, I could not venture to say. As the eventful day drew near, the excitement became prodigious. Special trains were advertised from Chalons, and even Dijon, which was forty-three miles farther off. Cabs, diligences, and vehicles of every description were put on the road between Villefranche and Lyons. The price of lodgings became suddenly augmented; and the hotel keepers placarded the town with modest announcements of beds at fifteen and twenty francs for the night.

These golden expectations were destined for once to be more than fulfilled. Visitors began to arrive for some three or four days beforehand, and on the last morning poured in by hundreds from every barrier. Not a wealthy land-owner, not a retired merchant, not a country gentleman within a radius of fifty miles, but brought out his antiquated family-carriage, and either travelled by easy stages, or posted up to the great manufacturing capital, to do honour to the greatest *tragédienne* that had trodden the national stage since the reign of Mademoiselle Mars.

The performance was announced for eight o'clock, and at half-past seven the fly came round to convey us to the theatre. Marguerite, who had been ailing and languid all the morning, wore a pale-blue dress of watered silk, and white roses in her hair; and

245

looked, though delicate, more than usually pretty.

The streets leading to the theatre were full of vehicles moving in two lines, and all in the same direction. The nearer we approached, the more difficult became our progress. By-and-by we stopped altogether, only advancing now and then at a foot-pace, and counting the minutes as they went by. Thus we crept on till within a few yards of the box-entrance, and then alighted. Monsieur gave his arm to Madame, I took charge of Marguerite, and in this order we made our way through the crowd as best we could; passed rapidly up the stairs, and through a double row of eager inquisitive faces; captured an attendant; and were shown, through a labyrinth of lobbies, ante-rooms, and corridors, to our box on the second tier.

Following thus at the heels of the liveried *domestique*, I was struck by the pale cheeks and faltering steps of my companion.

'What is the matter, *petite*?' I exclaimed. 'Are we going too quickly for you? Are you tired?'

Marguerite shook her head, and pressed her hand to her side.

'Not tired,' said she, 'but faint, and very nervous. Do you know, mademoiselle, I ... But I am almost ashamed to confess it!'

'Confess what, my darling?'

'Nay, you would think me so foolish!'

'Indeed, I will do nothing of the kind. Pray speak, or I shall begin to fancy a thousand things.'

'Well, then, I - I have such a strange feeling to-night, as if something were about to happen. I wish we had not come.'

'This is mere excitement,' said I, soothingly. 'You will forget it when the play begins.'

But she shook her head again, and repeated -

'I wish we had not come!'

By this time we had arrived at our box, and were ushered in with great ceremony by the attendant. The orchestra was just finishing the last bars of a popular overture, and, as we took our places, the curtain rose.

The piece was *Adrienne Lecouvreur*. The great actress whom we were met to see had no part to play till the second act, and so we paid at first more attention to the audience than the stage. The house was crowded to excess in every part; the pit was paved with heads; and the gallery presented an amphitheatre of faces, terminated only by the ceiling. For a long time the actors were inaudible, and the private boxes continued to fill when there was no longer standing room in any other part of the theatre. We amused ourselves by singling out those whom we knew, either by sight or personally. As for M. Delahaye, he was in the seventh heaven. Oiled, ringleted, and perfumed, he *posed* himself in the seat nearest the stage, so as to be seen to the best advantage; swept the house with his lorgnette; exchanged bows with his friends in the boxes; and wore his rings outside his gloves, that nothing of his splendour might be lost in this auspicious occasion.

'There is Grandet,' said he, 'in the stalls, and General Max beside him; and there is the Count de Beauvilliers and his young wife; they have come all the way from St. Etienne - positively! And I see Nicoud and Millary; and yonder, in a box as good as our own - as good, Madame Delahaye, as our own - that creature, Baudin - Baudin of Chalons - my tailor!'

Madame could not help smiling.

'Really, my dear,' said she, 'I do not see why Baudin should not have as good a right to a box as any one else, provided only that he has the money to pay for it.'

M. Delahaye put on a countenance expressive of horror; but, recollecting that horror was an unbecoming emotion, dismissed it immediately.

'My angel,' said he, impressively, 'your sentiments are democratic and vulgar, and break my heart. Pray let me never hear you speak in that afflicting strain again.'

Madame looked down and was silent, and Marguerite turned the conversation by pointing with her fan to a stage-box, and saying -

'Look, papa! There is Monsieur Deligny, and I think he sees us.'

It was M. Deligny, and the customary bows were exchanged. I leaned back in a shady corner of the box, and observed him attentively. Pallid of complexion, spare of figure, faultlessly, but plainly dressed, and manifesting in his every gesture the easy bearing of a polished man of the world, he was a person whom, once seen, it were impossible to forget. He seemed to be, like Faust's familiar, the very embodiment of the keen, cold, comprehensive intellect - the very type of a sceptic, or a critic. The box in which he sat was large and commodious, and contained several other gentlemen. One among these (a bronzed, black-bearded man, in a braided frock) appeared to be M. Deligny's especial friend, and engrossed most of his conversation. I could not help observing, however, that when the critic spoke, the others listened, and that his opinion was constantly appealed to. To judge by the disdainful lip with which that opinion was given, and the smiles with which it was received, one might readily guess that it was seldom very complimentary.

Scrutinizing him thus, I was reminded of the dinner at Madame Vaudon's, and of the antipathy which sprang up, almost at the first glance, between him and M. Hamel.

'Had I been in his position,' thought I, 'a stranger and a public character, I should hardly have liked to make M. Deligny my enemy.'

Just at this moment the curtain rose for the second act, and, for the first time, the house became profoundly silent. The scene represented the green-room of the *Comédie Française*, and the actors, costumed for their various parts in Bajazet and *Les Folies Amoureuses*, were seen coming, and going, and conversing among themselves. Some few unimportant phrases followed; expectation rose to its height; every eye, every glass was turned upon a door to the right of the scene, and, in the midst of the living hush, she entered.

A tall, slender woman, dark-haired, small-featured, and sad looking, with something intense and unfathomable underlying the pale composure of her face. With deep-set eyes, that glow like consuming fires, and with a physical organization so fragile, that it seems almost as if the storm of applause now breaking above her head might alone be sufficient to destroy her! Yet she is unmoved and calm as marble, and, when the tumult has abated, delivers the first lines of her part in a sonorous, deliberate tone that travels round the house like the rich notes of an organ.

I can never forget the thrill that traversed every fibre of my frame when that marvellous voice, in all its depth and melody, first fell upon my ear. It took away my breath, and I was so absorbed in my own emotion as to forget to observe how others were affected. The play became to me only Adrienne Lecouvreur. I saw no one else, heard no one else; forgot theatre, audience, stage, everything and every one save that frail heroine, with her burning eyes and her inspired gesture.

The piece went on. She loved, she doubted, she was jealous; and she bared her fierce jealousy as a surgeon with his knife might bare the shrinking nerves and quivering muscles of a wretch diseased. It was no longer acting; it was the living agony - the study of the artist Parrhasius.

Then came the scene in which she confronts her rival. Actress and princess, face to face, read each other's souls, and, in the presence of the man whom they both love, take up the deadly weapons of a secret hate. From passion to lamentation, from defiance to tenderness, from tears of joy to smiles that mask her torture, she passes with the fearful subtlety of truth! Her eyes dilate and blaze; her voice, gathering power and intensity, vibrates with scorn, and crushes her rival to the earth! Spell-bound and trembling, I lean my head up against the partition, and neither speak nor move. Thus the curtain falls upon the close of the fourth act, and then, and not till then, do I observe that M. Hamel has entered the box, and occupies a seat beside my own.

'I am very sorry,' says he, bending over the back of Marguerite's chair, 'but I could not get away sooner. I had hoped to be in time to escort you to the theatre.'

'And I,' replies she, 'am only grieved that you should have lost so much of the piece.'

'Oh, that is of little consequence. I have seen her play this very part three or four times already in Vienna.'

'And what do you think of her?'

'Think of her!' echoes M. Hamel. 'I think her one of the most appalling geniuses that ever lived. She is scarcely human, and reminds me of the Lady Geraldine of Coleridge, or of that most fearful of creations, the living-dead Morella of Edgar Poe. But, *à propos* of things unpleasant, is not that my quondam antagonist, Monsieur Deligny?'

'It is, indeed. How he stares at you!'

'Hah! does he? Nay, then, I have eyes and an opera-glass as well as he.'

And half laughingly, half haughtily, M. Hamel levels his lorgnette full upon the stage-box opposite. But the contest is unequal, and he is only one against many. No less than seven glasses are directed upon him from M. Deligny's box, and he of the bronzed face and braided frock appears to be speaking earnestly. The rest lay down their glasses and listen - raise them again and gaze intently - are interrupted by the rising of the curtain for the last act, and so relinquish the war of eyes, at least for the present.

And now it is Adrienne, and Adrienne alone, upon whom the attention of all these thousands is riveted. She is changed, she is suffering, she is in despair. Her voice is feeble, her step falters, and the light burns faintly in her eye, as in festal-lamps that fade and flicker towards morning. A strange air of exultation is apparent in her gestures - a bitter exultation wrung by her own sufferings from the memory of a by-gone tenderness. Her tones have a weary, thrilling, penetrating significance, which finds an echo and a sympathy in every breast. Then comes the fatal bouquet, poisoned by her rival; and then that reconcilement which is all too late, that outpouring of triumph, and passion, and wild joy, which rends the last frail thread of reason and hurries on the fever of dissolution.

And now the poison begins to work. Visible first in the tremulous tone and listless attitude, it next shows itself in the wandering eye, the seeking hands, the memory that betrays, and the tongue that will not do its office. She fancies herself once more in the presence of her rival; she believes herself acting, and upon the stage; she rises, inspired by the ghastly energies of death, and recites passages from Corneille! Then her strength fails; she again recognizes her lover; she struggles, oh, how piteously! with the pains that consume her; and, convulsed already with her last throes, cries aloud for 'life! ... life! ... one day, one hour of life, oh, God of mercy!'

Can this be all unreal?

The curtain has fallen. The great actress, who now, alas! can delight us never more, has appeared and reappeared, gathered her bouquets and wreaths from off the flower-strewn stage, and bowed her last farewell to the people of Lyons. The plaudits continue long after she has withdrawn, and are not yet over when we rise to leave the theatre. There is an after-piece to come, but none of us care to wait for it. Her voice is still ringing in our ears, our pulses are yet throbbing beneath the influence of a great emotion, and there is not one among us, unless it might be M. Delahaye, who would willingly remain to dissipate that impression. So we go down, much in the order that we arrived, excepting only that Marguerite and I take each an arm of M. Hamel's. The crush-room is so full, and the gentlemen both meet so many acquaintances, that it is a long time before we get out as far as the grand staircase, and even then we can proceed only by one step at a time.

When we are about half-way down, we find ourselves brought suddenly face to face with M. Deligny and his friend. Marguerite is at the moment looking back up the staircase, fancying that she has descried the Vaudons at a distance. I alone am witness of the scene that follows.

Checked by the stream from above, and wedged in by the numbers below, we are brought to a temporary standstill. M. Deligny does not choose to recognize M. Hamel, and, most probably, has forgotten me altogether. Instead, therefore, of exchanging salutations, they stare haughtily at each other like perfect strangers.

Then M. Deligny presses his friend's arm and murmurs some inaudible inquiry, to which the stranger, fixing his eyes full on M. Hamel's face, replies distinctly -

'Yes; in the Brazils.'

It takes several moments to tell the events of one, and this brief episode took place so rapidly that before I well knew what had happened, it was over. In another second the crowd had swept them past, and Marguerite, looking round once more, said -

'I really don't think it was the Vaudons, after all ... but, *mon Dieu*, Alexis! what ails you? You tremble - are you ill?'

And then I saw that M. Hamel had turned dead white, even to his lips, and looked faint and bewildered, like a man just roused from sleep.

CHAPTER XXXV

COMING EVENTS

It was now April. A month had passed by since the night at the grand theatre, and we were still in Lyons. No events of any importance had occurred since then, either in the town, or in the bosom of the Delahaye family. M. Hamel had come and gone as usual; Marguerite's spirits had continued improving as before; M. Alexander had repeated his visit but once, and then only for a single evening; and M. Delahaye and I continued to play at chess 'every evening until further notice.' Nothing, in short, had happened to ruffle the still waters of our daily life, and yet an important change was on the eve of taking place.

Marguerite was about to be married.

It was sudden, but not wholly unexpected. Ever since they had been affianced, M. Hamel had remonstrated against a long betrothal; and now that our darling's health was re-established, and the early spring had set in with unusual splendour, he never ceased to importune for a speedy marriage, or to point out the delights and advantages of a wedding tour at this season of the year. The consent of her parents once obtained, Marguerite was soon persuaded; and so, almost before we were aware of it, April came round, and the appointed time drew nearer every day.

Always impatient, M. Hamel had, during the whole of this last month, manifested a degree of anxiety which surprised even his betrothed. He urged on the preparations with a haste for which there was no necessity; was nervous, irascible, and exacting; and, though an inconveniently early date had already been conceded, continued to entreat with feverish eagerness for the remission of six, or four, or even two days from the appointed time.

'I feel,' said he, 'as if every moment were fraught with danger and uncertainty - as if an invisible hand were outstretched above our heads, and might at any instant snatch her from my side! If I be importunate, it is my love that makes me so. If I offend, blame not me, but the fears and hopes that beset me night and day. Till she is mine, I am nothing - not even myself. I can settle to nothing - do nothing - think nothing, but with reference to her; and not till I am assured that no power on earth can part us, shall I again be happy and at rest!'

And so it came that they were to be married on the sixteenth, and that the contract was to be signed the evening before, in the presence of a small party of friends and relatives. Also the wedding was to take place in Lyons; an arrangement which, if it were in some respects expensive and inconvenient, was in others wisely made. In the first place, it was desirable that the bride's trousseau should be purchased and made up in an important capital where the fashions were found in as great perfection as in Paris. Secondly, it was thought that a return to Montrocher might possibly induce a return of Marguerite's despondency, and awaken recollections now quite laid to rest. Thirdly, it was M. Hamel's intention to carry his young wife direct to Florence for the May season, bringing her home, about July, through North Italy and the Tyrol; and as, to carry out this project, they must take the steamer from Marseilles, it was very properly decided that, instead of travelling to Montrocher and then travelling back again, they should avoid all this unnecessary fatigue by remaining quietly at Lyons, which was already eighty miles on the way.

So letters of invitation were forwarded to certain aunts, cousins, and godfathers, of whom I had never heard before; and Monsieur Delahaye engaged rooms for his guests in a neighbouring hotel, after the manner of those potentates who, on special occasions, do assemble together more guests than they have royal palaces to accommodate; and there were rumours of gifts; and discussions on the subject of laces and orange-flowers; and long consultations about bridesmaids; and, above all, there was rejoicing and jealousy among the milliners and haberdashers of the good city of Lyons.

'A letter for ma'mselle,' said Pierrette, coming into my bedroom one morning with the missive on a salver.

I was awake in an instant.

'A letter for me!' I exclaimed. 'Where can it be from?'

'From Chalons, I think, ma'mselle, by the post-mark,' replied Pierrette, opening the shutters and admitting a flood of yellow sunlight. 'I felt sure it was for you, because the postman could not pronounce the name, and I could not read it.'

'Certainly, an excellent reason,' said I, laughing. 'Thank you for acting on it, Pierrette: the letter is quite right.'

Pierrette courtesied and left the room, and I hastened to break the seal, for the writing was Dr. Bryant's.

In ran thus:-

Chalons, April 7, 18—.

'MY DEAR LITTLE GARTHA,

'After more delays and broken promises than I should care to count, behold me here at last, within visiting distance of yourself and Lyons! You will, no doubt, tell me that I have come at precisely the wrong season, and that I should either have shared in the Dionysia of the vintage, or helped to tell ghost stories round the yule fire on Christmas-eve. I am fully prepared to admit the justice of these, your anticipated reproaches; but, my dear little Gartha, I come urged by a stronger motive than either the autumn or winter festivities could have held out to me. I don't care much for grapes till they have been half-a-dozen years in bottle; and I have no curiosity to taste that most melancholy of exiles - a French plum-pudding. You, and you alone, are the object of my journey.

'The fact is, that I have heard how Mademoiselle Delahaye is about to exchange your yoke for one still heavier; and, foreseeing that from that day forth your occupation's gone, I thought I could not do better than cross the Channel and fetch you home in triumph. So prepare to be gone when the wedding is over; for my holiday must not be a long one, and Brookfield, remember, is doctorless!

'I have a thousand things to talk over with you when we meet; which I hope may be very soon. I have, however, only just arrived, and for at least a few days my movements must be regulated by my cousin's engagements. Among other things, I am charged with a message from Mr. Williams, our Brookfield lawyer. In obedience to your wishes, he has lately looked through a variety of old documents relating to your father's affairs, and has forwarded some of them for your perusal. Had you not called on him for the express purpose of learning these particulars, I should have advised you not to rake up the ashes of the past. The wrong is done, the money is gone beyond recall, and it can only grieve you to know what might have been. Lost siller, little Gartha, is never worth counting.

'You will be pleased to hear that poor old Janet is hale and sulky as ever. She has taken of late to rearing poultry, and as she is no bad hand at a bargain, does well in her new profession. The moor-house, I hear, will be pulled down, to make way for the railroad which is to connect us with Durham. The Brookfield church has just been furnished with a new peal of bells, which I may say are wrung out of the pockets of the parishioners. Young Brandon has sold his business and gone to the deuce; old Grimsby died last January of bronchitis and beer; I have been obliged to part with my pony, and cannot easily get another to suit me; and last week there was a shocking murder close by - of kittens.

I believe I have now given you a complete summary of our local news, and long to hear all yours in exchange. By-and-by, I have brought you some money - your half-year's dividend on the 400l. in the funds.

'Let me hear from you soon, and tell me the earliest day that you can fix for your return to England. Ah, little Gartha! when I once get you back, I will not easily part with you again.

'Ever your friend and guardian,

'EDWARD BRYANT.

'P.S. My cousin tells me that I must not hope to see you before the evening of the fifteenth, when, I understand, there is to be a party at M. Delahaye's, and they are all invited. It is a long time - more than a week; but I suppose I must have patience.'

I read the letter twice through. That he should be actually arrived, and that he should have taken this journey for me, me who - it was too much even for my stoicism, and I blotted the paper with grateful tears. It relieved my mind also of an anxiety that had weighed upon it for the last month or more. Neither Monsieur nor Madame had yet, it is true, spoken to me on the subject of my departure; but ever since this marriage was decided, I knew that I must leave, and had lain awake many a night considering where I should go, and what I should do next? Sometimes I had thought of trying to get a situation in London or Paris; sometimes of attempting to open a school in Lyons, where there were English residents in plenty.

Now, however, my good old friend's invitation tempted me with the prospect of a holiday, and gave me leisure to mature my future plans. Dear, dear Dr. Bryant! how full of thankfulness is my heart this morning: and yet -

And yet, somehow or another, I shall be sorry to leave Montrocher!

CHAPTER XXXVI

HAND AND GLOVE

'At last Gartha! at last!' exclaimed Dr. Bryant, taking both my hands in his, and leading me away into the farther room. 'There - don't speak for a moment - let me look at you. So, so! how well and young she looks; ten years younger than when we parted a year ago!'

'My kind friend,' said I, half laughing, and half crying, 'have you come all the way to France to teach me vanity?'

But he only smoothed my cheek with a tremulous hand, and repeated - 'so, so little Gartha! a year - a whole year!'

'Has it seemed so long, then?'

'It *has* seemed long, and yet it has gone by quickly. Time flies faster and faster as one gets old, Gartha.'

'Nay, dear sir, you must not yet begin to talk of age!'

He shook his head, and smiled sadly.

'Whether I talk of it or not, I feel it, Gartha,' said he. 'This last winter has tried me severely. I cannot bear our bleak moor-winds as bravely as I used; or start out of my bed upon a midnight journey without being almost as ill as the patient I go to visit. I fear I shall have to give up before long, and make over my practice to a younger, and a better man.'

As he said this, I observed him more closely, and saw that he did indeed look grayer and thinner than when we parted. His voice, too, was less steady than ever; but this might be from excitement, for it was the night of the party given in honour of the signing of the contract, and the rooms were filling fast.

'I wish you would do so,' said I, sighing. 'Yours is an arduous profession, and I do not see why you need labour in it longer. I am very glad that you have taken this holiday.'

'So am I; for I don't believe I should have got you back easily without it!'

'Take care! I may escape you yet!'

'Eh? what do you mean? How can you stay here after - after your pupil is out of your hands?' asked Dr. Bryant, nervously. 'Surely you are not going to get married too?'

'Married! Indeed no - not I; but in case I procured another situation ...'

'Don't think of it - don't name it,' interrupted he. 'If you knew how I have built on taking you back with me to England, you would not even entertain the idea of it. Gartha, my dear little Gartha - I have not many more years to live, and I don't know what I shall do if you will not spend them with me!'

More moved by this appeal than I cared to show, I pressed his hand, turned away my head, and said -

'Well, dear friend, we will not talk of that at present. Time enough when this wedding is over.'

'True - true. Let us change the subject. Who is that pretty girl with the black ringlets? Is she the bride- elect?'

'No - she is a cousin, I believe, from Mâcon. I never saw her before. Yonder stands Marguerite, in a white dress looped with roses. She is talking to an old lady near the piano.'

'Ah, she is pretty too; but looks pale, poor child!'

'Yes; she has but lately recovered from a nervous illness, and has been out of spirits all the day. I shall be glad when she is really married and gone; for another week of this excitement would be enough to kill her.'

Dr. Bryant put on his glasses and looked at her attentively.

'Poor thing! poor thing! I heard all about it,' said he. 'What about the *fiancé*? Do you like him?'

'He is handsome and accomplished.'

'H'm! rather an evasive answer! Matilda Vaudon lauds him to the skies, and so does her daughter.'

'Well, M. Hamel is very fascinating.'

'But he has not fascinated you?'

'Not yet, certainly. However, if he only makes Marguerite happy, I will cast my prejudices to the winds, and laud him as heartily as the rest. Do you see that cheerful-looking little man now talking to Madame Delahaye? He is a member of your profession, and his name is Grandet.'

'I have heard the Vaudons speak of him. What uncouth, surly, shock-headed individual is that beside him?'

'Monsieur Alexander Delahaye - Marguerite's uncle.'

'Indeed! I never saw any one who looked more disagreeable in my life.'

'Then it is the old story of the husk and the kernel,' said I; 'for a better heart never beat beneath a rough exterior. He is very eccentric, very blunt, very churlish; but ...'

Dr. Bryant changed colour, and seized me by the wrist.

'Who is that man?' he interrupted, eagerly.

'What man?'

'There - there! He has just come in - he speaks to Madame Delahaye, and now turns to her daughter. Who is he?'

'Why, the very person we were talking of just now. That is M. Hamel.'

'Monsieur Hamel!'

'Yes - the bridegroom.'

'Oh, heavens!'

And Dr. Bryant half rose from his seat, sank back again, and uttered a sort of smothered groan. His pallor and his agitation alarmed me.

'Good God!' said I, 'what is the matter?'

He wiped the cold drops from his forehead, and looked fixedly at M. Hamel before replying. Then, turning to me, -

'Gartha,' said he, solemnly, 'if I did not believe it to be impossible, I should say that yonder man was - your aunt Eleanor's husband!'

For some moments I scarcely comprehended the sense of his words. My aunt Eleanor's husband - the worker of my father's ruin! The room swam round before my eyes, and I turned sick and giddy.

'No, no,' I faltered; 'it is impossible! It cannot be!'

Dr. Bryant shuddered, and covered his eyes with his hand.

'It is twenty years now since last I saw him,' said he; 'and yet the resemblance - so exact - only the changing of the hair from black to grey - every feature the same ... Oh, that I had some proof!'

An idea - a revelation, flashed upon me.

'Stay here till I return,' said I, and glided from the room.

I was not three minutes absent, and, coming breathlessly back, brought with me that little carved-ivory box containing the miniature, which I had hidden away during Marguerite's illness, and which had remained in a corner of my box ever since.

I opened it, and placed the locket in his hand.

'Tell me,' said I, 'whose portrait is this?'

He looked, and gave it back in silence. One glance at his face was enough. I knew his answer before he uttered it.

'His wife's.'

Here then was 'confirmation strong' - here the secret of that haunting face, that, seen dimly through the mists of many years, came back upon me like the vision of a dream. My father's sister - my poor, heartbroken, betrayed aunt Eleanor! My own faint and far-away remembrance of her needed but this clue. I comprehended all now, and the reminiscence and the portrait identified each other in my mind, fitting together like the two fragments of a broken link.

For several moments neither of us spoke. My thoughts were tumultuous and confused, and I could see by Dr. Bryant's face that his own were no less troubled. When he did go on, it was in a voice that vainly struggled to be calm.

'Gartha,' said he, 'we must not suffer this marriage to take place.'

'Alas! how are we to prevent it? What can we say? That he defrauded my father twenty years ago; that he squandered his wife's fortune; and that, through his misdeeds, I am comparatively penniless ... This is much; but is it enough? Should we be justified in over-whelming a whole family with distress; in ...'

'Hush, hush! You know not what you say,' interrupted he, with increasing agitation. 'You do not know half. You ... I *must* speak; but, oh! what a painful office!'

'Stay - there is another course. Consult first with M. Alexander. He is clear-headed, prompt, and energetic; and, above all, he is no friend to M. Hamel.'

Dr. Bryant gave utterance to a sigh of relief, and nodded acqui-escence; so I left him to seek for M. Alexander in the adjoining *salon*. But I was too late. The guests were already crowded round a small table at the farther end of the room. The notary had arrived, and was drawling through the tedious formalities of the contract. Marguerite was leaning on her father's arm; and M. Alexander, hemmed in five or six deep, was standing beside the man of law, and reading the document over his shoulder.

Baffled and perplexed, I stood beyond the circle, and hoped that he might chance to look up presently.

Meanwhile, the notary read on -

'Whereby the contracting parties are mutually bound in law: and the aforesaid Marguerite Hélène Delahaye, having by the consent of her parents and guardians taken upon herself the above-named obligations, does give and consign to the aforesaid Alexis

Xavier Hamel -'

'*To whom?*' interrupted a clear, grave voice.

The notary broke off suddenly - the crowd about the table fell back - every eye was turned in the direction of the sound - and there - there, in the shadow of the doorway stood Monsieur Deligny, accompanied by the same dark stranger who was with him at the theatre a few weeks before.

There was a brief silence. Then M. Alexander pushed his way through, and confronted the intruders.

'What is the meaning of this interruption?' said he, angrily. 'Who spoke?'

M. Deligny took a step in advance, and replied -

'I did.'

'Well, sir - well! What then? What is your business?'

'My business,' said M. Deligny, with quiet dignity, 'is the business of a friend. I come to save an honourable family from disgrace, and a young lady from a most unhappy alliance.'

At this M. Hamel flushed crimson, stepped haughtily forward, and was about to speak; but the other checked him by a gesture, and went on -

'My communication,' said he, 'must be made to M. Delahaye himself. I have only, therefore, to request that the reading of the contract may be suspended while he favours me with a few moments of private conversation.'

'Sir, this is an insult - an intrusion,' interposed M. Hamel, speaking fast and hoarsely. 'The reading of the contract must go on. If you have anything to say, it must be said to me, sir - to me - when ...'

'I have nothing to say to any one but the father of Mademoiselle Delahaye,' said M. Deligny, without deigning even a glance towards M. Hamel.

Thus directly attacked, Monsieur Delahaye turned an appealing face first upon M. Hamel, and then upon his brother - hesitated - hemmed - and knew not what to reply.

'This is really,' said he, 'a - a most unprecedented and perplexing visit. I - positively I - that is to say, my daughter - eve of - ahem! matrimonial alliance - gentleman of distinguished position - high personal and professional merits -'

'I presume,' said M. Deligny, with increasing coldness, 'that you allude, monsieur, to the person calling himself Alexis Xavier Hamel;

260

but I must be permitted to undeceive you. This man is an impostor. His name is not Alexis Xavier Hamel; and he never took orders in his life.'

M. Delahaye sank, with a gasp, into the nearest chair; but M. Hamel sprang forward to face his accuser.

'It is a lie!' he cried, furiously. 'It is a lie, and I demand satisfaction - instant satisfaction!'

M. Deligny turned upon him, for the first time, with a bitter smile.

'Were you what you pretend to be,' said he, deliberately, - 'a minister of the church - you could not ask it of me. Being what you are, I refuse to give it.'

A blow aimed and intercepted - Hamel held back by M. Alexander - Deligny pale and disdainful - Marguerite shrinking to her mother's side - a crowd of wondering faces all about - This was the strange picture of which I was all at once a witness.

'Let there be an end of this,' said uncle Alexander. 'Say what you have to say, Monsieur Deligny. If this person has imposed upon us, he has also imposed on others, and the more public your disclosures are, the better. Who is he?'

'His name,' replied M. Deligny, impassable as ever, 'is Larivière - Alexis Amédée Larivière. He is a native of Chartres, and began life in Paris as a notary-public. In the year 18— he became first agent for, and then director of, a bubble speculation conducted by a party of adventurers calling themselves the "Ural Mountains Diamond-Mining Company." Vast sums were collected in various countries; but especially in France and England. The bubble broke - hundreds of families were ruined - the fraudulent directors absconded with seven millions of francs; and Larivière fled to the Brazils. Tracked to Rio Janeiro, he was given up by the Portuguese authorities, removed to French Guiana, tried at St. Louis, and condemned to fourteen years of penal servitude in the mines. Having had time, however, to dispose of his share of the plunder, Larivière was taken with only a few hundred francs upon his person, and all search for the money proved ineffectual. Before seven years of his term of punishment had expired, he found means to effect a daring escape, was supposed to have floated down the Marawina in an open boat, and was probably rescued near the coast by some European vessel. From that time to the present, Alexis Amédée Larivière was never seen or heard of more.'

A subdued murmur ran round the room, and Marguerite sobbed audibly. But Hamel himself stood by pale and stern, with arms folded on his breast, and eyes that flashed a sullen fire at every fresh disclosure.

'Go on, sir - go on,' said uncle Alexander, with grim satisfaction.

M. Deligny bowed, rested his elbow on the piano, fell into a negligent attitude, and continued -

'I have said that the convict Larivière disappeared utterly; but I have yet to inform you that about four years after his escape, one Adrien Beaumarchais, called Count de Beaumarchais, made his appearance at Vienna, and there resided with extraordinary splendour during a period of several months. I have been at some pains to trace out the subsequent career of this person; but as my inquiries only date from a few weeks back, I must be pardoned if the gaps in my narrative be frequent. The Count de Beaumarchais gave himself out as the only survivor of a noble French family which had taken refuge in Mexico during the Reign of Terror, and there accumulated a vast fortune by commerce. Popular and accomplished as he was, however, the count became the victim of court curiosity. Some indiscreet genealogist discovered that the family of Beaumarchais had been extinct since the beginning of the seventeenth century, and the count found himself regarded in the light of an impostor. From Vienna he withdrew to Baden, Homburg, Ems, Wiesbaden, and every similar haunt of *parvenu* adventurers and *soi-disant* nobility. He became a gambler; lost and won fortune after fortune; was detected in the act of concealing a card; and was compelled once more to beat a hasty retreat. Lost sight of for another year or two, we find him in 18— appearing as primo basso at the Venice theatre, in the part of Caspar, and under the name of Savarino. He fails, disappears again, and returns upon the scene after a long absence - this time as travelling tutor to a young Englishman of fortune, and under the new *alias* of Alexis Xavier Hamel.'

A cry of rage burst from the lips of M. Hamel. He seemed as if he would have sprung upon the speaker, but was again held forcibly back by M. Alexander.

Deligny acknowledged the obligation by a careless bow, and proceeded -

'Prefacing his name with the title of Reverend, we now find him conducting his pupil through Europe and part of Asia, aspiring towards church patronage, and for the first time in his life, seeking peace, retirement, and respectability. A living is promised to him by the father of his pupil; but he forfeits it through his own culpable indiscretion. He initiates the young man into the mysteries of the gaming-table, is dismissed from his tutorship, and is glad to accept a remote appointment at the town of Chalons-sur-Saône. Beyond this point I need not go. Whether as Larivière, Beaumarchais, Savarino, or Hamel he is still infamous, and still the same. Notary, director, convict, count, actor, tutor, and mock-priest, he stands before you now, and I stand here to unmask him!'

'It is false!' exclaimed the accused, with wild vehemence. 'It is false as hell!'

'It is true as heaven!' replies Deligny, solemnly, 'and I am ready to prove it.'

Whereupon uncle Alexander nods approvingly, and Monsieur Delahaye, fanning himself with his pocket-handkerchief, is heard to bewail the delicacy of his nerves.

'In the first place,' said M. Deligny, 'I beg to introduce to you my friend, Don Manoel de Campos, Governor of the fortress of St. Pedro, at Rio Janeiro. Having seen the said Hamel five or six weeks since at a public theatre here in Lyons, he is prepared to identify him as the convict Larivière.'

The dark stranger stepped forward, laid his hand upon his heart, and said with a deep sonorous accent -

'It is true.'

'And, farther still, I have the written testimony of the *chef de police* at Vienna, and a letter from the father of the young Englishman with whom he was travelling a year ago. If this be not enough ...'

'If this be not enough,' said Dr. Bryant, rising and coming forward, 'then I also am willing to bear witness to at least the first part of this gentleman's disclosures.'

Exclamations of surprise broke from the lips of all present, and even M. Hamel fell back a step, and started at the sight of this fresh accuser.

'You!' he faltered. 'Who are you? What do you know of me? I never saw you in my life!'

'You have forgotten me,' said Dr. Bryant, with great agitation; 'but I remember you well. I knew you the moment you entered this room, though it is more than twenty years since last I saw you.'

'Twenty years!' murmured Hamel, with an air of bewilderment.

Dr. Bryant glanced round, and, seeing me standing at a little distance, took my hand in his, and led me forward.

'Look at this lady,' said he, 'and tell me how it is that for so many months you can have met her almost daily without being struck either by the features or the name of Gartha Wylde?'

The last tinge of colour fled from Hamel's face, and left him lividly white.

'Gartha Wylde!' he echoed, faintly.

'Ay, daughter to that Martin Wylde whom you robbed and ruined - niece to that Eleanor Wylde (your most unhappy wife) whose fortune you squandered, and whose family you disgraced! Monsieur Delahaye - this man is indeed Larivière! I knew him in England twenty years ago. He was then agent for the Ural Mountains Diamond-Mining Company. This honourable and respectable family was utterly ruined by him, and by him this orphan-girl is reduced to poverty.'

'Oh, brother Alexander! dear brother Alexander!' cried M. Delahaye, looking the picture of helpless indecision. 'What shall I do? What shall I say? Has nobody a bottle of salts to lend me? Alas! my poor nerves!'

'Do, indeed!' said M. Alexander, savagely. 'Do! Don't you hear that this parson of yours is a common felon, and haven't you the spirit of a man to stand up and order him out of your doors?'

But before her father could answer, Marguerite had disengaged herself from her mother's clasp, and was clinging to M. Alexander's arm.

'Oh, uncle Alexander!' she cried, imploringly, 'don't *you* turn against him, too! You are condemning him without proof! How can you be sure that all these things are true?'

'Unless they were true, mademoiselle,' began Deligny, compassionately, 'we should not ...'

'Silence!' she said, interrupting him so fiercely that he started as if he had been stung. 'Silence, sir! You hated him from the first. This is your plot, and I disbelieve every word of it, from beginning to end!'

Her eyes flashed - her colour rose - she looked almost heroic in her indignation. Then she turned to her lover, and every feature melted into tenderness.

'Alexis,' she said, earnestly, 'Alexis! Tell me that you are innocent, and, though all the world should abandon you, I will trust you for ever!'

A gleam of triumphant joy passed over his face, and was succeeded by such a look of determination as I had never seen there before. It was as if some fresh hope had been opened to him, and, despite all difficulties, he had resolved to profit by it.

'I *am* innocent!' he cried, passionately. 'Marguerite - my own Marguerite, I *am* innocent, and I shall live to prove it! Trust me, defend me, wait for me, and the time shall soon come when I will answer my enemies as they deserve! Ah, Marguerite, if I only know that you believe in my truth, not a lie that has been spoken this night will have power to harm me!'

So frank and fervent were his accents, that Marguerite uttered a cry of thankfulness, and I, for the moment, felt my conviction shaken. Even Deligny hesitated, and uncle Alexander's brow relaxed somewhat of its severity.

'Suppose,' said he, doubtfully, 'that we are accusing the wrong man after all? It is a long time since either of these gentlemen have seen Larivière, and if there should be any mistake of resemblance ...'

'Not in my case,' interrupted Dr. Bryant. 'I would swear to him with my last breath!'

'And I also,' said Don Manoel, 'though his hair has turned from black to white since then. But,' and here he raised his voice, and his eye glittered keenly, 'there need be no hesitation about the matter. All felons condemned to the mines of French Guiana are branded with a cross on the palm of the right hand.'

There was a moment of dead blank silence, during which M. Hamel's lips were seen to move without the utterance of a sound. Then he looked despairingly towards the door; but uncle Alexander's iron grasp was upon him in an instant.

'Take off your glove,' said he, sternly. 'Take off your glove, or, by heaven! ...'

Before he could pronounce the threat, Hamel had dealt him a fierce blow, and dragged him half-way to the door, in the effort to get free! For one brief second all was struggling and confusion. Then I heard the words 'consummate hypocrite!' and saw - Hamel held back by Deligny and the Portuguese; uncle Alexander forcing open the clenched hand, about which the glove was now hanging in shreds; Marguerite fallen senseless at her mother's feet; and, there - there in the unwilling palm, a deep red cross seamed indelibly upon the flesh!

Another instant, and, by a mighty effort, he had snatched the hand away and broken from them.

'All's over,' said he, hoarsely. 'The game is played out - you've won - enjoy your triumph, and take my curses with it! Stand back there - I *will* see her again!'

And thrusting those aside who had crowded between them, he forced his way to where Marguerite was lying with her head against her mother's knees. He stood for a moment looking down upon her; then lifted her in his arms, and kissed her pale cheeks tenderly. No one stirred. No one raised a finger to prevent him. They knew they had to deal with a desperate man, and that now, at least, he was no longer feigning.

'Farewell,' he murmured. 'Farewell, my last, best, only love! Forget me, and may another make thee happier than I ever could have made thee!'

With this he kissed her again, and a heavy sob broke from his lips. Then he carried her to a sofa, laid her gently down, and without one glance right or left, and only a stunned despairing look upon his face, walked straight out of the room, and down the echoing stairs.

CHAPTER XXXVII

UNCLE ALEXANDER'S PRISONER

Another week went by. We were still in Lyons, and likely to remain there; for Marguerite lay dangerously ill of brain fever, and none could tell how soon she might recover, if at all.

Of Larivière (or Hamel, as I prefer to call him) nothing had been seen or heard since the night of the contract-party. Information of his story had, however, got abroad, and we were told that a warrant was issued for his apprehension. He was not in Lyons, that was very certain; and he was not in Chalons, for his lodgings there, said uncle Alexander, were closed up and deserted. He was gone, in short, no one knew whither.

Sitting one morning in the darkened bedroom where Marguerite lay moaning in her flushed and restless sleep, my attention was drawn to a scratching upon the panels of the door, and a subdued cough or two in the outer passage. I opened the door, and saw M. Alexander. He laid his finger on his lip, peeped cautiously in at Marguerite, and beckoned me away into an adjoining room.

'Look at this,' said he, bringing a folded paper out of his pocket. 'I saw a bill-sticker at work with them on one of the quays a quarter of an hour ago, and I got this one from him. They'll be all over Lyons before night.'

It was a placard minutely describing the size, features, voice, and general appearance of 'one Alexis Amédée Larivière, *alias* Alexis Xavier Hamel, late of Chalons-sur-Saône, escaped convict from the colony of Cayenne, branded in the right hand with a Greek cross, etc., etc.'

'Humph! that's a pretty thing to be published throughout the department, isn't it?' growled uncle Alexander, seeing that I had read and laid it down in silence. 'That will attach a delightful notoriety to Marguerite's name, especially if he's caught and brought back in irons, won't it?'

'It is a great misfortune,' I replied, sorrowfully.

'And there's no help for it.'

'None, indeed.'

'Unless ...' said uncle Alexander, hesitatingly, 'unless ...'

'Unless what?'

'Unless it were possible to get him out of the country; ship him off to America, for instance. What d'ye think?'

'That it would be the best thing in the world - the only thing to keep a second trial out of the papers. But, then, he is nowhere to be found.'

Uncle Alexander stroked his moustache, and shrugged his shoulders.

'But if one could find him,' suggested he; 'does he deserve to escape? Wouldn't it serve him rightly to be sent back to the mines, the scoundrel?'

'Not if you know of any means of saving him, as I seem to

think you do!' I said, earnestly. 'He is a brave man, be his sins what they may; and remember, sir, that, with regard to Marguerite, his only crime was loving her too much.'

'I believe he really was in earnest, as far as that went,' said uncle Alexander.

'I'm sure of it, sir.'

He thrust his hands into his pockets and paced backwards and forwards for a few minutes, thinking profoundly. Then he wheeled suddenly round, peered quite into my face, and said - 'You're a good little soul, and you've more common sense than anybody in this house. Put on your bonnet, and come out with me directly.'

To which, although it was the civilest speech that I had ever heard from M. Alexander, I replied no otherwise than by going straight away for my bonnet, and obeying him instantly.

As we were going down the stairs, we met M. Delahaye coming up. Seeing us together, he looked surprised, and would have spoken; but uncle Alexander laid his hand on his shoulder, and said, 'I want her - particular business - back in half an hour,' and hurried me on before his brother had time to reply.

Passing down beside the river, and through one or two side streets, I saw copies of the placard pasted up here and there against the walls, and round the trunks of trees. Then I found that we were taking the road towards a kind of little stable-yard and coach-house that had been rented by M. Delahaye for the accommodation of his horse and chaise ever since the first few weeks of our establishment in Lyons.

'Do you know where you are?' said uncle Alexander, pausing before the gate with the key in his hand. 'Have you ever been here before?'

'Oh, yes; several times.'

'Humph! and may you be trusted with a secret?'

'I think so; but if you doubt it, I can go back again.'

He smiled grimly, threw open the gate, motioned to me to go in before him, and then locked it again from the inside. We were now standing in a little square yard, with a pump in the middle, and some small stable-buildings enclosing it on two sides. I looked round; but saw nothing at all mysterious or new about the place. Uncle Alexander then took a bright, queer-shaped key out of his waistcoat-pocket, pointed with it to the door of the chaise-house, and said -

'My secret's in there!'

The colour rushed to my face, and my heart beat quickly.

'Monsieur Hamel?' I exclaimed.

But he only shook his head; undid the padlock that secured the entrance; made me go in first as before; and then, leaving but a little bit of the door ajar, went round to the back of the chaise, and disappeared in the gloom at the farther end of the outhouse.

'Where are you?' I heard him say. 'Come out, I tell you! come out directly!'

'Oh, m'sieur! please, m'sieur! Oh, do, please, let me go, m'sieur!' cried a shrill voice that sounded familiar to my ears, but which was certainly very unlike the voice of M. Hamel.

'Let you go, indeed!' returned uncle Alexander, in his gruffest tones. 'We shall see about that, *parbleu*! Come over to the light!'

And with this, for my eyes were now growing used to the darkness, I saw him lay hold of some object crouching in the corner, and return towards me dragging a small ragged boy by the collar. One glance at that frightened face and diminutive figure was enough. It was Pierre Pichat.

'Look at this plotting, good-for-nothing little vagabond!' said uncle Alexander, administering a series of shakes and cuffs for the better assistance of his rhetoric. 'I caught him about two hours ago skulking down a by-street, and tearing one of those infernal placards off a dead wall. What were you doing that for, you precious scoundrel? - hey?'

'I - I don't know, m'sieur!' whimpered the boy, sticking his knuckles into his eyes.

'Don't know? Why, you said you didn't know two hours ago! Haven't you had enough prison yet? Or must I help your memory with a horsewhip?'

Master Pierre drew down the corners of his mouth, and closed his eyes, and prepared to howl; but uncle Alexander clapped his hand over his lips, and unexpectedly smothered him.

'If you dare to do that,' said he, 'I'll thrash you as you never were thrashed before! What have you done with your livery, you miserable villain? What brought you to Lyons at all? Where is your master? Speak, or I'll hand you over to the *gendarmes*, and have you carried to gaol before you're an hour older.'

The boy's teeth chattered and his knees knocked together with terror; but he never answered a word.

'Oh, very well,' said uncle Alexander, taking down a short throng-whip that hung behind the door. 'I see you're determined to have it.'

Something in the half-cunning, half-resolute expression of the lad's countenance struck me.

'Perhaps,' said I, 'he would be less obstinate if you told him you meant to be a friend to his master.'

The keen eyes lit up suddenly, but were as quickly averted and fixed upon the ground.

'Humph!' growled uncle Alexander. 'What good would that do? He cares little enough about his master, I'll swear.'

Still he looked down and said nothing.

'I shouldn't wonder if he came here to betray him to the police,' added his tormentor, still balancing the whip in his right hand.

The boy's face grew scarlet. Dusk as it was, I saw it.

'It's a lie!' said he, and burst into a torrent of tears. 'I'd die for him, I would! I'd ... I'd ...'

From this moment our point was gained. Uncle Alexander replaced the whip, lit his pipe with great satisfaction, and walked up and down the yard outside, leaving me to accomplish the rest - while I, having taken my seat upon an inverted bucket, drew the boy to my side, and did my best to soothe him. Even now it was no easy task to win his confidence; and what little he did confess was extracted from him slowly and reluctantly.

That M. Hamel was somewhere in concealment, and that he knew the place of that concealment - that he had come into Lyons for the express purpose of gathering what news he could - that he had thrown aside his livery in the fear of recognition - and that he was trying to tear down a placard to carry back with him to M. Hamel; these, after long questioning, were the only facts that I succeeded in eliciting. Argue as I might, he would not reveal his master's hiding-place.

'It's a long way from here,' said he. 'I've promised not to tell where; but it's a long way.'

'How far?'

'I don't know how far, ma'mselle.'

'Farther than Villefranche?'

'Oh, yes - much farther.'

'Farther than Mâcon?'

'Ever so much farther, ma'mselle.'

'Farther than Chalons? Surely not farther than Chalons, *mon enfant!*'

'*Mais, oui,* ma'mselle. It's farther than Chalons - a good bit farther! But I won't tell you, ma'mselle. I wouldn't tell him' (pointing through the chink of the door to M. Alexander, who was getting very impatient), 'not - not if he whipped me from this till midnight!'

The boy's constancy, troublesome as it was, delighted me.

'You are a brave lad,' said I, laying my hand upon his shoulder; 'but we cannot save your master without your help.'

And with this I went out and consulted M. Alexander. After we had discussed it three or four times over, we went back to the chaise-house and negotiated again, much as two besieging generals might parley with the commander of a resolute but exhausted garrison.

He had promised not to tell, and he would not; so this time we played the Jesuit with him, and our diplomacy succeeded. We persuaded him to observe his promise to the letter, but to transgress it in the spirit; or, to be plainer, we got him, in consideration of our friendly intentions, to agree that M. Alexander should go back with him to the place of his master's concealment - he only reserving the right of silence till M. Alexander found out the locality for himself. Even then he looked doubtful, and half repented.

'You are sure you will save him?' said he, piteously.

'Save him!' cried uncle Alexander. '*Tonnerre de Dieu!* Do you take us for spies or executioners? Upon my life, I've a great mind to horse-whip you, after all!'

With which consoling observation, he coolly locked up his prisoner as before, and walked away.

We went on silently after this, and my thoughts ran upon Hamel.

'What a strange power of fascination he possesses,' said I, unconsciously following up the train. 'He seems to have power to win the affection of the ignorant, and the admiration of the educated with equal facility. Under other influences, he might have developed into a great and good man!'

Uncle Alexander shrugged his shoulders and made a wry face; for he hated anything like sentiment.

271

'Every blackguard's a hero spoilt!' said he, curtly, and went striding on like the Colossus of Rhodes.

This elegant aphorism quite put a stop to my moralizing; and not another word was exchanged till we were almost in sight of home. Then M. Alexander came to a sudden halt.

'Can you be ready in an hour?' asked he.

'Ready! for what, pray?'

'To go with me, of course. Impossible to get on without you.'

'Surely you cannot be in earnest?' said I, by no means relishing the idea of this vague expedition.

'In earnest! I'm always in earnest,' replied uncle Alexander, impatiently. 'I couldn't have managed this morning but for you; and if that boy changes his mind by the way, and refuses to go on, what should I do without you? Besides, you'll conduct the other matter better than I could. Women always succeed in these things better than men - they talk better - they smooth away difficulties ... in short, you must go!'

'So it appears; but what will Madame say?'

'I'll settle that.'

'And then Marguerite, who is ill ...'

'Let her mother attend to her. That's her place.'

'I do not really see how I can be of use to you,' I persisted; 'but still, if you think it really necessary ...'

'I do think it really necessary,' interrupted he, crossly. 'I want you to settle matters with the parson. I don't want to have to talk myself. I ... but there's a steamer going up to Villefranche at half-past two, and you have only three-quarters of an hour to get ready; so be quick!'

CHAPTER XXXVIII

FLED AND GONE!

We were on board at half-past two; and by a quarter before three had steamed away from the great quays, and left the spires and bridges, with all their glorious background, clustered picturesquely behind us.

It was the first time that I had been upon the river, or seen the approach to Lyons from this side. Much, therefore, as I had already admired the city and its environs, I now thought it ten times more beautiful than ever, and stood leaning against the side of the boat, utterly absorbed in the splendour of the panorama which was being unfolded before me.

Hills, fortresses, wharves and landing-places; houses abruptly interspersed with huge *aiguilles* of dark granite; and waterside hotels, with pleasure-gardens and summer-houses overlooking the river, stretched on and on for many miles on either side, following all the bends of the stream, and varying the scene at every turn. Now we passed a great rock, with a cavern in it, and a statue standing inside, half concealed by a natural canopy of creeping plants - now a line of uniform barracks, with a troop of horsemen riding out to the sound of military music - then more green hills, and forts, and colonies of manufactories, sending up wreaths of smoke that glittered in the sun - then a rock-island, connected with the shore by a slender bridge, and crowned by an antique turret, from which Charlemagne watched the march of his Paladins eleven centuries ago - then scattered fragments of pointed granite starting up from the bed of the river, which boils and eddies round them as the waters of the Rhine chafe round the sunken summits of the Seven Sisters - then precipices, clothed with trees down to the water's edge; elegant country mansions dotted over the slopes of the hills; gardens, all radiant with the delicate white and pink blossoms of the almond, apple, and cherry-tree; and little white towns; and nestling villages, and forest-like plantations, and the river growing ever wider and wider, till we come at last to Villefranche, and the bell on the landing-place warns us ashore!

I was very sorry to leave the boat; and when M. Alexander came hurrying up from the farther end, where he had all the time been keeping guard over his prisoner, I could not help saying so. To which observation, having no soul for the picturesque, he only replied -

'Bah! scenery, indeed! what *is* scenery, I should like to know? Water - trees - rocks; the same thing over and over again perpetually. I hate scenery!'

Hurried from the steamer out upon the wharf, from the wharf into a cab, and from the cab into a yet unfinished railway station, I had neither time nor inclination to dispute this point with my companion. Besides, it is ever useless to argue upon matters of taste, when, as in this case, one's opponent happens to have no taste at all.

By the time the train started, it was just six o'clock. We had a second-class carriage to ourselves for almost the whole journey, and as soon as it got dusk M. Alexander tied his pocket-handkerchief over his head and dozed in a corner. By-and-by, having been regaled with a prodigious supply of bread and meat on board the boat, master Pierre followed his captor's example, and fell into a heavy sleep; whilst I, wakeful and uneasy, watched the darkening landscape, and thought alternately of M. Hamel in his unknown hiding-place, and Marguerite tossing on her bed of fever. Thus the hours went slowly by, and the night grew profoundly dark. I could just see the outline of the banks and signal-posts along the line, but nothing beyond, unless the occasional twinkling of a distant light, or the red haze that hovered over a town. At Mâcon we stopped for a few moments, and a burly guard came bustling in to inspect our tickets; but this was the exception, for ours was an express train, and we shot past the stations with the speed of the wind, seeing only a sudden blaze of gas and a flying picture of a platform and bystanders. Then I also fell into a troubled dream, in which Marguerite, and my father, and M. Alexander, and the old moor-house, with its three gaunt poplars, were linked together in painful confusion; and then I awoke again, roused by a sudden stoppage, a sound of many feet rushing to and fro, and a rough voice crying, 'Chalons!'

Hurrying out now with that bewildered haste that follows an uneasy sleep, we find that it is already ten by the station-clock, and that a slow misty rain is coming steadily down; so we make our way into the waiting-room, dragging the sleepy boy between us, and decide upon going first of all to the *Lion d'Or,*, and there hiring some vehicle in which to pursue the remainder of our journey; for master Pierre has said that we can do so by no other means, as our destination, whatever that may be, lies inland towards the mountains.

Wet, and dreary, and deserted are the streets of the quiet town as we thread them in the rain on our way to the *Lion d'Or,*. There are scarcely any passengers on foot, no shops open, and but few lights anywhere. At the little auberge they are already putting up their shutters for the night; but there is a capital fire in the kitchen, round which the family are sitting at their supper, and here we find warmth and a hearty welcome together. Uncle Alexander then orders the solitary chaise of the establishment to be at once prepared, calls for hot wine and toast, and borrows a stout railway-rug for our better protection against the inclemency of the night. The landlady is all this time in a fever of curiosity, and assails us with all kinds of indirect questions.

'*Ciel!* what weather,' she exclaims. 'What a pity that m'sieur should have to drive all the way to Montrocher at this hour! M'sieur is unusually late upon the road to-night.'

'Humph! it *is* late,' replies uncle Alexander, sipping his wine.

'Nothing the matter at Montrocher, I hope, m'sieur?'

'Not that I know of, Madame Barthelet - not that I know of.'

'And the family, m'sieur, I trust they are well, and enjoying their stay at Lyons?'

'Pretty well, I thank you, Madame Barthelet. This is good wine - Volnay, I think?'

The landlady drops a courtesy.

It is Volnay - m'sieur's own Volnay of the year before last, of which she (Madame Barthelet) has the happiness to possess more than eleven dozen.

The conversation then languishes, and the clock in the corner strikes eleven.

'It will be twelve before m'sieur reaches Montrocher,' observes the landlady.

No reply.

'I - I suppose the servants have forgotten to forward m'sieur's own chaise to-night?' pursues she, twirling the corner of her apron in a paroxysm of inquisitiveness.

'No, no - I did not order it,' replies uncle Alexander, quite coolly, but with a peculiar twinkle of enjoyment at the corner of his eye.

'Oh! m'sieur is going home *unexpectedly* - and ma'mselle along with him. OH, INDEED!'

A pause, during which the chaise is heard to come up to the door, and a voice outside the window cries, 'All ready!'

'Good-night, Madame Barthelet,' says uncle Alexander, starting up immediately. 'Good-night. You shall have your chaise back some time to-morrow.'

'My son will drive you, m'sieur, with pleasure, and bring it back to-night if it will save you trouble,' gasps the landlady, following us

275

into the porch.

But uncle Alexander shakes his head, helps me in, and throws the reins to Pierre Pichat.

'This lad is here on purpose to drive me, Madame Barthelet,' says he, 'but I thank you all the same. Besides, I may want the chaise to-morrow. Good-night.'

Whereupon we drive away, leaving our hostess of the *Lion d'Or,* utterly mystified, and incapable of even executing a courtesy.

It is now pitch dark, and the rain keeps getting thicker and heavier. Pierre sits on the shafts and drives, and uncle Alexander, smoking away inside the extinguisher-hood, growls, and grunts, and grumbles incessantly. Passing, by-and-by, through a dismal little miry village, we hear the cocks crowing and the church-clock striking the hour of midnight. Then we get among the hills, where the roads are steep and stony, and the wind howls like a chorus of Banshees. Here the boy is forced to dismount and lead the horse, and so we plod on for a weary time, till we come to a place where three roads diverge. Having chosen the best and broadest of these, he resumes his seat on the shafts, and cracks his whip merrily, while M. Alexander, peering forward into the mist, exclaims -

'*Mille tonnerres!* 'Tis the Santenay road that he has taken, after all!'

And it is the Santenay road, beyond a doubt; for soon we are climbing that steep mountain-side, and traversing that straggling village-street which I so well remember to have passed, under far other auspices, well nigh a year ago!

Arrived at the upper end of the village, master Pierre touches his cap, and says that we must alight here, and walk the rest of the distance. So we reluctantly obey, and the chaise is left in the yard of a little inn close by, where a sleepy ostler rolls out of a stable and takes charge of it wonderingly; and then we tramp on a little farther, with the boy going before us as a guide, till, coming to a halt before the gates of M. Gautier's lodge, he pulls the bell, and, turning to us again, says -

'In here, m'sieur, if you please.'

'Now may the devil fly away with me if I didn't suspect as much!' mutters uncle Alexander, with a shrug of his broad shoulders. 'The little villain has dared to hide his confounded master in my nephew's house! Upon my soul, I've a greater mind to thrash him than ever!'

Just then a window is thrown open, and a peevish voice cries - 'Who knocks?'

'I - little Pierre.'

'*Ah, dâme!* You keep bad hours, *petit* Pierre! This is the second time that you have brought me from my bed within the last eight days. If I were your mother, I'd ...'

With this the voice dies away in yawns and mutterings; the window is slammed violently down; a long pause follows; and then one great wooden gate sways reluctantly back, and Monsieur Gautier's fat porteress, clad in a cloak and night-cap, and holding a lantern high above her head, appears on the other side.

'But you are not alone! Who are these people? What do you want?' cries she, planting herself in the way. 'Ah, *Ciel!* M'sieur Alexander of Montrocher! A thousand pardons, m'sieur - and Ma'mselle Marguerite also? Ah, no - not Ma'mselle Marguerite, I declare! And to think that I should be seen in my night-cap - oh, blessed Mary!'

Whereupon, being suddenly overcome by the recollection of her personal appearance, the fat porteress resigns the light to Pierre Pichat, and beats a sudden retreat into the fastnesses of her lodge.

Tired and anxious as we are, we cannot keep from laughing as we follow the boy and lantern up the avenue. It is a dreary avenue now, and the scant gleams strike upon a network of bare wet boughs at every step we take.

'In what part of my nephew's house have you stowed away this precious master of yours - hey, you scoundrel?' says M. Alexander.

'In - in the tower, m'sieur.'

'Humph! then, of course your mother knows all about it - supplies him with food, and so forth - Hey!'

'Yes, m'sieur.'

'And your father? He's in the plot, too, I suppose?'

'No - no, m'sieur! We did not dare to tell my father. M'sieur Charles left everything in his care when he went away - and - and father's a strict man - and ...'

'But supposing he heard a noise! What then?'

'Ah, bah! then he would think it was a ghost. There are plenty of them up there!' replies Pierre, with a sly laugh, and extinguishes the light.

'*Diable!* what have you done that for?'

'Because we are coming in sight of the house, m'sieur, and father is so watchful now that M'sieur Charles is away! Walk as softly as you can, please, m'sieur, for we must go round to the side-door. I have a key that fits it in my pocket.'

And so we steal over the bridge, and past the great ivied tower, in which there is no sign of life, and make our way round to the farther wing, on the side of M. Charles's apartments.

Pierre then unlocks the door, and in another moment we are all inside, and surrounded by the deepest darkness.

'I keep the matches in the library,' whispers the boy. 'Wait here till I come back.'

We stand with suspended breath, and hear him glide gently down the passage. Then there is the cautious turning of a doorhandle - the falling of a gleam of sudden light across the floor - a cry of terror, and ...

Do my senses deceive me, or is it indeed Monsieur Gautier who, pale, but resolute, stands before us with a heavy stick in one hand and a lamp in the other?

'My boy Charles!'

'Uncle Alexander!'

The stick is flung aside and uncle and nephew grasp each other's hands in hearty greeting.

'When did you come home?' 'What brought you here?' 'Why did you not write?' 'What is the matter?' and a hundred such questions are poured forth by both. A few hurried words of explanation follow. M. Charles, grown weary of wandering, and hearing that certain lands in his neighbourhood are put up to sale, has hastened home to conduct the purchase of them. He returned only yesterday, and to-night has been sitting up to examine his steward's accountbooks. His story is told briefly enough. Ours takes longer to relate, and touches on a painful subject; but uncle Alexander is a man of few words, and half a dozen rapid sentences serve to convey the outline of all that has lately happened.

In the meanwhile, Monsieur Charles has turned from white to red, and from red to white again in the course of three or four minutes; and Pierre has fallen on his knees in the middle of the floor, overwhelmed with terror and contrition.

'Oh, pray forgive me, M'sieur Charles!' he cries. 'Pray forgive me! Father knew nothing about it - it's all my own doing - I knew he'd be safe here, sir!'

'*Here!*' repeats M. Gautier, in a deep voice. 'Here!'

'Yes, in the upper floor of your old belfry-tower, of all places in the world!' ejaculates uncle Alexander, shaking his fist ominously at the penitent.

But M. Gautier seemed to be neither indignant nor surprised. He was, instead, deeply affected, and stood leaning against the mantel-piece with his face averted, and his eyes shaded by his hand.

'Here, under my roof,' he said, falteringly. 'It is well - and I am glad - for her sake - poor Marguerite!'

Pierre started up, hardly believing the evidence of his ears.

'*Comment!*' cried he. 'You are not angry with me, M'sieur Charles? You will not give him to the gendarmes? You will save and protect him?'

'Yes, though it were at the peril of my life,' replied M. Gautier, solemnly. 'Uncle Alexander, let us go to him. There is a door of communication up stairs by which we can enter the tower without disturbing Madame Pichat. Pierre, take a light, and bring me the keys that hang just inside the door of the housekeeper's sitting-room; and tread lightly, lest you should wake Jacqueline.'

But the boy, instead of obeying, lingered and looked down.

'If you please, M'sieur Charles,' said he, reluctantly, 'I - I think I have those keys in my pocket.'

Cousin Charles looked at him gravely, but kindly, and took them without a word. He then lit a small hand-lamp, surmounted by a tiny globe, and preceded us up the great staircase. The uninhabited rooms looked just as bare, and echoed as dismally, as ever. Seen by this faint light, they wore, perhaps, a still ghostlier aspect than when we traversed them so merrily, and threw open their shutters to the morning sun, a year ago.

Arrived at the upper chambers, the farthest of which opened upon the third story of the tower adjoining, we trod more cautiously, and whispered more softly than before. At the door of communication we paused and listened. All was profoundly still. Even the raving winds were hushed, and the rain had ceased to patter on the panes.

'Let me go first,' said the boy, eagerly, 'and I can tell him who is here, and what you have come for.'

So we drew back and waited, while he unlocked the door and went in. We heard his footsteps go down the passage, and die away upon the dust of the deserted floors. We heard him call whisperingly upon his master's name, once, twice, thrice - each time more distinctly than before. Then there was a moment of dead silence; and then he came hurrying back, pale and frightened, and trembling from head to foot.

'He is gone!' stammered he. 'I looked for him - I called him; but he is gone!'

'Gone!' echoed M. Charles. 'Did you go up into the loft?'

'N-no, m'sieur, I was afraid.'

'Afraid! Give me the lamp.'

And M. Charles again took the lead, and again we followed after. The first chamber was bare and dreary, and showed no signs of habitation. The second contained an old carved chair and table, transported most probably from the loft above, and a rough bed of horse-rugs and blankets. There was a watch, an empty cup, a book, and half a loaf on the table, and some few articles of wearing apparel lying here and there about the room. I looked at the watch. It had stopped at nine o'clock, and lay there blank and speechless. A vague, dull apprehension fell upon me, and I shuddered.

'He is up stairs if anywhere,' whispered M. Charles, and led the way out upon the landing, and up the crazy ladder.

Dreading to go forward, and yet not daring to remain behind, I followed. When I had nearly reached the top, a rat came rushing past, and I clung with a frightened cry to uncle Alexander's arm.

'You have nothing to fear, mademoiselle,' said our leader, stepping into the middle of the floor, and holding the lamp up with a steady hand. 'There is no one here.'

The light fell feebly and flickeringly around, revealing the fantastic outlines of the piled-up lumber, casting a circle of bright radiance just by M. Charles's feet, and leaving the roof and corners of the loft in utter darkness.

'Humph!' muttered uncle Alexander. 'Then he has escaped without our help, after all!'

We turned to go; but the boy sprang forward with a piercing cry, and pointed to some dark object yonder in the gloom.

'My master!' he gasped - 'My dear master!'

Oh, heaven! it was, indeed.

An open pocket-book was lying beside him; his rigid fingers grasped an empty phial; he had fallen face downwards, and his silver locks hung trailing in the dust. He was dead, quite dead, and had been so for hours. Not a thought now in the busy brain - not a pulse at the beating heart - not a spring of all that wondrous mechanism but was shattered and still.

Silent and awe-struck, we stood about the body, and uncle Alexander lifted the pocket-book from the ground. The open page contained these pencilled words:-

'I have carried a subtle poison concealed for years about my person. It is the key to eternal peace, and to-night I use it. Life has no joy left for me, and no hope. It is a game which I have lost; a race in which I have been distanced; a fever of which I am weary. Marguerite, farewell!'

We passed it silently from hand to hand, and read it each in turn. Then M. Charles bowed his head, and stood as if in prayer.

'He has indeed escaped,' said he, solemnly, 'for ever!'

CHAPTER XXXIX

MULTUM IN PARVO

Dr. Bryant, after all, went back to England without me. Marguerite, in her sickness and calamity, needed my presence more than ever; and had my affection been even less devoted, I could not have left her at such a time, and in such a state. I loved her as if she had been my own young sister; and if I tended her with more than common solicitude, it was through no desire of praise, but for her sake alone.

Her illness was severe and lingering, and there came a time when even the physicians despaired. But her youth saved her. The crisis went by, and she recovered slowly. It was, however, many weeks before she could leave her room, or cross the floor without assistance. When she was at length able to do so, and could bear to be driven out daily in a carriage, change of air was prescribed. We then took her by easy stages to Geneva, pausing on the road to spend some days beside the deep-green waters of the lake of Nantua, which lies so high and tranquil in its nest of rustling pines up among the summits of the Jura.

Arrived at Geneva, M. Delahaye engaged a small villa just beyond the town - a fairy place, solitary, and beautiful, where a poet might have been content to live for ever. To our right lay the spires and bridges and old wooden houses of the Cité - to the left, the far-spreading shores and mountains of Savoy. Straight before our windows rose the peaked and solitary Mole, and Mont Blanc, hooded with clouds, like a ghostly friar. Our garden sloped down in terraces to the water's edge, and all day long the light Swiss barques skimmed by on their wing-like sails, or floated, picturesquely idle, round about the town; looking like aquatic birds of some strange breed and bright fantastic plumage.

Here Marguerite continued steadily to improve, and drank in new life with every breath of air and beam of sunlight. Sometimes she sat for half the day under the shade of the acacias at the end of the garden, whilst I read aloud; or, oftener still, reclined for hours in our tiny skiff, gazing up dreamily into the depths of the blue sky, or trailing her hand through the still bluer waters that rippled round the prow.

What her thoughts were at these times, it would be hard to say; for she spoke but seldom. Pensive and abstracted as an opium-dreamer, she seemed under the influence of some unearthly calm, more like the peace of sleep than the serenity of waking life. She never spoke of the past. She neither wept, nor sighed, nor lamented; but, steeped in a languid melancholy, suffered the days and hours to float on unheeded. It was as if some spring had ceased to act, some chord to vibrate. At times I almost doubted whether her memory was not itself impaired, and whether the great sorrow of her life had not burnt out even its own record in her brain. Be this, however, as it might, she basked in the warm sun; and breathed the pleasant air; and revived like a flower after rain, passively, indolently, without effort, and without enjoyment.

This state of indifference grieved, and sometimes alarmed me; and I took every opportunity of rousing her to a sense of the reality and beauty of material life.

'Look, Marguerite,' said I, one evening, as we drifted with suspended oars across the glassy lake. 'What a glorious sunset! See those violet shadows in the hollows of the mountains - see that troop of winged clouds sailing to the west! In the face of such a scene, is it not a privilege to live?'

She gazed up steadfastly into the sky, and paused before replying.

'Perhaps so,' she murmured at length; 'but, oh! it were a sweeter privilege to die!'

And so, with the faintest ripple of a smile upon her parted lips, she closed her eyes, laid her head wearily upon my knees, and slept, or seemed to sleep.

This is but one instance taken from many, and I only quote it in evidence of the condition of her mind at one especial period.

The next phase was restlessness, and we greeted it as a change of happy omen. She tired of Geneva and its environs - even of the blue lake and the sentinel peaks of Savoy. She fancied to visit Chambery, and when she had been in Chambery but a few short days, longed to travel southwards, and breathe the breath of Italy. She had but to wish it, and she went. We crossed by the pass of the Mont Cénis, and for two more months wandered hither and thither amid the northern shores and cities of Piedmont and Lombardy. This life of intellectual and bodily activity worked miracles upon her. The sight of palaces and pictures; the study of strange manners, and of a new and musical language; the atmosphere of art that seems to inform the very air of Italy - all braced and developed the natural capabilities of her mind. Her conversation became more thoughtful, and her aspect more womanly. With the improvement of her taste, her desire of knowledge was increased, and her power of observation intensified. Her melancholy thus gave place to earnestness; and her countenance grew sweet and serious, like a Madonna of Giotto. Nor was this all. The luxurious climate, the journeys by land and sea, the glories of the rich autumnal season, served, each and all, to invigorate her health, and repair the last lingering evils of her former illness. She grew in stature as in mind, in grace of person, as in beauty of soul - 'sweet are the uses of adversity!'

The autumn was not yet past when we began to retrace our steps. Returning through the Simplon and a section of Switzerland, we loitered homewards by Chillon, Freybourg, and Soleure, and arrived towards the last days of September, at the quaint old town of Basle, beside the rushing waters of the Rhine.

Here, not quite unexpectedly, and yet not by positive appointment, we were joined by uncle Alexander and M. Charles. It was a quiet meeting, and conducted without any show of peace-making, or any painful explanations. They shook hands like friends after a brief absence; and, had I been a stranger, I should perhaps have wondered why they each looked embarrassed, without even guessing that the cousins had once been lovers, and betrothed.

But they had both altered since that time; Charles no less than Marguerite. He, too, had suffered, and his lesson had been a bitter one.

'I thought to teach,' said he, one day when we chanced to be alone, 'and instead of teaching, I was severely taught. My domineering pride is all gone now; but it is too late. We are friends, and I see plainly that I need never hope for more. She never loved me, and, dear as she was to me, I disdained to cultivate her affections. Alas! I was rightly punished. I lost her, and lost her for ever!'

I tried to console him, but it was of no avail.

'She is greatly changed,' I said. 'She is a thoughtful woman now, and better fitted to appreciate you than she ever could have been without these trials. Have patience - make no attempt to press your suit - be content first with her friendship; and, having once gained that, it will be time enough to think of love.'

He thanked me; but shook his head, and doubted still.

We spent a fortnight going down the Rhine, and a happy fortnight it was. Sometimes we went by the steamer, sometimes by the river-road, and sometimes, when the distances were short, by a pleasure-boat with four rowers. Every morning, about twelve or one, we landed to lunch by the water-side under the shade of the cherry-trees, or up among the ruins of any feudal castle that chanced to be at hand. In the evening we dined and put up for the night at the nearest village inn; sometimes remaining there for the next day or two to explore the surrounding neighbourhood. Thus we staid awhile at Bingen, to visit the oak-forest of the Niederwald; at St. Goar, to follow the windings of the delicious Schweitzer Thal; and at Coblentz, to row up the sylvan Lahn, and drink the bitter waters of Ems.

Marguerite, finding that Charles paid her no lover-like attentions, grew daily more cheerful and at ease. Monsieur, equipped with all kinds of eccentric travelling garments, played the distinguished tourist to his heart's content, and presented himself at the *table d'hôtes* every evening in the most dazzling and elaborate toilettes. Uncle Alexander, although he did profess to care nothing for scenery, enjoyed this vagrant life after his own fashion, and took a turn at the oars, or lay smoking at the bottom of the boat in his wide-awake and shirt-sleeves, as indifferent to appearances, and as contentedly shabby, as if he and his brother came from two opposite hemispheres. As for Madame and myself, we read, worked, and admired, and agreed that we had never been so happy in our lives. Was it not the fulfilment of all that I had longed for so ardently? Was it not the realization of those girlish dreams that, long ago, pictured the ocean in place of the dull moor, and turned the clouds to snow-clad Alpine peaks? Yes, I had indeed found the 'word of power,' and that word was - duty. I had laboured lovingly in my vocation, and, I think, faithfully. I was rewarded now in the gratification of desires long cherished, in the esteem of my employers, and in the knowledge that my pupil was restored to health and elevated in character, if not by my means wholly, at least, through circumstances in which I had borne no inconsiderable part.

Reflecting thus, and enjoying to the utmost my pleasant holiday, I still sighed, and asked myself - What next? Marguerite had passed suddenly into womanhood, and spoke my language fluently. I could not hope now to be retained much longer in my situation, and, granting even that I remained awhile as her companion, I saw prophetically what at last must happen.

For, however ill-assorted at the time of their engagement, Marguerite and her cousin were now by no means unsuited to each other. His character had softened, while hers had strengthened. He had learned to be indulgent, and she to be firm. Starting from opposite extremes, they now met on tolerably equal ground, and, for the first time, rightly understood each other's value. They were already friends. They would soon be lovers. Once lovers and betrothed again ... Heigho! I must either make my home among strangers, or e'en go back to my native North, settle down at Brookfield as housekeeper to Dr. Bryant, and never again see the blue mountains and golden vines of Montrocher! The one alternative was as bad as the other, and the thought of change lay heavy at my heart.

Our tour ended with a week in Paris, and we arrived in Burgundy just one month after the two gentlemen had joined us at Basle - nearly one year since we started away to spend the winter in

Lyons. A year! a whole year! It seemed a long time, because so much had happened, and we had been so far.

Claude and Marie were married now, and lived in a pretty cottage a little way beyond the village. They were supremely happy, and their only matrimonial regret was that 'Ma'mselle Marguerite' should never have been bridesmaid after all. I have reason, however, to believe that this disappointment was atoned for when their master's daughter stood as sponsor at a certain christening, not many months after our return. With the exception of this one change, we found everything at Montrocher precisely as we had left it. Coming back thus towards the beginning of the winter, it was easy to imagine that we had never been away at all, and that Italy and the Alps were nothing but a dream!

The winter passed away, and the spring-time came back, and I saw my prophecy fulfilled with the blossoming of the first violets. Charles and Marguerite were betrothed again. She loved him now, and her love was based upon esteem. Proud of his position, his intellect, and his many noble qualities, she was prouder still of his affection, and only lamented that she had not valued it before.

'How was it that I did not learn to love you sooner?' I heard her murmur one evening as they stood apart, watching the rising moon.

'Because, *chérie*,' said he, bending low, and twining one of her glossy ringlets round his finger, '*I* had not learned to woo!'

CHAPTER XL

CHEQUE - AND MATE

'I'll tell you what, monkey - except to the pair of fools that are going to get married, a wedding is the most stupid and tiresome piece of business upon earth!'

It was after breakfast, while we were still sitting round the table, and uncle Alexander was in one of his odd, half-disagreeable, and half-jesting moods.

Marguerite looked up and smiled, and cousin Charles ventured on a remonstrance.

'I'm sure, sir,' said he, 'we give you no cause for complaint. You are out all day, and the preparations ...'

'Hang the preparations,' interrupted uncle Alexander, savagely. 'I'm sick of them. There are pins all about the carpets, and needles sticking in the seats of all the chairs; and it was only yesterday that I sat down on a bonnet!'

'And that bonnet was mine, monsieur,' said I, looking grave at the recollection of the misfortune, though the rest were laughing.

'*Yours* - with all those flowers and bows about it? I thought you knew better.'

'Mademoiselle is to be one of the bridesmaids, uncle Alexander,' said Marguerite, coming to my defence; 'and she must dress like the rest. The bonnet is a very quiet bonnet, indeed! Adèle Vaudon would have had them trimmed with Valenciennes lace, and with the flowers outside; but that Mademoiselle objected so decidedly.'

'Humph! I'd better have said nothing about it,' growled her uncle, pulling at his moustache with both hands. 'Let us change the subject, Charles, and talk of business.'

'Business, sir?' repeated M. Gautier. 'Whose business?'

'Your own, of course - and Marguerite's. My time is precious, you know - especially at this season. I've not even looked at the settlements; but you've made all right without me, I dare say.'

'The preliminaries,' said M. Delahaye, with great dignity, 'have been, I believe, arranged upon an unexceptionable basis; and are likely to be productive of indubitable gratification to - ahem! the negotiating parties.'

'The translation meaning that you are all content - hey, brother Jacques?'

M. Delahaye looked furious, and was about to speak; but uncle Alexander pulled out a great, shabby, leather pocket-book, tied round with red tape, and, turning to M. Charles, continued -

'You've looked forward to something from me, I suppose, at some time or other. There, don't interrupt me - I know all you're going to say, and I've no time to listen to it. People call me rich - at all events I'm not poor; and I can afford to make the monkey a pretty present to add to her dowry. But, mark me, I hate *expectations*. I give what I choose, and give it now for the pleasure of seeing you enjoy it. Don't look to my death for a farthing, any of you, or you may be strangely disappointed.'

Marguerite changed colour, and her eyes filled with tears - Monsieur Charles could keep silence no longer.

'Your death, sir, under any circumstances, could never be otherwise than a loss to me,' said he, looking proud and pained together. 'I am not a money-lover - I have lived for science all my life, and, perhaps, I place too little value upon wealth. At all events, you - you who have been my best friend ... my second father ... my ...'

His voice shook and he looked down, while uncle Alexander fidgeted uneasily in his chair, and seemed about to sacrifice the moustache altogether.

'*Mille diables!*' he exclaimed. 'What do you mean? You're as explosive, all of you, as if you had been brought up upon gunpowder and lucifer-matches! I'm a plain man, and I can't talk like a dictionary; but I don't mean to affront you, boy. There, let's say no more about it. I've this bit of paper for you and the monkey, and all you have to do, is to take it and say "thank you." Now go and be married as fast as you like; and don't get tired of each other any sooner than you can help.'

With which pleasant valediction, uncle Alexander clapped his hat upon his head, and stalked out of the room, leaving Monsieur Charles standing, silent and irresolute, with the unopened paper in his hand.

For some seconds no one spoke or stirred. Then M. Delahaye wiped his eye-glass on his embroidered handkerchief, gave a preliminary cough, sauntered carelessly across the room, and, laying his hand affectionately on his nephew's arm, said -

'You - excuse me, my dear Charles - you have not yet investigated the - ahem! May I be permitted?'

M. Gautier handed it to him without a word, and turned his head studiously away. His pride and his feelings had both been hurt, and he could not quickly forget it. M. Delahaye, on the contrary, could scarcely control his impatience; and as he unfolded it, the paper fluttered in his hands.

'Ha! a cheque ... I pre-supposed a cheque,' said he: 'for - let me see - eh? How much? Impossible! No - yes - my dear Charles, your - your uncle Alexander has the - the unparalleled generosity to give you ... what do you suppose?'

'Really, sir, I have no idea,' replied M. Gautier, half-smiling.

'Two hundred and fifty thousand francs!* Two hundred and fifty thousand francs, payable at sight! Charles, shake hands - Marguerite, embrace me! Ha! ha! Two hundred and fifty thousand francs! *Vive le roi!*'

And Monsieur, forgetful of his dignity for the first time in his life, actually laughed aloud; kissed his daughter; executed a *pirouette*; and ending by sinking, exhausted, into a chair, and fanning himself with his pocket-handkerchief.

As for Charles, he stood bewildered, and had not a word to say; whilst I, feeling myself *de trop*, stole softly from the room, and left them to discuss their family affairs in private.

I went straight to the garden, took my work with me, and sat down to spend a quiet hour in the summer-house. Though still the early spring-time, it was deliciously warm and sunny. The birds and *cigales* were trying which could make themselves heard the loudest; and Pedro, basking and blinking on the gravel path, let the flies settle in swarms upon his coat, and was too lazy to shake them off.

I was thoughtful, and rather sad; for I had that very morning begun my letter to Dr. Bryant, and was going back to England a week after the wedding.

The life of a teacher is, after all, melancholy enough - made up of partings and sacrifices! How much we give! How little we receive! How soon we are forgotten! I had never been so happy in my life as during these two years at Montrocher. I loved Marguerite dearly, and there was no member of the household, down to the dog Pedro, for whom I did not entertain some degree of attachment. And yet how soon it would be over! Kind and generous as they were, I was nothing to them. How long should I be remembered? Who would regret me? Should I ever again meet any of them upon earth?

I dared not answer my own questions. My work fell to the ground, and, covering my face with both my hands, I sobbed bitterly.

I cannot tell how long I wept. I am unused to give way to emotion, and when I lose my self-control, it is with difficulty that I regain it. I do not think, however, that I remained long thus; for when

---

* £10,000, English.

once my tears flowed freely, the heavy sobs gradually ceased, and the paroxysm died away.

'I'm glad you've stopped that noise, at any rate,' growled a well-known voice close beside me.

I looked up; saw uncle Alexander sitting on the opposite seat; turned hot and cold, red and white all in one minute; and knew not what to say. There was an interval of dead silence, during which he continued to stare at me from under his bushy brows, and (having, of course, his meerschaum in his mouth) puffed slowly and solemnly, like a Turk at a divan.

'What's the matter?' said he, presently.

'Nothing, n-n-nothing at all.'

I was struggling hard to be calm, but my voice shook in spite of me.

'And yet, just now, you were howling like a macaw,' said uncle Alexander. 'Are you fond of howling? Do you often do it?'

Feeling too much annoyed, and still too hysterical, to venture on a reply, I snatched up my work, and rose to go. But his gigantic grasp was on my wrist in a moment.

'Sit down,' said he, authoritatively. 'I want to talk to you.'

The stronger will prevailed, and I obeyed mechanically. Then there was another long pause, during which I had time fully to recover my composure, and to wonder what this grim companion had to say.

'I'm two hundred and fifty thousand francs poorer to-day than yesterday,' said he, at length; 'and that's a large sum.'

'It is, indeed,' I replied. 'You have been very liberal, sir.'

'Then it's your fault,' said he, turning sharply upon me. 'It's your fault altogether.'

I was so amazed at this unexpected accusation that I could not utter a word.

'I've heard all about it,' he continued, expelling the smoke in short angry puffs through his nostrils, which gave him a perfectly diabolical appearance. 'I know your match-making propensities! *Sacr-r-r-re nom de Dieu!*'

'My fault - my match-making propensities!' I stammered. 'In heaven's name, sir, what is it that you mean?'

'I mean, that but for you and your counsels, Charles would never have made it up with Marguerite; this marriage would never have taken place; and I should still have my two hundred and fifty thousand francs in my pocket. There, can you deny that?'

I could not have kept from smiling had it been to save my life.

'If I really have helped to bring Charles and Marguerite together,' said I, 'I shall be only too happy to confess it. But I lay no such flattering unction to my soul. Fate would have done it for them without my interference.'

'Fate never abstracted two hundred and fifty thousand francs from my banking account,' grumbled uncle Alexander.

'Nor added it to mine,' I retorted, still laughing. 'Upon my word, sir, I think it a pity you should have given the money if you meant to repent your generosity for ever after!'

'Humph! That's my business. I'm a rich man. I can afford to repent of it if I please.'

'An expensive luxury! Allow me to congratulate you.'

Uncle Alexander brought down his clenched fist so heavily upon the little rustic table, that Pedro started from his doze and uttered an apologetic whine.

'*Vingt-cinq milles diables!* You are the most aggravating, satirical ... Stop! there's another trifle I should like to point out to you. You've not only robbed me of two hundred and fifty thousand francs; but you've thrown yourself out of your situation! You won't be wanted here when Marguerite is married and gone!'

'Thank you, sir, - I did not need to be reminded of that,' I said, stiffly. 'I have already written to Dr. Bryant, and - and I leave Montrocher the week after next.'

'The devil you do!' ejaculated uncle Alexander, quite taken by surprise. 'You are in a monstrous hurry, it seems!'

I looked down, but said nothing.

'Glad to go back to England, I suppose?'

Still I made no reply.

'What do you mean to do when you get there - hey?'

'I scarcely know yet; but I think I shall be housekeeper to Dr. Bryant. He is getting old now - looks upon me as a daughter - was my mother's earliest friend, and ...'

'And so you mean to sacrifice the best days of your life in nursing and gruel-making for the next ten or twenty years! Ugh! You exemplary Christian!'

I felt the tears once more welling to my eyes; but drove them bravely back.

'I have no other resource, sir,' I said, 'and duty, after all, has its own rewards. I would thank you not to discourage me with my future - it is quite dreary enough already.'

Uncle Alexander glanced sharply at me; then, fixing his eyes upon a certain pebble in the gravel, fell into a deep study, and smoothed his moustache contemplatively with his thumb and forefinger.

'I wonder,' said he, after another interval of silence, 'that, with all your taste for match-making, you never got married yourself!'

'For two good reasons, sir. In the first place, though you persist in asserting the contrary, I have no taste for match-making. In the second place, I have never had an offer of marriage in my life.'

I spoke with some irritation - for M. Alexander generally contrived, somehow or another, to put me out of temper. He listened gravely, continued to stare at the pebble, and said -

'Never had an offer! Humph! I'm surprised at that.'

'The first polite observation I ever heard you make, monsieur!'

He gave a sort of grunt and smoked on, never looking up or changing his position. A silence longer than any of the others now ensued. At length I again gathered up my work, and prepared to go in; but he, without ever turning his head, once more put out his hand, and said -

'Not yet.'

So I sat down with an impatient sigh, and began to stitch diligently.

'You think yourself a mighty clever accountant, don't you?' he next asked, in the same musing tone.

'Not at all,' I replied, surprised at the change of subject. 'I know the multiplication and addition tables, and a little of book-keeping; but I pretend to nothing more.'

'Well, that's enough. Now, make this calculation for me: you are, let me see, how old? Thirty-five?'

'Thirty-two, if you please.'

'Oh! thirty-two. *Eh bien!* how many years do you think you have to live?'

'How can I guess? Perhaps as many more,' I answered, laughing, and wondering what would come next.

Uncle Alexander nodded twice or thrice, with the air of a man who adds up figures in his mind.

'I am forty-six,' said he; 'and, as I come of a long-lived family, it is just possible that I may last thirty or thirty-two years longer. My father died at ninety-four ... what do you think - hey?'

'I should say it was very likely indeed, sir, and I'm sure Marguerite ...'

'Never mind Marguerite,' interrupted he, plucking hard at the moustache. 'Make the calculation - add up the items - and tell me if you don't think it a pity that you and I should live alone for thirty-two years, when we might as well be happy and comfortable together?'

I was struck dumb, and the needle dropped from my fingers.

'Well, what do you say?' said uncle Alexander, laying down his pipe, and looking up suddenly in my face. 'Shall we be married to-morrow fortnight?'

———————

I am not going to confess any thing - not even that I had for a long time unconsciously entertained something more than a liking for gruff, eccentric uncle Alexander. Perhaps I only found this liking out when I thought that I was about to leave Montrocher for ever. Perhaps it made me very happy to discover that he was equally averse to let me go: but I shall certainly not acknowledge either of these suppositions, however near the truth they may happen to be.

We were not married quite so hastily as M. Alexander proposed. We waited for rather more than two months, till Dr. Bryant could be present at the wedding. When he did arrive it was for life. He had sold his practice at Brookfield, and came, not only to play a father's part at the altar, but to end his days in Chalons, near the Vaudons and myself. He is still living, and, though some years have passed away since these things happened, not one familiar face has yet vanished from our circle. M. Delahaye still practises the shake, and has lately taken to the guitar. Charles and Marguerite, linked each to each, 'like perfect music unto noble words,' are happier than tongue can tell, or pen relate. He lives but for her love - she for his honour; and thus they

'Walk this world,
Yoked in all exercise of noble ends.'

Remote from them and us, in a lone corner of a wild churchyard, high up among the mountains north of Santenay, lies the dust of that misguided man whose strange and fatal history I have here recorded. It is a bleak and solitary spot, where the winds rave more keenly, and the bitter grasses grow more scantily than elsewhere. His grave is nameless. His story is almost forgotten. Peace be with him - peace and forgiveness.

THE END.